Running From Redemption

Presented by

Cyril Gillion

Product of
CGpublishing

Running From Redemption
CG Publishing

Publisher's Note:

This book is a work of fiction. Names, characters, places and incidents are products of the author's imagination or are used fictitiously. Any resemblance to actual events or locales or persons, living or dead, is entirely coincidental.

COPYRIGHT © 2010
by
CYRIL GILLION

ALL RIGHTS RESERVED.

NO PART OF THIS BOOK, INCLUDING COVER DESIGN, MAY BE REPRODUCED IN ANY FORM BY ANY MEANS WITHOUT PRIOR CONSENT OF THE PUBLISHER, EXCEPT IN THE CASE OF BRIEF QUOTATIONS USED IN REVIEWS

Manufactured in the United States of America

I S B N
978-1-4507-1329-0

AUTHOR'S NOTE

Success is the loneliest place to travel if no one is there for the ride. And if God is not on the GPS, then that ride is headed for disaster.

On this voyage as an author, I picked up a few people along the way.

To my family: There's no better support system I could ever have. Through each of you I receive the bitter with the sweet. Know that I love all of you, and I take pride in representing the legacy wherever I go.

To my extended family: Janine Knowledge Mitchell, Recia Turner, NaSheka Williams, Wilson Fervil, and Katrick Nelson, whether it was looking over proofs or calibrating ideas, I cherish the invaluable advice that was constantly given.

Keith Sanders, this is our second project together. Thank you for your artistry and expertise.

To priceless people that assisted in promoting my work: V.J. Prophete of VJ Promotions, Dee Dee Roc at 90.5 FM, and Marcus at Bella Donna's, it's been a pleasure working with each of you.

To Bridgette, a.k.a. Gorgeous, they say that diamonds melt at 1300 degrees Fahrenheit, yet somehow through the fire you kept your natural form. Thank you for catching me when I trip, never letting me fall.

Last and certainly not least, to you, the reader, the ones that keep the wheels spinning on every writer's journey. Along with reading *Running From Redemption*, make sure you go out and grab it's prequel, *The Other Side of The Pillow*. Not only will you love it, but it will put any unanswered questions into perspective. Want to know the best way to keep a smile on an author's face ... keep buying their books!

Running From Redemption

1

The only sound sweeter than hearing the bullet was hearing him die, begging for life.
"Don't kill my daddy! Please Ms. Angel, don't kill my daddy!"
Maybe in another lifetime, or with another woman, the words of his six-year-old daughter would have some bearing.
But because of the past they had no bearing. And because of the past I shot him again, this time putting the bullet where it counts.
"Nooooo!" his daughter bellowed.
She bites my leg like a loose pitbull, pain making me curse in volumes. I threw her to the floor, showed her my gun, gave her the Lucifer eye.
She freezes.
Then I pointed the gun back at her father, the .45 planted at his chest.
"I beg you, Angel!" he told me. "Don't ... kill me ... in front ... of my daughter ... she's ... only six years old."
"I know," I replied, sneering at him. "The same age I was when you killed my mother in front of me. But this has nothing to do with Devilla. This is 'bout me and you. This is 'bout—"
"Run, Devilla! Run and get—"

Another bullet exits my gun and tears through his muscular flesh. He stumbles, then staggers, tracks his blood throughout the white walls of my living room, but he refuses to fall, refuses to die, a cat with nine lives is staring me in the face.

I shoot him again. Shoot him again. Shoot him again.

The immortal man falls to his knees with his body trembling like he's having a seizure, eyes spinning in circles as he sees his own death.

He howls for mercy.

But mercy doesn't live in this apartment.

Then he drew in his fists to fight his own death, did that while I smiled at his persistence.

"Please, Ms. Angel. Leave 'lone my daddy ... leave 'lone my daddy."

Her disoriented father – 6'2 with a gorilla frame – crawls in my direction before stopping at my feet and falling helplessly to the floor. At his greatest moment of pity, I placed my right foot on his chest – the spot where bullets tore – and I dug into his wound with my four-inch stiletto heel, a zebra on a lion that craved sweet revenge.

"Look at me!" I demanded, grabbing him by his bloody shirt. "Take a good look at the last eyes you'll ever see!'

He opens his mouth as if he wants to speak, but words have been replaced with blood.

"You're dying today!" I told him. "God or no God, you're dying today!"

I stared into his eyes like the lady grim reaper, like no one is here to wake him or clean up the mess. Being face-to-face with the man who murdered my mother, the man also known as my stepfather, makes me want to do a lot more than just kill him. For dying is easy. Anyone can die. But then again, keeping him alive isn't fair to the living. Breath should be a privilege. Not everyone deserves it. That's why I didn't hesitate to point the gun at his forehead, and before allowing him to take his final breath, I squared my shoulders, squeezed the trigger, and—

"*Drop the gun!*" a voice hollered. "*Drop the gun or we'll shoot!*"

My stare went towards the living room door where two policemen had entered my apartment, both drawing guns, both giving strict orders to relinquish my weapon.

With unfinished business at stake, I told them, "In case y'all haven't noticed, I'm the victim here."

"One more time ma'am, drop it or we'll shoot!"

Itching to pull the trigger, they sneered at me as if they weren't bluffing.

But neither am I.

Taking William's life at this present moment is more important than anything else in this unfair world, including risking my own. I've lived for this day. Thought about it every day of my life. From the images. To the scenery. To placing his body in an unbeknownst grave. I've dreamt of this very personal moment.

And with that vengeance another thought came to mind.

I quickly grabbed the arm of William's daughter, little Devilla, and I aimed the .45 at her light-skinned temple.

Devilla screams.

Cops lowered their weapons and removed stern looks, then switched those looks with eyes of concernment.

"Be easy," they pleaded. "Be easy with the girl."

I smiled. "Either y'all get out my house or I put a bullet in her head!"

"Please don't," one said, calmly shaking his head. "You don't wanna do that."

"Oh yes I do."

"Oh no you don't ... now just drop the weapon ... everything will be okay ... just lower your—"

"Silence!" I demanded. "In case y'all failed to notice, I'm the bitch with the gun!"

Face filled with trauma, Devilla shakes in my arm like a fish on a hook, her bright eyes watering with tears of pain.

"At least give us the girl," one of the cops said. "Give us the girl and you'll get what you want."

"You sure about that?"

"We're sure ma'am ... we're sure ... whatever it is, we'll get it ..."

"Okay then, can you give me back my mother? Huh? Can you bring her back?"

They never answered.

"Didn't think so!"

More silence.

"Everything's gonna be fine," a cop said, talking to Devilla. "We're gonna get you out of here alive. I promise you."

I sneered. "Don't make her promises you can't keep."

Four blue eyes immediately looked at me, the eyes of policemen from two different worlds. One of the cops – the one doing all the talking – was a veteran policeman with hairs of gray. He had a plump, round face with a heavy physique, and he was playing the role of a negotiator. But the other one – the taller cop with a clean shaven face – was a scrawny man that looked very young. Young and scrawny meant inexperienced, never been tested. It meant he was only trained to do his job. Not trained to kill.

The negotiator said, "Tell us what you want, Ms. Inghram. Tell us and we'll—"

"How do you know my name?"

He hesitated, said, "All of this is just a big misunderstanding ... that's it ... just a misunderstanding ... We're on your side ... You have to trust us okay... But if you don't trust us we can't help you ... Now tell us, Angel. Tell us what you want."

"Right now I want you to shut the fuck up!"

"Need a car? A phone call? Anything you—"

I pressed the .45 deeper into Devilla's temple, and as she screams for mercy I looked his way. "Say one more word and I let loose a clip. Believe that!"

Dead silence.

I looked back at Devilla. "Now where are William's car keys?"

Stuttering, she answered, "They're ... over there ... on the carpet."

I glanced over at the keys that'll lead me to my freedom, keys drenched in blood at the tip of William's feet. The cops watched me as I contemplated on grabbing the car keys, their eyes daring me to reach for my deliverance. My eyes double their dares. Eyes retorting that nothing will stop me from grabbing that metal, that my freedom costs more than the price of their badge.

After a ten second stare down, I smiled at the young, skinny cop that was ill-experienced. "You! Slowly walk over there and get me those keys."

The negotiator intervened. "Okay, Ms. Inghram ... whatever you want. But first let us check on the victim. Looks like he's bleeding to death."

"Then let 'im bleed."

"Sorry Angel but we can't do that ... I'm giving you something so give me something in return ... at least give me the victim."

Thought about it, then nodded, "Okay, but drop your weapon on the floor."

He hesitated.

"Drop it!" I demanded.

His gun fell to the carpet as he motioned to William. I ordered him to move slowly, watched him as he communicated to his partner in a cop-coded language, then he repeated to Devilla it would be okay.

With a hand to William's neck, the cop reacts in a way that says it's too late, a reaction that made Devilla shout out in tears.

"Get an ambulance!" the officer said to his partner. "He needs an ambulance!"

"You're not calling anyone!" I barked. "Not until you reach over and give me those keys."

They silently communicated in that cop-coded language again, subtly plotting my arrest, then they slowly tossed me the keys to William's truck.

I smiled a devious smile, did that as I peeked out the blinds of my 3rd floor apartment to see if any more cops were hiding downstairs. Time was winding down. Time to make a move.

"Just because you don't see them, it doesn't mean they aren't there," the negotiator said.

Then he took a step forward.

I took a step back.

"Think about what you're doing young lady. You look like a smart girl. Don't throw your life away on something so—"

Another step forward.

"Don't move!" I said.

He puts his hands in the air. "No problem, I'm backing up. And as you can see, my gun is on the floor. I'm no longer carrying."

"You're not, but he is," I replied, looking at his partner that was ready to pull the trigger.

"Larry!" the negotiator snapped. "Put your goddamn gun on the floor!"

Obeying orders, his partner followed his lead.

"You see that, Angel? No more guns. No longer do you have to be threatened. Now do you trust me?"

Looking at the front door of my apartment that was three feet away, I took a deep breath, told him, "I trust no one," then I slowly backed out my apartment, watching their faces, and with Devilla as my hostage, I forced her to run down the steps as fast as she could.

"Code 416!" a cop yelled. "Code 416!"

All hell broke loose as NYPD called for back-up, which meant I only had seconds to run down six flights of stairs and climb into William's jeep.

I pointed the gun at Devilla and ordered her to run faster, panic chasing panic, fear chasing fear, we ran for our lives for two separate reasons, like red-nose pits were right on our trail.

Then I heard hard boots.

Boots from the law.

"Hurry!" I hollered at Devilla. "Move faster!"

With one flight of stairs remaining, I nearly trampled over Devilla to make it to home base. Almost slipped. Did slip. Slipped so hard that one of my heels fell off and got caught in the staircase.

The heel is a pink stiletto. Two hundred dollars.

But two hundred dollars will have to take a loss today.

"Get in the truck!" I ordered Devilla.

With one shoe on, I duck-walked to the driver-side of the unlocked jeep, my adrenaline pumping like a runaway slave.

"Stop her Dave! Stop her!" a voice yelled as I slammed the door of the jeep.

Before I could throw the jeep into reverse, another police car drove up behind me to block my exit to freedom. I smashed the entire hood of the car so I could clear up some space. NYPD ran in front of the vehicle with guns pointed at the windshield.

"Freeze," they yelled, sneering at me. "Get out your vehicle! Get out your vehicle!"

Spectators are on standby. Dozens of Brooklyn natives are witnessing this uproar, some gathering on sidewalks, others peeking out windows; my problems becoming their satellite dish.

Then, from nowhere, a rock came flying at the head of a cop, a rock thrown by a member of the neighborhood.

"Why don't you pigs get the fuck from 'round here," the crowd yelled. "Leave her alone."

Together we stand or united we fall. That's the golden rule of Brooklyn.

Trying their best to ignore the thunderous crowd, the cop car behind me turned on his loud speaker and shouted at my truck, *"Get out of your vehicle!" Get out of your vehicle with your hands in the air and you won't be harmed!"*

I roared my engine hard, an implication that I wasn't down for that plan, did that as I glanced at Devilla and told her to strap on her seat belt.

"Throw the keys out the window and exit the vehicle! Exit now and you won't be harmed!"

Deemed to do the unthinkable, I rammed my foot hard on the gas. Didn't think twice about running over cops as their eyes got big as plums – the jeep coming to claim their fate – and they dived towards the concrete like Olympic swimmers, surprised at a woman that was trying to escape.

Then bullets came flying.

Life-threatening bullets.

Bullets shooting at my tires. Denting up doors. I saw those guns in the rear view mirror that shot at one jeep, the one I was driving.

With angst on my bumper, I bent a left on Fulton St., another left on Grand, and I flooded the jeep fast and hard before making a right on Atlantic Ave. Cars are coming from both directions. It's 5pm. Rush hour traffic. The time of day when New Yorkers are at their lowest tolerance, and in Brooklyn, it's twice the tension.

A police car rear-ends my bumper, causing Devilla to duck in a startled state. I hit the gas, switched a couple lanes, but he catches up and rear-ends me again.

Devilla cries, "Why are they hitting us?"

"Why do you think?" I answered. Then I grabbed my gun. "The hell with this!"

With one hand on the wheel, I inserted the .45 with another clip before aiming out the window at the cop on my bumper. "Rear-end this!"

I fired at the cop's tire but only connected with the side mirror.

Before aiming again, I told Devilla, "Take the wheel!"

"No."

"Take the wheel right now, Devilla!"

"No."

I showed her my gun to remind her that this wasn't up for a discussion.

She complied, eyes stretching wide.

Then I stuck my .45 out the window and fired at the cop's gas tank. Fired twice. Watched him yield to my ammunition and swerve towards opposite traffic, nearly meeting an early death with Plexiglas.

I reclaimed the steering wheel from Devilla and made a strong left on Vanderbilt Ave. Tried to blend in with traffic. Kept riding until I drove up on Grand Army Plaza, a tourist beehive that connects to a park, but tourism didn't stop me from speeding up as I maneuvered on Butler, then I made a right on Flatbush Ave, the busiest street in this borough.

Running From Redemption

In my rear view mirror was a black Monte Carlo that had sped up beside me, the Monte Carlo of an undercover cop. To my surprise the cop is a woman. Can't make out her face, but I see long hair blowing out the back of a police cap.

"Pull over!" she yelled. "Pull over right now!"

I ignored her request and shot at her windshield. Glass shatters, but not before she swung her car up against my jeep.

The jeep jerks. Nearly threw me out the window.

I looked over at Devilla. "You okay?"

Her lips trembled. "Uh huh."

The cop rams into us again, this time veering us into another lane.

I shook that undercover cop by bending a left on 7th Ave., cut off a Dodge Civic and nearly ran into an SUV.

The SUV driver flips me the bird. "Asshole!"

I instantly took to the back streets, made a right on 4th and a left on 2nd where another cop had suddenly appeared. On this street – inside Park Slope Neighborhood – there are fewer traffic lights but a lot more people are traveling on foot. I blew my horn for pedestrians to move, then I approached an elderly woman that was crossing the street, a cane in one hand and a brown bag of groceries in the other. Never taking my foot off the brakes, I pressed the horn to get her attention. She freezes, eyes locking with death. Groceries fell from her hands and splattered the payment. Thinking she's too panicked to move, I shifted the car towards the sidewalk, knocked over a parking meter, sideswiped a newspaper stand that airplaned onto the street, recklessly forced a right on 4th Ave., all while Devilla squeezed her seat belt like a teddy bear, that seat belt being her guardian angel.

I glanced in my rear-view. Five-O was gone.

Actually, the cop had pulled up to my driver side to try and close me in, a cop doing everything possible to end a reckless chase that I was destined to win.

And then I saw death.

Death sat at a four-way intersection ahead of us, the type of death that's never been friendly to open caskets. If I tested my luck I was sure to be dead. But if I stopped on brakes I was sure to go to prison.

Either way my breaths were limited.

Choosing to test my luck, I glanced out my window at the cop beside me and gave him a sneer; he returned the grimace. Then I looked at the road as death winked at the both us.

Speed against speed.

Guts against guts.

Neither car is willing to yield to the intersection in front, our fate giving us the come-here finger while licking its lips.

Devilla begged me to slow down.

Instead I drove faster.

We mashed those gases and tested our limits. But within twenty feet of the intersection, before becoming closed caskets, I heard tires shrieking while trying to slow down, the tires of NYPD who suddenly pressed the brakes.

I mashed the gas pedal and never looked back.

Then I held my breath. Closed my eyes. And with every nerve in my body, I drove through that four-way intersection.

Drove while Devilla screamed to the top of her lungs.

2

Seize the moment.
    There comes a time in every person's life when they must seize the moment.
    For most of us that moment comes when we're least expecting it, a time when you've counted your losses and surrendered the hunt, then right at the peak of dropping your rifle, there goes that deer, staring you down, its beautiful eyes waiting for you to seize the moment.
    And then it flees.
    Now gone forever.
    On September 21st, the day I had a chance to murder my stepfather, there was no way I'd let that deer get away.
    Why?
    Well I used to have dreams. My mother used to tell me that no matter what people take from you, they can never take your dreams, and she preached to keep dreaming because if you dream long enough, someday your dreams will become a reality.
    My dream was to be on a billboard in the center of 46th street and Broadway, overlooking the eyes of many New Yorkers.
    Well I got my dream. I got my face on that billboard. But with that publicity, I also got words that read: *America's Most Wanted*, outlined in bold letters.

Unlike your typical criminal, I'm not a product of my environment. This caramel sistah was once crowned Salutatorian of her high school class, a top ten national merit, two years of making the dean's list, law-school student, scholarships galore, plus a bag of medals that could cover your living room wall. I was on a first class ticket to success, bypassing my contemporaries that stared jealously in the rear view.

But eventually every fast car meets a brick wall.

My brick wall was the day I became a killer. I'd killed a man who should've died years ago, the first commandment I'd broken with pride and dignity. Truth is he deserved it. Not death. No man deserves death. But he did deserve the bullet I gave him, no matter where the bullet might've torn.

There were a total of four shots. Two shots to the chest. One to the head. And one to the groin, just to show him how much I meant business. He begged for his life. Begged for an existence that he so vastly took for granted, but in my world, there's no such thing as second chances.

Twenty years ago my mother begged for that same life. She was gunned down by her husband in front of my eyes, slain by the same man that I killed with pleasure. That man went to prison when I was six years old, and from then on I went to school to set my sights on becoming a lawyer, pledging to prosecute as many criminals as possible if given the chance to live out my dream. Becoming a lawyer was the only way I knew how to avenge my mother's death, my train ticket to restoration. Somehow I thought that journey would bring contentment in my life, but truth is, it only heightened my tensioned flame, and I was still lacking real happiness.

Real happiness didn't show its face until my darkest hour, and it snuck up on me with broad shoulders, a masculine scent, and hazel eyes that glowed a block away.

His name was William Randolph, a brotha from the streets with a suburbs mentality – tall, warm smile, light brown complexion, and a breath-taking physique that was the eighth wonder of the world. William showed his face at a time when I was just picking up the pieces from a bad relationship, a time when men was considered trash on the ground.

But this man was different. With William it was love. And that love was considered unparalleled, the type that grandparents reminisce about on their front porch wearing penny loafers, grooving to the beat of a rocking chair. Yes, yes, yes. Very few women ever get a chance to feel what I felt with William Randolph. But love wasn't all that came in the bag. In essence, I was given a companion, an adviser, and considering that William was sixteen years my senior, I also fell on the lap of a father-figure, which is something I never had growing up.

William made me look at things from a different perspective. He was the perfect teacher. Taught me the difference between a tragedy and a testimony, and how one person's tragedy could be another person's testimony. He taught me forgiveness. Demonstrated the art of compassion. Showed me how the power of understanding can be the cure to anything intolerable. Just when I thought God had spat on my life, hope was restored with a man that came gift-wrapped on my front doorstep.

But love came with a price. A price stuck on a bullet.

On September 21st I threw away that love, packed love in a box and returned it back to sender. William Randolph didn't turn out to be the fallen angel that he perceived to be. With a background check and the internet on my side, William was revealed as an ex-con, a man who served a ten year prison sentence for killing his wife in 1989. That same year my mother was murdered by her husband, stripped from this existence before my very eyes, and it was then that I started puzzling the pieces together, back-tracking dates that linked William to the inevitable, then finding out that the woman William murdered was no other than my mother, Anna B. Brown.

So that would make him my stepfather. Felony of all felonies.

Since the age of six I was told by my aunt that my stepfather was murdered in prison. The night I heard the news I wept like a widow, not because he was dead, but because his blood was on someone else's hands and not mines. I wanted to kill him myself, wanted that blood dripping from my own acrylics. But now – after twenty years of being in the dark – I finally realized my aunt had been lying, and the rock she'd thrown to the bottom of the ocean had surfaced to where it showed me the light. My stepfather was not really dead. Instead, he started a life after prison that was lived in utter secrecy. That life included living under a different name, a different look, and worst of all, bedding the daughter of his ex-wife that he'd murdered years ago, that daughter being myself.

Love caused me to lay with my mother's murderer.

Love allowed Satan to drink from my refrigerator.

Because of that love I had to make a choice. I chose the road that involved a silver bullet and a four inch slide, pushed by a trigger with a mind of its own. I shot William Randolph with satisfaction, and had the police not busted through my door I would've kept shooting until my fingers went sore, until blood flooded the carpet of my living room floor.

If God never gave me anything else he gave me that sweet revenge. But sweetness quickly became bittersweet when a third party was placed at the scene.

Her name was Devilla. Little Devilla. The biological daughter of William Randolph, Devilla was a six-year-old who was going on thirty. Light-skinned. Freckled-faced. Long tangled hair. Deep dimples. And light brown eyes that resembled her father.

For that is my only regret.

Not William, but Devilla.

She's a replica of me when I was six-years-old, and considering that we both watched our parents die at our feet, looking at her was equivalent to staring dejavu in the mirror. Sometimes I wake up at night in cold sweats, staggered from hallucinations of Devilla's face. I see her little hands reaching for her father. I see her long tangled hair, her fire-red cheeks. I see her staring at me with William's eyes, the look she gave me during the massacre, the tear that ran down her face as she begged me to let loose the man that gave her life. And that same little girl is staring me down as I sped down the interstate, looking for cops.

"Could you pull over, Ms. Angel?" she asked. "I need to go potty."

I corrected her dialect. "You need to go potty or you need to use the rest room?"

She gives a who-gives-a-crap face, then answered, "I need to use the rest room."

"Very good ... But you can't go now. Not until we find the right place to stop."

It's been twenty six days since I kidnapped Devilla. Twenty six days since I left a dead father lying in an apartment with enough evidence to frame O.J. Simpson - the same apartment that was leased in my name so I couldn't go home.

For twenty-six days I've had no home.

I live on wheels and sleep on dashboards, and the only rent I pay is to the Chevron gas station that keeps the engine running in my hard-top convertible. Hotwired from the garage of a Macy's parking lot, I've rode this car through twenty-four states, rode my car like Westerns ride their horses. Because I had taken the girl, everywhere I turned there were pictures of our faces. On sidewalks. On light poles. In Walmart along with other retail stores. Cops wanted my head for x amount of dollars and Devilla was my meal ticket to staying alive.

Today, while riding pass the tips of the Grand Canyon in Arizona, I was on my way to Las Vegas, Nevada - that beautiful city infested with sin. Wasn't going for the sin though. I was going there to scoop up my passport that took weeks to process, that along with a fake I.D. I had gathered from a private source.

I was leaving the country. Leaving for good.

All I needed now was a couple hundred dollars for a plane ticket.

"There!" Devilla blurted out, pointing towards a rest stop that is crowded with people. "What about there? Don't they got restrooms?"

"Like I told you before, Devilla. No stopping at places that's filled with people. Someone might recognize us."

Dimples tightening, she dropped her eyes back into her lap and resumed playing with a Tinkerbell doll.

I told her, "The next rest stop is twenty minutes away. We'll stop there okay."

She nodded.

To you and the rest of the world I'm nothing but her kidnapper. But to Devilla I used to be a woman much more. After getting romantically involved with William Randolph, I started taking on the role as being Devilla's mother, a role I took on cold turkey after good sex and false promises. I came into their lives at a time when William Randolph was still trying to rid those demons from his past. Demons of narcotics that he sold for the dollar. Demons he tried to hide from me.

William Randolph was a single father; every dirty dollar set aside for the molding of his little princess. From enrolling her in the best private school to buying her top-of-the-line clothes, William spoiled little Devilla like age old milk, and from the time I stepped into the picture Devilla tried to knock me out that picture. That six-year-old girl drugged me to boot camp and back as I kissed her little Tinkerbell ass in every way possible. Hated her at first. Hated her before hate grew into love. Love for a girl that I now wished I had birthed from my own womb.

And she loved me back. Loved me like a mother. But the price of revenge made all of that change, and no longer am I the woman who fixes her blouse, plays hide and go seek, or sneak into her bedroom late at night to deliver strawberry ice cream. Now - with the exchange of a bullet - I'll always be one woman and one woman only in Devilla's eyes. Her daddy's killer.

Ten minutes down the road we approached an exit that carried a Denny's to the right.

Eyes lightening up, Devilla pointed out the window. "There. Can't we stop there?"

"Not yet."

"But why?"

"Like I said, too many people."

"But I gotta use the bathroom ... gotta go right now."

"Then I suggest you reach into the backseat and grab yourself a bucket. Otherwise, sit back and wait."

She puckered her lips and folded her arms. "I hate you!"

"You what?"

"I hate you! Wish my daddy never met you."

"Yeah, well I wish your daddy never met me too. Otherwise, you and I wouldn't be in this predicament."

Sneering like a baby leopard, she shot me a fuck-you stare before going back to playing with Tinkerbell.

I let a few minutes pass before I delicately told her, "I'm sorry for what I did to your father ... but what you don't know is that a long long time ago he ... he took someone special from me too ... not saying that two wrongs make a right. But at the same time ... I just couldn't control the moment."

Her unforgiving face never loses its scowl, a six-year-old that wanted to crumble up my apology and throw it out the window.

At times I feel guilty. Guilty because I love Devilla and I didn't want to add this segment to her life, nor did I want to endanger her on this unpredicted journey. But no matter how much I loved her I wasn't ready to free the birdie from the nest. Not until I got my passport. Not until the feds were completely out of range.

After five more minutes of driving, I eventually approached the exit that Devilla needed in Kingman, Arizona. Located in a secluded area, there was nothing around except sycamore trees and a rundown gas station, and after glancing at my quarter-filled gas tank I decided to kill two birds with one stone.

Ten minutes.

That was the agreement I had with Devilla, ten minutes and ten minutes only to use the bathroom, grab us some snacks, and be back on the road to hit our next destination, but my words fell short to her bowels that bubbled inside the passenger seat, and before I could whip the convertible into the gas station, Devilla quickly opened the door to head for the toilet.

"Hold on!" I stopped her. "You stay by my side at all times, never go in front. Understood?"

She nodded while holding her stomach, those bowels now playing hop scotch.

"And aren't you missing something?"

She reached back into the car for a baseball cap and a pair of black shades, her hidden disguise from the outside world. I shaded myself in the same attire, took no chances when it came to my freedom.

Gun stored in my purse, I clinched her hand like mother and daughter and walked towards the gas station watching our backs. Before going inside, we bumped into a family that was walking to their car. Mother and two daughters. Asian descent. Both girls were the same age as little Devilla.

I smiled at them in passing. But I suddenly got frightened as one of the little Asian girls stopped in her tracks, slung back her head, those dark beanie eyes now staring at Devilla, then pointing at Devilla while yanking on her mother's shirt. I stutter-stepped, almost panicked, then realized it wasn't Devilla who the little girl had recognized. It was Tinkerbell on the back of Devilla's blouse.

An upset Asian mama snatched her daughter's arm and dragged her to the car, anger implying that Tinkerbell was not in the budget.

I tightened Devilla's hand and walked on. Walked into the gas station where a young skinny white boy was working behind the counter. Twenty-one at most, he had spiky dark hair that shot up into an ocean wave, lip and nose piercings, was 100% the Gothic type. Wearing black Vans shoes that were kicked up on a wooden chair, his eyes were engrossed into a Marvel Comic Book, so engrossed that he never even saw Devilla and I standing at the counter.

I tapped on the counter to grab his attention. "Excuse me, but is there a bathroom inside this—"

"Be wit' you in a sec'," he said, cutting me off while taking those eyes back to his comic.

I reached across the counter and shut-closed his literature. That was considered murder in his eyes.

"For the second time," I told him. "Where is your bathroom?"

"Outside by the garbage dump okay."

"Good. Now we're finally getting somewhere."

He sneered. "Anything else?"

"If it's not too much to ask, give me two packs of skittles, two orange Fantas, and twenty on pump four."

I went into my purse for twenty-five dollars, twenty-five taken from the eighty I had total. Cash was getting low, was damn near broke, and I didn't have a plan for buying that plane ticket.

No plan except my criminal thoughts that were preaching a sermon.

Seeing no one inside the gas station except me and Comic Book Boy, I ran my nails across the .45 that rested within my purse. Thought about robbing the joint. Quickly reconsidered. Would've done so if it wasn't for the hidden cameras checking me out. Wasn't worth the risk.

Out of my purse came twenty five dollars that I handed to Comic Book Boy with a stranger's smile. He returned my change and a silver key to the bathroom, then he said, "Make sure you bring this key back to me okay. There is no duplicate."

Zipping up my purse, I walked Devilla out the gas station and around the corner to the bathroom, inspected it first, then reminded her that she had eight minutes only to shed those pounds and under no circumstances is she to sit on that filthy toilet.

As she handled her business, I stood outside the bathroom door. Stood and watched the world that was constantly watching me. More cars drove up to the gas station. A Chevy Taurus. Grand Prix. Tahoe. All different shades of people that I put in my photographic memory bank, observing them to see if any were potential threats. In the fugitive world you can never put your guard down for one minute. That would be considered suicide.

Eventually my nose caught a whiff of a foul odor in the area. Thought it was Devilla, but no six-year-old bowels should smell that awful, then I noticed it was the garbage dump that sat across the grass. Amongst that trash was two dozen vultures flying over a dead carcass, they all fighting for a meal that'll allow them to live another day. Like humans, it's every vulture for themselves, the recession forming a pandemic amongst all species in this cosmos. One vulture had given up on the fight and decided to take another course of action. It found its supper around a light pole that had a flyer thumb-tacked on all corners, a flyer that grabbed my attention to make me step in that direction. The closer I approached the light pole the more I saw a face that resembled mines. I did a double-look. Saw me again, also saw a message beneath it that read:

FBI wanted.
Felon on the loose.
Armed and Dangerous.

That message followed with another picture of Devilla.

Missing person's case.
$20,000 to any leads of our whereabouts.

I stood up straight. Looked around. Eyeballed the world for any eyes that weren't minding their business, and after seeing no spectators, I quickly snatched down the flyer to crumble it up, tossed it in the dumpster, and I sped-walked back to the bathroom to snatch up my little meal ticket.

I banged on the door. "Devilla, Hurry it up. We gotta move."

"Okay ... just another moment."

A minute later I heard the toilet flush, heard the belt of a little girl pulling up her pants with the sound of water running from the faucet.

But a minute after that the door never opened.

I paced around in a circle. Bit at my fingernails. Got impatient.

I knocked again. "Devilla, wipe your little butt and let's go now."

No answer. Only the sound of running water.

Impatience started hammering at my nerves, told me that either she fell in the toilet or was going after the longest crap award. Motherly instinct kicked in. I pulled out the key to force myself inside, but inside that bathroom was no Devilla. No foul odor. No sign of a little girl insight.

The faucet was turned on full blast, water running faster than the thoughts in my head, paper towels all over the floor, the toilet seat being down, and on top of the toilet seat was footprints. Tinkerbell footprints. That animated character had left its mark from the back of the toilet to the dirt-filled walls, then up to a window that opened to freedom.

Looking outside that bathroom window, I screamed for Devilla to stop, but my meal ticket was running for her life through the patchy grass. Saw her glance back with freedom running deep in her eyes, freedom that would've outran Cunta Kinte any day, those Tinkerbell shoes kicking up dirt as if they were ready to be airborne. Natural instinct told me to climb out the window and go after Devilla, but common sense intervened, reminded me that these breasts would never fit, not even slicked down with oil.

"Dammit!" I yelled, jumping off the toilet.

I left the bathroom and ran across the street in her direction, ran into a mini forest of bright sycamore trees while trying to find her, noticing she was out of sight.

I searched that tree trunk heaven while screaming her name. Got no response. Screamed again. No answer except a flock of vultures that filled the sky, humming in search for another dead carcass. I tried to think like a six year-old and look for their ideal hiding spots. Started running in circles. Then walking in circles. Did that while kicking up leaves and looking through trees. Baby Tinkerbell could be in a rabbit hole and I'll never even know.

Eventually I saw that the wilderness led to a construction site on the other side of the street, and behind that hazardous site was the noisy freeway, nowhere else to go. I kept calling for Devilla like a Christian for Jesus, my echo trying to call her too. Fatigue set in. Titties started soaking in my bra from getting cooked by the sun, had to be at least a hundred degrees out here with an overcast of hell. Wanted to call it quits, but concernment wouldn't allow me to throw in the towel.

Then I saw footprints. Sketched in the dirt.

A clue that Devilla was near.

The footprints had large gaps in between them, another clue that she was still running for her life. I followed that trail of the cat, became anxious, but suddenly the footprints stopped, shifted right, and met up with larger footprints that no longer had the trademark of Tinkerbell, but instead the trademark of Timberland – a pair of Timberland boots. The footprints showed Timberland and Tinkerbell joining forces, then fleeing trough the dirt, leaving a trail of zig zag patterns that quickly became blurred, shadowy, and fading into a non-existence that led to another FBI flyer, *Felon on the loose*. Saw my picture mean-mugging me while lying on the ground, a Timberland footprint stuck on my papered face.

For there was a third wheel at the party.

An uninvited guest.

I stopped moving and looked around for that mystery, saw no one, heard no one, but knew someone was near, perhaps watching me from the distance.

Thinking that if they found Devilla they would find me too, I left that construction site and hoofed it back towards the gas station for my car, all while never looking back, cursing in my mind, jumping in the car, cursing some more, and after breaking a nail from slamming the door, I cursed out loud from the searing pain.

Angry and sweaty, I roared up the convertible, only to see Comic Book Boy coming out the gas station with his animated literature at his side.

He yelled out, "Eh lady, you mind returning that bathroom key?"

I shot him the finger and sped away.

3

Thirty minutes later on a heavy traffic freeway, I was flooding my car at 90 mph, heartbeat racing, cutting drivers off, was glancing in the rear view mirror every ten seconds for the closest-looking car that resembled a cop.

I had grabbed a different ride. Also switched up the wig. The convertible was left in a hotel parking lot and replaced with a car that I stole at gun point. Stole it from a couple. A couple getting busy. I ran up on a young Latin woman that had her face buried in the pants of a lust-filled man, told the man that he had two seconds to give up the keys before I gave his woman an extra hole to breathe out of, then I sped off quickly, wearing a ski mask, left the man standing with a limp penis and a half-naked shell-shocked lover.

Now driving a different route, I was fifteen minutes from Devilla's disappearance, fifteen minutes from the landmark that could lead feds to my capturing. The next sign to Vegas read 87 miles. The logical part of my brain begged me to make a U-turn and forget about my passport, but the illogical part held a stronger debate; it reminded me that although Devilla had broken loose, she posed no threat, because in her mind we were on our way to San Diego, California to head for the border.

Cops would be at that border. And I'll be in Vegas.

Thinking I had shaken the feds for a second time, I popped open the glove compartment to search my new whip, started looking to see if the lovebirds had left anything behind for my grabbing. I closed it back shut after seeing nothing profitable, nothing but a signature on stacks of papers that read Hertz Rental; the love birds must've been on vacation because this wasn't even their car.

I kept my search going stringently. Ran my fingers through the console to look for spare cash. Instead I found lotion, three pens, and a bag full of mints. No money in the ashtray. No change in the seats. I'd stolen a car more naked than skin.

I stretched my arm in the backseat and accidentally got my hands on a large gift bag with items encased in decorative wrapping.

Jackpot.

Wrapped in that paper was all Louis Vuitton. Louis Vuitton belt, Louis Vuitton pants, and a Louis white purse that brought on a smile, every item carrying lucrative price tags that totaled to $1,626.57, paid for by Visa. At the bottom of the bag was a handwritten note:

> *Happy Birthday to my beautiful Sole'.*
> *Hope you enjoy this day.*
> *Love, Solomon*

Seeing that the note served me no purpose, my eyes went back to the Visa receipt, and I started looking for credit card digits.

xxxx xxxx xxxx 7368.

Double jackpot. But four digits alone wouldn't get me what I wanted.

I picked up my untraceable phone to call the Luis Vuitton store, and I pretended to be the wife of Loverboy who had purchased these items.

"Thank you for calling Louis Vuitton," a clerk answered at the store. "Edward speaking."

I became over-dramatic. "You bastards overcharged my card!"

"Excuse me?"

"Me and my husband just bought a few items from your store and there's no way we spent 3,000 dollars! Y'all better straighten this out and straighten this out fast before I—"

"Okay ma'am. Calm down for a second. Did you say you purchased something from this store?"

"Yes goddammit. And you bastards overcharged our card. You know what that means you moron? It means I can't pay my bills until your company—"

"Hold on ma'am. Just calm down."

"I am calm!"

"Was your purchase made today?"

"Don't you listen? Are you deaf? I just said yes!"

He took a deep breath as if he hated the fact that the customer was always right, and he came back with, "What did you purchase?"

I gave him the Louis items, then I started breathing impatient breaths as he searched inside the system.

He said, "I remember this order; it was made this morning. But the name on the card is from a man."

"For the fourth time, that's my goddamn husband!"

"Solomon?"

"Yes, we have a joint account."

"Well I'm sorry ma'am but there must be some type of mistake. It looks here that you were only charged once for these items."

"Not according to the credit card company. They said your stupid store charged me freaking twice!"

"Okay okay. Just give me a second ... You paid by Visa ... a debit purchase... Can you verify the last four digits of the card?"

I looked at the receipt, answered, "7368."

"Expiration date of 9/14/2012?"

"Yes goddammit yes!" I hollered, writing down the date while focusing on the highway.

"Well I'm sorry ma'am but I only show one payment."

"And I show double payment, so I suggest you look again."

"If you bring in your credit card statement, we can take a look at it together and go from there."

"I don't have no damn gas money to be turning around and riding to y'all store all because your stupid system made a mistake and charged my fucking card twice you—"

"Ma'am, ma'am," he says getting nervous. "I'ma need you to calm down so we can—"

"I will not calm down! I will not calm down! We're talkin' 'bout a thousand dollars missing and you expect me to be calm." I took a hard breath. "Are you sure you looking at the right purchase?"

"Yes ma'am."

"Card ending with 7368?"

"Yes.

"And the first twelve digits?"

"636282496624."

Jackpot. I tried to keep up by scribbling on the receipt, and I repeated, "6362 ... 8249 ... and 66 what?"

"6624. Visa debit. The system show this as the account # that you and your husband used. Is that correct?"

I switched lanes while jotting down the last two digits.

"Ma'am," he repeated. "Is that account # correct?"

Knowing I had talked my way into someone's personal account, I smiled, hung up the phone, then I called the credit card company to get a balance of what was in loverboy's account.

But I reached a dead-end. One I didn't see coming.

I was missing the Card Security Code on the back of the card, and there was no way of sweet-talking the man that worked for the credit card company, not without verifying an address, date of birth, social security number, and a password. He started asking me unnecessary questions as if he was prying for information, and it was then that I realized what was going on. Loverboy had previously called to cancel his credit card, and I was being set up for credit card fraud. I hung up instantly, which sucked because I was stuck with expensive items that I could not return.

Then I thought of Vegas.

A hustler's paradise.

If I upped my sex appeal, I could sell these items on the Vegas strip in a matter of minutes. Figured I wouldn't get much for the pants or belt, but the handbag could earn at least five hundred dollars. That was more than enough to purchase a one-way plane ticket and get out the country by tomorrow.

In the midst of calculating my net worth, I noticed the traffic was gradually starting to slow down on US93. I eased the gas pedal from 90 to 70. Then 60 to 40. Then 30 to screaming a mouth of foul language, wondering what the hell was causing a delay.

Traffic jam. A place where people got impatient, road rage spread, and horns sang in unison to loud cursive anguish. I poked my head outside the window to check out the problem, but I wasn't able to see past an eighteen wheeler, nor could I switch up lanes to get a better view. After thirty minutes of only covering two miles, I noticed people getting more impatient, cars cutting cars off, and the driver behind me kept riding my bumper, was two seconds from getting out my vehicle and shooting a bitch through the window, my temper now rising to the roof. Because I was thirty miles from Vegas, trapped in Boulder City,

I figured that the high-end traffic was from people wanting to see The Hoover Dam, but according to locals, that tourist attraction is only heavy between the hours of 10 – 3pm; it was now approaching nightfall.

Then I heard sirens.

Heard cops nearby.

My neck spun like an owl as I ducked in my seat, temperament leaped from aggravation to a strong sense of paranoia, probably because for every cop-like tune there was an officer I felt who was coming for me.

Or coming for Devilla.

Coming in droves.

While waiting stationary in that traffic jam, I saw a half dozen police on the opposite side of the highway that sped behind a raucous ambulance. Flashing lights chasing flashing lights, they zipped across the grass that connected both highways, then they weaved into the cracks of this chaotic jam, leaped out their vehicles, strapped on equipment, and rushed towards an accident lightning in flames.

I felt relieved, became relaxed.

While a person in a car was struggling to breath I breathed fresh air from that monkey off my shoulder.

But it was only so long before that monkey would re-appear.

Devilla.

She was still out there. Still flapping her wings like a lost little birdie.

More than likely that birdie had reached another nest.

And now vultures were coming. V-shaped formations. Tracking the features I left behind.

Thirty short miles took two long hours, not counting the traffic once entering the city.

I'd finally reached Vegas – home of the moneymakers and heaven for the sinners. A place that has always been on my top places to see list, just never planned on seeing it as a criminal.

Although I'm here on business, it was hard to ignore the magnificent scenery that Vegas had to offer. I was passing through a street called Dean Martin Drive, bumper to bumper traffic, a street that seemed like it had no end. Palm trees covered both sides of the street. That reminded me of sunny South Florida, only difference was that

Vegas trees were lit up light Christmas. Tall luxurious hotels sat on both sides of the street: The MGM. Treasure Island. The Bellagio. Caesar's Palace. Each hotel owned a grand casino and massive colored waterfalls that shot into the sky, dozens of rainbows coloring the night. Lights flashed from every angle to attract tourists like honeybees. There were truckloads of people that crowded the street. From Black, to White, to Asian, to Native American, I saw ethnic group after ethnic group. Seemed like the United Nations was having a party and the theme was to bring a friend. Camcorders. Throw-away cameras. Cell-phones that could do everything but fly. Everyone wanted a snapshot of greatness, and the more I blew my horn the more they cluttered the streets, people looking into skies like Christ was fixing to burst through the clouds at any given moment.

I looked in the passenger seat and saw my hustle bag, got back focused. Hoping someone could point me in the right direction, I tried grabbing the attention of three Caucasian girls that were crossing an intersection, each wearing purple spandex tights with long spiral hair that fell down their backs, highlighted with strips of pink. Looking to be in their mid-twenties, they were dancing to a soundless beat, liquored to the core, six legs doing a jacked-up dance that was completely off rhythm. They were thin-shaped, make that pencil-shaped, and for some strange reason they had taken off their heels. Three Paris Hiltons gone wild.

I let down the window to grab the attention of the one most sober. "Y'all know where the Vegas Strip is located?"

One shot me the finger while the other two laughed, then they went back to doing their jacked-up dance.

I sped up, drove off.

A half-block down the road was a Latin couple that was holding hands. They were dressed in all white, both wearing shirts that read, *What happens in Vegas*, followed by three question marks. The man has his hand on the woman's rear, gripping it with pleasure, and the woman smiled back at his kung fu grip.

I loud-talked the man to try and test my luck again. "Hey there! You know where the Vegas Strip is located?"

They looked at me like the tourist I was, then turned to each other and giggled. My temper replied what the hell is so funny.

The Latin guy yells, "You're already on the strip, baby ... all of this is considered the strip."

I screamed out thanks and kept moving right along, but not before the man winked at me and seductively decided to stick out his tongue.

I ignored the gesture, kept moving right along.

After searching and searching for a parking space, I lucked up on an empty parking meter on one of the back roads, a few streets down from the party. Then I quickly changed into my hustlers outfit. Skin tight jeans. Open-toe heels. A black ruffled blouse that showed some cleavage, I dabbed on some oil to set off a sparkle.

Wigs. I had dozens of wigs. From constant ducking and dodging the police, one day I was Halle Berry, the next day Vivica Fox, and depending on the stakes, there was always the black Marilyn Monroe. Tonight I did Halle. A short brush-cut wig that was low on the sides, I wrapped up my hair to pack it beneath and spritzed it down before getting out the car.

Then the gun.

Almost forgot the gun, needed it in case some shit popped off.

After sticking it inside the holster of my ankle that hid beneath my jeans, I popped open the trunk to snatch up my trinkets. Coach purse in hand. Bracelets in purse. Started up the one-way road that was a quarter mile from the strip, a back road that was too dangerous for a woman to be traveling herself.

Urine. Sex. Alcohol. Cigarettes. Each of those smells paid rent to this street, distinctive smells that was a clear indication of my whereabouts. I had stumbled in Satan's playground. The land of the nightwalkers. A place where brains have been replaced with breasts and booty is worth more than a PHD, a stench that made me heighten my pace as I stepped over used condoms and broken Heineken bottles, potholes in the road, nearly broke a heel.

On this one-way street - a street darker than a coffin - estrogen dominates the entire area. Every corner is run by the power of the stiletto or the lining of the thong, cars passing through at the pace of a drive-by, and each driver is glancing in their rear view mirror for the right woman to fill their passenger seats.

There's an old saying that goes, *In order to run with the Jones's you must watch how the Jones's operate.*

That saying stuck in my head as I strutted this block where hookers began to eyeball me vigorously. The hookers ranged in all shapes and sizes. Some full-figured. Some skinny. Some carrying assets faker than a humanized clone. Some barely eighteen. Some eighteen times three. Some looked like they've been hooking for decades, as if a pension plan came with the deal.

Then I felt a hand.

Someone had grabbed me by the ass and spun me around. I became stagnate. Throat got tight.

In front of me was a dark-skinned man that looked to be in his mid-forties. Medium-build. Smile on his face. But the smile changed after telling him to let go of my goddamn ass. He lets go and says, "It's okay, Beautiful. I just wanted to make sure it was as soft as it looks."

He licks his lips and caresses a shabby-looking beard. Green pin-striped suite. Chains around the neck. Everything about this man said raggedly pimp, from the shiny gold shoes to the hair that was permed with a bad rinse.

He asks me, "So what's your name, Sweet Thang?"

I became frank. "Not interested."

"Not interested huh? That's not a good name for a sexy woman like yourself. How 'bout I call you Caramel?"

"How 'bout no?"

He starts circling around my frame as if he was calculating the amount of money I'd bring to his empire. "Yes ... yes ... yes," he mutters while staring down my shirt. "Caramel fits you good. Why don't you pull those bad girls out to give Sweet Willie a better view?"

"Who?"

"Sweet Willie," he repeated, licking lips once more.

"Okay then, Mr. Sweet Willie. How 'bout you get a better view of this." I gave him the finger and told him to go find some other girl to play with.

His face fills with anger. "You disrespecting me?"

"For the last time, get out my face and go find some other girl to pimp."

More anger in his eyes, knuckles turning into fists. No longer does he represent the smooth pimp persona. He's now a disrespected pimp that's waiting to unload on a bad-mouthed woman.

I turned my back on him to walk away. But then I felt a hand grab me by the neck. A hand that made me reach for my ankle to pull out my gun, but before I could bend down, he yanked my wrist to beat me to the punch, then tells me, "Listen here you ho—"

"Let her go!" someone yelled from afar.

Across the street was a slender, fair-skinned woman who was coming this way, pissed-off pace, her walk just as stank as mines.

"Don't you dare touch her!" she yelled.

Four-inch heels. Silver-chain belt. Dreadlocks crawling mid-way down her back with hell in her eyes that glowed in the night, she stopped in front of me and lashed at the pimp, "Back off, Whilly! Back off now!"

With a hand to my throat and a doubt in his eyes, he contemplates on letting me loose. Then he glared back at the fair-skinned woman, glared at her like a leopard intruding on a life or death meal.

He yells out, "Dammit, Snow! Why you always gotta come round here playin' supa-sava-ho. This has nothing to do with you."

"When you're messin' with one of my girls, it has everything to do with me."

"One of your girls? How so?"

"Don't matter. Just take your dirty hands off of her okay."

"Or what?" he says, whipping out a blade. "Now get lost befo' I take this to another level."

The woman reaches behind her back, pulls out a pistol, and she aims it at the one place on his body that's able to think.

In a calm voice, she tells him, "We can take this shit to any level you wanna take it to."

His eyes widen with fear. "Oh I see ... so it's like that."

"It's like that."

Silence.

Realizing he had no win, the pimp counted his losses, released my throat, and he walked that loud green suit right back into the darkness.

The woman slowly stores her gun back into its rightful place, did that while looking around to ensure no cops were on standby. I looked around too, heartbeat slowing down, thinking how I should've been quicker on my feet for that raggedly pimp.

Then I looked at my savior, the chick known as Snow. "You were willing to kill a man for a woman you don't even know. How come?"

"Because it was my first instinct," she answers, "and I always go with my first instinct."

"Instincts can get you killed."

"Or they can save lives."

I nod my head. "Well for what it's worth ... thanks for being there."

"No need to thank me. Something tells me you would've done the same for me."

I look at her as if she's off her rocker. "Sorry, but I'm not that type of woman."

"What type of woman?"

"The type that meddles in other people's business. If I don't know you, I keep it moving."

Running From Redemption

"That's easy to say, but even the most heartless person has a heart sometimes. And usually, in life or death situations, the heart will surely overpower the mind."

She says that with conviction, as if those words were once said to her and they're now being passed down to me; first two minutes in Vegas and I'm already getting advice from a hooker. How strange?

I thanked her again, then I turned my back to walk away, didn't have time for useless conversation.

"Wait a second!" she hollered.

I turned around, pulled in my lips. "What do you want?"

"Your Louis Vuitton bag."

I looked down at my purse, then back at her. "Only if you're willing to take a bullet for it."

"Oh no honey. It's not like that. Just wanna know how much you're selling the bag for."

"Who said I was selling it?"

"Oh please. On this street you're either pushing pussy or pushing retail. And if you were hooking, I'd be the first to know. So don't BS me, how much is the bag going for?"

"Okay then. Three hundred."

"Three hundred for a fake purse?"

"The purse isn't fake. It's 100% real and it's ... anyways ... you interested or not?"

"I'm very interested. Just not in the purse."

An unpleasant thought struck me like a tumor.

I told her, "Let's not get this twisted okay. I appreciate you having my back and all, but in case you thought I was a dyke—"

"A dyke?"

"Yeah, and I ain't—"

"Wrong chick," she said, her voice unintentionally rising. Inclination tells me I've insulted her, which is good, because that answers my question.

She straightens her face, "Just so we're clear, know that I'm not a lesbian. I like men. Only men. Lay up with a different man every night. Strictly dickly."

"Well that makes two of us."

She laughs. We both laugh at something we finally can agree on. Afterwards, she reaches into her pocket to pull out a cigarette, fired up her smoke, then offered me a hit.

I declined.

She says, "A school girl huh? Good for you."

As she inhaled, I turned my attention back towards her wardrobe. She might not be a lesbo, but with fishnet tights and Cuba-dressed boots, she was definitely a night walker. Her dreadlocks were skinny and spirally, followed with red highlights burning at the ends to go with her fair-skinned complexion. She was slender like me, just a cup size smaller, wore a rust orange top that suffocated her breasts. On the front of that shirt was a half-naked woman sitting on a motorcycle, followed with the words, *I PUT THE SIN IN SIN CITY*!!

I'd be lying if I said she wasn't pretty. If I was a hooker, she'd be competition.

I told her, "So the pimp referred to you as Snow. How come?"

"Isn't it obvious," she answered. "I'm a shade from being albino. Besides, it was given to me by my father. Hell, that's 'bout the only thing that bastard ever gave me. That and this money-making body."

She started blabbering about her life, a life she claimed she resented to the grave. Like me, her mother was murdered when she was a kid, never knew her father either, had to be raised by the relative with the most patience or whoever was the highest bidder. She comes from a broken home. Broken homes usually reflect broken hearts. And that brokenness mirrored her perception of the world.

But although our foundation was similar, our outlook on life was different.

While I went to school all my life, she stopped going after the sixth grade, told me how the streets were the best teacher a person could have and she wouldn't trade that education for all the professors at Harvard. She was content with being who she was, a lateral move-maker. I on the other hand was stuck on progression. A life without progression is a plane crashing down. I didn't act as if I was better than her, because my shit didn't have the scent of fresh roses either, but then again, regardless of my present circumstances, I wasn't a hooker. Wasn't tossing around my body for a green piece of paper. I had pride. Had integrity. Two simple words that separated us, made us see the world from two different glasses.

One view we did share were our thoughts on men. That was to never trust them, and always remember that a man's word only goes as far as his erection. She confessed stories about men that once screwed her over, about men on the streets, and how she grew stronger from each heartbreaking encounter. She confessed that she's been hooking for twenty years, running the streets since the age of sixteen, then explained how this became her life by choice and not by chance. She was much older than me. Ten years my senior. But aging and stress has skipped passed her life because she still looked like she could pass for twenty-one, and in her eyes, the look raised her clientele of men.

Our conversation went on for almost a half hour. She did most of the talking, and I just stood there like a priest behind a confession booth, listening to her stories, all while milking her for information on Vegas, my new hiding spot. I noticed she wasn't interested in my life one bit, never even asked me my name. The few questions she asked I gave false answers. In my eyes I didn't owe her the truth. Didn't owe her anything. The truth meant the will to trust, and when you're a felon on the run, you can't trust anyone.

After finishing up her confessions, she said, "You know what? I've got big money coming in tonight. How 'bout we make this money together."

"Together?"

"Yeah. You know like partners."

I pressed her brakes. "Sorry but I don't do partnerships. I work alone. Always have. Always will."

"Why?"

"Because when it comes to money, the only person I trust is Mr. Benjamin. And if you're not cautious, even he will stab you in the back and wind up in someone else's pocket."

She laughs, "Never heard it put like that before. That's clever."

"Yeah, but it's real."

She brings another cigarette to her mouth, holds in her smoke, then lets it out with a slow release.

She says, "I'll tell you what else is real. The money you're trying to make alone will never amount to the money we can make together."

"Yeah, and how is that? I hope not hooking, 'cause I don't get down like that. These goods are not for sale."

She smiles. "Girl, hooking only pays the bills. Any chick with a hole can stop a car. But I'm talkin' 'bout somethin' else. Somethin' that takes certain skills."

"Well unless it's an ATM machine down the crack of your butt, considered me uninterested. There's nothing you can offer that I haven't tried already, especially when it comes to money."

"Okay then, suit yourself. But you're missing out on some real money here."

"Yeah? How real?"

She straightened her face, dished the girly smile and gave a womanly glare. "Real enough to where you can stop hustling purses. I'm talking thousands of dollars in one single night."

My hearing sense became more alert, ears flaring out like a German Sheppard.

She adds, "Not to mention, the gig doesn't even require much."

I swung at her pitch. "Exactly what type of gig are we talkin' 'bout?"

"Three words: The Mirage Hotel."

"Excuse me?"

She goes on, "Ever done a bachelor party?"

"Not lately."

"Well get ready, 'cause here's your chance."

I tilted my head to let it circulate, considered it, but it didn't sound good enough to take the bait. Bachelor parties require people, lots of people, which meant I could possibly be recognized by the wrong person.

I told her, "Nah, I'm not interested in this bachelor party thing. Last thing I need is a bunch of fat, greasy guys tugging at my g-string."

"What if I told you that those fat, greasy guys were paying us ten grand for one session."

I dropped my jaw. "Ten grand?"

"Ten grand each … tax free … not including tips."

She smiles a confident smile as if she's gained control, a poker face waiting to collect a ton of chips.

Meanwhile, I did the calculation of ten grand in my head. Added the comma. Carried the one. Damn, ten grand. It was a helluva lot of money. Money I could never get on these streets.

Thinking there had to be a catch involved, I spun that wheel of fortune, asked her, "What type of men pay twenty large for a bachelor party?"

"Rich men. Established men. Men that come to Vegas for all the wrong reasons, dreading going back to a married man's life."

"And how do you know these men? Were one of them your clients?"

"Like I told you earlier, I'm the queen on these streets. When big money comes to Vegas, I'm always the first to know. Hell, I would do it myself but they requested two girls."

"And what about these other women out here?"

"What about 'em?"

"Why haven't you tried to team up with one of them?"

"Girl pa-leeze. Have you seen the girls out here? They don't got half of what it takes to make a c-note, let alone ten stacks. But you on the other hand..." She looks me up and down, takes in a smoke, her eyes glaring at my body like a prisoner on work-release. Then she smiles while blowing fumes into the night. "You got a different look ya know ... an innocent look. You fit the profile that men are looking for?"

"Which is?"

"A young naïve pussy that's straight out of Melrose place." She giggles. A giggle more creepy than funny. "Oh yes, girl. With your type of figure, we can make a whole lot of money ... So what do you think? Sounds good?"

Questions run through my head like gladiators, but then again, any answer she gave would be questionable, which left me repeating the same dumb question. "Exactly how much did you say was involved here?"

"Ten grand each ... that's five up front, five afterwards ... not including tips."

"And how do we know they'll pay?"

"Because one, they have too much to risk if they don't pay, and two, these are not strangers. These are men I know. And one thing they know is that no one underhands Snow and lives to tell about it. End of story."

I thought about the money, about how it could help me, thoughts on top of thoughts while juggling more thoughts.

Ten grand, Angel.

Ten grand vs. ten cents in my pocket.

Might not seem like much for a corporate woman, but for me right now, ten grand looked more like ten million, was enough money to get lost in another country, perhaps start all over and never look back.

I rubbed my fingertips together, tugged at my hair, a trademark of mines when decisions are hard.

Cars continue to pass us full of testosterone. Nightwalkers are still on the stroll, women circling the block like hungry cheetahs. A few of them recognized Snow in passing. Some said a word or two. Others saluted her with a wave as if she was the matriarch of these streets. She acknowledged each passer to show me her status, but in between useless conversation and mist filling dark skies, there were dead silence between me and Snow, silence building a brick wall as she waited on an answer.

"Exactly how many men are we talking here?" I asked. "Ten? Twenty? Fifty—"

"What does it matter, college girl? Look, I'm through with the questions. You're either in or out. Your choice."

She stood up straight, hands on her hips, brushed locks away from an impatient face.

I thought about how I didn't know this chick from a can of paint. But even if I did know her, she was still considered a woman, and one thing I don't do is other females. I learned that from mama. Another woman could care less about you and their always waiting to stab you in the back, if they haven't cut you already. Last thing I needed was another woman friend.

But what I did need was money.

No friend like Mr. Benjamin, even if it meant befriending some woman.

Going against the grain, I took a deep breath and told her straight up. "Let's do it."

4

The time was 10pm. Bachelor party would start in twenty minutes.

I was on the fourth floor of the Saraha hotel, room 409, just finished towel-drying my hair after showering up. All my sexy outfits were laid out for tonight's mission; I was indecisive of what to wear. As far as the disguise goes, my choices of wigs were one of a kind. In one pile there was the short school-girl, cream colored wig while the other wig was more business-woman like, a mocha brown with long spiral curls down my back.

Then the phone rang, an unfamiliar ring-tone coming from my purse. The caller's number was unknown. I let it keep ringing; not answering unknown calls is a universal rule. A second later I heard the doorknob rattle, sounded like someone was breaking and entering in my hotel room. I froze. Told myself that housekeeping better have a damn good reason for bulging in, unless they wanted to get shot.

But housekeeping doesn't wear four inch heels.

The woman coming through the door was no other than Snow, doing what she does best, intruding. Whether we're on the street or indoors, that hooker-stroll will always be her Naomi Campbell walk.

Snow is wearing a short leather skirt with a thick chain belt, her multicolored locks tied in a pin. A tight leather top is hugging her arms like she's about to play the next cat woman. Make-up is professionally done.

"Snap snap, sexy," she says. "We don't have much time."

I asked, "How the hell did you get inside? I only have one key."

She smirks. "Don't sleep on my skills, Hun. The power of the tit will cause a desk-clerk to do anything. Now where's the bathroom?"

"Straight ahead."

She walks over to the mirror, starts pulling at her eyelashes, all while reaching into her purse. Out of the purse comes an extra pair of eye-lashes.

I ask, "What are you doing?"

"What does it look like? I'm getting prepared. Putting on the final touches."

Her hands go back and forth into her bag of tricks, pulling out everything from make-up to push-up bras to Lee press-on nails to hazel contacts. If there was an award for the fakest chick in Vegas, she'd win hands down.

Then she tosses some clothes on the bed. Similar to hers. Leather pants with a strapless top.

She says, "That's your outfit for tonight ... our theme is leather."

I looked at the skimpy top, then put it up to my 34D's.

I asked her, "Are you serious? I can't wear this."

"Why not?"

"Because my tits will die of suffocation that's why ... in case you haven't noticed, I'm a black girl. Gimme somethin' that's not so tiny."

"That's all I got, Angel. Besides, the tighter the sexier."

"Thought I was playing the innocent school-girl look?"

"Change of plans. Now hurry up. We don't have much time."

I rushed into the leather pre-school outfit, fastened the zipper midway up my top with light glitter laying on my chest. I also wore black lipstick and big earrings. Snow convinced me that the dark wig with flip up curls would go best, told me that I looked like Janet Jackson at the super bowl, when she lost her mind and flashed a tit for millions of viewers.

Before we leave, Snow says, "Wait. Forgot something."

She goes back into the bathroom and unzips her bag. Out comes a long black whip. Thick and curvy. Dominatrix style.

I asked, "What you plan on doin' with that?"

"What does it look like?" She slings the whip against the wall to create a fierce sting. "I plan on whippin' some ass with it."

I laugh at her like she's gone too far.

She smiles back at me. "You'll be surprised at the things that turn men on."

"Oh trust me, I know. But you don't really plan on hittin' someone with that thing do you?"

"I will if they get outta line ... we gotta keep control up in there."

"Whatever. Just don't aim that thing in this direction while you're keepin' control."

"That reminds me," she says, pulling out another weapon. This time it's a big white paddle that's also used for spanking. She holds it in the air next to the whip. "Which one you want?"

I suck my teeth at her. "You crazy ... I'm not spanking anyone."

"Trust me, Angel. They like it. I be having those rich men hollering my name while I paddle them. Ooooh Snow ... Ooooh Snow."

We both start cracking up.

"Why don't you keep them both for yourself," I told her.

"You sure?"

"Very sure. I have my own tactics for getting tips."

"Ok then, suit yourself. Guess that means I'll get all the fun."

We left the room and headed towards the elevator, making our way towards the eleventh floor, the floor of the bachelor party.

The elevator stops on the seventh floor and an elderly Asian couple enters.

I ask, "Going up or down?"

"Up."

"Floor?"

"Eleventh."

The couple looks to be eighty years old, hair completely grey, their backs hunching over as if they're about to throw in the towel of life. Aside from age, their clothes spoke of youth, the man wearing a tank top and shorts while the woman wore even less, a tube top clinging from big saggy breasts. Mardi Gras beads hung around her neck. I don't wanna know where she got those beads, and her tube top had italic words that read, *I'm old ... but so what.*

Apart of me wanted to laugh, but that would've been disrespectful. Then I saw the man peeking at my breasts that are bunched in leather. Eyes pop out his head like he's seen the messiah and what makes it worse is that he refuses to be discreet about staring.

He licks his old lips, his ways of letting me know that he may be old, but so what.

I tense up. Don't know how to react. It's this type of behavior that makes me think Vegas is the sickest place on earth.

The elevator doors open to the eleventh floor. Snow said the party was at the last door on the left, which is where all the noise was coming from.

I got ready mentally. Put on my stripper face. Whatever face that was supposed to be.

At the door comes a white guy. Medium Age. Skinny. A low brush cut. Pretty boy look.

He sticks his head out the door and whispers, "You ladies are the strippers, right?"

"That's us," Snow confirmed in a sexy voice.

"Okay, then. Wait right here for a moment."

He shuts the door in our face. Snow and I look at each other in disbelief, bewildered.

The door re-opens. Same guy with the pretty boy look.

Snow tells the guy, "What the hell is wrong with you? Y'all want us to do this or what?"

"You bet we do," the man whispered. "What are y'all names?"

We think of creative fictitious names.

Snow tell him, "Snow White and Angelica ... that's what you can call us."

"Okay Snow White and Angelica ... Follow behind me ...They don't know you girls are coming."

He takes us inside a large room that's equivalent to a presidential suite. I immediately got cold feet, butterflies building a cocoon in my stomach, but I tried my best to shake those feelings aside. The man leads us down a hallway to where the other men are lounging. A white wall separates us from the action that's about to go down. Sticking his head from out the hallway, he yells in a feminine voice, "Fellas! Brace yourself for the main event! Meet Snow White and Angelica!" The guy signals for us to show our faces and he snaps his fingers like he's pulling magic out of a hat.

We burst onto the scene like we're the main event of the night, and the moment we set eyes on our audience they went ballistic.

What was a nice hotel has now been replaced with lots of beer and men screaming, "Take it off! Take it off!" They had no other care in the world. Nothing else was more important than this moment right now.

Soon I started to notice things that changed the whole scenery. There were two women in the back of the room. Gay looking women.

Women with broad shoulders and arms bigger than 50 cent. They were just as rowdy as the men in the room. Both were eyeing me down as if they wanted to rip off my clothes.

I turned my attention to Snow and asked her what the heck is going on.

"What you mean?" she replies, leaning into my ear.

My face imprints lines of confusion. "What I mean is there are two women sitting in the back."

"So?"

"So, you never told me there'd be women in the room." Then I spoke clearly so she wouldn't misinterpret my next set of words. "I'm not strippin' for no females. Period. That's where I draw the line. So until you get rid of Venus and Serena, I'm leaving right now. I ain't tryna—"

"Angel, everyone in here is a woman."

"What?"

"These are transgender women, which mean they recently had a sex change, and they are now men."

"What?" I repeated in disbelief.

I started processing her statement, tried to swallow it, consume it, but I coughed it back up, words too shocking to digest.

I looked around at the transgender women. All women dressed as men. Some formal dressed. Some sporting mustaches. None had hair past the neck. A dozen dikes were rocking the same brush cut.

Making sure my eyes weren't playing tricks on me, I watched one slowly in passing, then looked under the chin for an atoms apple.

There was none. Neck was as smooth as mine.

Freaked out, I jerked at Snow's arm. "Oh hell naw! Forget that!"

"Angel what's your problem?"

"I can't do this!"

"Why not? It's not like you're having sex. Only showing a little skin to get paid."

"Maybe to you. But where I'm from, women don't strip for other women unless they really wanna do something else. I'm outta here!"

I turned my back on Snow and shot towards the door, started pushing through women while never looking back.

Then I felt a hand on my ass.

One of the transgender women had touched me without permission. Touched me in a place where only a man can touch.

Instincts made me over-react, and I hit that bitch so hard to where she almost caught the Holy Ghost. "Don't you ever put your hands on me again!" I hollered.

Thinking she'd back off, she came back at me with twice the momentum, a zombie on a steady pursuit for flesh. She winks at me, says, "Wow, Sexy. So you're the aggressive type ... I like that ... now slap me again, mommi." She stuck out her tongue. "I like dat roughness."

I turned my back on her to keep it moving, and then I felt another hand on my shoulder, this time the person being Snow.

I tell her, "Forget it, Snow. I'm leaving and there's no way you're gonna change my—"

She flashes a fistful of money without speaking. Benjamin Franklin is now staring me in the face, daring me to resist his charm.

I held my ground by saying, "Just because you're flashing money, it doesn't mean I'll bite."

She puts the money in my hand.

That changed everything.

"Don't act like you don't wanna take it," she said. "This is 'bout making money remember, or did you forget?"

"Making money never included stripping for lesbians. I've got too much pride to—"

"Pride is a poor woman's word, Angel. Don't compromise this type of money for something as foolish as pride."

I gave no reply, my eyes going back and forth between the money in my hand and the women in the room.

I could've rebelled. Could've left her trapped in this room with the rest of the estrogen army. But ten grand was at stake and it wasn't backing down.

In a strong voice, Snow said, "Now I'm gonna ask you one more time, Angel. Are you in or out?"

I swallowed hard. Inhaled the moment. Told mama not to turn over in her grave as I answered, "Fine. Let's do this."

Snow smiled as if she'd won the lottery, then grabbed my hand and pulled me back into the limelight.

Afterwards, she grabbed the attention of all the transgender women. "Listen up, everyone. I need the groom to come to the center of the room to get his reward. My girl Angelica got something in store for ya." Cheers go in the air as one of the transsexuals take center stage. From face alone, you can't tell whether she is a woman or man, don't know whether the doctor finished the job or forfeited in the middle.

Snow pulled out a chair for the woman to sit, then tied her hands behind her back so she couldn't move. I approached the woman slowly, seduced her like a man, danced an exotic dance while holding my breath.

The woman smiled in delight. Gave me her attention.

I grinded a little more without touching her, couldn't build the nerves to touch her, and in my shyness Snow joined the party by grinding her leather all over the victim. Snow did it like a pro, like she owned the moment, the main attraction to my opening act.

Something tells me she's done this before. Either she's a great actress or is really enjoying the moment. I tried to play catch-up. Didn't want to be outshined by her magnificence. I sped up my rhythm and grinded harder to the beat.

While in the grove, someone from the audience shouted out, "Take it off! Take it off!"

Snow played to the crowd and decided to drop her little top, revealed the breasts of a woman in her late thirties. The crowd stirred at Snow's splendor, started feeding her the attention she deserved by placing dollar bills inside her slit.

But not just one dollar bills.

These were the type of presidents that didn't come with wooden teeth. Money worth grinding for.

That raised the stakes for me. Made me compete.

Not to be outshined, I unsnapped my bra to show the crowd what real black tits should look like, my perky upgrades shifting the attention in a new direction.

Dollar bills fly at me like paper airplanes.

I grabbed as many dollars as possible, so many to where there was no more room in my panties to store them, was whirling that crowd that continued to holler, "Take it off! Take it off!"

I touched my toes, dropped to a split, shook one cheek like a magician with a wand, tricked out the other, clapped them together, my little tush rolling like rims on a car.

Money over pride.

Money over pride.

I performed lewd acts thinking money over pride.

As the bachelor party got wilder, my bawdy behavior caused the women in the room to lose their minds, and with lust leading the way, they suddenly ambushed me and Snow, dancing on us, grinding on us, started dropping their tops as if they had no conscience, as if they were auditioning for girls gone wild – or men gone wild – a pack of famished wolves that fought over meat.

Then the music stopped.

Everyone freezes.

In came policemen that have come to ruin the show, policemen with handcuffs intending to do damage.

My heartbeat fired through that bloody chamber.

"Everyone get on the ground!" they yelled. "Get on the ground right now!"

My optimism hoped the policemen were part of a skit, but then they pulled out guns. Real guns. And that instant terror illuminated the room, electrified my fear to no end. I looked around this hotel room for an exit, only saw one-way in and one-way out, that one-way being blocked by a K-9 dog that was held on a tight leash.

"Get on the ground!" They re-iterated. "Get on the ground or we'll make you!"

"For what?" the groom asked. "Can't you see that this is a bachelor party?"

"Was a bachelor party ... As for now, it's an LVMPD party. Jimmy search the room!"

The officer snaps his fingers at the four-legged cop, that pointy-nose K-9 obeying all orders. Proficiently trained, the dog makes its rounds through the master suit, started sniffing under the couch, sniffing over tables, behind counters, rugs, kitchen, bedroom, was sniffing all over for that hidden white monkey.

"This is ludicrous," the groom yelled out again. "You're ruining my fucking party. So unless you have a warrant I suggest you—"

The dog barked in the bedroom.

Barked like a witness that just seen a corpse.

Out of that bedroom comes the sniffing beast, and in his mouth is the lost white monkey, was enough dope in that bag to build everyone in this hotel room their own private prison.

"You asked for my warrant. Well here it goes right here," the cop said.

I nearly fainted on the spot. Saw my end coming. Deeply considered jumping out the window of this 11th floor as my nerves were stuck in an ice-covered wall.

Face to the floor, I glanced over at Snow. That poised mature stripper who once had no fear was now shaking like a petrified adolescent, was just as panicky as me in a curled up position.

But she's not the one who should be panicking.

She's not the one who's wanted for murder.

"*Everyone in here put your hands behind your back. You're all being taken in to custody.*"

My soul melted like wax.

Back-up police busted through the doors like cops with a vengeance, and instead of bringing drinks to the party they decided to bring handcuffs – cuffed each transgender woman one by one until this whole party was completely cleared out.

Snow and I were the last ones to go. They allowed us just enough time to cover up our assets before cold metal was slapped on our wrists, the beginning to my long anticipated end.

With bags of cocaine and twenty thousand dollars now stolen by the feds, I walked out that hotel room half-naked. Walked out with a hundred bystanders witnessing my demise.

5

Two days later I was sitting in a jail, looking at a wall, thinking of a plan.

I had yet to be arraigned.

Because of the sudden influx of inmates, the courts were two days behind their usual schedule, and I was informed my arraignment would take place tomorrow.

After getting arrested, Snow was transported into a different police car than me. Because of her they had found guns on us both. Two . 45's were packed into a little black bag, and considering that I was wanted for murder, they had enough evidence to engrave my initials on a personalized cell. One cop tried to get me to open up and explain my reason for carrying a concealed weapon, but I wasn't stupid enough to open my trap without a lawyer.

Then again I had no lawyer.

I was on my own. No representation aside from an appointed lawyer from the state, and having one of those were equivalent to slicing your own throat, which was feasible for my current situation.

"Inghram, on your feet," someone said.

That voice was the voice of the guard, hopefully coming to give me good news. Usually the guards in this jail are women on steroids, but this particular guard wasn't that big. 120 pounds at most. If necessary, I could take her down.

"What is it?" I replied.

"You have a visitor."

"Huh?"

"Someone is here to see you."

"Here to see me?" I asked, making sure she didn't have the wrong inmate.

I slowly rose from my bunk bed, not knowing what to expect of this visit.

"Unless you wanna stay your butt inside, get a move on it," she demanded.

She unlocks the cell, opening my pathway to freedom. Around her waist is a Billy club, a taser, and a set of dangling keys – all within reach of my grabbing – all staring at me like puppies at a pet sale.

Temptation dared me to reach for the keys. Double dared me.

My fingers started twitching as I looked around to ensure no other guards were in the perimeter. Coast was clear.

I glanced back at the keys, that slave mentality running through my head like a butt-naked Cunta Kinte. If Cunta could escape his massa on one foot, then I certainly could get these keys.

Then I heard footsteps. Heard a voice yell out, "Vicky, I also need you to grab cells three and four for visitation. I'll take this one."

That voice was another guard coming to her rescue, making me leave the criminal world and come back to my senses. I told myself that there'd be plenty more chances to escape, but this wasn't the right time.

Once the guard took me to the visitation area I was told I had thirty minutes to sit on a hard metal seat and communicate through a sound proof window that was three inches thick, telephone in booth. The only problem is that there was no one on the other side of that window, which made me wonder what the hell was going on.

I turned to the guard and asked, "Where's my visitor?"

"Wait a moment," she says. "They'll be here in a sec."

"Yeah, well whoever it is, you better let them know that I ain't got much time, unless y'all gonna gimme an extra thirty minutes."

"Sit down," she ordered.

I sat down and waited impatiently, wondering who the heck was here to see me. I knew no one in Vegas. No one. That meant this would be the visit from hell or one that'll save my life.

After doing a process of elimination, I looked up and saw a person coming right towards my window, a blur of the undisguised visitor.

It's a woman. A woman rocking hard-bottom shoes and a mean walk, sunglasses glued to her face.

I recognize that walk from anywhere. Whether she's on the Vegas Strip or in a penitentiary, that hooker stroll is one she cannot shake; it's the stroll of no other than Snow. Snow the prostitute. My partner in this back-fired plan.

She's dressed in a police detective attire – blue dress shirt, black dress pants, hard-bottom shoes, and a badge on her waist that was accented by a gun. Her fire-red locks are pulled back into a professional ponytail, Corporate America style, and she's not flaunting the extra garnishes that present her as the dynamic diva. No lipstick. No big earrings. No wild acrylics. No make-up to mask her imperfections. Nothing about her represents the hooker I met on the streets, her secret life. In front of me stands a totally different woman. Totally different agenda. She's now known as Officer Jenkins according to the nametag on her shirt, and in her hand is a black duffel bag that I hope has nothing to do with me.

She sits down, crosses her legs, removes her sunglasses to give me a better look at her face.

I look at the face of a cop. The face of a malicious woman. A liar. A scam artist. A bitch I'd drag all over this jail if a thick glass wasn't separating us.

I picked up the phone in the booth as she did the same, not knowing if I should speak to her or bang this phone all over the soundproof window. Meanwhile, she grabs a pack of Newports from her back pocket, pulled out two cigarettes and a lighter.

"Wanna smoke?" she asked, pointing a cancer stick towards the window.

I don't respond. My wicked glare says everything I'm thinking, everything she already knows.

"What's the problem?" she asks. "Don't you smoke?"

I sneered. "Not from people that cross me."

"Oh come on, Angel. I know you're not getting sensitive over this whole thing ... If it makes you feel any better, know that what happened back at that hotel, that was all business. Nothing personal."

I gritted my teeth, that inner K-9 ready to do some bloody damage.

Running From Redemption

She goes on, "Well the past is the past. But at this point you gotta roll with the punches, you know. It's like they say ... when life throws you lemons you—"

"Throw back rocks," I replied, letting her know I'm pass the cliché bullshit.

She took both cigarettes and set them on fire, smoked them one at a time, then two at the same time, a hardcore smoker.

She says, "Tell you what, Angel. How 'bout we play a little game? It's a game called, Honesty. Don't worry 'cause the rules are simple. You be truthful with me and I'll be truthful with you. I mean, we both could use a stress reliever, so how 'bout it?"

Her face loses its grin and becomes flat with no emotion.

She says, "William Randolph."

I became attentive. Sat up straight. Made sure I heard that name correctly.

"What did you just say?" I asked.

She smiles. "That's right. I knew that name would wake you up. I said William Randolph. You know ... your stepfather ... the guy who murdered your mother, Anna Brown, when you were only six years—"

"Keep my mother's name out your mouth!" I snapped.

She smirks. Her expression saying she's hit me where it hurts, a blow I never seen coming.

"I never said you'd like this game of honesty, Angel. But then again, it's a game that must be played." She puffed her pollution while I held my breath, toyed with my anger from behind that glass. "Boy does God have a way of letting people see the light," she says.

"Excuse me?"

"A year ago you were attending one of the most prestigious law schools around, getting ready to clean up our streets with your intellect and your good instincts ... but now look at ya ... look at where your good instincts has gotten you, right here in the same hell where you wanted to put others." Her laughter relishes. "Talk about Carma ... bet your ass wish you would've stayed in Miami ... bet you wish you would've never taken that scholarship in New York. See where the good road leads you?"

Baffled from the truth, it was no secret that she knew my story. I wanted to ask her how much she knew already, but her facial expressions told me she knew quite a lot.

"Well if you think you're gonna get me to talk, I suggest you think again," I clarified. "Because I'm not speaking without a lawyer."

"You don't have to say anything," she replied. "I already know why you killed William. I also know why you ran for your life after murdering him, leaving him lying in his own blood for the police to clean up."

"So does every other normal person who watches the news. So what makes you so unique?"

"Well for one, my badge. And two, well ... let's just say we share some things in common."

"We share nothing in common."

"You sure 'bout that? Because like you, I also once lived in Brooklyn's apartments known as *The Estates*."

More shots fired at my past as I asked her, "Who are you?"

"A cop you don't wanna fuck with, Angel. I took you down before and I'll take you down again."

I hesitated, repeated, "Who are you?"

She reaches into her black bag and pulls out a shoe. The shoe is a stiletto. Dull pink. Open toe. 7 ½.

For I knew that shoe from anywhere. It's the same shoe I'd worn the day I shot William, the one I left on the steps of my apartment when trying to get away. In order to get this shoe she had to be at the crime scene. Or was she? All I remember was two cops storming into the apartment. Both cops being men. But then again, when I was fleeing the scene, a third undercover cop came from nowhere, and due to the circumstances, I never saw that cop's face.

Now I can put a face with a badge. That undercover cop was Snow.

"Yeah, I knew you'd figure it out," she said. "You thought you'd gotten away. Thought you'd crossed all your T's and dotted all your I's, that you had escaped prison to live a new life of contentment. But you underestimated one thing Little Girl ... you underestimated the woman behind this window."

I grimaced, grabbed the collar of that inner K-9, told it to sit.

She went on, "About *Brooklyn Estates* apartment complex, thank God I changed my address years ago, but it doesn't stop me from visiting my sick mother who does still live there, a mother I pay a visit to once a month. Just so happened that the day I was visiting my ill mother was the same day I heard shots coming from an apartment, an apartment where an insane woman was shooting a man. I guess you can say I'm a natural cop because I wasn't on duty the day you went nuts, but seeing that you had dodged NYPD, seeing that you were about to get away, my cop instincts told me I had to do something.

You should be lucky because you're the first person to ever escape me on the run. Or at least you almost—"

"How did you find me?" I asked.

She puffed one of the cigarettes, lounged back in her seat, slowly blew out those greenhouse gases with a gratification that said she captured Carmen Sandiago, her biggest fish of the month. "I didn't have to find you, Angel. You found me instead?"

"What the heck you talking 'bout?"

Truth is after you shook me that day I took it very personal. Took it so personal that I'd been looking for you for months, and quite frankly, I thought you had hijacked it out the country somewhere, had left this part of the world for good ... But then you left tracks. Tracks left in California. Tracks that led me right up your alley." She giggles to herself. "It's funny ya know ... with you thinking I was actually a hooker ... You see, I knew that the only way to gain your trust was to show you I'd kill. That's the reason you were introduced to the pimp, Sweet Willie."

"You mean that was a set up?"

"Planned it perfectly don't you think? I know I know. Kudos for Snow. Truth of the matter is I was playing you the entire time. From the time I met you on the street corner until the time we got busted at the party, it was all staged. I could've taken you down sooner. But that bachelor party was also a case I was working on. Figured I could take down you and those she-males at the same exact time."

One muscle shy of exploding, I asked her the question that stayed on my mind. "Why would you do this?"

"Let's just say it's complicated," she answered, flashing a wicked grin. "Besides, why I did it is not important. I'm here for something else. Here because I need you. We need each other."

"I need nothing from you."

"Oh come on, Angel. I thought we already had this conversation about letting your pride get in the way. Now whether you wanna accept it or not, we need each other. And what I need from you is ..." She comes closer to the window, smoke illuminating our space, and she whispers in the phone, "I need you to do a job for me ... a job that involves the killing of a cartel."

"What? Kill someone? Are you out of your whacked out mind you crazy—"

"Lower your voice." She came closer to the window. "I need you to do this for me, Angel. I'm serious."

"So am I. And right now, the only person I want to kill is you."

"You don't mean that."

"I don't? Let me out this bitch and I'll show you how much I—"

"You're just angry right now. But what if I offered you something to reduce your anger. Let's say ... a hundred grand."

"No."

"Why not?"

"Because this isn't about money. I'm not taking an innocent person's life."

She laughs in my face as if my comment is a joke. "Come on, Angel. All of a sudden you want to talk ethics. Well whether you realize it or not, you're a killer. Will always be a killer. Even with all the medals behind your name, with all the academics, you're still a killer."

"Yeah, well that's up for the jury to decide, not you ... Besides, since when did a police investigation consists of killing cartels?"

"For the department it's an investigation. But for me it's personal, personal with a lot of money involved. But don't worry about all the logistics behind it, just know that you'll have top-notch protection, and when it's all said and done, your name won't be affiliated with it whatsoever."

Thinking she was a dirty cop, I said, "So let's get this straight ... you want me to kill a drug lord ... by myself ... all so you can cover it up and get rich on the side?"

"Sloppy way of wording it, but yes."

"Go to hell, Snow."

I hung up the phone and rose from my seat, but before turning around, Snow flashes a picture against the hard window. The photo is a little girl's face. Light-skinned with dimples. Wild tangled hair. A face to die for.

That little girl is Devilla, the daughter of William Randolph.

A ball forms in the pits of my stomach and causes me to sit back down.

I picked up the phone. "What the heck is this?"

She smiles. "Don't play dumb with me, Angel. You know exactly who that is."

"Where is she? What did you do to her?"

"Calm down," she says. "Besides, I should be asking you that question, because according to the cops, Devilla's case is still being treated as a kidnapping by you, the infamous Angel Inghram—"

"Where the fuck is she?" I repeated.

Running From Redemption

"In a safe place. A place where you'll never get to. And believe me, a lot of bad things can happen to a little girl like her. So sweet and—"

"Lay a hand on her and I'll fuck you up! You hear that, I'll fuck you up!"

I slammed the phone against the window, did that as the guard rushed over to calm me down. My blood burns. Rage is unparalleled.

Snow demands for the guard to let me go, telling the woman, "It's ok, Rhonda. It's ok. Angel just got a little emotional, that's all."

The guard released me, then backed up so I could finish my phone call. I sat back down. Took everything inside of me to sit back down.

Meanwhile, Snow grimaces at me as if she now has the upper hand. "Uh-huh," she says. "I thought the death of your mother was your only soft spot, but now I know you actually care 'bout someone else."

My face turns into a cactus. "You must be taking some serious PCP to think you can come inside here and pull this off. You think blackmailing me is gonna get you what you want?"

"Oh no, Angel. I wouldn't call it blackmailing. You see, blackmailing is such an aggressive word. I'd rather call it … negotiating … that's all this is …. a negotiation."

"You're not gonna get away with this you bitch!"

"I'm not? Says who? You? Angel Inghram? A woman that's not only wanted for murder, but kidnapping a child. Do you know how much time you'll get for those crimes? Huh? Do you? You've been to law school, so you know all about how the system works, and right now, your voice means nothing more than a prisoner on death row."

"Maybe not. But how you gonna explain a murder to the DA? Or the Mayor? Or even the Governor? Don't forget that I also have friends in high places."

Her eyes sharpen. "Don't try to play rough with me, Angel. Play rough me with me and I'll put you so far in prison to where you'll be wiping your ass with cement. Trust that ok."

"Don't matter. I'm going to prison for life anyway."

She smiles. "So you think."

"What?"

"The only reason you're in here right now, caged behind that window, is so I can show you how serious I really am. But really, your fingerprints have been switched, which means you appear in the system as a totally different person. So in retrospect, there's no Angel Inghram on file."

"What?"

"I know I'm full of surprises. According to our databases, Angel Inghram is still on the loose, has yet to be captured. Everything about you reflects someone else. From description. To DNA. To the tests the doctors done when you were first booked inside, I controlled all of that. Why you think you haven't been arraigned yet? You thought it was just a coincidence?" A bigger smile shines on her criminal face. "So you see, Angel, right now I'm the HBIC in your little world, but if you act right, you still have a little chance of a life."

This whole situation was getting more twisted and twisted. Every five minutes a new ball is dropped.

"But don't ever threaten me again," she said. "Because with just the flip of a scanner, I can book you right back into the system, can make your pathetic life a living hell. You got that?"

I don't respond.

She says, "Now enough with the back and forth. Are you gonna get with the program or do you wanna continue to play hardball?"

"How do you know that time you let me out this jail, I won't turn my back and take off running?"

"Because you're not stupid, Angel. We both have something to gain here, and you of all people have nothing to lose ... actually, I forgot, you do have something to lose." She puts the picture of little Devilla back up against the window, then gave me a dirty stare. "Think hard, Angel. Think very hard."

That ultimatum scared me, caused questions to play racquetball inside my spiraling head. *Could I really kill a man for money?*

I've killed before, but under different conditions. Conditions that were necessary for the cause, necessary for my own survival. No matter how much of a bad person this drug dealer was, he was still considered a person, still someone's brother, someone's child, someone's husband, or even worse, someone's father. I lost my father at birth. Both parents taken by an unmerciful God. Daddy was on his way to the hospital, driving at midnight, racing to the hospital to see his pregnant wife, until a drunk-driver switched lanes and interfered with the plan.

Daddy never made it. Never got a chance to see his wife birth a baby-girl named Angel Inghram, seven pounds thick with her father's smile. As daddy fought to stay alive inside an ambulance, mama was fighting on the miracle bed, struggling to push me out of her womb.

Life exists as life enters this world.

Death and deliverance on the same doorstep.

Running From Redemption

That day was a bitter-sweet day. When the doctor first broke the news to my mother – while she was holding me in her arms – her fragile body almost collapsed on the miracle bed that day. That day there were no happy faces in the delivery room. No claps of celebration or balloons of excitement. No champagne glasses. No bumper sticker on a car that read, *It's a Girl*. All I got was tears of sadness, heavy hearts, and people saying, 'She looks just like her father.'

I'd lose a leg to have a father in my life, to be a daddy's girl in some man's eyes. And if I could I'd kill that drunk-driving bastard who turned me into a bastard's child, I would do it without thinking, no questions asked. But as much as that hurts, it hurts even more to know I could be responsible for the death of a child, especially an innocent child like Devilla. I didn't want that death on my conscience, didn't want that blood on my hands.

Snow had Devilla hostage. Had the closest thing to a daughter in these brown eyes of mine. I'd taken the life of her father the same way that drunken driver had taken my father's life.

And somehow I felt I owed her something.

I owed her life. Even if it meant taking someone else's.

"So do we have a deal?" Snow asked.

I glared into her eyes with the phone to my ear, unwillingly muttered, "Deal."

6

Whenever you make a deal with the devil there must always be a back-up plan.

My back-up plan was simple: I didn't have one. Didn't have no coastguard to pull me above water, and there was a good chance I'd drown.

The time was 2am. Lights off for all inmates, but I heard keys rattling the lock on my cell.

I rose up on the bunk bed, speechless.

"Suit up," the voice whispered, tossing me a uniform.

The intruder was no other than Snow, the red tips of her hair now glowing in the dark as if Satan had come here to bail me out.

"What are you doing?" I asked her.

"What does it look like, Angel? I'm getting you out of jail."

"Thought you weren't supposed to come 'til tomorrow. What happened to—"

"Listen, there's been a change in plans. Now unless you wanna stay in this place until eternity, I suggest you get a move on it."

Asking no more questions, I stripped off my inmate clothes and climbed into popular attire. Blue collar shirt. Khaki pants. Flashlight. Billie club. To walk out of jail as one of them, as a prison guard, is something they'd never see coming, the ultimate disguise.

"Make sure you don't leave anything behind," Snow whispered. "Here, dump your clothes in the bag. And hurry up."

Snow locked up the cell while I watched our backs, then we hurried through darkness, trying to be discreet, passed other inmates cells as they watched us heading for a gut-wrenching border.

"Hey Angel!" a woman said, recognizing my face. "Get me out too."

I glanced back to inquire about the voice, but Snow pulled me by the shoulder and said, "Keep it moving."

We made an abrupt left at the end of the hallway, passed the after-hours service desk, then came to the part where guards have to use their badges. Snow swipes her badge. A red light tells her to try again. Second swipe. Same response. And now we're starting to panic like barricaded mice, robbers who sought the wrong exit of escape.

"Need some help," a voice said, coming from a distance.

The person walking towards us is a white male guard, Harrison Ford with a wider nose.

Snow staggered at the man's presence, then she stammered, "Shucks."

"Who is he?" I asked.

"Chief of police."

"What?" My heartbeat raced down paranoia alley. "Why the heck is the chief—"

"Just be cool ok."

Being cool meant turning my face so it wouldn't be recognized.

"Snow? Is that you?" the chief said. "What on earth are you doing in here?"

"Oh nothing ... just checking on a prisoner I recently booked ... remember Sandra Davis ... killed her husband in self-defense ... the one getting ready to do twenty."

"I remember."

"Well rumor has it that she's attempting to break out tonight. I was just making sure she was still in place."

"Ain't nobody breakin' outta here," he said sternly. "Even if I have to stop 'em myself. But that has nothing to do with you. After what happened this week, you shouldn't be anywhere around these prisoners."

"I understand, Captain. But I was just—"

"Trying to bring more fire down my back. Is that what you want, Snow?"

"No, Captain."

"Then act like it," he snarled. "You already know the hot water that our department is in already."

Remaining silent, I kept my head to the floor like a child in the midst of company.

"And who are you, Ms. Santiaga?"

No response.

Wondering who Ms. Santiaga was, I glanced at my shirt, and right there in bold letters my nametag spelled it out. I looked at Snow, my reaction telling her, *"Why the hell would you give a black woman a Spanish nametag?* She sneers as if I better get with the program and answer the chief's question.

I looked at the chief, Harrison Ford's twin, impatience climbing his irritated face that was turning to cement.

I told him, "Oh ... I was just hired a few days ago."

"Yeah, by who?"

My mind goes blank as notebook paper, and I try to think of a description that fits every person. "Uuuhhh ... I forget the guy's name. But he has a low haircut, broad shoulders—"

"Bushner. You're talkin' bout Bushner."

"Yeah that's it. Bushner. The name was at the tip of my tongue."

"Bushner hired you? Well that's strange ... Bushner never hires anyone."

"Actually, Angel is just kidding," Snow said, jumping in to save me. "She's not really one of the guards, Captain. At least not yet. She's a trainee."

He shakes my hand as I breathe the breath of a CPR victim, knowing that was a close one.

"And how do you know Snow?" he continued.

"I beg your pardon?"

"You and Snow? Y'all were heading out together. How do you ladies know each another?"

You are one nosy ass chief.

I swallowed, said, "We know each other from ... from—"

"Club Pleasures," Snow said, interfering.

The chief looked astonished. "Club Pleasures? But isn't that a—"

"Swingers Club. I know."

Swingers? I thought. *Is that the best lie she could think of?*

"I'm sorry," the chief said. "Didn't know you and Mr. Marcello was..."

"Into swinging, I know," Snow said. "It was actually his idea. He introduced me to this life. And once I met this beautiful woman here ... well ... I've been swinging ever since." She smiled and smacked me on the butt, damn near made me smack her in the face. Then she turned to the chief. "Isn't she a peach?"

His cheeks turned reddish pink, as if he wanted to edit the conversation and delete Snow's remarks.

Stuttering, he says, "I ... I think I'm gonna be leaving now ... need me to let you ladies out?"

"Please."

He quickly scans his badge against the door, and the green light appeared for us to exit.

I exit jail.

I exit jail untouched.

I exit jail as a free woman.

But then, in the middle of us exiting, the chief yells, "Hey Snow! One more thing!"

My heartbeat paused as we turned around, anxiety crawling down our backs. The chief stares us down, then turns up his nose as if something isn't right.

"What is it?" Snow asked.

"Despite the allegations, I personally wanna say you did a fine job on that Gibbons case ... don't know how you was able to track down that much drug money, and I know the DA might be on our ass, but thanks to you, we finally have some leverage ... Nice work detective."

"Thanks, Captain."

"So how'd you do it?"

Snow hesitates, then flashes a crooked smile at her boss. "Let's just say I had a darn good teacher."

"You're a very bad liar," Snow said, turning her nose up at me as we walked to the car. "If anyone ever said you're a good liar, they lied."

"Whateva. I'm not the one who told your boss that we met in a Swingers Club. How brilliant was that?"

"I only said that because you couldn't think quick on your feet. It's like I told you before, Angel, you gotta learn how to roll with the punches."

"Yeah, well the next time you grab my ass, I'll show you how quick I can roll with a punch."

Making it towards home base, Snow unlocked the door of a black Mustang parked outside the jail. The car had tinted windows. Marvelous paint job. Looked like it just came straight from the dealership. I wondered if a cop's salary was enough to afford a car of this caliber, maybe so, but it had me thinking she probably had a gig on the side, a gig that involved getting her hands real dirty.

Speaking of hands, Snow told me to reach mines into the glove compartment to pull out something special.

"What's in there?" I asked.

"You'll see."

The glove compartment drops out stacks of cash, Benjamin Franklin duplicates in thick rubber bands.

Shocked, I asked Snow, "What is this?"

"It's what you call money," she joked. "In America, we use that to regulate checks and balances."

I stare at the most money I ever saw in my life, a lifelong dream that I'm now afraid to touch.

"Go 'head and take it," Snow said. "After all, it's yours. Fifty large to let you know I'm serious ... You'll get the other fifty after finishing the job."

She reaches into her backseat and tosses me a black duffel bag. "Here. Stack 'em in there."

"Wait a sec. Is this money clean? How'd you get it?"

"See that's your problem, Angel. You ask too many unnecessary questions." She shakes her head at me. "Take the damn money. And just to clear your conscience – yes, the money's clean."

Without second-guessing, I started stuffing money in the bag like it was getting ready to walk away, not leaving a single dollar around.

"So does this mean we're good?" Snow asked.

I pressed her brakes. "Not exactly." A little girl's life was still at stake and to me that life is priceless. "Before we go anywhere, I wanna know where Devilla is."

That statement throws her to left field. I stay at home base, then she grins as if she was testing my morals.

I repeat, "Where is Devilla?"

"In a safe place."

"Which is?"

"At this point and time it's none of your business."

"Yeah, well until I know that she's alive, me and you have no business at all."

I threw the duffel bag into her lap to show her I'm serious, that Devilla's life is worth more than dirty money.

She smiles. "What's the problem, Angel? Don't you trust me?"

My face hardens with disdain. "Show me Devilla or show me back to my cell. Your choice."

My ultimatum surprises her, causes her to look away. Something tells me she's afraid to show me Devilla, reluctant of opening that door because of what I'd witness behind it.

I tell her, "Show me Devilla now!"

She looks back at me.

I cut my eyes at her deeply; put on my Angela Bassett face to show her that this was non-negotiable. Inside that Mustang, outside the parking lot of a jail, Snow sucks her teeth, opens her pocket, and she raises a blue-tooth to her ear with a cell-phone emerging from her pocket.

I wait.

She says, "Hey, everything alright over there ... and where's the girl ... what do you mean she went to the bathroom? Thought you were supposed to keep an eye on her ... huh ... how does a six-year-old tell you what to do ... am I paying her or paying you dummy ... what ... well act like it then..."

Snow carelessly has the phone laying in her lap. My wandering eye peeks over her shoulder to track down the number she called. 585-24 ... *Darnit*. She changed positions, leaned on the door and turned the phone face down to her knee. "*I don't wanna hear anything else, just put her on the phone right now ... Put her on the phone I said ...*" My chest clinches. Throat got tight. Time freezes as I waited for Devilla to get on the line.

Snow says, "Hi, Devilla ... I got someone who wanna say something to ya." She hands me the phone with the evil eye. "Make it quick."

I pick up the phone, my lips quivering. "Devilla."

"Ms. Angel ... Ms. Angel ... Where ... where are you?" she cried.

Her voice tells me that she's frightened. Been frightened for quite some time. Just knowing she's alive makes me breathe again. But there was still that ball in my stomach, the pain of knowing I got her in this situation.

I ask her, "You ok? They haven't touched you have they?"

"No but ... she said if you don't finish the job by Saturday ... she's gonna ... she's gonna kill me ... I don't wanna die, Ms. Angel ... I don't ... I don't wanna—"

"Stay calm, Devilla. Just stay calm and do everything they tell you and hold on for a little while longer ... just a few more days."

"Okay." Then she quickly said, "I'm in a dark room with a shovel and a long knife and—"

"That's enough!" Snow said, snatching the phone away.

My heart retracted into a sponge that covetously soaked up every ounce of my blood.

"Don't let me come down there!" Snow said, snapping at the person on the phone. "Handle that little girl!"

The phone clasps shut, shattering that glass within me. Behind that glass is Devilla's face. My only weakness. My responsibility. This phone call solidified the importance of this situation. It woke me up. Pepper sprayed the truth in my eyes.

Angrily, I told Snow, "If anyone lay a finger on her ... I swear ... I swear ..." I raise my fist and allowed my expression fill in the blanks. "Ugghh!"

"Be smart," she said with a crooked smile. "Devilla's fate is just a phone call away."

She flips the phone back open to provoke me, daring me to get out of line. Right then I wanted to rip out her throat and lay it on the dashboard of her Mustang. But this wasn't the time. So I left planet insanity and came back to earth.

"Good choice," she said. "I knew you weren't as stupid as you look."

7

Save me, Ms. Angel. Save me.

Devilla's words were pounding in my head like a tenacious tumor, my brain building a collage of her face.

The only clues she gave was a dark room, a shovel, and a long knife.

All meant death.

In an undercover Mustang with tinted windows, Snow drove me down one of the busiest streets in Vegas, ignoring the speed limit like a narcissistic cop that owned the road. Drunk college kids flew past us with heads out the window, beer cups in hands, all screaming as if they were auditioning for *The Fast and The Furious*. Thinking that Snow would stop them and deliver a ticket, she actually did the complete opposite and allowed them to keep riding, then justified it by saying she was a detective, and she was only concerned about going after criminals that matter.

I shifted topics, asked her, "So who is Mr. Marcello?"

"Huh?"

"The chief of police mentioned a guy named Mr. Marcello. Who is that? Your lover?"

She takes a deep breath, sighs hard, confirming that I've pushed a button. "Actually, he's my husband."

My jaw drops. "Your husband? You mean to tell me that a man actually married you ... wow." I giggle silently, but she doesn't find it very amusing.

"Laugh now, but that bastard won't be my husband for long."

"Why not?"

"Because he's your target."

"Come again?"

"He's the man you gotta kill."

My brain downshifts, kicks into fourth gear of thought. "Hold up hold up hold up. Let's rewind for a second ... You mean to tell me that you snuck me out of jail, all so I can kill your husband ... You're joking with me right?"

"Does it look like I'm joking," she said, horns sticking out the sides of her head. "I want him dead ... want it more than anything I ever wanted in my life ... I can't wait to look at his casket ... fake tears in my eyes ... mourning his body ... carrying red roses ... dark limos around ... Hell, I already got my black dress picked out."

My throat tightens. Don't know what to say next to this psychotic woman. Every minute this situation gets more twisted and twisted.

I wondered what her husband did to be hated so much. Or what he didn't do. Did he physically beat her? Screw with her head mentally? I mean, here is a woman that has it all: Beauty. Brains. A well-respected job as a detective. If love was determined by someone's resume then she'd be crème le creme, the apple that sits highest on the tree of women.

But someday every apple gets worms. I'm just curious of how hers came about.

I ask her, "So what happened?"

"Huh?"

"Why do you wanna kill your husband?"

"The same reason any woman wants to kill her husband ... payback."

"Yeah, well your payback is a little over the top, don't you think?"

"My husband owns a chain of restaurants. Two in Vegas, three in New York, and three in California, all the big cities."

"And you wanna kill him for that?"

"But that's not where he makes the bulk of his money. You see he's also a drug smuggler. But not just any drug smuggler. He's the biggest supplier on all the West Coast ... do you know how it feels to be a cop and know that your husband is doing more crime than any criminal out there? It tears you up inside."

"But didn't you know that all along?"

"Men never bring all the truth into a marriage. They always have skeletons in the closet. You see, when me and my husband first got married, all I knew was that I had a wealthy man that loved me to death, did things for me that men don't usually do, and took me places that you never see in the hood. He's Dominican, and Dominican men treat their women different than Americans ... from pulling out chairs ... to opening doors ... it's a totally different experience ... Then I watched how good he treats his mother, and for me that put the icing on the cake because a man will always treat a woman the way he treats his mother ... I thought my husband was a damn good man. I mean, I did until I started noticing things that made me speculate ... things as simple as phone calls at three in the morning, or late nights at work ... At first I thought it was women. But then I noticed something bigger ... something more dangerous ... you see, one night while I was sleeping, a man broke into our house and woke me up with a gun in my face ... I almost peed my pants because at that time I'd only been on the force for a week, and the whole time the man was screaming, 'Where is the dope? Where is the dope?' Luckily, my husband was in the bathroom at the time, and when he came out he put a bullet in the guy's skull, brains splattered all over my sheets ... that was the scariest night of my life, and it was then that I found how my husband makes his real money .... A couple days later my husband flew me to Dominica to show me where he keeps his stash ... showed me more drugs than I'd ever seen on the force, enough drugs to send him to prison for life ... he knew I was a cop, but he still wasn't willing to give up that lifestyle, even though he promised to only remain in the game for a year longer ... Now of course, nine years later, we're still where we started."

"Then why not just turn him in? You're a cop, so I know you can set up a sting operation to get him busted."

"And risk not only my career but my life. Are you nuts? Everyone knows that if a husband is a drug dealer, the next step is to investigate his wife. And with me being a detective, they'll attack me with everything they got."

"So why not just get a divorce?"

She looks at me as if that's a stupid question, then asks me, "You ever been married?"

I don't respond.

"Well then," she said, "you'd never understand. When a woman takes those vows she feels as if she has two obligations: One, to fulfill that man and all his needs. And two, to make sure no other woman tries to fulfill him. That's it."

"In what world are you living in?"

"The real world ... I mean don't get me wrong, you do have those times where you wanna call it quits, but then you think about all the time you've invested, and one thing us women don't wanna do is waste time."

"So if you love 'im that much, then why do you want him dead? Why kill him now?"

She pulls out a cigarette and lights a blaze, allows the nicotine to consume her.

She says, "He wants a divorce."

"Did he tell you that?"

"No, but I can tell. A wife can always tell."

"Yeah, well that's even better. At least now you'll get half."

"Wrong. You see I signed a pre-nup. So if we split, I leave this marriage with exactly what I came into it with. Not a damn penny. I mean unless…"

"Unless what?"

"Unless he cheats on me. Infidelity will grant me half. I made sure to add that clause to the pre-nup. But then again my husband is smart. He's not gonna throw away his money for ass on the side. Well, at least not ass I'll know about."

"So you admit he's cheating."

"I suspect he is. But truth is, I don't wanna know if he is or isn't. Just want 'im dead, that's it. I refuse to let some trick come between me and my money."

Trying to shed light on the situation, I said, "But you're a detective."

"So?"

"So even with a divorce, you wouldn't struggle that bad financially."

She sucks her teeth. "Please, you think detectives make a lot of money? They might bring in more than the average cop, but when you consider the long hours, the constant running around to find a clue, it's like pulling teeth out of people just so you can have a lead, it's like you're working for peanuts … Not to mention, my husband is the reason why I made detective."

"Yeah?"

"He put in a good word, worked his magic downtown, and just like that he convinced them to hire me, the same way he can convince them to take the job away. It's like he owns me. No matter which direction I walk, I'll always be walking towards him, and he gets off on knowing that."

Now I see why she wants to murder him. She has no other cards to play, and she doesn't have enough confidence to be on her own, which is downright sad.

She continues with, "A man's love is different from ours, and they can never be fulfilled no matter what you do ... you see men are like children and to them you're nothing but a toy ... a toy they love for the moment, until another toy comes along that's more intriguing ... what's tricky is that the toy is not always a woman ... it can be drugs, alcohol, gambling, anything ... and when you're married, it only gets worse."

"I feel you on that," I said, watching her go ten miles over the speed limit.

What she was experiencing is the marriage my mother had. The man comes in with one personality, then leaves out with three or four more, expecting a woman to adapt to his corrupted world. The same thing happened with my stepfather, William Randolph. He intruded into our lives and convinced my mother to adapt to his lifestyle. He was also a drug dealer. Banged women on the side. I knew exactly what she was going through.

The Mustang crosses an intersection as we ride the streets of Vegas. Snow is now going sixty in a forty-five zone, steadily puffing her cigarette as if she's in another world.

I ask, "Are you okay?"

She ignores my question, then carries on. "After all these years, I can't believe he has the nerves to want a divorce... after all I've done for him ... washing his clothes ... cooking ... cleaning ... even had to wipe his ass here and there."

"What?" I said in disgust.

"That's right. He had a stroke once. Had to be rehabilitated for months, which meant he couldn't do nothing for himself ... couldn't even clean himself."

Watching her now go 65 mph, I put on my seat belt.

"I should've sent him to his mama, let her wipe his ass ... but naaah, me being the stupid wife I was, I dealt with the situation like a woman."

70 mph. I got nervous, watched her eyes become dark as the night, watched us zip pass cars like drag racers at Nascar.

"You might wanna slow down," I mumbled.

A face of fire, she continues to feel the situation at hand. "I stuck by his ass through thick and thin ... when he needed a half-mill to pay off an oversize debt, who you think helped him smuggle the money?"

I held my breath, kept replaying the message that every kid is told: *Never ride in cars with strangers.*

"I gave it to 'im!" she hollered. "Smuggled it right from my own department, money the DEA needed for a case."

80 mph. Her face becomes red as her dreadlocks.

"Slow down," I told her.

"I was there for him when no one else was."

"Slow down!"

"Through thick and thin."

"Slow the fuck down!"

"Through rain, sleet, or snow. So when you ask me why I want to kill him, I can give you a hundred—"

"The car in front of you!"

She slams on brakes and the Mustang slides under a red light, nearly colliding into a Mazda.

A man sticks his head out the Mazda, hollers at Snow, "Crazy, bitch!" He cursed a few more times before driving off.

I caught my breath as Snow catches her conscience.

"Look here!" I said. "I don't know what's going on with you and your husband, but if you don't get yourself together, we're gonna be the ones six feet under ... not him!"

She comes back to earth, breathes hard. "I'm sorry ... guess I got a little beside myself."

"Besides, where are we going anyway?"

"My house."

"Your house? That's not a good idea."

"My house is the safest place for you to be right now, at least until our business is over. Also, my husband don't get home until Saturday, which gives us four days to prepare."

"So what's the plan?"

"In order to kill my husband, you're gonna have to do it when his guard is down.

"Which is?"

She smiles, licks her lips. "The graveyard."

"Say what? I ain't killing this man at some graveyard. Can't I just feed 'im some rat poison and call it a day."

Running From Redemption

"No. That's too risky. My husband doesn't go anywhere without bodyguards, and he pays them lots of money to keep him well-protected."

"Wait hold on. Did you say bodyguards? I don't know what you might have thought, but I'm not some contract killer. I mean, I might be trained at using a firearm, but that's about it. You might need someone else. Someone who's—"

"Exactly like you, Angel. Someone who'll go undetected."

"Then how do I pull this off if he has protection like you say he does?"

"Every Sunday my husband goes to the cemetery to mourn his father. It's the only place he goes alone. Never takes his bodyguards because that's his personal time of solemn, don't want anyone around while he's grieving. Your job is to be in that cemetery before he arrives, this Sunday, making sure he never leaves."

"Okay … And then what?"

"That's it."

"Just show up and cap 'im just like that? In broad daylight? What if someone sees me?"

"They won't. He goes to the cemetery at night."

"And? Other people visit cemeteries at night too. I mean, how the hell can you assure me that I won't get caught. Is there a spot at the cemetery where I can hide with a gun? What about cameras? Like I said before, I'm not some damn assassin you know."

"Well for a hundred grand, you best think like one. Hell, I don't care how you do it. From the bushes. In the trees. You could hide behind a goddamn tombstone for all I care. All I know is I want him dead as a doorknob when I get back from vacation. No mistakes. No excuses."

"Vacation?"

"I'm leaving for New York this Sunday. Leaving for a week to visit my mother, already got it marked on my calendar at work. So in case you thought the wife would be the prime suspect, know that my alibi is all set to go."

I turned my head. "Exactly how long have you been planning this?"

She takes her eyes off the road, all smiles. "Long enough, Angel. Long enough."

Inside that passenger seat, I started mentioning all the things that could interfere with this plan, and every answer she gave said her bases were covered.

But those were her bases. Not mine.

At the end of the day I had to cover myself, just in case Snow tried to cross me again.

I had my own plans. Plans that Snow knew nothing about. Plans involving a woman I could trust.

And this time, I knew the perfect person to call.

8

Snow made a right turn on Martin Drive as the scenery quickly changed. Unlike the typical streets of Vegas, we ride on a road that no longer toasts to the party life – a street filled with beer cans and bottles, shoes hanging from power lines, and addicts circling the block to find their next fix. Men ride shirtless on bicycles, swerving through the road, and women are walking around barefooted. In Miami we call those women dirty-foots. Their clothes are torn. Breasts are exposed. Hair is sticking up as if it's pleading for a perm.

A bunch of bad kids are playing on sidewalks as if curfew is when the sun comes up. No parental supervision. No police. No rules besides the golden rule of the streets, and that rule is to never enter the ghetto as a tourist.

Especially at night.

Ignoring that rule, Snow turned the Mustang inside an apartment complex called Shady Pines. Actually, the *S* was missing from Shady and the *I* was missing in Pines, which made the complex look even more run down. A cigarette to her mouth, she slowly backed into a parking space, did that as the entire neighborhood was eyeballing our car to see who we were, and I braced myself for the unexpected.

"What are we doing here?" I asked Snow. Thought you said we were going to your house?"

"We are. But I had to make a stop first."

No one from the neighborhood recognizes our car and their glares quickly turned hideous.

I tell her, "You sure we're at the right place."

"Are you afraid?"

"Just being careful. After all, we're not from 'round here and I'm not even strapped."

"Don't worry. I'm a cop remember. So as long as you're with me, you're safe."

"Very reassuring," I replied sarcastically.

"I'll only be a minute. Stay in the car."

She cuts off the headlights, rolls down the window, and flicks her cancer stick into the night. Next, she takes out a pair of handcuffs and rattles them in front of my face, tells me, "I don't suppose I have to cuff you to the steering wheel ... or do I?"

I gave her my best sinister face imaginable. "Do what you want."

She smiles. "Be a good girl until I get back."

A cop attitude with a stripper walk, Snow strutted towards the apartment building like she was queen of the streets, gun on her waist, badge under her shirt, her colorful locks blowing freely in the night to catch the eyes of lurking men who sat on the steps. She owned their attention. Made them watch her like a stripper in church. One fixed his lips as if he wanted to holler, but then he saw her badge and respectively declined.

Meanwhile, I pulled out my cellular to make an important phone call. I was about to contact the most rudest, close-minded, no-nonsense, fiercest woman on the planet: Cuqui – a woman as crazy and abstract as her name.

Cuqui is the best friend I ever had, the sister I never had, my cohort in crime in spite of the consequences. She's black mixed with Spanish decent, but her skin color is more on the black side. Like me, she grew up in the projects of Miami, Florida; Liberty City to be exact – and from our first encounter we clicked instantly like magnets without a choice, from the first time we met at the lunch table in sixth grade. Although we ate at the same table we never spoke, but we quickly realized that there was a common denominator that linked us.

That common denominator was Cedric Mitchell, the cutest boy in school.

Cedric was a scrawny light-skinned kid who always rocked the smoothest pair of British Knights shoes, had the flyest S-Curl around, and during that time the S-Curl was the Bentley of hairdos. Cedric would always write me poetry; I'd quiver at his rhymes, at his lustful prose, even felt the need to share them at lunch with the other girls, bragging about my boyfriend, of how my Bentley was the shit and they had Honda Civics. But in the midst of my arrogance, Cuqui pulled out a poem that was identical to mines. Same rhymes. Same prose. Same handwriting and signature of my new boyfriend.

I quickly realized that Cuqui and I were driving the same Bentley – Cedric Mitchell, the only difference was how he labeled us: You see I was Butter Pecan while he called her Chocolate Swirl, and together we were the laughing stocks of school, everyone calling us double scoops.

But to Cuqui it wasn't funny.

And she wanted this to end.

Plus she had to live up to a well-earned reputation of being the most feared girl in sixth grade, a girl always sent home for misbehaving, getting referrals, bullying other girls, and her second home was the principal's office. Here was a girl with more ass-kicking medals than Lucy Liu, and out of all the girls in school, why did I have to be the one who shared her darn boyfriend.

One hot day, with a mean face, knee-high stockings, and a Jansport backpack on her shoulders, Cuqui stepped to me in the middle of the cafeteria about my boyfriend, or her boyfriend, a girl ready to settle this once and for all.

Contrary to her, I was labeled as the new girl who had been at this middle-school for only two weeks, and to the other girls I had to prove myself, had to show them my value by stepping to their bully.

Cuqui asked, "So you're the one they call Angel Inghram?"

Without thinking I sarcastically replied, "Only one me," and from the crowd's reaction I knew that wasn't good.

"How long you been wit' my man?" she said, getting straight to it.

"Yo' man?"

"That's right. My man! Besides, who do you think gave me this?" She opens her backpack and pulls out a narrow box that read *Jewelers*. Inside the box was a beautiful bracelet. Yellow gold. 14 karat. A gift she claimed had come from my boyfriend.

You see I had a bracelet that was identical to hers, autographed from the same author. The only difference is that her name was engraved along the bottom. Mine wasn't engraved at all, which meant her bracelet made more of a statement.

Refusing to be defeated, I reached into the sleeve of my shirt and revealed the same present. "You mean this bracelet," I said, sucking my teeth. Then I ran my fingers across the 14k to show her my jewelry was just as flawless.

Realizing we both had been two-timed, she stepped into my face, her big fists clasped, and she bit her bottom lip like an undefeated fighter who saw her next match.

I got a little scared. Actually, I was scared shitless. But mama always told me that whenever you fear something, you face it head on. And with those words in my ear, I stood on my toes and stuck out my chest, showed her that unlike the other girls I'm willing to fight, that pride over fear won't let me back down.

The crowd watched us. Girls dropped their pop-sickles to wait for Cuqui to drag me across the cafeteria floor, but surprisingly she didn't.

Instead, she said, "Let's see what he has to say about this. Follow me."

Together we clinched our bracelets and walked to the other side of the cafeteria, the side where all the eighth graders sat. Sixth graders were not allowed to mingle with eighth grade boys, but that didn't stop us from coming to foreign ground; we wanted some damn straightening. Not only us, but other girls stomped behind us like the million woman march, a bunch of angry girls following two activists with ponytails, breasts starting to perspire in our training bras.

The lover boy, Cedric Mitchell, was yapping with his friends about all the girls he had recently kissed. He was in a trash-talking zone with his back turned so he couldn't see the stampede of girls behind him.

Without further ado, Cuqui grabbed Cedric by his shoulder and spun him around to face us. He panicked. Looked at us like we were security getting ready to escort him to the principal's office.

I flashed him the bracelet and said, "Explain!"

His mouth was outlined with milk after digging in a plate of steamed chicken, mac & cheese, an apple, and those awful veggies they serve at lunch. He looked like he was trying to muster a lie, so I snatched the bracelet from off my wrist and threw it in the mac & cheese, then repeated, "Explain!"

He looked around as the crowd became silent as a jury, a dozen girls waiting for his response.

Cuqui said, "What's the problem, Cedric? Cat got your tongue? Why the heck we have the same bracelet?"

She flashed her bracelet to show him the evidence, but still no response. Then one of his boys stepped in and said, "Y'all chicks betta get off my dog ... comin' round here startin' all dat drama ... y'all betta take y'all butt back to the other side of the cafeteria befo' we—"

"What?" Cuqui said, getting in his face. "What you and yo boys gon' do?" A dozen girls stood behind her and waited for him to jump, but after seeing his boys not backing him up, he lost the tough-guy act and yielded to the power of numbers.

Cuqui proceeded, "That's what I thought ... Now as for you Cedric, why do we both have the same bracelet? Are you dating both of us? Huh? Give us an answer! You think we're stupid?"

Questions flew at him like racquetballs and he couldn't get a word out.

With a straight face he told Cuqui, "I never bought Angel a bracelet. I only bought one bracelet, and that's yours."

Extremely shocked, I got in his face. "What, Cedric? You tryna tell me that you ain't buy this bracelet?"

"That's right," he said, not going back on his word. "I never bought a thing."

"Cedric, you just bought this last Saturday. And you wrote me a poem to go with it."

I didn't have the poem in my possession. All I had was my word against his.

He turned to Cuqui and said, "I swear on my daddy's life I ain't buy that bracelet. That's not my even my style."

"What???" I said in disbelief.

"The bracelets are the same," Cuqui said, jumping in to help me. "If you ain't buy it, then where did she get it from?"

"I don't know where she got it but she ain't get it from me."

He yanked the jewelry from out the plate of food, my 14 karat royalty smothered in Mac & Cheese. After wiping off the back, he ignored my presence and turned back to Cuqui. "Look baby," he said. "Her bracelet doesn't even have her name. But yours does ... see that ... you see that?"

He brought it closer to Cuqui's face to prove his innocence. She looked confused, as if she didn't know what to believe.

He said, "Trust me, baby. I only got one girl. And that's you."

My heart fell into my stomach, nearly causing me to hyperventilate. He actually had the audacity to call her baby, in front of me, confirming what he thought of our relationship, that we had none. Done. Barred from existence.

I turned his face back to mine, our love hanging on a string of hope. "So what you sayin,' Cedric? You sayin' we ain't together. Huh? Is that what you sayin?"

He looked into my eyes of misery, no remorse in those brown eyes of his. "Me and you was just kickin' it, Angel. Nothing more. I just wanted to see how the booty worked."

That rock hit my chest at 90 mph, nearly caused me to black out. His friend said, "Dang, Cedric. That's messed up cuz."

"Yeah, but it's the truth," Cedric said, his body language backing up his words.

Mortified, I started pulling at straws. "So what about all the poems you wrote me... all the walks to class ... huh, Cedric ... answer me ... all the times you were calling me at night when you knew I ... you knew I couldn't receive phone calls ... or what about the nicknames ... thought I was your Butter Pecan ... huh ... you lying son of a..."

My eyes started to water. Tears became a thunderstorm down my cheeks.

I was hoping he'd feel empathy, a trickle of remorse, but he stunned me by saying, "Come on, girl. All of that was just game. Don't you know game when you see it ... Besides, you was gaming me too. And game recognize game. So deal wit' it."

Not caring, he blew me off in front of everyone, booed me off stage at his own little Apollo. I felt weak. Felt inept. My equilibrium was lopsided and I didn't know whether to faint or vomit. Walls closed in. Every image was becoming condensed.

All I kept thinking was this bastard had embarrassed me in front of all my friends and Cuqui was safe while I struck out.

But no one embarrasses Angel Inghram.

Not him. Not Cuqui. No one.

Right at that instance, as blood from my heart spilled to my cerebrum, I regained consciousness, picked up my pride, and as everyone awaited my next move, I bit my lip and held my breath, then with no hesitation, I cocked back and punched him right in the face, hit him harder than I ever hit a boy before.

He fell onto the cafeteria table like a fish without water, completely traumatized, a hit making the shocked crowd drop their jaws. Then he got back up, surprised that I socked him, and I raised my fist for another sucker punch, wanting to show him that although I'm a girl, I will box like a man.

With a busted lip, he said, "Ho, I don't usually hit females, but I'm' bout to tear yo ass up!" He drew back to return the blow, but before he could hit me Cuqui punched him from his blind side and surprised the both us. "You're a liar!" she hollered. "I knew you liked her the whole time!"

Somehow we fed off each other, and just as he tried to hit her, I swung at him again, this time landing a fist into his back, watching him stumble into a delusional state and hit the floor again.

And from there it was hell.

We jumped on his back and tag-teamed him like hyenas on a cheetah, punching him, choking him, digging his face into the plate of mac & cheese, not caring about the consequences that we'll encounter.

His boys tried to break it up but the girls interfered. And a massacre started. All hell broke loose in that cafeteria. Soon, teachers and administrators were diving in the crowd to end the middle school mob, looking for the students that started the fight.

Five minutes later I was making my first trip to the principal's office. Both me and Cuqui. And the whole time while being questioned I was thinking of my Aunt Terry, hoping they didn't call her, knowing if she came to the school I would get an ass whipping, the type of ass whipping that Cedric wanted to give. But to my surprise, Cuqui blamed everything on herself as I sat looking confused; she told the administrators that she started the whole commotion. They didn't believe her entirely, but her words did lessen my punishment to three days detention while she got suspended for a week.

Till this day she never said why she stuck up for me. And till this day I never fixed my lips to ask.

Maybe because I already knew. I knew that in spite of us wanting to fight one another, I was the only friend she ever had, the only real friend, because no other girl had ever stood up to her. Since that day we became inseparable, would go on to rule junior high together, always having each others backs.

Although we took different paths in life, neither of us ever talked to Cedric again. He'd see us in the hallways, in the classroom, at school parties, and whenever he'd fix his lips to speak, one of his boys would remind him of the cafeteria scene, and that was enough for him to hold his words. Till this day Cuqui and I still laugh about that, because it sparked our circle of sisterhood, became the commencement of a long-term friendship.

You see it took a boy to bring us together, but a man will never tear us apart. That was the first promise we made as a pack. To always have each other's back when necessary, no matter how hostile the situation was.

Right now my situation was hostile, and the only person I could genuinely count on was Cuqui. She was my Ace of Spades. The last card for me to play. And while waiting in the car, phone to my ear, I rung Cuqui's phone again and again.

9

"Who the hell is ringin' my goddamn phone this time of night? Unless you're the police, you betta have a damn good reason!"
My best friend was at her lowest tolerance, but I couldn't hang up.
"This is Angel," I muttered.
"Who?"
"Angel."
"My girl, Angel?"
"Yeah."
"Angel Inghram?"
"Yeah."
"Scotts Projects Angel Inghram?"
"Cuqui stop playin'. Now this is me."
A long silence came over the phone, as if she was surprised to hear my voice. We haven't talked in months.
She tells me, "Bitch, you got some nerve callin' me after all what happened? Don't you know every cop in Miami is lookin' fo' yo' ass ... Every five minutes they bangin' on my door talkin' all dis mess of how they gon' take me in if I don't tell 'em where you at and talkin' junk 'bout if I don't tell 'em they gon' hold me fo' conspiracy to commit murder and I'm like y'all betta gon' 'bout y'all business' cause

I don't know where Angel is and if I did know I ain't telling y'all cause I ain't no snitch and—"

"Cuqui!"

"What?"

"Slow down for a sec. Now I'm calling you because I need a favor."

"A favor? Ho you must be out yo' ignorant ass mind to think I'm 'bout to do a favor for you. If anything, I need you to do me a favor because I've been protecting you for the last three months. The police even went as far as to show up at my job asking questions 'bout you. You got some gas money? 'Cause I'm tired of taking long routes home just so I can dodge the police. I've been—"

"Cuqui!"

"What bitch?"

"Shut up and listen to me."

"I am listening. But I already know where this conversation is goin' and I ain't tryna hear it."

Cuqui has a tendency to go motor-mouth when she's against something. She also curses a lot, which is something you have to get used to.

On the contrary, Snow was still in the parking lot of Shady Pines Apartments, speaking with two buff black guys in gold chains and white T shirts, Suge Knight look-a-likes. I sat in the passenger seat of the Mustang, impatient, wondering what was taking her so long. At first it looked like regular talk, but then I noticed some sort of exchange between them.

Over the phone, Cuqui said, "Angel, you there?"

"Yeah."

"Well start talkin' 'cause you wasting my minutes."

"Hold on for a sec."

The men gave Snow a manila envelope. Safely sealed. Looked like some sort of package.

I swallowed a baseball. Didn't know what was the relevance of that package, but I wondered if it played a part of Devilla's kidnapping. Or death.

I rolled down the window to hear them talking, breathed the thick smoke from weed clouding the air. They spoke low. Kept their conversation so cryptic to where all I heard was ... *be careful with this ... make sure you don't leave it lying around.*

Meanwhile, Cuqui told me, "I'm hangin' up, Angel. I gotta—"

"Don't," I stopped her. "I need you."

"For what?"
"Because—"
"Did you kill William?" she asked.
"Huh?"
"Don't play stupid with me, Angel. I'm talkin' 'bout William? Did you kill im or not? I need to know."
I pull myself together before telling the truth. "Yes."
"Oh hell naw ... hell naw ... all this time I thought it was an accident and you really killed 'em ... bitch, what type of weed were you smoking to do something like that? You must've been—"
"Cuqui!" I said, trying not to raise my voice. "Right now this isn't about William. I'm in a lot of trouble and I need you to do something."
"Do what?"
"I need you to come to Vegas."
"Come where?"
"Vegas. I need you to catch the quickest flight to Vegas."
"Vegas? The hell with weed. You must be smoking crack."
"I'm serious, Cuqui."
"So am I. In case you haven't realized it, I gotta go to work in the morning."
"Forget about your job. As far as money, you'll be taken care of."
"Yeah, how so? You gon' pay these bills? You gon' sex the rent man for me? Last week my light bill was $250 alone. And I'm not gon' mention my car note ... shiiiiiiit ... that with insurance almost broke my back. So unless you gonna—"
"Ten thousand dollars."
"Say what?"
"I'll pay you ten thousand dollars to come to Vegas, plus all your expenses while you're here."
Silence comes over the phone. She's speechless. Money is the only thing that talks louder than Cuqui.
"Fine," she said. "Guess I could use a vacation. I mean, a sista has been workin' hard and all."
I smile. "Thanks, Cuqui. Now I want you to—"
"Hold on, hold on, hold on," she said. "Not so fast Flo Jo ... Number one, what's my purpose for coming to Vegas and number two, where did you get so much money?"
I looked in the rear view mirror. Snow was still talking with both men, but they had taken their conversation upstairs to the third floor. Lights flashed from that apartment where window blinds were torn.

"You still there?" Cuqui asked.

"I'm here."

I couldn't tell Cuqui where I got the money, at least not right now. For Cuqui hates the police. Hates them with a passion. One time she was dating a guy for two months before finding out he was a cop, then after he confessed, she immediately broke it off, gave him a bogus story about how she became a born-again Christian and she was practicing abstinence. She despised the police just that much.

Cuqui repeated, "Well, I'm still waiting for an answer, Angel. How are you able to give me ten grand? You rob someone?"

"I didn't rob anyone. Just know that the money is safe. I'll explain it all when you get to Vegas. But in the meantime, I need you to be on a nine o'clock flight tomorrow morning, if not earlier."

My eyes went back to the third floor to watch Snow and the two men. The men started pacing through the apartment, kept throwing their hands in the air as if they were trying to get their points across. I couldn't hear what they were saying, but their body language said this was no longer a friendly conversation, and with the look on Snow's face, it was evident that anger was circulating in the room. Lots of anger.

Before I could blink, I saw a gun rise in the air, vivid as ever, pointed directly at one of the men.

Then a shot fired. Another shot; blood splatters all over the apartment window.

"Jesus Christ!" I said, not believing my eyes.

"What is it?" Cuqui asked over the phone. "What was that noise?"

"Nothing ... nothing ... I gotta go—"

"What?"

More shots are fired. The window shatters into pieces and a body drops from the third floor, crashing on top of a blue Chevy Impala.

I peed my pants. Make that crapped my pants.

"Dammit! Gotta call you later, Cuqui—"

"But—"

"Bye! And remember what I told you! Vegas."

I clasp the phone shut with my brain going a hundred miles an hour. The impact of the dropped body sets off the alarm of the Chevy Impala, that earsplitting sound causing every light in the apartments to flash on. Doors flew open. Windows came up. The dead had risen to life.

Then I heard screams. "She killed Tony! She killed Tony!"

Everyone starts pointing at one person, and that person is no other than Snow, walking down the steps as if she's untouchable, as if she's the fourth Charlie's Angel.

Nervous as hell, my first thought was to get the heck out this neighborhood. I looked around, saw the keys already in the ignition, car was cranked and ready to go.

I jumped into the driver seat of the Mustang, told myself that Snow would have to find another way home. But there was only one problem. One big ass problem. This car is a stick-shift and I only driven a stick once in my entire life.

While thinking what to do first, Snow opened the passenger-side door.

My heart jumped.

"You tryna leave me?" she said in a calm voice.

"Are you crazy, Snow? What the hell is your problem?"

"I don't have a problem. But we're gonna have a huge problem if you don't get this car going right now."

I panicked, became short on breath. "I don't ... remember ... how to drive a stick."

"Be calm," she said. "Now just press your left foot on the clutch. All the way down."

I did as I was told. Fingers trembling. Face starting to sweat.

Snow threw the car in first gear and said, "Now easily press the gas while letting your foot off the clutch."

A gunshot burst through our back window to insinuate we've overstayed our welcome.

"Do it now!" she yelled.

I mashed the gas so hard to where I almost burnt a whole in the motor. The car skidded off, but not before more gunshots were fired.

Snow yells, "Again! Mash the clutch!" I did the same routine as she threw the car into second gear.

The engine roars, wheels spinning like a car ready to be airborne.

I took off fast. Drove hard. Drove like the devil was on my ass in the rear view mirror.

Bullets continue to hit our car, all shots coming towards the driver's side. I glanced out the window. Seems like everyone and their mama had a gun, including teenagers with shirts off, kids rocking bandanas, each determined to keep us trapped in their beehive of violence.

Snow pulled out her gat to return the ammunition, firing back at anyone and everyone who was shooting at us. "Come on!" she yelled. "That's the best y'all got!"

I tell her, "Stick your head back in this window before a stray bullet hits!"

She doesn't listen, and she continued on her shooting spree as if she was immortal.

"Turn there!" she said. "There goes the exit."

Nearly crashing into the sign that read Shady Pines Apartments, I flooded the engine to get out this death trap. Gunshots were nonstop. Even after we were up the street, people were still chasing us in the rear view mirror, running after the car like zombies in a Rated R Thriller.

I rode the Mustang until the coast was clear, looking for the nearest place to pull over and regroup. Five blocks ahead was a Chevron gas station. Clean area. Better part of town.

I zipped into the gas station and mashed on brakes. Face flushed. Wrinkled forehead. I got out the car and slammed the door, told myself to run fast as I could, to get far away from Snow as possible.

"What are you doing?" she yelled.

"Running from a crazy bitch!"

Footsteps run after me. Cold metal is placed at the back of my head.

"Turn around!" she said.

I turned to face her head-on. Faced her 9mm that is pointed at my forehead, staring me in the face with no leniency.

She tells me, "A hundred grand says you're not going anywhere."

"Yeah, well it's gonna take more than that to get me back into that car."

People stare at us. Innocent civilians pumping gas had stopped to give their undivided attention, shocked at what they were witnessing.

Snow waves her badge around to show everyone her status. "It's okay people. I'm a cop."

The moment she takes her eyes off me, I snatch the gun from her hands and point it at her temple. The crowd held their breaths. People were terrified. Then I grabbed her by the shirt and pulled her to me, my fingers ready to pull the trigger.

She says, "Point that thing at me and you better be ready to use it."

"Open up!" I demanded.

She opens her mouth and I stick the gun down her throat, letting her get a taste of her own medicine.

I tell her, "If it wasn't for the life of Devilla, you'd be a dead cop right now." I take the gun out of her mouth and point it at her chest.

"And you'd be in jail," she replied. "So we both have something to be thankful for. But remember that I got the little girl ... Devilla is in my possession, which means I got the power."

"Only for so long."

She hunches over and sticks her eyes into the face of the 9mm, does that as if she's begging me to shoot.

She says, "Just so you know, I'm not afraid of dying."

"That makes two of us."

"I can see that. But what I don't see is your logic behind your actions. I mean, I don't understand why Devilla means so much to you anyway."

"A skank like you could never understand."

She laughs. "You have one helluva mouth to be so young. But that's all you got ... You see, Angel, your life will never be the same. Even after this is over, you can never go back to law-school, can never live out your dreams of becoming an attorney."

I held the gun tighter. "Fuck you." Told her the first thing that came to mind.

"It must suck to be you, Angel. To know you exist in a world where you'll always be the hunted, constantly looking over your shoulder, trying to escape the law because you could never be a part of it."

"And you're the law?" I said, pointing the gun at her throat. "Is this what you call the law? You?"

"I'm the law. The system. The police. All of that wrapped into one badass bitch. That's me! But you ... you're an underachiever. You're what they call an imbecile."

Her words became a knife into my back, the blade penetrating me deep. She was trying to deface me with cruelty, wanted to show me that I was on her level, that my life was as jacked up as hers, a crooked cop with nothing to love but a badge.

She says, "How does it feel to be an imbecile? To know that all your days of law school led to this?"

I cocked the gun. "Keep running that mouth ya here. Keep on talking."

"What you gonna do, Angel? Kill me in front of all these people ... at a gas station ... Remember that I'm a cop. So in case you're thinking about running again, remember that if you kill me, you won't get a block."

"That's fine with me. I'll take my chances."

"I know you would. Because unlike me, you can't control your emotions. Emotions led you to killing William and they're also telling you to kill me right now."

I sharpen iron with iron; tell her, "You mean the same emotions that make you wanna kill your husband?"

Her face mutates from calmness to aggression. "Don't ever compare yourself to me, Little Girl. You'll never be me. You see I'm a businesswoman. Something you tried to be, but never quite succeeded at."

"And you never succeeded at marriage, which makes us both failures doesn't it? Your husband doesn't even love you. No one loves you. How can you be respected as a cop when you're not even respected in your own home?"

"Homes can be replaced, Little Girl. So can love. But where's your home, Angel? New York? Miami? Vegas? Pick one. You have no home because you'll forever be on the run, always running like the criminal you are. Like you're the scum of the earth. What's the difference between you and a rat that's looking for a hole, squirming for a new habitat?"

The knife goes deeper into my back, but I restrained myself from pulling the trigger and blowing out her brains.

She goes on, "As far as I'm concerned, you're better off dead because alive you're useless ... You're not living. Just existing. So how 'bout you do us both a favor and gimme the gun."

"And what if I don't? What can you do to me that haven't been done already?"

"Kill the girl," she said, reaching in her pocket and showing me Devilla's picture. "Consider this your last warning, Angel. Because the next time you step out of line, I'm gonna call the men who are holding Devilla, give them the order, then I'm gonna put the phone to your ear and let you hear her make a sound you never heard a little girl make. A sound that will haunt you for the rest of your pathetic life."

My face began to burn, eyebrows slanted as a sharpened blade.

She goes on, "Besides, if you shoot me that'll only scare these innocent people out here. And you don't wanna do that now do you? You don't have the heart to do something like that."

She smiles. People continue to watch us like an accident on the side of the road. No one moves. Everyone is ducking behind cars, waiting for Snow to do her diligence as a cop and take me down.

Hard to admit it but she was right. I couldn't do this like this. Not with all these people watching. And even if I did so happened to kill Snow, that wouldn't necessarily save Devilla from being killed. Couldn't take this type of gamble on Devilla's life.

Snow says, "So this is how it's gonna go. I need you to let me take the gun away from you, then I'm gonna throw you on the ground and force your hands behind your back so I can cuff you."

"How 'bout I just hand you the gun and eliminate all the unnecessary foolishness."

"No, Angel. That's too simple. The people out here gotta fear the police. But on the same token, they gotta know the police are doing everything possible to protect them from criminals, even it means putting our lives on the line. You got it?"

"Let's just get this over with."

Doing as we discussed, she strips the gun from my hands, turns me around, and forcefully handcuffs me with pleasure, acting as if she's auditioning for CSI.

"On your feet!" she said, shining for the audience.

People raise their heads as she escorts me back to the car. Faces full of excitement, everyone started to applaud her like an actress getting ready to win an academy award. "Good work!" they all screamed. "Very very good work, Officer!"

In unison, they turned their noses at me as if I got what I deserved, then stared at me the way America stared at Saddam Hussein when he was first captured and hung by a rope. To them I was equivalent to the rat that Snow mentioned earlier, the scum of the earth.

But to them she was a hero.

The badge made her a hero.

I wanted to get angry. Wanted to let them know that the real criminal is the cop, the one who has me in handcuffs.

But at this point that was utterly useless.

Snow said, "You see what you did, Angel. You just restored the public's faith back into our justice system. Take a bow," she joked.

She placed me in the backseat of her undercover whip.

More strangers applauded for justice. More citizens became fans.

10

I held my temper all the way to Snow's house.
We shared no words. No eye contact. Just two women with fierce units on their faces, both out to do business and get on with their lives.

Snow's house was in the suburbs of Vegas, an area known as Green Valley. She lived in a gated community. Very peaceful. Far from a house the average woman can afford, or man for that matter. You had to pass through security before entering the gates, and then there was a machine for entering a pass code. Snow showed the security guard her badge. He yielded to her. Looked at her as if she could take away his job with a phone call, fake smiles exchanged between the two of them.

Her house was bigger than I ever would've imagined. It was two stories. All white. Looked like a mansion making love to another mansion. The price on the house could've easily gone for 1.5 million on the market, even with the state of the economy. The lawn was gigantic, grass so green to where it looked fake. Beautiful garden. Every flower known to man was vacationing in this woman's front yard.

If I didn't know any better I'd think we were in the Hamptons. The place was mind-boggling. Made my Brooklyn apartment look like the apartment from *Good Times*, while she was moving on up like the Jefferson's.

Snow parked her Mustang in a garage big enough to hold a dealership. In the garage was also a Black Mercedes. Silver Maybach. Range Rover. But weirdest of all, there was an old beat-up truck that was parked there too, a truck that somehow fell into the wrong garage. After exiting the car, she walked to the front of the house and turned on the sprinklers.

She tells me, "Come to the back. Let me show you the love of my life."

I stopped in my tracks. "Love of your life. I thought you said your husband was out of town."

"No silly. Not that love. I'm talking 'bout Macho."

"Who?"

She walks to the backyard and opens the fence to a yard that stretched longer than a football field. I was speechless. Majority of black folks have yet to receive their two acres, but she already had hers. All that was missing was a mule.

She yells into the open field. "Macho! Where are you?"

Out of the darkness comes the biggest freaking dog I ever saw in my life, looked like a bear running in our direction. Thinking the dog wouldn't stop running, it jumped on top of Snow and threw her to the ground, started licking her face as if they were lovers. She didn't resist. Kissed him back. Rubbed his head. Turned him over and tickled his belly. "*You miss mommy*," she said to him. "*Did you? I knew you'd miss me but mommy was out taking care of business ... oh it's okay ... I'll take you next time.*"

After their foreplay was over, the dog looked in my direction and stared at me as if I was interrupting something special. I froze. The dog stood on its legs. Licked its lips. Gave me a look that said I either join the party or get the hell out his yard. My choice.

Snow says, "Angel, this is my dog Macho." Then she turns to the dog. "Macho, say hello to Angel Inghram."

The dog barked. Told me I don't got much time to make a choice. I sized him up. His breed was a Rottweiler. All black in color with strips of brown going alongside his mouth. That mouth was bigger than my head with a long tongue, and slob was pouring out the left side of his grill. I noticed there wasn't a leash on this monster, and right now, a sista didn't have the proper shoes for jumping over this fence.

Snow says, "Why don't you come and pet 'em. He doesn't bite."

The dog barked again, gave a look that says he does bite, and I better not believe a word she says.

I told Snow, "That's okay."

"You sure?"

"I'm sure."

"Okay then. Suit yourself. But you're missing out on the cutest dog ever." She turns back to the dog and starts tugging at his cheeks, then she starts talking to him like a baby in a crib. *"Isn't she missin' out my little snack 'em cakes ... she don't know that you're the best doggy in the world ... you've been a good doggy for mama while I was gone? Huh? Were you a good doggy?"*

She looks back at me with a face that says she's on cloud nine.

"I'm sorry," she said. "I love my dog. Macho means everything to me."

"I can tell. Looks like you've built him a nice-size doghouse?"

"Well technically, that's not considered a doghouse. It's actually a shed. But because I love my little Macho so much, I turned it into a doghouse. *Ain't that right little pumpkin,*" she said, tugging on the dog's cheeks again. "And word of advice, Angel: While you're staying here, don't ever come in this backyard without me, because if you do, Macho will tear you up clean. Not even my husband goes in this backyard because Macho is only used to one person." She turns back to the dog. *"You hungry little Macho? Huh baby? You hungry."*

After Snow sat out a plate of dog food for her beast, we left the backyard to enter her house, unlocked the double doors of her honeycomb hideout.

Snow flicked on the lights to reveal the heart of the rich. I never been in the Whitehouse, but I can imagine it looked something like this. There was a living room inside a living room. Cozy fireplace. Marble Floor. Vaulted ceilings with lights shining down on us like angels. A beautiful oriental rug extended from the front door to dining room and to the left was a plasma television that belonged in Times Square.

In the midst of admiring her crib, a woman of tan complexion walked into the living room. She was a middle-aged lady but had a good figure for her age. Short and petite. Full lips. Honeycomb complexion dipped in more than one ethnicity. Thick, bushy hair ran down her back like a canyon. Hair long enough to tie at her ankles.

Snow says, "Angel, this is my maid ... Maid, meet Angel Inghram."

Now I know who owns the old truck, I thought.

"Welcome?" the maid said.

"Thank you," I replied. "Nice to meet you."

The woman looked nervous, as if she was a part of an institution that held her hostage. I could see it in her eyes. Eyes telling me to get lost before I become a lost soul.

Snow says, "I gotta give Maid credit for keeping this place tidy. Without her, I don't know what I'd do."

"Is that right?"

"But watch out, Angel. Maid sees and hears everything."

She calls her Maid instead of calling her by her real name, and I resented that. It shows no respect for this woman or her line of work.

Snow says, "Well sit down, Angel. Make yourself comfortable."

I sat down on a black leather couch. A couch long enough to sit an Indian Village.

She asks, "Want something to drink? Water? Wine?"

Thinking she'd spike my drink, I asked for the clearest liquid. "Water would be nice."

"Then water it is." She takes her eyes to the maid. "Take care of Angel for me. Also show her around the rest of the house. I'm going to go upstairs and get out of these clothes."

They went their separate directions and left me sitting on the couch. I glanced over to the right, saw a wall full of vivid pictures. Suspicion told me to inquire about the faces that made up Snow's world, so I walked over and did just that. There were many photos of Snow. Photos of her younger days when she was in her twenties, before her hair metamorphosed into multicolored locks. On every photo she looks beautiful, doesn't seem like she's aged a bit. She has pictures with many important people, her smiling with celebrities like Jada Pinkett, Star Jones, and Tichina Arnold. Then there are photos from the police force. Her flashing smiles with the chief of police. District Attorneys. Lawyers. Even judges. I now see why she feels she can't be touched. She knows everybody and anybody that is somebody.

There was one particular man that she shared the camera with a lot. He appeared to be Columbian. Very handsome. An older man that carried a boyish glow, very well put-together. I imagined the man had to be her husband, the man she was paying me to kill. The photos show them doing normal things people do in a relationship. Kissing. Dancing. Lying on the beach on summer vacations. Even saw wedding photos of them cutting the cake, Snow throwing the bouquet, the day she stood before a preacher and said *'til death do us part*.

Pictures always tell what a person is feeling; they never lie. And on every photo her husband is showing no emotion while Snow is smiling like the sun, two minds in different places that came on one photo. But on other photos he's ecstatically happy. He's fishing with the Mayor. Hugging Fidel Castro. Posing with people in prominent positions. Senators. Congressmen. Governors. Wow. On one photo he's even shaking hands with the president, a powerful man that knows powerful people. And it was my job to take him out.

I picked up the photo to get a better view of the man I was paid to kill. He didn't only have a handsome face, but it was a face that looked familiar. I thought about where I'd seen him. Took in his green eyes, his thick mustache, that dark mole on his face that was tattooed in my memory, not too many people walking around with those distinctive features.

Then the picture dropped.

The picture dropped from my hand and hit the tile floor, an unexpected drop from sudden memory.

"Yuh k, madam?" someone asked.

I turned my stare. In a broken English voice, it was the maid, coming back into the living room with a glass of water in hand.

"Yes ... Yes I'm okay," I answered, picking up the photo.

The man in this picture was the same man I'd stumbled upon in the parking lot of a hotel. The same man I had caught with a beautiful young woman that was half his senior. Long-legged. Ethnic features. A super model giving him more than a catwalk. That erotic behavior was less than 24 hours ago, the same time I burst on the scene with a mask on my face and put a gun to the supermodel's head, ordering Snow's husband to give up the rented car before I ended the life of his mistress.

That moment – with his pants at his ankles – was the first time I met Snow's husband. The only scary part is that he's yet to meet me.

The maid said, "He boss husban' ... he gud mon."

"A good man? You sure about that?"

She nodded yes, then handed me a glass of water. "Fa yu madam. Anting else?"

"No thanks. And please, call me Angel. I'm nobody's madam."

"A'rite."

"Good. And what's your name?"

"Montreal."

"Mon-what?"

She sounded it out. "Mon-tre-al."

"Got it. Montreal. Ms. Montreal."

She concurred with a smile, the sound of her name bringing her joy as if it's been stricken from her existence, as if no one in this house ever addressed her that way.

But I had intentions on finding out more than just her name. Considering that she was the maid, her eyes and ears made her very informative when it came to the business of this mansion, and everything within it. The first two minutes I found out her heritage. She was born in Peru, raised in Jamaica, and that explains her accent and beautiful dialect, the linguistics of patois. She spent the latter part of her life living in different parts of the states, moved to wherever the money looked best.

As I inspected the maid's life, she took me through the rest of the house, showed me the dining room, kitchen, patio, and den. According to her there were twelve rooms and six bathrooms altogether. In the hallway leading to the dining room there was a large painting of Snow on the wall. The illustration was identical to Snow's image – mean, wicked, and deserted – and the bottom of the painting also had words written in French: *Respecter ma maison ou ma feuille.*

I ask the maid, "Do you know the meaning behind those words?"

The maid giggles. "It mean respek mi house or leave."

I laughed behind her. "Yep, that's Snow all the way."

"Le mi show yu to yuh room."

"Which is?"

"Upstairs."

"Upstairs?"

She nodded yes.

Thinking she was leading me to a flight of stairs, she stopped in the center of the hallway and pushed a button. From behind the wall a door opened.

I ask, "What are you doing?"

"Tekin' de elveter, Angel. It fasser."

"What? This house has an elevator. Oh hecks naw ... now I'm really jealous."

After stepping off the elevator I walked down a long hallway that had multicolored ceramic tile throughout. Above me were beautiful chandeliers that hung from the ceiling, all going in a row like plantation trees. More paintings covered the walls. Beautiful paintings of Marilyn Monroe, Madonna, and Diana Ross. Three back-to-back divas.

The maid says, "Dis yur room."

She opens a door at the end of the hallway for me to enter. The room was not over the top like the rest of the house. Nothing fancy. Just a queen-size bed with all the necessary amenities for the average person's stay, but I noticed that the bed was not made up.

In the blink of an eye the maid ran over to start stripping down the comforters and sheets, also tossed the pillow to the floor.

I wondered what the drama was, but then I looked down and saw something that nearly ruptured a blood vessel. Beside the bed was an unwrapped condemn. Gold Color. Slightly opened. *MAGNUM* sketched across the box. The maid hurried to pick it up before I noticed it. Then she ran over to the television and pressed eject from the DVD player. My eyes skipped to the dresser as I noticed a DVD Cover lying face up. The DVD was entitled, *Once You Go Black* and beneath those words were two black chicks tag-teaming a happy Latin man.

My jaw drops.

The maid grabs the box like it's a bomb equipped with a timer, ejects the DVD and covers it up.

I pickup my jaw.

Carrying a handful of skeletons, she turns around in a panicked state and stares at me as if she wanted to die. "Mi sorry, madam. Pleez no ... no tell boss a'rite."

"It's okay," I told her.

"Pleez no tell boss. Boss fiah mi if—"

"I said it's okay. I'm not telling anyone. Your secret is safe with me."

She left the room with her heart racing as fast as her steps, left with her skeletons wrapped in sheets.

I chuckled some more, then lounged on the bed.

While sitting on a naked mattress, I checked the phone in my purse and saw that I had four text messages from Cuqui.

Text 1: *Why'd you rush me off the phone? Everything okay?*

Text 2: *Hey Angel, it's Cuqui. Checkin' on u. Call me back.*

Text 3: *Dammit, call me back!*

Text 4: *Bitch, this is my last time checking on yo' ass okay. Call me back!*

I replied with two texts. One saying I was okay. The other reminding her to be on that early morning flight.

I dropped the phone back in my purse and placed it on the dresser, a dresser that had more photos of Snow shown with her high-profile acquaintances. Judge Judy. Judge Mathis. Condoleezza Rice.

In one photo there was a woman by her side. No celebrity. No political figure. Just an ordinary woman that looked like Snow. Figured it must've been her sister due to the albino skin and the high cheek bones, only difference is that this person had a chubbier face, was at least forty pounds heavier.

It was at that moment that the maid strolled back in with sheets for the bed, her embarrassment still lingering from the incident earlier.

I looked back at the unrecognizable photo, then glanced back at the maid.

Eyes and ears. Eyes and ears. If anyone could tell me something about Snow, it was sure to be the maid.

She said, "Fresh linen fresh pillows for yur be'room."

"Why thank you."

When I asked her about the woman on the photo, she answered, "Boss. Dat boss."

"Snow? The woman on this picture is Snow?"

She nodded yes.

I looked back at the photo, looked back at the chubby face that was much rounder than the Snow who lived in this house.

I asked the maid, "When was she ever this big?"

"No big. De boss wes preg-"

My eyes light up. "What did you say?"

She put her hands to her mouth as if she had said too much. "Nuntin. Nuntin et all."

She turns her back to walk out the door.

"Wait!" I said, stopping her in her tracks as she knows she's busted. "Turn around."

"Sorry madam but me need leave. Got clean downstairs."

"You're lying. What is there to clean at 1am?"

She thinks of something to say, but there's a rat in the house and she knows I smell it.

"Exactly," I said. "You have something to tell me don't you?"

"Me have nuntin—"

"Don't lie!"

She turned around to face me. "Pleez madam. De boss kill me if—"

"Don't worry about Snow. I can deal with her myself. But what I need from you is to know what happened."

Lips trembling, she holds her mouth like it's a loaded gun.

"Just say it," I repeated.

I waited. Got nothing. Couldn't pull those lips apart with a set of pliers.

Desperate, I pulled the last card in the deck, a card that reads blackmail. "How do you think the boss would feel if she knew 'bout your little secret? About how you were sexing a man in her house while she was gone?"

"Pleez no ... me ... me need job."

"Then I suggest you cooperate because I know a lot of unemployed women who wouldn't mind having your job."

Considering she was a sweet lady, I didn't want to go the blackmail route, but I had no choice.

"So what's it gonna be? Are you gonna tell me or what?"

She contemplates on my proposal before deciding to choose the path of employment. "K ... K ..." she says, raising her palms in the air. "But dis private. If boss esk yuh hear nuntin' from me."

"I won't tell a soul."

Gathering her words, she eventually said, "De boss kill beh-beh. Boss kill beh-beh."

"Who killed baby? Snow? What baby?"

"Yes. Beh-beh lon' to boss."

"Snow killed her own baby?"

"Yes."

That brick hit me in my stomach as I tried to re-group, then asked the maid to repeat her last words. After she confirmed her statement, I motioned to the door and glanced down the hallway, ensuring that Snow didn't hear our conversation. Snow's bedroom door was closed shut.

I walked back to the maid, sat on the bed, held her hand, and asked, "How do you know this?"

She dropped her head.

"Take your time and speak slowly."

"K ... K ..." More wrinkles indenting her honey-comb face as she swallowed a bucket of paranoia. "One day wen cleanin', me 'ere boss mad wit' husban' over tele'fon. De boss cry en curse, sey if not for yu, wud not kill beh-beh."

I tried to translate, said, "You heard Snow crying over the phone, telling her husband that if it wasn't for him, she wouldn't have killed her baby?"

She nodded yes.

I said, "But why? Why would he make her do something like that?"

"Mi 'ere boss sey she bun wit' nudder mon."

"Cheating? Are you saying that Snow cheated on her husband and had another man's baby?"

She shrugged her shoulders as if she wasn't sure, as if she only got a taste of that phone conversation.

She went on, "Erd boss sey no forgive 'im. She miss 'er lil' beh-beh. She wan more beh-behs but cunt mek more beh-behs."

"Why can't she have more babies? Did he make her have surgery?"

More shrugging of her shoulders to insinuate uncertainty. Getting the facts out of her was more useless than milking a dry cow.

I said, "Are you sure that you heard what you heard? You absolutely positive."

She nodded yes.

"And how do you know that Snow doesn't know you were listening that night?"

"She no see mi. Me very quiet dat night ... preten' clean ba'room."

"You pretended to clean the bathroom?"

"Uh-huh. Boss be'room crack en door. But boss no see mi." Her eyes became fearful again. "Pleez no tell boss. De boss evil. Bod. Very very bod."

This was murder at its highest peak. Calamity at its darkest hour. If Snow could kill her own child with no conscience, blood of her blood, then what she'd do to someone else child was unmentionable. Devilla's words replayed in my mind. *Save me Ms. Angel. Save me.* I let the maid off the hook from answering any more questions. All other information I could get for myself.

In my thought process, the maid repeated, "No tell boss. No tell boss."

I reassured her that my lips were sealed. "You have nothing to worry about, Ms. Montreal. Your words are safe with—"

"I see you ladies are getting acquainted," a voice said, coming from the door.

I turned around, quivered in my seat, sat up straight as the maid jumped from the bed. That voice was the voice of Snow, the devil intruding in the room with a grin on her face. I didn't speak. Neither did the maid. Silence controlled the airways and the only noise was the maid breathing hard, looking at Snow like a slave on the verge of being lynched.

This, indeed, was a dilemma.

11

Snow stood in the doorway with her arms crossed, leaning against the wall.

She wore a long housecoat of Versace material, purple color, and house shoes on her feet. Her locks were swooped in a bond that sat high on her head, covered by a purple head wrap, and the red tips fell down on her face like poison ivy from a wild growing plant.

I wondered how long she's been standing there, how much she'd heard from this dark conversation between me and the maid.

She smiled at me. I smiled back. Didn't give her the perception that she was the center of the conversation.

Meanwhile, the maid felt a need to say something. "Me jus tell madam 'bout pardy."

"What party?" Snow asked, squinting her eyes.

"Surprise pardy nes week … yuh know … de one yuh wan' me plan Mr. Marcello birday."

"Ooohh okay. That party … So what do you think about it, Angel?"

"About what?"

"About the party? That is what y'all were discussing right?"

"Oh yeah … I think it's a great idea. Birthdays only come once a year and you must cherish each one."

Snow looks at the maid. Looks at me. Then back at the maid with an inquisitive eye.

The maid was trembling harder than a murderer taking a polygraph test.

Snow says, "On second thought, there's been a change of plans. I think I'm gonna cancel the party. I have something else in mind." Her eyes come to me. "Isn't that right, Angel?"

"Yeah, me and Snow decided to do something a little less extravagant."

"You see," Snow said to the maid. "So don't worry about planning anything."

The maid asks, "But what 'bout udur guests. Mi ready call hunred of his frens, sen cards. Whad me tell dem—"

"Doesn't matter?" Snow snapped, cutting her off. "I don't care what you tell 'em, as long you make sure it doesn't happen. Just because you're a maid it doesn't mean you have to think like one. Now leave us."

Speechless, the maid drops the bathroom towels on the bed. "Good night, Angel."

"Good night."

She leaves the room as quickly as she came, her long hair running to catch up.

I remained sitting on the bed with my hands behind me, then locked my elbows and crossed my legs. Snow didn't speak. She just walked the room like a parent does a teenager, inspecting anything that was out of place. She stops at the window seal and props her body against the wall, faces me.

She says, "I don't want you talking to Maid."

"Jealous?"

"Just careful. She's not to know your purpose for being here. No one's to know your purpose for being here."

I asked, "Exactly what does the maid know already?"

"Only what I want her to know."

"Which is?"

"Enough to cover our asses, Angel. That's it."

"And you trust her?"

"Darn right I do. Trust her more than I trust my own husband."

"Why?"

"Because she fears me, Angel. The first step to establishing trust is imbedding fear; that's something you ought to know."

"You should also know that fear ignites betrayal; or worse it can lead to murder. The more someone fears something the greater chance they'd kill it. It's the reason we kill spiders. The reason we kill snakes. The reason wives kill their abusive husbands."

She sneers at my indirectness. "My husband is not abusive and I'm not killing him because of fear. This is bigger than fear, something your little finite mind could never understand."

A telephone rings.

It's coming from the house phone sitting on the dresser. Snow rushes over to the caller id, smiles, then picks up in a cheerful voice. "Hey, Honey ... oh nothing, just here with my cousin ... Angel, the one I was telling you about ... remember I said she'd be staying with us for a while ... of course I told you ... I'm sure we talked about it ... that's because you never be listening when I talk ... okay ... okay ... so when are you coming back .... What???" Her tone shot into a boisterous thunder. "Are you serious? The 6th is not until two weeks from now ... no that's not what you said ... that's not what you said ... I remember 'cause that's not what you said ... well what's keeping you there, and what am I supposed to do while you're gone ... fine ... fine ... No I do not have an attitude ... no ... no ... I don't have a ... yeah well ... well the next time you have an assignment, it'll be nice if you remembered that you have a wife. Just once!"

She hung up in his ear, left him with nothing but a dial tone.

I uncrossed my legs and sat up straight.

"Something wrong?" I asked.

No response. Just a woman pacing around the room with hands on her hips, doing her best to keep her act together.

Once the pacing stopped, she said, "There's been a setback in plans. Instead of my husband getting here tomorrow, he won't be back from Dominica until two weeks."

"Why the sudden change in plans?"

"Something popped up."

I knew what popped up. Knew exactly what popped up. His adulterated penis had changed the plans to make its own plans with a promiscuous model. I knew because of what I had seen in that parking lot that day, that a husband who was supposedly in Dominica on business was right down the street with a fake Naomi Campbell. Snow didn't know this. But I did. And I sat on that ace-of-spades. Sat silently with a plan.

Snow told me, "But this doesn't change anything. The plan is still going down when my husband gets back. Same place. Same time."

The phone rang again.

"Don't get that!" Snow said.

The caller ID said *Unknown*, but the look on Snow's face said it wasn't a bill collector.

Snow ignored her husband's call and waited for it to end. More ringing. No answer. More ringing. No answer. She blocked out the tune like a mother does a crying baby, but eventually, the ringing got the best of her, caused her to race towards the phone, grab it with two hands, then she threw the helpless phone at the guess room wall, threw that ringing phone with all she had.

The phone chips the wall and falls to its death. I jumped in astonishment, thinking this bitch must be on some type of medication.

Fingers rubbing at her temple, she says, "I outta kill them both."

The next morning I awoke in Snow's guest room, fighting the sleep of a relentless nightmare.

And it's the same damn nightmare I've always had.

The same damn nightmare that made me a woman.

A woman at six. Barely a girl. Watching the gun being pointed at mama as my stepfather accused her of stealing cocaine. And I watched as mama had stood in my way to protect the life she cared for most. She cried don't shoot. Cried for mercy.

But mercy never stopped his gun from blasting to take the life I cared for most.

And mercy never stopped my gun from blasting to give karma back its unpaid debt.

Six rounds of justice. Thought I could sleep. But now – instead of watching mama beg for her own life, the nightmare is of him begging me, begging not to shoot, and I always awake at the same exact point where Devilla is screaming to leave 'lone her daddy.

Neck sweating, my eyes got stunned by the sun through the guestroom window. I glanced at the clock. 11 am. Morning was clocking out for Afternoon's shift and I wondered how I had slept so long.

Rising from the bed I heard a knock on the door. It was the maid, Ms. Montreal, coming in the room and tapping on the dresser, her thick dark hair swinging at her side. "Good morning, madam."

"Thought I told you to stop calling me that."

"Sorry. Me been waitin' to wake yuh."

"How come?"
"Brunch downstairs."
"Brunch?"
"Da boss gon to work. She sey she be bac 4 pm. Yu get clothes en closet."
"Okay, give me a second and I'll be down."

I went into the bathroom to shower up, took off my short brown wig and placed it on the back of the toilet. Mama always said to never take a shower in other's people's houses. Said it was disgusting, that everyone doesn't live by the same sanitary principles. I inspected the shower before climbing inside. A gold walk-in shower that was absolutely spotless. Gold sink. Expensive mats. Marble floor with a tiger painting hanging over the toilet, five-star resort type stuff.

After getting out the shower, I left that foggy bathroom to sit on the bed, then I lotioned my legs while looking in the mirror, started examining the rest of my body.

I detected flaws. Many flaws.

Although I'm only 125 pounds soaking wet, I saw flab trying to creep around my thighs, followed with cellulite peeking under my left butt cheek. My stomach was still tone, thanks to a gazillion crunches a day, but my booty could use a little inflation. Cuqui told me that doggystyle sex would fix the problem, told me she got her blessing by getting on all fours and being illicit, but if that was true, then I should have a butt like Serena Williams by now. Breasts were my most valuable assets. All natural D cups. Sat up like trophies. I call 'em the moneymakers. The only problem is that they wore heavily on my back, and after observing them for so long I noticed flaws in them too, that one of my breasts sat lower than the other, also thought I saw a lump in the right one.

I walked to the other side of the room to meet the walk-in closet. And I instantly fell in love. According to the maid, these were clothes that Snow never wore, yet still they were more expensive than some people's cars. There were four racks in total, each rack had been layered by order of apparel. Versace coats. Formal dressers. Stylish tops. Killer skirts. Made me feel like a member of *Sex In The City*, like I was shopping in a city that exceeded my expenses. I turned my back to see what else she had in store, and behind me was a goldmine, something so extravagant that I nearly had an orgasm.

Shoes.
Shoes for days.

An array of designers were assembled in the closet. From Louis Vuitton, to Ferragmos, to my favorite, Manolo Blahniks, I had never seen so many expensive shoes at one time. I tried on one of the Blahniks. Reached for another pair. Then reached for another. And another. One more. I was a kid in a candy store, now trying on shoes just to try them on. Posing. Modeling. Strutted that catwalk. Tyra didn't have shit on me because I was so full of myself right now.

After the party was over, I reached on the top shelf for some knock-about clothes. Threw on a white T-shirt, some blue Capri Pants, and a pair of blue Sandals for my 7 ½ foot.

I took the elevator to the first floor of a house that wasn't mines, went into the kitchen and sat on a stool where the maid came over to bring apple juice.

What was on the menu?

Everything that I don't usually eat. I was served pastries, mixed fruit, crackers & cheese, bagels, and English muffins. I looked around for some meat, some sausages or ham, but there was none in sight.

The maid said, "Boss careful whad she eats. She vegturin."

"A vegetarian? No wonder she is the way she is. She ain't got no meat in her life."

The maid laughs, "Yu funny, Angel. Yuh remind mi of mi daughter."

The maid classified this meal as brunch. But where I'm from – in the projects of Miami – there was no such thing as categorizing a certain meal, because it was all considered food no matter the time of day. I've ate breakfast at dinner. Dinner at breakfast. From sugar sandwiches to syrup sandwiches to peanut butter without jelly sandwiches, I grew up with an aunt that didn't care what she served you, as long as you got served, you got what you got.

The maid said, "Need sometin else?"

"Yeah, I need us to finish our conversation from last night."

She freezes. "Tought we finish."

"Not exactly. You never told me how you met Snow. How did you end up working for her?"

"Mi use to be gud frens wit' 'er mutter."

"Her sick mother in New York?"

She shook her head yes. "Mi knew Snow wen she was lil' gal. Kep 'er wen 'er mutter was gon."

"So you know her quite well, meaning that you know other things about her too?"

She shook her head no. "Kep 'er wen she small. Dat's it." Then she gave a one-sided smile that had room for inspection, as if she was lying, or hiding something, the truth etched all over her face. I wondered if she knew about Devilla, if she knew where Snow was hiding my little girl, and even greater, if she knew my purpose for being here.

Before pressuring the maid for any more information, the cellular rung in my pocket.

The caller was Cuqui, my best friend. Heard her yelling through the phone before I could put it to my ear.

"Angel, where the hell yo' ass at?" she asked.

"Are you ... you at the airport?"

"That's right, waiting on you heifer. And you need to hurry up because it's hot out here and my eyeliner is starting to run."

Not wanting the maid to hear the conversation, I whispered, "Cuqui, I don't have a car. You're gonna have to catch a cab to get where I'm at."

"What? Are you out yo' rabbit ass mind, Angel? You betta come pick me up."

"I'm not that far from you, Cuqui. It's 'bout a thirty minute drive that—"

"Oh hell naw, Angel. This wasn't part of the contract 'cause I know what you told me and I ain't got dementia I done already flew on this long boring plane ride and had to eat pretzels while listening to a cryin' ass baby who wouldn't shut up for nothing in the world and not to mention waitin' another hour for a delay in Texas I went through all this crazy stuff and now you tell me that I have to find you in a cab. Bitch I hope you payin' me extra 'cause I ain't equipped to deal with this foolishness and I don't even ..."

I dropped the phone to let her ramble on. The maid was looking at me in awe, wondering who was talking so loud through the receiver.

I asked the maid, "You think you can give my friend directions? She's at the airport."

"Yes."

I handed the phone to the maid. Even with the phone to her ear, I could still hear Cuqui saying, "Who the hell are you and where the hell is Angel? I can't even understand yo ass."

The maid wanted to give the phone back to me but I told her to never mind Cuqui and just continue to give her directions. Twenty minutes later a cab pulled into the driveway. Climbing out the backseat was a woman with a pink weave, a suitcase in hand, and a mean unit on her face.

The cab driver tells her, "You forgot something."

"Forgot what?"

He rubs his finger together as if to signal for a tip.

Cuqui tells him, "Nigga I just gave you $25 for the cab fare. You betta take your tip out that $25."

"Ma'am, I drove you for more than half an hour. Any distance that long should require a tip plus regular fare."

She gives him a harsh look and flashes the middle finger. "Tip this! And next time spray some Febreze in that stink dirty cab."

He cranks up the engine and floors out the parking lot, wishing he never had made the trip.

As Cuqui walked onto the front porch, I saw that she was just as elated to see me as I was to see her. Snow ordered me to stay in the house at all times, told me that violating that rule would be the result of a bullet being put into Devilla's head. Although she never mentioned it, I knew that visitors were also off limits. That's why I ordered the maid to never allow this visit to get back to Snow. I didn't have a plan for Cuqui – nothing besides booking her in a hotel that was nearby Snow's house – but one thing I knew was that I needed her in Vegas, needed her in case gasoline spilled on an unidentified match.

Cuqui greeted me with her usual hug when she saw me. "Girl, yo titties get bigger and bigger every time I see 'em."

I smiled. "I know right."

"Now all you gotta do is keep working on that white girl booty and you'll be aiight. You been doin' what I told you?"

"What's that? Oh, you talkin' 'bout the—"

"Ghetto Palates."

I sucked my teeth. "Girl that stuff don't work."

"Maybe not fo' you. But fo' me, it kept my booty tight as a rock." She bends over. "Don't act like you don't see it, Angel. Don't act like you don't see that bodacious ass."

I cracked up as she says, "My man been hittin' that thing so good to where I now have an apple bottom. And I ain't even shame to make it clap for 'im."

"Girl you crazy."

"Call it what you want but it works."

The maid was peeking through the window to watch Cuqui do her tricks, wondering who the heck I had brought to the house.

Cuqui was a dark-brown woman that looked mixed with something you could never figure out. Her eyes were brown and full of life. Had thick eyebrows she kept arched all the time.

She stood a couple inches shorter than me. A full-figure woman. Thick in all the right places that men cared about. Her breasts weren't as big as mines, but she had enough to make due. She did everything possible to keep her mid-section trimmed. Also had thunder thighs to go with her killer backside.

Above that backside is a set of eyes and below those eyes are the words, *I See You Looking*. A diamond is sketched across the nape of her neck and a shining star goes around her bellybutton. The back of her hand shows a rose that is fully detailed, thorns and vines poking out in different colors. That must've hurt. Her name is written on her arm in Chinese symbols. The other arm has the numbers 305 (Miami's area code), and a dragon blows fire down one of her legs while lilies and tulips cling to the other, but nothing is more vivid than the cherries coming down her thighs, cherries dripping red syrup with the words, *wanna taste?*

I ask, "When did you get so many tats?"

"Oh girl, they just kinda snuck up on me one day."

I looked at her hair. It was bright pink with strips of black, made her look as ghetto as she wanted to be. Although she had long curly hair, she never showed it. Instead she always rocked a weave. Loved horse hair the way a kid loves French fries. She's also materialistic. Always have to be first in line with the latest styles, the latest cell phones, even if it means going broke or losing the electricity in her house. She loves jewelry too. Can't go in public without six bracelets on her arm, 18K gold necklaces, and the biggest set of earrings you ever saw that sat on her shoulders. Never wears costume jewelry. Cuqui says it's for fake people and one thing she'll never be is fake.

She asks, "And who the hell you know that live way out here in the boondocks?"

"No one. Just a woman I recently met."

"Shiiiiiit. Unless that woman is Hilary Clinton, she must have two coochies to afford a house like this. A house this big should be illegal."

"You think this something; wait 'til you see the inside of this joint." When we walked through the door, Cuqui did exactly what I thought she would do, lose her mind. She was walking through the house like a tourist at a theme park, touching anything and everything that was in her reach.

She says, "Angel, can you believe that this house has an elevator."

"I know that, Cuqui."

"I can't believe it ... An elevator ... A damn elevator." She moves towards something else that captures her attention: Snow's painting hanging on the wall. "Is this the lady that live here?"

"Yeah ... That's her."

"Is she accepting applications? 'Cause any money she has, I wouldn't mind having a piece of it."

Cuqui runs her finger across the painting, admiring the artwork.

"No touch dat!" the maid snapped, coming down the stairs. "Boss no let anti one touch paintings."

Cuqui takes a step back. "And where the hell you came from Ms. Short Stuff? Who are you?"

"Me live dis house."

"Is yo' name on the lease?"

"No, me de concierge. Me look afer house when boss gone."

"So in other words, you ain't shit."

The maid's face fills with anger, her thick hair rising to the top of her head. She points her finger at Cuqui and says, "Respek mi yankee."

"Who the hell you calling a yankee you banana boat riding—"

"Banana boat! Banana boat!" The maid's eyes aged five more years from Cuqui's disrespectful comment. "Mi no come banana boat yuh bumbaclott mi es citizen yuh—"

"Banana boat. Raft. On a mule's ass. Ain't no difference to me how you got here—"

"—sketel yuh dun know mi yuh—"

"—take yo—"

"—bumbaclott—"

"—ass back where you—"

"—Mi got passport yuh rassclat—"

"—came you short ass—"

"—respek boss house or lev!"

I walk over to get in between them. "Hold on for a sec! Just hold on! Now Cuqui, this is Ms. Montreal. She's the maid in this house."

"Well she betta maid her lil' butt back upstairs 'cause—"

"Shut up, Cuqui!" I turned to the maid, watched her bite her lips as if she wanted to teach Cuqui a little respect. "Now Ms. Montreal, it's very important that you don't tell Snow about Cuqui being here. You got that?"

The maid's face turned into stone, and before agreeing not to tell, she snarled at Cuqui and muttered, "Rassclat."

Not knowing what a rassclat was, Cuqui ignored it and allowed the maid to walk off. Then we went our separate ways. Cuqui and I sat in the living room as Ms. Montreal dusted the dining room, still eyeballing my friend as if this wasn't over.

I whisper to Cuqui, "See what you did. Now you pissed her off."

"Ask me do I care."

"You haven't been here more than a minute and you're already starting stuff."

"Whateva, she'll be aiight ... All that woman needs is a social life."

"Think so?"

"Know so ... Being cooped up in a house all day will drive a person crazy. That's why she so uptight. She needs some friends, entertainment, anything."

I laughed. "Don't let her age fool you though. She's gettin' more entertainment than you can imagine."

"Oh really?"

"And gettin' paid for every minute she's not on the clock."

"I bet. She looks like she has a secret life."

"A secret life is putting it lightly."

"Yeah?"

"Hell yeah. Like I said, don't let her age fool you. That woman probably gets more lovin' than you."

"Than me? Shiiiiiiiiiit ... That must be a whole lot of lovin'."

Cuqui kicks off her heels and puts her foot on the couch, making herself at home. I peeked over my shoulder to see where the maid was cleaning. She was still in the dining room.

Then I whispered to Cuqui, "When I got here last night, I caught the maid with an open condom wrapper hid beneath the bed."

"What? Stop playin'."

"Surprised me too. And girl what makes it even worse is that the condom wrapper was gold."

"Magnum?"

"Magnum LX."

She laughs. "Get the hell outta here. You lyin'."

"I swear."

"On yo' mama's grave?"

"On my mama's grave."

Cuqui glances back at the maid, a look of disbelief, and she shakes her head. "Damn."

"I know girl. Same thing I said."

"Do you know how long it took me to find a Mandingo brotha?"
I laughed at her.
"I'm serious, Angel. Niggas like that are like winning the lottery."
"You ain't lyin'. And that's not all of it girl."
"Oh no?"
"What put the icing on the cake is what she had in the DVD player."
"What was it?"
"A DVD of a naked Latin man that was getting serviced by two black chicks."
"For real?"
"That's right girl. The biggest dick you ever saw in your life."
"And he was Latin?"
"Something like that. All I know is that regardless of his race, he had the dick of Mandingo's uncle."
We both fell to the floor laughing, not able to control ourselves.
Cuqui says, "Damn, me and her should hang."
It felt good to kick back and gossip with Cuqui, kind of took me to a place where I haven't been in months. The practical side of me isn't designed for laughter. It's constantly reminding me of reality, that I'm a convicted felon who's wanted for murder. But Cuqui has a way of making you lose that practical side. She's full of life. Full of fun. Ever since we were little she'd find ways to humor a bad situation, the water bringing life to a moldering plant. She always told me that I'll go on to do great things, because she believed in me when belief wasn't there. She said I was her better half, the one there to keep her from going over the edge. But now the roles are reversed. Now I'm the one on the edge, the one whose one step away from hitting ground zero. And who's there to save me from going over? Cuqui is.
I tell her, "Thanks, Cuqui. Thanks for coming way out here for me."
"Don't tell me you getting sensitive on me."
"I'm serious, Cuqui. It means a lot."
"Well it better mean ten grand 'cause that what you told me over the phone."
"I said that?"
"Don't play wit' me, Angel. And by the way, where my money at?"
"So the only reason you came is because of ten grand?"
"Hell yeah. Shiiiiiiiit. Times are hard. And that's not only me talking. The economy can also cosign on that. So yes, ten grand

means a lot right now." She sat there for a few, speechless, then she burst into hard laughter. "Girl you know I'm just BS'ing. Even if you said you weren't giving me a single red cent, I still would've come."

"You serious?"

"Okay then. I might be exaggerating a little, but you get my point. I ain't gon' let nothing happen to my girl."

"It's good to know that."

Silence sits between us.

She says, "But you do have the ten grand, right?"

I laugh. "You see, I knew it, Cuqui. You ain't no good."

"Whateva," she says, flipping back her weave. "Don't get mad at me 'cause I'm tryna get paid."

"What if I told you that I had a hundred grand?"

Her mouth drops. Eyes bulge out like a fish. "A hundred what?"

I silenced her. "Shhhh. Lower your voice ... well really I got fifty right now. I get the other half when the job is finished."

"What job? Wait, I think I need a drink for this one. God only knows what you 'bout to tell me."

I called for the maid who was doing work in the dining room. She comes into the living room with a more relaxed face than before.

I ask, "Could you get us something to drink?"

"Whaa'd yuh ladies like?"

"I can go for some dark liquor," Cuqui said.

"Actually, she'll take some juice. We both will."

After the maid delivered our drinks, she headed upstairs to continue her cleaning. My eyes followed her until she disappeared, didn't want her eavesdropping on our conversation.

"Cuqui asks, "So what's the deal with this Snow chic? Who is she?"

"She's the devil with tits. Actually, make that the devil with tits in a police uniform."

Cuqui's eyes light up. "She's a cop? You mean to tell me I'm in the home of a cop?"

Shucks. I forgot how much Cuqui hates cops.

She tells me, "Angel, you know how I feel 'bout cops."

"I know I know. But unfortunately for me, it's either here or jail. I mean ... she knows about William."

"About the murder?"

"Yes. She was one of the officers at the crime scene. One that I took on a high-speed chase."

"Really?"

"And she's been chasing me ever since."

"So what does she want? Why are you in her house and not in jail?"

"I was in jail. But she snuck me out of jail to blackmail me into doing her dirty work."

"Which is?"

I wanted to tell her about the plan of killing Snow's husband, but it wasn't the right moment. The maid was sweeping upstairs in the center of the hallway, and although she was cleaning, I had a feeling that she was listening in.

I signaled to Cuqui that I'll tell her in a few. In the meantime, Cuqui rose from the couch to walk over to the shelf, picking up the picture of Mr. Marcello.

She asks me, "Who is this?"

"That's Snow's husband."

"This is her husband? Damn, talk about fine."

A door closed upstairs. The maid was in Snow's room.

I hesitated, then murmured to Cuqui, "He's also the reason why she wants to pay me a hundred grand. He's my assignment."

"Assignment? What type of assignment involves you, her husband, and a hundred grand?"

I tried to think of a way to say it without actually saying it, but before saying anything, Cuqui put her own context clues together, and she came out the mouth with, "Oh my gosh. She's wants you to sleep with—"

"Hush. Now before you go assuming, it's not what you think."

"Bullshit, Angel. She looks back at Mr. Marcello's picture with a face of delight. "Geez, Angel. This man is sexy as hell."

"So?"

"So, are you out of your mind? This lady wants to give you a hundred grand to sex her husband and you ain't down with that. Shiiiiiiiit, I'll fuck 'im for free."

"I know you would. That's because you're nasty."

"Call it whateva you want, but for a hundred grand I'll be nasty and paid." She stares at the picture and licks her lips, acting like this is the best news she had all week. I knew I needed to tell her the whole story, but the words are not coming easy.

Cuqui says, "And he's Spanish too?"

"Dominican."

"Same thing. Either way that makes it better. Those Spanish men know how to get it down in bed. Girrrrrl, I had one of 'em last month and when I tell you that Spanish men can put it down. Trust dat ... They puts it down!" She closes her eyes and shakes her head, acting as if she's having an orgasm. "Girl that man sexed me so good to where I'm still feelin' the vibrations."

"Anyways, listen to what I have to—"

"That man knew he could put it down. Put it down so good to where I got on my knees and prayed to Jesus, thanked him for bringing a man like that in my life that—"

"Cuqui—"

"—knew how to do a sista good. Hell, he put it down so good to where I almost made a trip to the alter and changed my last name to—"

"She's gonna kill 'im."

"Say what?"

"She wants me to help her ... kill ... her husband."

The room gets quiet, air solid as ice.

Cuqui drops the picture and stands immobile, her shoulders tensed, lips trembling. There's more fear on her face than a white woman in Harlem.

I tell her, "I know what I said sounds bad. That's why I need you to help me."

"Oh hell naw. Hell to the naw naw, naw. You want me to help you? Are you crazy? She throws her hands in the air and paces through the living room. "I'm not with dat, Angel. I'm telling you right now I'm not killing any—"

I jumped off the couch and put my hand to her mouth to quiet her. "Shhhhhh. Don't talk so loud. The maid will hear us. And why are you being so over-dramatic."

"Over-dramatic? You tell me you want me to help you kill—"

Another hand over her mouth. "Don't say the word," I whispered. "Don't say the darn word."

"Okay okay. Well, you tell me that you want me to ... you know ... take someone out, and I'm the one being over-dramatic? What the hell did you expect me to say because I know you ain't think I'd go through with this. You lied to me."

"I didn't lie. Just didn't tell you the whole truth. Now sit for a sec."

"For what?"

"Just shut up and sit down."

She saunters back to the couch, looking at me as if I'm a stranger, as if I'm not the woman she's known for the last thirteen years.

She says, "Please tell me that this is one big joke. You're fooling with me right?"

"I wish I was but this is real." I take a deep breath, let out an exhausting sigh, then lean in to start whispering. "According to Snow, her husband owns restaurants ... but he's also a drug smuggler, supposed to be one of the biggest cartels on all the west coast."

"Huh?"

"That's how she affords to live in this house; her husband is worth millions. But the thing is, he wants to leave her for another woman and she's determined not to let that happen. That's why she's plotting his murder. To collect all his earnings."

"But what does this gotta do with you?"

"She's blackmailing me to help her do her dirty work. Tells me that if I don't go through with it killing her husband, she's gonna put me back in jail ... Then she tried to bride me with a hundred grand. Gave me fifty up front. The other fifty after we finish the job."

"And you actually wanna do this?"

"What the hell you think? Of course I don't. But time I turned her down she tried to get real."

"What do you mean?"

"The day I killed William, I took off running with his daughter. Remember Devilla?"

"Of course. How could I forget that bad lil' demon."

"Well I used Devilla as a hostage to run from the cops that day. But once I was free, Devilla got loose and ran for the cops. Unfortunately, the dirty cop she ran into was Snow."

"Wow. The odds of that happening."

"Thing is, somehow Snow found me after she found Devilla, knew exactly where I'd be. And once she found me, she tricked me with another money scheme that involved a bachelorette party."

"A bachelorette party? You mean to tell me that you stripped for women?"

"That's another story. But the point is, after she busted me with her little sting operation, she paid me a visit in jail the next day and told me that if I don't kill her husband, she'd kill Devilla."

"Damn. How do you know she's serious? I mean, do you really think she'd do that to a little girl?"

My face transmutes to anger. "Hell yeah she would, Cuqui. She's killed before and she'll kill again."

"Wait a second. Did you say killed before? Killed who?"

Before taking my voice into an undertone, I glanced upstairs to ensure the maid was nowhere in sight.

Cuqui repeated, "Killed who?"

"I saw her kill two men last night. Shot 'em without even thinking, in front of a whole apartment complex, while I was on the phone with you."

"What?"

"And that's not half of it. Some years back she killed her own baby."

"What?"

"Killed it because she couldn't have the father."

"Are you serious? That's crazy."

"Crazy is putting it lightly. A more suitable word is psychotic."

"And how do you know all of this?"

"Because I know her weakness."

"Which is?"

"The maid ... The maid hears everything. And last night, when she saw me and the maid talking, she almost had a conniption. Hell, I wouldn't be surprised if the maid was next to take a bullet. So you see what I'm up against."

Cuqui scratches her head as if this is too much information at once.

She tells me, "Why the hell did I ever pick up the phone when you called? I should've done you like I do the bill collectors."

"I know I know. But I didn't know who else to call."

"You should've called Jesus. Because I'm not a miracle worker. And it's gonna take a miracle to get you out this mess."

I clasped my hands and gave a hard sigh. "Does that mean you're gonna help?"

"Help you do what? Get killed? I say you're better off running for your life."

"I can't do that."

"Why not?"

"Because Devilla needs me. She's only six years old."

"And? Whether you've realized it or not, Devilla is not your child and she damn sure ain't mines. I only got one child and her name is Shaquana."

"And what if this happened to Shaquana? You'd give your right arm."

"If this was Shaquana we wouldn't be worrying because Shaquana ain't gon' run into the hands of a cop. If anything, she'll be tryna get as far away from the police as possible. She's just like her mama."

I laughed. "Girl you got problems."

"Besides, you should've listened to me from the beginning."

"What you mean?"

"I told yo' butt a long time ago that you didn't have to go to NYU. Didn't I?"

"Oh okay. So now you gonna throw that up in my face."

"Just stating the obvious. I also warned you about William. That he could be crooked. If you would've listened to me from the jump, we wouldn't be in this predicament."

I smiled.

She asked, "What you grinning for?"

"You said the word *we*, as in we're in this together."

"No bitch. I meant you. The police ain't after me."

"Uh uh," I said, disagreeing. "You already said we. Can't take it back. So I guess you're gonna help me right? You got my back?"

She hesitates, then sucks her teeth. "I guess I do. The same way I had your back in the 6th grade, when Cedric was 'bout to whip you like you stole something."

"That's jacked up. You didn't have to go there."

"I had yo' back then, and I got yo' back now … Truth is, I'm tired of having yo' back. I got a back on me too ya know. When you ever gonna have mines?"

I kiss her on the cheek. "Thanks, girl. I owe you big—"

"Don't be kissin' on me ho. We might be close but we ain't that close."

After we came to a mutual understanding, the maid came downstairs smiling while dressed in a different outfit. She was rocking a turquoise dress with loose-end ruffles. J-Renee heels. Dark blue Pearls clung around her neck with her hair in an updo, diamond clips clinging to each side, and she was all dolled up with foundation and eye shadow as if she was heading to a Senior Prom. I was stunned.

"Looks like someone is dressed for action," Cuqui said. "Where you goin' sexy?"

I pinch Cuqui's leg.

"What?" she mumbled.

"Hush."

"For what? All I said is she looks good."

The maid says, "Mi goin' out, Angel. Be bac lil' bit."

"Okay."

She grabs the keys to her rundown truck. "If de boss calls, tell 'er mi wen to get groceries for de house."

"I bet," Cuqui mumbled. "Do those groceries include a pickle?"

I pinch that arm again.

"Ouch!"

"Not another word, Cuqui. I mean it." I look back at the maid. "Cool. I'll give Snow the message."

After the maid leaves, Cuqui whirled in mirth.

I tell her, "You play too much."

"Sorry but I couldn't hold it in."

"Well I'm glad she's gone."

"Why?"

"Because now I can get busy, if you know what I mean." I give Cuqui the eye, the one involving a crooked smile.

She says, "Oh I see where this is heading and I want no part of it."

"You don't even know what I'm 'bout to say."

"I don't gotta know. I saw the eye."

"What eye?"

"The eye you give when you're up to no good and want my participation. Well it's not gonna happen."

"Just listen. Now in order to get Devilla back, I need to beat Snow at her own game."

"And what's that?"

"Prying. I'm gonna find everything there is to know 'bout this woman. From her family. To her ex-boyfriends. Her likes. Dislikes. Health. Hobbies. Even down to her panties."

"Geez, girl. You crazy for real."

"Just determined. I refuse to let this psychotic woman get the upper hand. She needs a taste of her own medicine."

"So where do we start? Her neighbors? The internet?"

I hesitated, then pointed my finger upstairs. "Her bedroom."

"What? Girl you must've lost your mind. I'm not going in that woman's bedroom."

"I'll go in. All you need to do is stand by the door and be on the lookout."

"What if she comes home?"

"She won't."

"How you know? I don't even know this woman and you think I'm 'bout to go sneaking 'round her bedroom. Hell, I'm not even supposed to be in her house."

"I know her schedule. She doesn't get home 'til six, which means we got three hours."

Cuqui scratches her head. "Uh uh. This don't sound right, Angel. And you know I always go with my first mind. This doesn't—"

"Come on, Cuqui. This woman has everything on me. Murder. Kidnapping. She has enough to put me behind bars for years. But what do I have on her? Not a darn thing. All I have is a bunch of allegations that wouldn't stand a chance in court. Nothing tangible."

Cuqui slouches against the wall to give it some thought.

She says, "Why do I have to go into her bedroom? Can't I just lookout from downstairs?"

"Downstairs is too risky."

"Why? I'll alert you if someone comes through the door."

"That'll be too late. I need you upstairs so you can see the entire neighborhood, which means you'll know if someone is driving up. Now come on. Let's do this before the maid gets back."

Cuqui looks up at the ceiling, rubs her temples, then she sighs. "Fine, Angel. Whatever you want I'm down. But you better be payin' me extra for this shit."

12

Making our way upstairs – which was supposed to be the easiest part – was not easy for Cuqui one bit. She was trembling up the steps, peeking over her shoulder, holding the rail like it was a life jacket.
I tell her, "Snow's bedroom is the first to the left. Now come your scary butt on."
"Girl, stop rushing me."
"Hurry up."
I turn the door knob to the room where Snow lays her head to rest. It's locked.
"Dammit!"
"What is it?"
"The door is locked."
"You see, Angel. That's a sign. That's God way of telling us to get our asses from up here. Don't ignore the signs—"
"Shut up. Now all we gotta do is pick the lock."
"Pick the lock? I'm not picking anything. That's breaking and entering."
I try to think of the easiest object that'll get me through this door. Something sharp. Something thin. Something pointed

Cuqui says, "I say we take our butts back downstairs. God has already gave us a sign that—"

"Hush. Now wait right here."

"Where you goin'?"

"Wait."

I ran down the hall into the guestroom, opened the closet to look for a hanger that was thin with a sharp tip, like those hangers from the olden days. I searched high and low. Threw around coats. Pushed jeans to the side. In the back of the closet was an old hanger covered with a long-sleeve white collar shirt. I yanked the shirt from its domicile, pulled the hanger apart, stretched it out to create the ultimate jagged edge.

I ran back down the hall, saw Cuqui twitching on the rail.

She asks, "What took you so long?"

"Needed something sharp."

I stuck the hanger through the door knob, started fiddling for the lock that'll get me into the promise land. I jerked left. Tweaked right. Peeked my eye through the key hole to look for a click, or a loose end that held the piece to this puzzle.

Cuqui tries to put her two cents in. "Pull the doorknob towards you and lift up on it."

"Like you ever picked a lock before."

"Did it once when I was sneaking up on my man."

I kept the tweaking going steady, took her advice and lifted up on the doorknob, pulled it towards me. Still no luck.

"Here, let me help you," she said.

A two-team effort, we poked and prodded at the door like addicts in need of a fix. Jerking. Yanking. Rattled that door knob for nearly twenty minutes, until the hanger was bent up from persevering work.

Then I heard a click. A click that turned the lock to all of our troubles, caused the door to Snow's bedroom to open up wide.

Jackpot.

Cuqui says, "Damn. This lady is living large. Really large."

We stepped into the biggest room I ever seen. There were more large paintings on the wall, Michelangelo paintings of naked couples from the olden days, flaccid penises with natural breasts of women that carried a forest between their legs, a time when nudity meant art and not a nest of pleasure.

She had three sets of dressers. All were made of cherry Oakwood trimmed in gold. Tall antique lamps. Enormous walk-in closet. King size bed. Massive gold mirrors that were clear enough to show every

Running From Redemption

impurity on your face. While wondering where to start, I didn't notice that Cuqui had already started her own investigation in the bathroom. At the break of me going to grab her, I heard her scream to the top of her lungs.

"What is it?" I asked.

"It's ... it's ... it's diamonds, Angel! Real diamonds!"

"What? Let me see what you talking 'bout?"

In her hand is a platinum necklace with round diamonds, more carats than I ever saw in my entire life.

I ask, "Where'd you find that?"

"Lying on the sink."

"Well put it back. We can't touch anything."

She turns up her nose. "Kiss my ass, Angel! This necklace is mine."

"Are you stupid? Put that thing down right now."

"But—"

"But nothing. Do it now. And put it back like you found it. We don't need your fingerprints smudged all over that thing."

She gazes at me like a little girl that's forced to give up her puppy and she slowly lays the necklace back in its proper place. Then she talks to it. "I'll come back for you, someday ... okay ... me and you are meant to be together, no matter how hard people try to tear us apart." She looks back at me. "You know I'll never come across another necklace like this one."

"Stop acting stupid and go stand by the window. You're supposed to be on the look-out."

As Cuqui leaves to assume her position, I thought about the best place to look for a lead, maybe the bathroom since there was already a discovery. I searched through their medicine cabinets, not caring about the rules of privacy while running my fingers through all of Snow's personal items. Tampax. Sinus Relief. Rubbing alcohol. Tylenol PM. Lithium Carbonate.

Lithium Carbonate?

That's a bipolar drug. I should've known Snow was on some type of medication from all the mood swings she has. Something told me to mix some Tylenol with her Lithium and put her out of her misery. I tampered with that thought, rode it until I hit a dead end that said it wouldn't work. Or maybe I could inject some alcohol in her tampons to give her the burn of a lifetime.

Another bad idea.

Finding nothing in the medicine cabinets, I shut the bathroom door to continue my search in the bedroom. The dressers were first. Started from top to bottom. Panty drawers. Pajama drawers. T-shirt. Shorts. Socks. I was doing a tornado through Snow and her husband's clothes and my only discovery was finding that her husband doesn't wear boxers, strictly a brief's man.

I glanced at Cuqui. Instead of watching my back through the window, she was filing down her nails.

I asked her, "What are you doing?"

"Looking out for you."

"Stop messin' with your hands and pay attention."

My next place to search was under the bed. I locked eyes with a black briefcase that was slightly open. I froze. Wondered what the briefcase had to offer to a stranger and if I should touch it or not.

I went for the gold.

Slid the briefcase from under the bed and flipped it open, thinking there would be money inside, but instead there were pictures, snapshots of different criminals before they were taken into custody, all types of people I didn't know. It wasn't long before I stumbled onto a picture of myself. Make that many pictures of myself.

I swallowed hard. Swallowed again.

There were photos of me in different cities. Eating in Boston. Driving in Detroit. Sleeping at hotels in Houston, Phoenix, and flirting with a man in San Francisco. This woman had been following me from the very beginning, knowing my every move.

I cursed out loud.

"What is it?" Cuqui asked.

"That lying bitch was right under my nose the entire time."

I looked around some more, scrambled through pictures like a pathfinder in search of a goldmine. Not only were there pictures but she also had personal info – things like my driver license, birth certificate, four previous addresses, and the icing on the cake, my SS number.

I shut the briefcase and slid it back under the bed, started walking around for more leads. I passed a dresser, chest of drawers, vanity table, night stand, chair, armoire, garbage disposal, then saw a place where I should've looked from the beginning.

The closet.

I opened the doors to her walk-in closet that was twice as big as the guestrooms. Never have I seen so many Armani suites in my entire life. Leather coats. Denim Jackets. Then there was Burberry,

Burberry, and more Burberry. Adjacent to the closet was a DVD stand that had a vase on top. The vase was engraved in italic letters: *1924 – 2009. Love you mom forever. You'll always be in our hearts.* Cremation stared me right in the face, a jar full of someone's mother's ashes.

Eyes still in the closet, I stared left at something lying on the same rack. It was a black object. Very round. An object out of my reach, but desperately needing some further inspection. I grabbed the futon in the center of the room and carried it back to the closet to get my hands on this anonymous object. Even after standing on the chair, it was still out of reach.

I whispered, "Cuqui ... come here ... come here quick."

"Why?"

"Need you to give me a lift."

"What?"

"Need you to put me on your shoulders."

She squints repulsively. "Your shoulders? We might be close, but we ain't that damn close."

"Girl come here. Think I found something."

Cuqui comes over to give me a lift, squatting as I climb onto her back.

"A little higher," I told her.

"What?"

"Higher."

"Can't you see I'm tryin' bitch? I ain't no bodybuilder. Now hurry up and watch your legs."

She plants her feet to the ground as I rise in a slanted position, her back against the closet shudders. I rested my elbow on the third rack and stretched for the disguised object.

Cuqui asks, "You got it?"

"Yeah ... yeah ... got it."

"Well what is it?"

To my surprise, it's a ten inch rubber dildo. Artificially erect. Black in color.

"Eeewww," I said, dropping it to the ground.

Cuqui looked down at the dildo and instantly got excited. "Damn! Look at that thing!"

Forgetting I was on her back, she reached for the sex toy like it was money on the ground.

I scream, "Wait! Wait!" But before she could keep her balance, I threw my hands in the air, bumped the closet shudders, and as gravity started taking me downward, I hit the floor harder than a reckless G5.

Then something else fell.

The pierce sound of glass.

I rose to my feet and dropped my jaw. Saw the death of a cremated vase, the second death of someone's beloved mother all scattered across the floor into a million pieces.

"What's that?" Cuqui asked.

I looked at her as if I wanted to kill her. "Are you insane? Those are ashes from a human being."

"What?"

"That vase was the cremation of an old woman! Someone's mother!"

"Really? I mean … what are we—"

"Dammit, Cuqui! See what you did!"

"How was I supposed to know to—"

"You should have never let me fall!"

"You fell on your own!"

"You dropped me goddammit!"

"Whateva … let's just find a way to hide it."

"Hide it? Hide it how? For Christ's sake, Cuqui, this is somebody's mother! Don't you think they're gonna find out."

At the break of us arguing, I heard a car door slam and an alarm chirp.

"Hold on," I told her. "You hear that?"

"Hear what?"

"Someone's in the driveway."

I ran towards the window and peeked through the blinds. "Oh my gosh! Oh my gosh!"

"What is it?"

"She's home."

"Who's home? The maid?"

"No. Snow's home."

"You mean the cop?"

"Yes dumbass! The cop."

Cuqui goes berserk. "Oh Lord! Oh Lord! I'm not even supposed to be in this lady's—"

"Shhhhh! Be quiet. Now let me think for a second."

"Dammit, we don't got a second, Angel! She's home right now!"

My mind goes haywire. "Okay ... okay ... I gotta find a way to get you out this house ... Quick, the window."

"What? Who you think I am? Gail Devers? I'm not jumping out no window."

"If Snow sees you in this house, we're both gonna be messed up. So the window is the only option."

I looked out the window and no longer saw Snow, but then I heard Macho barking out back.

I told Cuqui, "On second thought, don't go through the window."

"Why?"

"She's out back feeding Macho."

"Macho?"

"Her Rottweiler."

Cuqui's eyes exploded. "Rottweiler??? You mean this chick has a dog. Oh hell naw!"

Panicked out, I started talking to myself. *Okay ... okay ... think Angel ... think fast.*

"Quick, Cuqui. Gimme the garbage can."

Moving without thinking, I grabbed a broom and swept up the glass from the shattered vase, then dumped the human particles into the trash, as much as I could sweep up. Any remaining ashes were swept under the bed to a new cemetery. I felt miserable, but time wasn't on my side.

Cuqui started running in circles from being paranoid. "Oh no! Oh no! I'm going to jail! I'm going to jail!"

"Shut up before she hears you!"

"You see what you got me into, Angel. I knew I should've followed my own mind."

"Too late for placing blame. Now come on. Follow behind me."

"Where we going?"

"Just follow."

We exited Snow's room and I locked the door behind us. Keys rattled at the front door. Keys eerie enough to rattle my insides. I peeked over the staircase and locked eyes with the living room's doorknob.

It opened.

The shadow of Snow was coming through the door, the outlining of her silhouette looking oh so evil.

Trembling, Cuqui whispered, "What ... what do I do?"

"The guestroom is the last door on the right. Go there and hide."

"Until?"

"Until I get Snow out the house. I'ma take her out the front door and when the door closes, that's your queue to leave through the back door. It's already open"

"What type of BS plan is that?"

"The only way out."

"But what if—"

"Do it now."

She flees down the hallway. I stand to my feet, our plan as weak as a public defender.

Meanwhile, Snow takes off her jacket and throws it on the couch. "Maid!" Snow yelled. "Is that you I hear? Where are you?"

"She's not here," I said, walking down the stairway.

Snow takes her eyes to me, staring at me like a stranger who stumbled into her house, like she forgot I was left here this morning. Dressed in Nevada's most feared attire, her face is as fierce as her detective wardrobe that hides the gun alongside her waist.

"Well well well," she said. "If it's not my favorite criminal."

"I see you've been looking in a mirror lately."

"How cute, Angel. But where's Maid?"

"You mean Ms. Montreal. Or do you not remember her name because you're so busy belittling her, so busy calling her Maid."

Her eyes sharpen. "Where is she?"

"Doing what a maid does. She went grocery shopping for the house."

"Without telling me?"

"Is that a crime tough cop?"

"Damn right it is in my house. I need to know everything."

A thump sounds from upstairs, the feet of my stupid friend trying to hide in the closet.

Then another thump. Another bang.

"What's that?" Snow asked, her eyes going upwards. "You heard that?"

"Heard what?"

Another bang.

"Heard that," she says, bracing herself. "Is someone in the house?"

"Not to my knowledge." I reach for Snow's arm, told her, "How 'bout we go outside. You never finished showing me your plants."

Her eyes read me. Eyes of a cop that's trained to sense the unusual. Taking no chances, she reaches for her gun to act on her instincts, and she starts walking up the stairway. I followed behind her with my heartbeat hammering my chest. Blood pumping, legs twitching, my face sweated from nervousness, not knowing whether to come clean or continue walking up these steps, gripping my fists like a woman that was clinching lost hope. Hope that Cuqui doesn't blow our cover. Hope that she's in a good hiding space. Hope that Snow doesn't slip up and put a bullet into my best friend's head.

At that moment Snow talked out loud. "Whoever you are, you've entered the house of a cop! Surrender now or leave this house in a body bag!"

I panicked, told myself that the risk wasn't worth Cuqui's life.

I grabbed Snow by the arm and turned her around. "Wait!"

Then we both heard someone screaming. "He's gonna bite me! He's gonna bite me!"

Macho started barking from the backyard, which let me know that Cuqui had jumped out the guestroom window. Snow and I started running downstairs. We ran through the living room. Zipped through the den. Tripped and trampled over chairs while running through the kitchen, then through the dining room, Snow running to kill and me running to prevent her from killing.

Snow threw back the door of the screened-in patio, then she cocked the 9mm. Cocked it faster than a Sniper on a rooftop, and she aimed the gun at my best friend.

"Don't shooooot!"

13

"Get down right now or I'll blow your little head off!"

That voice was the sound of Snow, aiming her gun at Cuqui who was ten feet in the air. I yanked Snow's wrist to point the gun in another direction, then told her, "Drop the gun!"

"What?"

I lowered her weapon, told her, "That woman is my best friend."

"Yeah, well your friend is scaring my damn dog."

Cuqui was trapped in the limbs of an oak tree, her body hanging from a branch while trying to shoe the dog away with one of her heels.

"Get doggy get!" she hollered.

Macho stood on its hind legs and jumped at Cuqui with its razor teeth, a dog determined to snatch her from the tree and sink its jaws into some dark human flesh.

"Somebody get this mangy mutt befo' I kick it in the face!" Cuqui screamed.

"Macho! Get over here! Get here now!"

A well-trained dog, Macho recognized its owner's voice and ran to Snow briskly, ran like a kid to an ice-cream truck.

"Sit, Macho. Sit!"

Snow puts Macho on a leash and gives it a light pat on the back. "Did she scare you baby? She scared my little doggy didn't she?"

Cuqui stayed confined in the tree, watching the dog in a frantic state.

I tell her, "The dog is tied up, Cuqui. So you can come down now."

"Hell no. Come down to get bit in the ass. I'll rather take my chances up here."

"Girl come yo' butt down!"

Snow escorts Macho to its doghouse as Cuqui slithers down the tree in slow motion, making sure her weave didn't get caught in the branches.

Snow yelled from afar, "Both of y'all stay there and don't move."

Cuqui whispered to me, "I'm going to jail. I'm going to jail. I'm going to jail. I'm—"

"Hush up. Now just stand there and let me do the talking."

Snow walked towards us with a unit on her face, a face that said her mind was already made up, that Cuqui's fate was already determined.

I spoke first. "I can explain. We were only—"

"Not now," Snow said, shushing me with her hand. "I'm the one asking the questions." She motions over to Cuqui, observing her features while giving a scrutinizing glare.

Cuqui says, "Well I'll let the two of you chat. I think I'ma be goin' now. Nice to meet you, Ms. Detective whoever you—"

"Not so fast!" Snow said, cutting in front of her. "Seems like we never got acquainted."

"This is all the acquaintance we gon' get today,' cause I gotta catch a flight. Now I'm sorry for being in yo' house and messing with yo' dog Micho, Macho, whatever his name is. But I gotta go so I can—"

"You're not going anywhere Ms. Motor Mouth!"

"Come again?"

"What is your name?"

"What you need to know my name fo'? I ain't do nothing."

"Never said you did anything. Just asking your name."

I got nervous, didn't know where their conversation was heading, but from knowing the two of them, I knew it couldn't be going anywhere positive. In one corner you have Snow – a psychotic woman who's missing a few screws – and in the other corner there's Cuqui, a woman missing the whole toolbox. Both were crazy. Both were short-tempered. Both had mouths of metal not used to bending.

Cuqui tells her, "My name is Cuqui?"

"Last name?"

"X."

"Who?"

"Cuqui X ... You know, like Malcom X. It's a religious thing. X is used for the unknown, a name used until I get back to my native land.

"Is that right? So you're Muslim?"

"As Muslim as it gets."

Cuqui was so afraid of Snow running her name through the computer that she was making up all types of lies.

Meanwhile, Snow reached into her pocket to grab a cigarette and lighter, then fired up her cancer stick and blew smoke in Cuqui's direction. "Quick question Ms. Cuqui X. Do you know the meaning of breaking and entering? Don't answer! Because according to the law, a person has the right to bear arms against any person who enters their home forcefully."

Cuqui replied, "Well that doesn't apply to me because I was invited in your home."

"Yeah, by who? Angel? Another guest in my house."

Cuqui stands speechless.

Snow continues. "You see according to the law, you broke into my house ... got caught ... then tried to run out the back where you were cornered by my Rottweiler. And you know what that means? Don't answer! That means I now have the power." She gets in Cuqui's face, stands nose to nose. "That means I don't have to arrest you, nor do I have to add more points to whatever criminal record you may already have ... It means I can pull out my 9mm, point it at your temple, and fill you with so many bullets to where you'll be shitting metal ... But you know what Ms. Cuqui X, no matter what you may think about cops, know that they can still be merciful, because that's the only reason why I haven't shot you already. Because of mercy ... I mean who knows? Maybe it's your lucky day. Or maybe I'm having a good day. But whatever it is, consider this as a blessing little girl."

Cuqui clasps her hands together and looks towards the sky, then she closes her eyes and bows her head. She says, "Please Lord. Please have mercy on me after I whip this lady's ass. I know I haven't been the best Christian, and I know you know my heart. But Lord ... Lord ... I have to show her that even though she has a gun, she don't know who she's messin' wit'. So please forgive me as I—"

Cuqui jumps at Snow as if to hit her, but I jumped in between them to set Cuqui straight. "Hold up, hold up, Cuqui! Allow me to handle

Running From Redemption 127

this!" Then I turned my attention to Snow. "Now like I told you before, I can explain."

"Explain what? That a hood rat was in my house without my permission."

"Hood rat? Who you callin' a hood rat?" Cuqui said, drawing back her fist.

I pressed Cuqui's brakes before she went over the top. "For the second time, Cuqui, let me handle this."

"You betta handle her befo' I put my foot in her high-yellow ass. Cop or no cop she ain't gon' disrespect me like dat ain't nobody gon' talk to me dat and I mean nobody my mama don't even talk to me like dat 'cause I ain't scared to go to jail hell I done been to jail befo' and I don't mind going back girl she must not know who she fuckin' with 'cause I ain't from round here I'm from the bottom and I'll show 'er how we get down in the south girl 'cause she don't know I'll get off in dat ass if she try me one mo' time ya hear 'cause—"

"Cuqui!"

She bites her lips, holding in her fist. "She just don't know I'll—"

"Calm down for a minute—"

"I don't care, Angel. She done tried me—"

"Relax! Now give me a second to talk to Snow."

Cuqui walks off towards the back patio, cursing out loud at everyone but herself.

I look back at Snow, her face full of anguish, eyes so tight her pupils could burst.

Snow says, "Did I or did I not make myself perfectly clear when I said no one is to know your whereabouts? Or did you forget?"

"I didn't forget anything."

"Then why is little Ms. Hip Hop inside my house?"

"I was just leaving," Cuqui said from afar.

"Cuqui hush!" I turned to Snow, anxiety going a hundred miles an hour. "I'm sorry. I'm sorry. My friend just so happened to be in Vegas and because I haven't seen her in a long time I figured it wouldn't hurt if she—"

"Save it," she said, smacking down whatever lie I was fixing to tell. "I already know ... You wanted to fill someone in on what I was doing, and why not start with your best friend."

"But—"

"Everyone's entitled to one screw-up, Angel. Consider this as being yours. And if you don't want your best friend to be on the back of a cereal box, I suggest you make sure that she keeps her mouth shut. Are we clear?"

I swallowed hard, told her, "Cuqui is not a threat. She's just a friend."

"That's right!" Cuqui yelled from a far. "I ain't see no evil speak no evil hear no evil nothing."

After telling my frantic friend to shut her mouth once more, I told Snow, "If you think I'm trying to cross you, know I wouldn't dare. I haven't forgot about our plan."

"Good," she replied, eyebrows going up. "Let's keep it that way."

14

Two weeks later.

    I was standing in the center of the guestroom, fully dressed, jazzed up in my skin-tight jeans that were low-rise cut, my high heels accompanied by Mr. Nine West. A white halter-top tugged at my breasts like a newborn, and between those breasts was an uneven heart from a white gold necklace.
    I was looking like a walking issue of King Magazine. Dark shades on my eyes. Shades worn so I wouldn't be recognized at the place I was going.
    I was heading to the airport to meet Snow's husband, Mr. Marcello, my only purpose for being here. His flight was due in just a half hour and Snow was rushing through the house to be there in time. The maid had just finished pleasing our stomachs with a gourmet dinner: Salisbury steak, white rice, asparagus, and red wine on the side.
    As far as Cuqui was concerned, Snow did more than enough to scare the living daylights out of my best friend. Scared her so bad that Cuqui wanted to duck-tape her mouth shut and hop on the first plane back to Miami, but I convinced her to stay. I gave her ten thousand dollars from the fifty Snow gave me and put my best friend in a four star hotel. Presidential Suite. Had to calm her nerves. And every five

minutes she was ringing my phone, talking about the extravagant amenities that the hotel had to offer: Jacuzzis, 24-hour room service, all-you-can-drink alcohol, and how she wanted to sex one of the bellboys.

As I was admiring myself in the mirror, Snow came through the guestroom to inspect my outfit, giving a look of distaste.

I asked her, "Somethin' wrong?"

"Most definitely. It's your shoes."

"What about 'em?"

"They're too ... too street ... your shoes make you look like a hooker."

My defenses go into full effect. "What you talking 'bout?"

"You're overly sexy."

"And?"

"And I don't need you dressing like a slut around my husband, might send out the wrong message. Don't forget that you're representing me okay. Supposed to be my cousin. And if you don't wanna blow our cover, I suggest you where some shoes that don't got so many inches. It's already bad enough that your fun bags are on display."

She walks over to the closet, shuffles through shoe boxes, and pulls out a pair of black low-wedge heels, closed toe, shoes with no sex-appeal what-so-ever. "There," she says. "Put these on."

I stare at her as if she's lost her mind. "You can't be serious."

"I am, Angel. And just a little advice for the future, know that most men aren't into provocative-dressing women. They prefer women that leave something to the imagination. You know, like myself."

If that's the case then why is your husband cheating on you?

Those words almost slipped off my tongue.

I told her, "I'll keep that in mind."

I've never taken fashion advice from another woman, especially a woman like Snow. But due to the circumstances I had to think level-headed. So I changed shoes, switched purses, and I sprayed on a whiff of her Tiffany's perfume before heading for the door.

Driving to the airport, Snow flooded the Mustang a mile a minute. She ran red lights and cut off cars, drove her undercover whip like a badass cop that owned the night, abusing her power. The whole time she was briefing me on her husband, about his drug trafficking that funded restaurants, hotels, car dealerships, even community programs that were so-called non-profit organizations. She also schooled me on his personal interests. He is a sports fanatic, favorite food is linguini, favorite actor is John Wayne, enjoys fishing, playing pool, and a hellafied trash-talker when it comes to the card table. Although he's Dominican, he's a renaissance man. He admires Miles Davis, Louis Armstrong, and all artwork from Jacob Lawrence. He's not a man of constant change, been sticking with the same routine for fifteen years, runs five miles every morning, visits the cemetery every Sunday night, and donates to the poor. Snow says he's intrigued by politics, says he's a walking debate, which meant we should probably get along fine.

We reached the airport in record-breaking time. A boatload of people were waiting in front of Delta Airlines, Gate E – the gate that we expected Mr. Marcello to be once getting off the plane – but Mr. Marcello wasn't there. No one from Flight 106 was there. The people at the gate were family and friends.

Snow started checking her watch while talking to herself, complaining about the poor service of Delta, and about how their aircrafts were always late.

She walked over to ask one of the attendants, "Any idea of when Flight 106 will be here?"

"About an hour ma'am."

"An hour?"

"Bad thunderstorms caused a layover in Chicago."

We sat impatiently in Gate E, shared that sentiment with other people that awaited their loved one's arrivals. Waited as time continued to pass. We looked at the clock. More time passed. Passed with strangers sparking conversation to shadow bad thoughts of Flight 106. All except Snow. She hoped for the worst. A plane crash meant cash for her that ultimately saves me the trouble.

And I thought of that trouble. Thought about life. Maybe because I was sitting in an airport – a well diverse place – the only place where two people can assemble in the same room, and one person laughs while the other cries, several entrances and exits throughout people's lives. Across the room there are families who wait for their boys to come home from Iraq, smiles plaguing across their celebrated faces. They all stand in a single-file line, exhausting their freedom of speech by wearing the same hate shirts. *Bush lied and thousands died. So thank God for Obama.* Other people in the airport are not so happy. Parents send their children off to college, sending them to a playground of partying, sex, drugs, and alcohol, a world where education consists of 10% of their lives, if that.

Then there are the couples. Couples forced to live long-distance relationships that never prosper due to the constant hunt of the man. An example of that is the couple behind me: There's an ordinary girl with an extraordinary guy who's looking everywhere but at his woman, and the girl is rocking an oversize shirt, comfortable jeans, and relaxed shoes that are certainly out of date. She resembled the girl-next-door-type while her lover resembled the pretty-boy type. Skinny jeans. Hard-bottom shoes. Collar shirt exposing his oiled-up chest, plus his hair was prettier than hers. He was too girly for a woman like me but to her he was Mr. Untouchable, because she was holding him harder than the luggage on his back with tears running down her cheeks. She begged him not to leave. Begged him not to leave her world and explore a world of his own. He consoled her sympathetically, saying it was only for the better. Then he kissed her forehead and buttered her up by swearing that he'll call every day, or email her, or text her, told her he'd do all those thing to keep the fire burning, but that'll never happen because men are so malicious, and he knows the relationship is finished once he boards the plane because the flight attendant is waiting to flirt, slipping him the digits right under a cup.

Everywhere I turn there are tears. Tears of pain. Tears of joy. Tears of long-suffering. Gratification. I was trapped in a delivery room of infants, and I felt isolated because I couldn't relate.

And why is that?

Because unlike these people, I had no intermediate family that was still living. I had no one to cry over or wish off at an airport in hopes of them coming back someday. My mother is dead. Father is dead. The blood of my blood has dried like a gas, forever desiccating into a form that has no touch, has no reach, unresponsive to my distant tears.

A whole hour had passed before flight 106 had finally arrived, and with that news it made Snow curse, upset that her husband was still amongst the living.

I started to get nervous. Wasn't ready to meet this man, let alone end his accomplished life. I thought about everything Snow told me in the car, had a memory bank of his entire port-folio. And that made it even worse. Made me get more nervous than I already was, knowing I was about to gamble with the most dangerous man in all of Vegas.

Snow says, "There he goes."
"Where?"
"Right there. Charcoal suit. Bodyguards with 'im."
I took a deep breath. Rubbed my fingertips. Got ready for the infamous Mr. Marcello, the man I robbed in the parking lot and jacked

for his ride, leaving his pants above his ankles. But unlike the man in the parking lot, the man I see is a total different man. The man I see has a new-renounced swagger, and he's walking with two big men on his arm, men bigger than big, like he was stuck in between two seven-foot stones.

And he was coming in my direction.

Coming with power.

All I saw was a dark suit moving, the face of a blur, a headless horseman protruding from darkness.

Under that dark suit was a bright red tie with a white button-up, the three colors of power. He was one of those men that stole the moment when entering a room. The type that looks like a somebody without needing to flash the VISA. The type that made me forget my purpose for being here, that my mission was simply to take him out.

Snow asks me, "You okay?"

"Yeah. Why?"

"You look a little jittery."

"Nah ... I'm good."

The more Mr. Marcello kept walking forward the more I kept seeing his pictures back at Snow's mansion, as if the images were finally coming to life.

He was medium-build. 5'11. A Dominican face that had the skin of a penny, very smooth, perfect bone structure to go with that copper complexion. He rocked a thick mustache. Powerful green eyes. Had a dark mole above his lips like an older version of Enrique Iglesis. Very good-looking for a man that appeared to be pushing fifty, and in any other world I would've been turned on by his sexiness, but death had a way of turning you off.

Snow told me, "Don't be offended if he pecks you on the cheek. For women, that's a common greeting for my husband."

"I won't be offended if you're not."

"I'm used to it."

She says that as if she despises it, as if marriage forced her to accept it over the years.

When Mr. Marcello walked up to his wife, he embraced her with a hug and told her how he was glad to be home. He kissed her. She kissed him back. Then she brushed back his hair and straightened his suite, prepping him like a privileged wife, like she was his pick in a lineup of women.

He told her, "Missed you, My Love."

"Me too, Honey. Couldn't wait for you to come home."

"Would've gotten home sooner if it wasn't for the governor. He wanted my take on industrial independence. Fuel efficiency. Wanted to know if I'd help invest money for more use of bio-diesel."

"And what did you tell 'im?"

"What else, My Love. Of course I couldn't say no to the governor."

He calls her, My Love. A pet name. Corny to me but she dug it with joy. To be a foreigner his English was as good as mine. I heard a little accent, but not too strong. That told me he'd been Americanized for quite some time, probably longer than I've been alive.

Snow asked him, "You brought back what I asked?"

"Of course. And we're gonna put it to good use later. Real good use."

Snow smiled an X-rated smile that said whatever he brought back couldn't be said in public. And then, "Honey, this is the cousin I was telling you about."

Her husband reaches to shake my hand. "Oh okay. So you must be Angel."

I shake death's hand with extreme discomfort, standing like a girl in the twilight zone.

He repeats. "Your name is Angel, right?"

"Yes ... yes ... that's me."

"Well if I must say, I'm truly happy to meet you."

There goes that twilight zone again.

"And she's truly happy to meet you too," Snow says, jumping in to save me from drowning.

Snow whispers in my ear. "Angel, get yourself together ... my husband is trying to introduce himself."

I tried my best to come back to earth, "It's ... it's nice to meet you too Mr—"

"—Marcello," he reminds me, flashing a smile. "My name is Mr. Marcello."

He says his name with conviction. A name built for dominance.

Then with strong eye contact, he tells me, "Looks like beauty runs in the bloodline."

"Why thank you ... thank ... thank you."

He turned back to his wife. "Can't wait to get you home, My Love. Is dinner prepared?"

"Made your favorite."

"Good. Because I can eat."

Running From Redemption

At that point another man snuck up behind Mr. Marcello and tapped him on the shoulder. Seeing that the bodyguards never reacted, I figured it must've been a man he knew. The man was also Dominican-looking and he had on a suit.

"You bastard, when you get here?" Mr. Marcello said with a smile on his face. "Thought you wasn't scheduled to leave until"—he looked at his watch—"9pm?"

"Flew American Airlines. Keep tellin' you that it's the best way to fly."

"Hi Sergio," Snow said to the man. "How's my favorite brother-n-law?"

"You mean your only brother-n-law?"

"Whatever."

They hugged each other like family, did that as Snow told me, "Hey Angel, meet my husband's brother. Sergio meet Angel."

I gave him my hand, and like Mr. Marcello, he kissed it too, kissed it willingly. I noticed that Sergio was younger than Mr. Marcello. Not much younger, maybe five years, saw the resemblance in their eyes that were both solid green. I noticed that unlike his brother he didn't have any bodyguards on his arm, or maybe he didn't want any. But what was obvious is that Mr. Marcello was the dictator in the family, the Godfather that kept everything together.

As Snow and her extended family socialized, Mr. Marcello's cellphone began to ring.

The Godfather answered with a hand to his ear to block out the noisy airport, then I heard him tell someone, "Yeah … huh … are you kidding me … that's impossible …"

His eyes squinted, forehead etched wrinkles of confusion. I tried to secretly listen in the shadows, my eyes and ears open.

"… I apologize … I sincerely apologize … anything you want me to do on my behalf, and I mean anything, I'm hands and feet there … okay … okay … see you then."

He hung up with a troubled face, the clasp of his cell phone causing Sergio and Snow to put their conversation on pause, as if their world was controlled by Mr. Marcello's stopwatch.

A concerned Snow asked her husband, "What's the matter, Honey? What happened?"

Eyes rising from the floor, Mr. Marcello told his wife, "Benito … Benito's brother is dead."

15

We left the airport in separate cars, me riding with Snow while an SUV parked on standby for Mr. Marcello and his bodyguards.

Snow takes out a cigarette and puts it to her mouth, breathing that polluted gas of death.

I tell her, "At that rate you'll be dead by fifty."

"At least I'll go out happy. Hell, better to die in mirth than to live a life of regret."

"True. But you're flipping that line and taking it out of context."

She goes on, "Besides, the only time I get to smoke is when my husband is not around. He doesn't like it."

"Wow. A dealer that doesn't like smokers. How ironic?"

"I know right. He thinks it's unladylike. That's why I try to get enough nicotine when he's out of town or I'll start going through withdrawal."

I suggest, "Can't you just quit?"

She turns her head as if that's another foolish question. "Can you quit having sex?"

No answer.

"My point exactly."

Snow drives the Mustang at a smooth pace. Cars speed pass her with no conscience, not knowing she's the police because of her camouflaged whip. I looked at the radar detector that sits on her dashboard, the device that clocks every driver's speed. Cars pass us going ten miles over the speed limit. Some even go twenty. In Vegas they ride their cars with no respect for the road, and I prepare myself for Snow to turn on the rainbow lights. But she pays them no attention, as if giving someone a ticket is beneath her, a process that involves too much time and paperwork.

My mind shifted back to the airport scene. Couldn't forget the look on Mr. Marcello's face after receiving that call.

I asked Snow, "So who is this Benito guy?"

Snow hesitated, said, "He's my husband's biggest problem."

"Meaning?"

"Benito is the leader of the Columbian mob, the most feared mob on all the west coast. What's ironic is, he's not even Columbian."

"I don't understand."

"Benito and my husband were under the same umbrella, way before both became leaders of their own mobs. Benito loved my husband. Taught 'im about the business, the first person to bring 'im inside. But then money went missing, money from a misunderstanding, and that sparked a whole lot of tension. As a matter of fact, it sparked so much tension that Benito crossed my husband by going left field."

"He joined the Columbians?"

"Not only did he join them, but he made it his business to clean up any profit my husband was getting, tried to put my husband's whole operation out of business ... For a while that sparked an all out war between the Dominicans and Columbians, lots of people got killed ... it took ten years to cease that tension, took a mutual meeting between my husband and Benito to end the violence ... Since then everything has become peaceful. Peaceful for about two years. But now – with the death of Benito's brother – I'm sure that tension would stir back up. It's only in their nature to think my husband had something to do with Benito's brother's death."

I took in everything she said, told her, "Your husband looked a little worried after getting that phone call."

"And he should," she replied with a satisfying smile.

"Is he always that closely guarded?"

"He has to be. Got more enemies than he has friends. But what he doesn't know is that the people closest to him are the same people that wanna stab 'im in the back. Like the two bodyguards that were on his arm."

"What about 'em?"
"They're in on the plan with us."
"What? Thought no one was supposed to know."
"Relax. They're harmless."
"Well why are you just telling me this?"
"Had to make sure you wouldn't chicken out first."
I shook my head, said nothing.
She goes on, "In case you're wondering why I didn't pay them to do it themselves, know that they're too stupid to pull it off."
"Wasn't thinking that."
"If you say so."
I nodded. "But damn. His own bodyguards wanna take 'im out. Whatever happened to loyalty?"
"Loyalty takes a back seat to the almighty dollar. You see my husband may appear to be nice, but truth is, there's not a genuine bone in his body. Because of the people he deceived in the past, he's now starting to reap the fruits of his labor. Everyone wants their payback, including me. And this time, no matter what it takes, I'm gonna end this. Nothing's gonna stand in my way of killing my husband."
She says *this time* as if this is not the only attempt.
Making her open up, I ask, "So you've tried this before?"
"More than you'll ever know. And each time something went wrong, one little monkey-wrench that messed up the entire plan. Last time the problem was a blond. Her assignment was the same as yours. But that woman got beside herself. She couldn't do it because she fell in love with my husband, and she lost sight of the mission ... So she left me no choice but to do one thing."
"Which was?"
"Kill her."
Unexpected words that hit me like a rock.
Then, from nowhere, she laughs out loud. The laugh of a person half-human, half-villain. "That's right, Angel. That woman tried to play on my intelligence. She thought I didn't know she was about to cross me. Well I knew it all along. Call it a detective instinct, but I always know something before it happens."
I ride in her passenger seat with my hands on my lap, eyes looking straight ahead. This lady had many skeletons. More secrets than Victoria. In my mind she was no longer a wife that was out to get even with her husband. She was a cold-blooded killer. Point blank. And worst part about it was that she had no conscience, no internal psychiatrist to tell her when to stop.

Snow says, "You see, that stupid blond got what she deserved because she thought she could outsmart me. But something tells me that I'm not gonna have that same problem out of you ... Am I?"

I don't answer.

She takes a puff of her cigarette. "Nah ... you're nothing like that other woman ... You see she was all about the money, and I don't trust money sluts ... But you on the other hand, you don't care about the money, nor do you care about death. But one thing you do care about is the life of an innocent child, and that makes you more willing to cooperate, makes you have a stronger motive to survive."

"I suppose. But tell me something, Snow. Why look for a gun when there's one in your hand."

She processes my words. "What's that supposed to mean?"

"Means what I said."

With one hand on the steering wheel, she told me, "If you're implying that I should kill my husband myself, know that it's more complicated than that."

"What's complicated about pulling the trigger? You've killed before. Many of times. So why is it so hard to pull the trigger when it counts?"

This was my reverse psychology approach to make her see that she wasn't the hard-head she thought she was.

"I don't need any satisfaction in killing him myself," she responded. "Just knowing he's dead is fine with me."

"Are you sure? Because I sense a woman who wants more. I sense a woman who wants that blood on her own hands."

"I'm a woman that thinks logical. And to kill my own husband, to leave traces of evidence that links him to me, that's illogical."

"So you're not afraid?"

"Of what?"

"Afraid you won't be able to pull the trigger yourself. That is the truth isn't it? You can hunt down criminals, kill innocent people, but when it's time to kill the man that matters most, your own husband, you can't gather yourself to do it alone. Go 'head and fess up. Isn't that the truth?"

Her face turned into a firecracker. "Fuck you."

"Why kidnap an innocent child and put on this whole facade, just because you're afraid to do your own dirty work? Huh? You're afraid aren't you? Aren't you, Mrs. Tough Cop?"

Her eyes turned red as the tips of her hair, nose flaring out like a raging bull.

I went on, "For goodness sake you animal, let the child go. Devilla has nothing to do with your incompetence. Why bring a six-year-old into the middle of your mess? Don't you have any mercy in your heart? If not for an adult then at least for a child. Don't make the same mistake and hurt another child."

"What? What did you just say?"

"Nothing," I replied, realizing I'd said too much.

"No, no, no. You said something."

"Said what?"

"Another child. What do you mean *another child*?"

"I didn't say anything—"

"Don't play wit' me, Angel! I know what I heard. How do you know about that incident? No one knows about that except me and my husband."

My own mouth had turned on me like a vicious Rottweiler. I had accidentally let the cat out the bag, spoken to soon. Snow wasn't supposed to know about the conversation that I had with the maid, how Snow killed her own child that was born out of wedlock.

Snow repeated, "How do you know?"

"Doesn't matter."

"How do you fucking know?"

I don't answer.

We come to a red light. Minutes pass.

In my peripheral vision I noticed that Snow had calmed down, but for some reason the calmer she got the madder I became, and after replaying the words that came from the maid, I started looking at Snow like the scum of the earth, a disgrace to all mothers, knowing my own mother was taken too soon. Then my emotions flared up and I told her, "You inconsiderate, thoughtless, heartless bitch. How does a mother do what you did and still sleep at night?"

She hesitates. "Maybe I don't ... Ever thought about that?"

"And you shouldn't!"

"Don't judge me until you know me."

"I know what you did to your own baby. That says enough."

She gives a hard sigh. "You think it's easy to walk around with this memory, knowing what I did? Huh? You think it's easy? Well I regret it every day."

"Then why'd you do it?"

"Because I didn't have a choice."

"You had a choice. You could've given the child to the father."

Running From Redemption

"And let another woman raise my baby? Over my dead body! Ain't no woman gonna take control of a child that belongs to me."

"Then you should've raised your own baby."

"That wasn't God's will."

"God had nothing to do with your cruelty."

She said, "God wouldn't bless a baby that was made out of wedlock."

"In what world?"

"My world. Besides, even if I wanted to keep the baby, my husband wouldn't allow it to stay in his house. He said there was no way he'd shelter another man's offspring."

"So you chose a man over your child?"

"Damn right I did. What else was I supposed to do?"

"Leave your husband and raise your freakin' baby."

"All by myself?"

"Women do it every day."

"Stupid women."

"No bitch. Women that love their children."

Her face pulsates with anger as if I'd said the unmentionable. "Say what you want but don't tell me I didn't love my child because I did! You don't know me okay. You know nothing 'bout my situation, all you know is what you see. My child was supposed to have what I didn't have as a child. A mother and father that was together, not split apart a thousand miles away. I refuse to repeat that single-mother cycle, playing mama and daddy like my mama did with me. So fuck you, Angel. You got that? Fuck you!"

I said no more, allowed her to have the last word because she obviously needed it. I could tell this was a touchy situation for her; it's probably the reason why she is the way she is, a woman with more issues than Fox News.

For the first time ever I was seeing a sensitive side to Snow, a side completely different than the bionic woman she claims to be. That sensitivity made me question the real reason why she wanted her husband dead. Was it just about money? Or infidelity? Something tells me the water runs deeper with extreme convolution.

Money can be replaced.

But children are irreplaceable.

That no longer makes her a woman of insecurities, but more so a woman who was out to get revenge. Revenge for a child that was restricted from her arms, a child not accepted by her own husband, is a pain that haunted her for all these years, and she now was at a breaking point, now ready to dispose of the man that forced her to make those regretful decisions, thinking it would somehow avenge the past.

The rest of the car drive was driven in silence.

We pulled into the driveway of Snow's mansion. Mr. Marcello and his bodyguards had beaten us to the house. With both bodyguards protecting his mansion, they were posted up on opposite ends of the porch, each facing forward like immobile statues.

I asked Snow, "Are they gonna stand out here all night?"

"Getting paid to do it."

Macho was patrolling the backyard while barking at our movements. Snow headed out back to go quiet him, did that as I walked into the house and saw Mr. Marcello who was heading up the steps to his master bedroom. I smelled his cologne that mapped his location. And I trailed behind him. Followed his scent. Then I went to the guestroom to take myself a shower, locked the bathroom door and called up Cuqui.

Although Cuqui was stationed at a luxurious hotel, it was still her job to be ready for the worst. However, for some reason, it took her four rings to answer the phone.

I got concerned, asked, "Everything okay?"

"Uh-huh."

"Did you do what I told you to do?"

"Huh?"

"The background report," I whispered. "The one I told you to get on Snow."

"Oh ... yeah ... working on that."

Then her breathing got heavy as if she was exerted.

"What are you doing?" I asked her.

No answer.

"Cuqui?"

"Yeah?" More heavy breathing. *"Get in between the toes,"* she said to someone. *"All in between the toes."* Then her words started to slur. *"Oh yes ... oh yes ... right there ... I knew you knew how to work 'em."*

My mind goes haywire. "Girl what's going on over there?"

"I got a fine-ass man in front of me. That's what's going on."

"Cuqui, you ain't supposed to be with a man. You supposed to be on alert."

"I am on alert. And so are my insides ... Hey, remember the bellboy I was telling you 'bout? Well that bellboy is ringing my bell right now, giving me the best pedicure I ever had. I'm at the Spa."

"The Spa? I told you not to leave the hotel."

"I didn't leave, Angel. The Spa is in the hotel downstairs, and when I saw him working there, you know I had to go up in there. Girl this man gives the best foot massage."

I took my ear from the phone and shook my head at the receiver.

Cuqui says, "And did I mention he has a twin. Girrrrrl, I'm thinking 'bout inviting them both up to my suite, might go 'head and get my ménage trios on. I mean, after all, I am in Vegas."

"Cuqui you better not invite anyone anywhere. You don't even know that guy."

"I know he can work some toes, and quite frankly, that's all I need to know right now." Then her voice starts to slur again. "*Oh yes ... don't forget the pinky ... yes ... oh yes ... that's right ... that pinky toe needs love too.*"

"Cuqui!"

"Anyways, girl I gotta call you later 'cause you bustin' up the groove."

A few hours later I was in bed, lights off, dozing off to sleep.

Bickering awakened me. Bickering coming from down the hall through Snow and her husband's bedroom. I tried to ignore it and go back to sleep, but then I heard keywords: *Vase ... my mother ... cremated ... vase broken.*

Listening hard, I slid off the sheets and sat up on the bed, tried to eavesdrop as much as I could. Mr. Marcello was yelling at Snow, telling her how his mother's vase was broken and quickly blamed her for committing the act. Snow told him it wasn't her doing, then started pleading her case of how she wasn't home when the incident occurred.

I tiptoed to the guestroom door, stuck my head into the hallway to listen some more.

"*It had to be you, Snow. Who else would've broken it?*"

"*Ever thought about the maid.*"

"*Oh now you wanna blame it on the maid. She wouldn't have done this.*"

"*Neither would I.*"

"*This has your name written all over it. Then you tried to sweep it up as if I wouldn't notice. Do you know what it feels like to see your mother's ashes in the trash can? Do you?*"

Snow pleaded to her husband. *"I told you I didn't do it, Honey."*
"Then who did?"
"Maybe it—"
"Fess up, Snow!"
"I'm not fessin' up to anything I didn't do."
"Make sure I have another vase by tomorrow!"

Snow yielded to the bark in her husband's voice. He made it well known that although she was the queen, she was still a queen that slept in his kingdom.

Then a door slammed. The slam of a man aggravated with his wife.

I started hearing footsteps. Hard-bottom shoes were stomping through the hallway, shoes pounding the staircase and walking through the living room, then through the dining room, and now into the kitchen. Because these walls were incredibility thin, and because the kitchen sat under the guestroom, I could hear Mr. Marcello's every move. Heard him scrambling through the refrigerator. Heard him using the microwave. And at that moment my curiosity started to fester. By any means necessary I wanted to get information on Snow, and what better way to get it than talking to her husband.

I rushed into the bathroom to quickly freshen up. Threw water on my face, pulled back my hair, got myself prepared for Mr. Marcello, rushing downstairs before he walked up. I passed Snow's bedroom door, noticed that there wasn't a light shining beneath. She must've taken her temper to bed.

While softly creeping down the stairs, I saw that Mr. Marcello was still in the kitchen. He was sitting on a barstool with late night dinner: Steak. Wild rice. Bottled wine on the counter. He was still formal dressed, all except the coat, and while staring at the dark bottle of wine, he sat at the table like a man that was tired. Or confused. Or troubled. Then he drunk from the bottle to numb those troubles.

I went towards the dishwater to grab myself a glass, did that while looking his way, then I said, "Got stress on the mind?"

He glances at me with no emotion, as if I was disturbing his meal. "Excuse me?"

"It's late. Usually when someone eats this late, it's stress-related."

"According to who?"

"According to most psychologists."

His buttons were undone. Chest was exposed. A white collar worker with a blue-collar body, the ultimate aphrodisiac.

Running From Redemption

I poured myself some wine as he put down his fork and decided to give me his undivided attention.

He said, "And you consider psychologists to be real doctors?"

"Anyone who enslaves eight years of higher learning is a real doctor in my book."

He paused, then said, "You know I tried a psychologist once. Never worked for me though. The advice that woman gave was no better than my Papa after having too much to drink."

I laughed.

He didn't.

And then he went on, "So I don't mean to disagree, but to me, psychologists are far from real doctors. They're full of nothing but theories. And if I'm paying you $200 a session, your advice better have no room for failure."

"But what about other doctors?"

"Such as?"

"Neurologists. Cardiologists. What makes them real doctors?"

"The fact that they prescribe tested medication as opposed to a made-up experiments for people to follow."

I challenge his ideology, tell him, "But not all medicines are found in a bottle."

"Meaning?"

"Although a psychologist wouldn't normally give you a pill, it doesn't mean their advice is not considered medicine. Like other doctors, they're experts when it comes to their field of work, and their clinical studies are tested the same way an oral medication is tested. Now just because the medication didn't work on you, it doesn't mean the medication doesn't work."

He sipped his wine, then slanted up a brow, his way of asking if I was through with the lecture, that at this hour of the night, he could care less about my methodological bullshit.

Truth is we actually shared the same beliefs when it came to psychologists. But debating was my way of breaking the ice, letting him know that I came with a brain.

Changing subjects, I told him, "Well I must say that you have a nice house. And as I told Snow earlier, I appreciate you letting me stay. Very sweet of you, Sir."

He swallows a piece of steak. "Sweet of me or sweet of my wife?"

A trick question, I thought. "Sweet of the both of you."

"Well just so you know, I let her have the final say. And thanks to her you had her vote."

I read between the lines, realizing that if it was up to him, I wouldn't be here. "Well I thank you anyways Sir. It's nice that—"

"Do I look old to you?"

"Excuse me?"

"My age?" he asked, straightening his face. "Do I look old?"

Another trick question.

"No, Sir," I answered.

"Then why do you insist on calling me Sir?"

His face detailed a sinister glare, not the face I saw in the airport, the one kissing my cheek, complimenting me, smiling in front of his peers. What I was seeing right now was the real man behind the suit, the man after business hours, a man who perfected the craft of putting it on and taking it off.

In the airport it was on.

Now it was all off.

He says, "You know what's strange? My wife never told me she had a cousin."

"Maybe she didn't feel it was necessary for you to know. I mean, when it comes to family, us women tend to keep a little to ourselves."

His thick eyebrow raises again. "Are you implying that my wife has secrets?"

I hesitated to answer, chose my words wisely. "I'm not implying anything. Just saying she probably never mentioned me because there was never a reason to, at least not until now. Besides, I've always been kind of a distant cousin."

"Distant?"

"Only come around when I'm needed."

"Or when you need somebody."

He's a smartass. I can tell he's a real smartass.

I say, "Just so we're clear, I'm not here to freeload off you or my cousin. And know that I'm only here until I make other arrangements."

"Such as?"

He stops eating and looks me in the eye, eyes saying I better have other options. The conversation that I planned is now speeding in a different direction. For some reason I'm getting the impression that this man doesn't want me in his house at all.

"I'm looking at a place on the East side of town," I answered. "Over on 15th and Marley."

"Is that right?"

"Yes Sir. I mean, Mr. Marcello."

Running From Redemption

He thinks out loud. "15th and Marley ... 15th and Marley. Are you referring to Manor's Village?"

"That's the one."

"What a coincidence. I'm currently working on a deal to own that property."

My eyes widen from a lie gone bad. "Is that right?"

"Just waiting for my lawyer to review the agreement."

I tell him, "Thought you owned restaurants."

"I do. But I decided to give Real Estate a try. This is my third deal."

"Don't you think it's a bad time to be investing in Real Estate? I mean, with the economy on the decline and all."

"Which is exactly why I gave it a try. When the market goes down, prices get lower. When prices get lower, it's the planet of the seller. See how that works."

I nodded.

"Besides, I'm a man that likes to gamble."

"Risk-taker huh?"

"Without risks, I wouldn't have gotten this far."

I become nosey. "And how far is that?"

"Living without worries. Highly successful. You know, those types of things."

"I notice you never mentioned happiness."

"Add that to the list."

We shared a laugh. Actually, I was the only one laughing. He just sat there like a bump on a log, analyzing me, reading me, staring at the woman that landed in his nest, like he'd seen my face on a channel where it doesn't belong and couldn't quite put it together.

I kept thinking about the car robbery, if he had recognized me when his eyes were full of panic ... nah ... I had on a ski-mask. Couldn't see my face.

Trying to gain control of the conversation, I asked, "So what about when it comes to my cousin? Are you happy there? I mean, after all these years ... is she still the only woman that catches your eye?"

"Getting personal?"

"Just wanna know for her sake."

"Or your sake?"

I don't respond.

He says, "Well I took those vows didn't I?"

"Years ago."

"And years to come, I'll still love my wife. Will always love my wife."

Knowing he was a liar, I replied, "You said you love her. That doesn't mean you're *in love* with her."

"That's one in the same."

"Not exactly. You see being in love means desiring her; it means wanting her the same as when you first got married—"

"Yeah yeah. Save the hoop-la. Not that it's any of your business, but last I checked, the scent between my wife's legs was just as fresh as it was fifteen years ago. So whether it's loving her or being in love, we have all of that."

"Yeah, well if that's the case then when's the last time you let her know you loved her."

"All the time."

"Flowers?"

"I don't know? Why?"

"Movies?"

He doesn't answer.

"My point exactly."

"What point?" he says. "You should understand that love changes when people get married."

"Love doesn't change. People change."

He shakes his head. "Now you're starting to sound like that psychologist I visited."

"Yeah, well it's been said that I have a knack for seeing things. And when I look in your eyes, I don't see a man that's in love."

"Okay then, Senorita. Tell me what you see." He folds his hands, looks into my eyes as if he's seeking advice from a psychic, as if I'm the Oracle of relationships. "Go 'head. What is it that you think you see."

"I see a man who wants the smell of a new scent."

"Excuse me?"

"A man who wants to be a man ... explore other options."

"Sorry, but you've got the wrong man."

"Do I?"

"Wrong man indeed."

"So you mean to tell me that after years of having sex with the same person, you never fantasized about a woman other than your wife?"

"I'm afraid not."

"Perhaps a woman you met out of town somewhere, someone waiting to do all the things that your wife doesn't do, the things she used to do?"

"No."

"Perhaps a younger woman ... young and innocent ... toned legs ... nice ass ... full breasts ... generous lips ... a figure that time and gravity has yet to destroy."

Looking at me as if I was hinting at something else, he asked, "Are we still talking about my wife?"

I smiled. "You tell me. I'm not the one that's happily married."

Thinking he would come forth and tell me about his parking lot lover, he glanced down into his dinner plate, then looked at me and said, "You and my wife must really think y'all are smart."

"Huh?"

"I can't believe this ... my own wife ... how could she do something like this?"

"Do what?"

He shakes his head in disbelief, disbelief so powerful it fades out my question.

Then his eyes became tight. "That bitch. That money-hungry treacherous cold-hearted bitch." I froze at his voice that became a low whisper, his eyes glancing upstairs as if he didn't want to awaken his wife. Then he picked up the fork and stabbed it into the gristle of his steak.

My throat jumped.

Mr. Marcello clinched his fists. "That bitch ... That deceitful, no good, double-crossing bitch. After all this time ... after all our quarrels ... now it all makes sense ... everything makes sense."

"Could you please say whatever the hell it is you're trying to say."

He stared me down like he was coming for blood, and after a long intimidating silence, he muttered, "I know why you're here ... Know exactly your purpose."

16

If it wasn't for the stiffness in my legs I would've ran.
If it wasn't for the fear in my heart I would've ran.
If it wasn't for little Devilla I would've ran.
But I didn't run. Didn't even move.
    Panic had me pressed against the refrigerator, trapped in the castle of a hardnosed king while the queen slept peacefully upstairs.
    And his face was a ticking bomb. Saw the detonator in his green eyes that had my pulse pounding with confusion. Then with fear. Then with downright terror. For I didn't know what was scarier – the look on Mr. Marcello's face or the fact that he had been silent for the last ten seconds, those seconds tip-toeing around a clock that ticked timidly.
    Then he reached over to pour himself another glass of red wine, as if the wine would relax him, but not even liquor could hide his menacing gaze, the mole on his cheek now doubling size.
    He said, "I tell you what, Senorita? However much my wife is paying you, know that I can double it."
    "Paying me? What do you mean by—"
    "Triple it."
    I kept that bamboozled glare in my eyes, pretended I had no idea of what he was referring to.

He told me, "Oh okay ... I see what this is ... you wanna play innocent-until-proven-guilty huh ... Well how 'bout this. I know my wife brought you here to sleep with me, all so she could have probable cause to get a divorce and take half my money for committing adultery. Now tell me, Senorita. Am I not right or am I not right?"

Seeing that he was way off base – that I had not blown my cover – I blew out a deep breath in relief.

He went on, "That is why you're here isn't it? To stop me from divorcing your cousin? To be a one night whore and get your cousin rich?" Then he laughed. "Well I tell you what, Senorita. If Snow wanna take me down, she's gonna have to do better than that."

Under any other circumstances – in any other galaxy – I would've slapped him right where he sat, would've shown him that no man gets away with calling me what he dared to declare.

For he'd disrespected me. Called me a whore to my face.

But being a living whore was more valuable than being a dead saint. That was my logic as long as he didn't know my real purpose for being here, that I was here to end his life. Without that knowledge he could never view me as any form of a threat, making me completely harmless in his little rich world.

Besides, I had a plan.

And a damn good plan at that.

It was a plan that him or his wife would never see coming. A plan that included a letter, a credit card, and a bag full of Louis Vuitton items that he purchased for another woman, a woman half his wife's age, a woman young enough to send a washed-up wife like Snow into a never-ending coma.

Mr. Marcello didn't know that it was me who robbed him that day. He didn't know that I was the one wearing the ski mask, the one that busted him and his Latin lover in a hotel parking lot doing illicit acts. He didn't know that I technically had the keys to his pre-nuptial, that I could slice his dividends in half if he kept his mouth running, that I had enough evidence to put the brakes on his wealthy life.

Snow wanted a marriage.

He wanted a divorce.

And then there's me. The third wheel. The one who witnessed the perfect infidelity at the perfect time, giving me the opportunity to play both sides of the fence.

If I could get Mr. Marcello to not leave his wife, to stay in Holy Matrimony, then Snow would have no reason to kill her husband, which would also give her no reason to keep me or Devilla hostage. That was my genius plan.

One stone. Two birds.

All I had to do was aim with precision.

With a prosecuting glare, Mr. Marcello said, "So you never answered my question, Senorita. How much is my wife paying you to open those legs?"

"A lot," I answered. "But not nearly as much as it's gonna cost you to do what I say."

"Excuse me?"

I smiled. "Sorry to spoil your fantasy, but I'm not here to sleep with you okay. You see I figured since you had enough gratitude to let me stay at your house, I'll show you the same gratitude by not taking all your money. But that's only if you're willing to cooperate."

He grimaced. "What on God's earth are you talking 'bout?"

"Tell me about your so-called business trip to Dominica, the one you lied about to your wife. That's what the hell I'm talking 'bout."

He kept a straight face, the look of a politician withholding information from the public. "My trip to Dominica was exactly what it was. A business trip."

"Is that right?"

"That's right."

Turning the tables, I fed him his own words by saying, "Oh I see. So you're one of those *innocent-until-proven-guilty* types."

He smiles.

I went on. "Well I'll put it on the table for you. How 'bout long legs ... thin waist ... dark eyes ... ethnic features..."

The smile on his face evaporates as shock began to harvest.

I go on. "Long flowing black hair ... high cheek bones ... a model's height ... and oh, young enough to still be sucking on her mama's titty." I chuckled. "That's right, Mr. Marcello. I know exactly who you're sticking it to when you're not sticking it to your wife. And I've got the evidence to prove it."

No response. His face begins to sharpen.

"It just makes me wonder you know. Why do powerful men always risk everything just to get next to a pretty face?"

He doesn't answer that question. Maybe because there is no answer at all.

Instead, he says, "So now that you got my attention, how much is it gonna cost me to make you go away?"

I smiled. "Typical rich man. Always thinking you can buy your way out of your problems. Well this time around there is no price."

"BS. There's always a price."

I sat down to join him at the table, decided to take a sip of his bloodshot wine.

I muttered, "What I want is simple. And it's definitely not money."

"Then what is it? What are you proposing?"

"Stay married. No divorce. Make that happily-ever-after phrase mean more than just a card from Hallmark."

He contemplated on that notion, then told me, "No deal."

"No deal? If I was you I'd think again. Because once my cousin receives this information, she'll have more than enough evidence to wipe your bank account clean."

What was a flat face quickly turned to madness. "Young lady, what makes you think you can come into my house and blackmail me? You must not know who I am."

"Looks like a man that was messy with his business, and as a result he's fixin' to get beat out his cash. But hey, don't thank me for that. Thank your wife for adding that clause to your prenup."

Madness turned into fury. "Is that right?"

"That's right."

"And what make you think I won't get rid of you by sunrise?"

"Because getting rid of me won't necessarily get rid of your problems. There's definitely a backup source."

"Oh is there?"

"You can count on it. Anything happens to me and my back-up source will finish what I started, including bringing in the Feds."

Fury turned into concernment. "Feds?"

"Oh what, you think I don't know how you fund your restaurants? Humph, just because I got perky breasts it doesn't make me a bimbo. I've done my research on you and your whole operation. And we both know that being a drug lord won't stand up in court. Don't fuck wit' me okay. Tick me off and I can easily become a bitch on roller skates. Wanna get gangsta and I get more gangsta."

Every emotion on his face transmuted to respect, respect for a woman that had him by the balls. And I was scared, little did he know. Never been so scared of what a person might do, but what I couldn't do is allow him to see fear. A dog that senses fear is a dog that will attack.

He tells me, "Just out of curiosity, why do you care so much about your cousin's marriage, or as you would say, 'a distant cousin'?"

"Because family is family, no matter the distance. You may be her husband, but I'm still her blood. And no one hurts blood. No one."

"And how do I know that after you're gone, some other blackmailing cousin won't come out the woodworks, only next time wanting money?"

"Rather than speculate, let's stick with the facts okay." I smiled. "So what's it gonna be, Mr. Marcello? Have we reached an understanding?"

He looked at the bottle of red wine as if he inherited more problems on top of the problems he already had. Then he rubbed his temples, stroked his thick mustache. "Very well, Senorita. Your game. Your rules."

"Good ... Now if you don't mind, I'ma head to your expensive guest bedroom and get me some shut-eye. And remember what I said ... holy matrimony."

Realizing that my plan was working perfectly, I rose from the table and left him sitting in the kitchen with nothing but thoughts, left him there confused and dismantled.

Then I scurried through the living room. Hurried up the stairs. My heartbeat working a double shift of constant paranoia.

Halfway up that stairway, I turned around to tell him, "And one more thing. As far as me leaving your house ... I think I'll stick around for a little bit longer."

17

The next morning I was awaken by a nightmare.

Not my typical nightmare, but one involving a light-skinned woman with a wretched face, fully dressed, standing over my bed with squiggly lines carved deep into her forehead, lines sketched with pores of anguish.

Or concernment.

"Get up," she whispered, glancing back at the doorway.

That creepy woman is no other than Snow, the devil looking down at me with fire red locks hanging inches from my face.

Trying to open my eyes, I did what people do when their unexpectedly awaken by someone. Looked around. Yawned. Wiped sleep from my mouth.

The comforter is suddenly snatched from my body.

"Get your butt up right now, Angel. We gotta talk."

"Hold your damn horses."

I rose from the bed and headed towards the bathroom.

She stops me in motion. "Where you going?"

"To pee ... Is that a crime?"

"Make it quick."

I go in to do my business, wondering what the heck is so important. Maybe she got nervous and decided to keep her husband after all, and now she was coming to call the whole thing off. Or maybe she agreed to let go of Devilla, perhaps because it came to her in a dream. An epiphany of some sort. Divine intervention. That optimism was wishing for the best, but you never can tell with a woman like Snow.

I flushed the toilet, washed my hands, and came out the bathroom to a Snow that was sitting on the bed with her legs crossed and a brown paper bag in her hand. Didn't know what was in the brown bag, but from the way she held it, I knew it wasn't liquor.

"Come sit," she said, patting the bed for me to lounge beside her. "You're gonna love this."

Fear stopped me in motion as she stared me down. She smiles. The smile of a conniving woman. The glare of a dog that looks friendly, but prone to bite if you invade its perimeter.

I tiptoe towards the bed like a hunter approaching a deer, but this time the deer is the one with the gun.

Snow said, "You know what, Angel? Something very strange happened to me this morning. Something that involves my husband."

"Let me guess. He told you how much he loves you."

"More so sexed me. He sexed me good."

"And you call that strange?"

"See I don't think you understand. We didn't just make love. We fucked. And we haven't fucked since ... since ... our honeymoon. I mean it's like ... he was a totally different man."

I thought about me and her husband's agreement, told her, "Well that's a good thing isn't it?"

"I just don't understand. One minute we're discussing a divorce and the next minute we're humping like rabbits."

I smiled. "So does this mean are arrangement is off? No one has to die."

She looked down at the floor as I anxiously awaited her verdict. Forget a penny for her thoughts. I was ready to pay hundreds.

Then I got straight to it. "What if I told you that your husband wants to stay married?"

She looked up with raised eyebrows, face switching channels, her ears becoming antennas with a good signal. "So you talked to my husband?"

"Briefly."

"And what was discussed?"

Running From Redemption

"Forgiveness. He told me how he knew he hadn't been a good husband in the past, but he wanted to make it right and work on his marriage."

She melted like candy in blazing summer heat. "All of a sudden he wants to work things out?"

"Well yeah. You know how men can be? Maybe he just needed some time to himself, time to think."

She didn't reply, just nodded.

I went on. "Or maybe he needed to talk to someone else. Sometimes a man needs a second opinion."

More nods.

"We both know that men don't always get it the first time around, but eventually they do get it."

As I fed her what she wanted to hear, a fluorescent light started to shine in her eyes, but that bulb only lasted for seconds, then it turned into darkness, as if bipolar intrusions had stolen her thoughts.

Snow said, "Or maybe that whore of his dumped 'im cold blooded and he"—her voice dropped into a whisper—"has no other choice but to come back to his wife, thinking she'll always be by his side. Well I got news for 'im. This wife of his got other plans. Big plans."

A knock appeared on the door, a knock that silenced her completely. Snow walked over to open the door, and sure enough it was the infamous Mr. Marcello, the king walking in with dark blue dress slacks and hard bottom shoes, hair half gelled, shirt unbuttoned, the collar unfolded as if he had stopped getting dressed to check on his wife.

Snow straightened up when her husband came through the door, his presence making her transform from lady assassin to innocent housewife.

She said, "Hey, Hun. Everything okay?"

"No, My Love. You seen my watch?"

"Which one."

"Gold Movado. Diamonds alongside the face."

"It's where you always keep it. Right side of the shelf. Second drawer to the bottom."

He smacked his head lightly. "Of course. Alzheimer's must be coming early."

"Seems like it," Snow joked. "What would a husband ever do without his wife?"

Wrong choice of words. Words that caused Mr. Marcello to cut his eyes at Snow, that prenuptial being balled up and cannon-balled at his face.

Then he noticed me in the room, noticed me sitting in my PJ's behind his wife.

He acknowledged me. I acknowledged him back. That awkwardness between us showed in his smile, as if last night's conversation was scribbled on the guestroom walls.

Mr. Marcello told his legal lover, "The guys arrived early to take you to the airport. Their waiting downstairs."

"Gimme a sec. Just catching my cousin up on some things to do while I'm gone."

"Anything I should know about?"

He squinted his eyes.

Her eyes opened wide.

I stood in the shadows and played my role, neither party knowing what was said about the other behind closed doors.

"Actually yes," Snow answered. "I was just telling her to stay away from you and all of your Godforsaken war stories. No boring my cousin with your experiences in Vietnam."

He chuckles. "If I recall correctly, those Vietnam stories are what hooked you good."

"So you thought," she said. "You hooked me good but it wasn't because of those stories."

His smile quickly vanished as if money was thrown at his face once more.

Snow said, "Anyways, if that's all you wanted then give me a second to finish talking with my cousin. Be downstairs in a few. And oh, your burgundy tie is hanging on the hat rack incase you forgot that too."

Eyes glued to his wife, the king slowly backed out the room with words unsaid like a rat was in his kingdom perfuming the air.

The moment he was gone Snow locked the bedroom door. Then she sat on the bed, slung back her locks, that innocent housewife transforming back into a lady assassin.

She whispered, "So this is how I want this to play out. My husband will be in that cemetery tonight at 10pm. At nine there'll be an empty black Land Rover parked in the driveway of 4600, a Land Rover that's totally untraceable."

"4600?"

"Here, let me show you for yourself." She takes me to the window to point at the mansion that sits adjacent to her house. "4600 is the address of the house next door. Don't worry because the house is completely vacant, now currently up for sale. The Land Rover that'll be in that driveway will be unlocked, keys inside. I want you to make your departure immediately after my husband makes his, and once you finish the job, be sure to park the SUV back where you got it. Someone will be here to pick it up later."

"But what about these nosey ass neighbors?"

"What about 'em?"

"What if someone sees me? They could draw out a sketch of my face. What if someone gets suspicious and calls the—"

"Police?" She flashes a grin. "Don't be so paranoid, Angel. In this neighborhood people don't call the cops. They call on me. The great thing about living next to a cop is knowing you'll always feel safe."

For my own advantage, I tried to dig deeper. "Who will be here to pick up the Land Rover?"

She smiles. "You would like to know that wouldn't you. Well if I was you, I'd leave this area immediately after the job is complete. Don't hang around to try and play detective."

"And what about Devilla? When do I get 'er back?"

"Give you those details later."

"Bullshit! Give 'em now."

"Not so fast Ms. Save-the-children. I'm not telling you anything until you live up to your end of our arrangement ... As long as my husband is alive, consider Devilla dead. Get my husband dead and I'll resurrect your little girl."

My face burned with fire.

She goes on, "Also, I got something for you to carry along on your journey. A lil' something for the ride." She reached into her purse and started digging around, then pulled out a small piece of tape that resembled a band-aid. "Your wrist," she said. "Need to put this on your pulse."

"A bandage?"

"Not a bandage. It's an NM Sensor."

"An NM what?"

"Nerve Monitoring Sensor. Detectives use these for interrogation purposes when they need leads on murder cases. It monitors your blood pressure, your heart rate, even pinpoints the address of your location. Think of it as a tracking device but to the third power."

"And why are you sticking it on me?"

"So I can monitor you from two thousand miles away. Need to know your state of mind while I'm in New York. How nervous you are. The places you're going. Oh yes, Angel. I will be monitoring."

I told her, "Don't you trust me?"

"Deal or no deal, in my eyes you're still a criminal. And I don't trust criminals one bit."

"But somehow you trust yourself?"

She grimaces. "As long as you finish this job you can think whatever you wanna think about me. Until then—"

Knocking pounded on the bedroom door. *"Hurry it up, My love. Your flight leaves in an hour."*

Snow shouts at the door. "Be right down, Honey!" Then she turned back to me. "And one more thing before I forget." She went back into her designer purse and showed me the brown paper bag she was carrying when first entering the room. Slowly going into the bag, Snow pulled out a fistful of human being ashes, the ashes of Mr. Marcello's mother.

I rose from the bed.

Snow sat up straight.

No words were exchanged between us. Just eye contact. Eyes that said I didn't have to admit that me and Cuqui was prowling through her bedroom; for she already knew.

In that moment of contention, Snow said, "Whatever it is you think you're looking for, I suggest you stop now."

"What's the matter, Snow? You afraid of what I might find in Pandora's box?"

She smirked. "The real question is, are you prepared for what's lingering inside?"

I swallowed hard. Swallowed the unknown that played the predecessor to another knock from Snow's husband.

"Hurry it up, My Love. My guards are waiting."

Snow didn't reply.

Instead, she opened up her hand that was filled with human ashes, then she closed it into a fist, drew in her lips, then turned that fist upside down into an hourglass, an hourglass that slowly poured the particles back into the brown paper bag, her way of showing me that time was ticking, the countdown before I took out her husband.

With a half-crooked smile, she said, "It's now 9am, Angel. That's approximately twelve hours before our deal goes down. Twelve hours before you make me the happiest woman on this planet ... Do me a favor, Angel ... Don't fuck up that happiness."

18

Ten minutes later I was peeking out the blinds of the guestroom window, watching Mr. Marcello see his wife off before she left for the airport, the bodyguard loading her bags into a black Suburban.

From her conservative style heels, to her buttoned up blouse, to her hair pulled back in a professional pony, Snow could've easily passed for a Wall Street woman, not knowing that beneath those clothes was a woman who could kill with the best of them.

Dark shades covered her eyes from the sunlight as she stood by the SUV, embraced in Mr. Marcello's arms. He held her tight, stroked her fire-red locks that sparkled from the sun, his lips speaking that lover language that made her smile.

Or pretend to smile.

Then I watched him close the gap to those lips as they began to speak a different language. They spoke in tongue. Tongued like teenagers in the back of the school bus. Their heads turning. Eyes closed. Noses stuck together with a delicate force, like lovers reuniting. He held her waist, grabbed her ass. Then he palmed a fistful of his own territory so she wouldn't forget it while boarding the plane, ultimate kiss.

After years of marriage he still kisses her like a new flame, and somehow I resented that. Resented her. A crazy whacked-out woman like Snow doesn't deserve a man, let alone a man of passion.

The prelude to their departure ended with Snow resting her chin on his shoulder, shades looking at the ground.

Then she looked up.

Not at her husband, but at the guestroom window where I peeked from inside. Made me look away. Made me wait for a brief moment before looking back through the blinds to see if she was still looking.

Indeed she was. Still looking. Her shades glued to my bedroom window while she rested in her husband's arms, and in that creepy moment she raised her hands in my direction to stick up a finger on one hand and two fingers on the other.

The #12.

12 hours.

That was her message. A message concluded with dimples diverging into a crooked grin, her way of saying I don't got much time to live up to my part of the deal. Then she left in the SUV, left that trepidation bubbling in my stomach.

I motioned from the window seal to take a morning shower. Before reaching the bathroom the maid came strolling through the door with new sheets in hand and pillow cases on her shoulder. The maid was in good spirits. She was snapping her finger and swaying her hips, doing that while slinging her long black hair to the beat of an imaginary Soul Train line.

Unnerved, I asked, "Are you okay?"

"Yes, madam. Me feel good."

"I can see that. But what's with the Harlem Shake?"

"Oh nuntin'… me jus… me happy dat … oh whad de heck. Da boss gon fo' weekend en me nev' felt better!"

She cheerfully walks over to do her usual chores, making the bed with a smile so tight it nearly choked her.

I continued my journey to the bathroom for a morning shower. The maid cracked the bathroom door to let me know she was leaving, said she'd be right back with a towel for me to dry myself with. I took off my clothes, wrapped my weave in a shower cap, set the shower to the only temperature that can rejuvenate me in the morning. Scorching hot. That stupid tracking device was still on my wrist. Snow said it was waterproof. But that proof wasn't its only purpose. This band was a reminder that I was still a criminal. State's property. It meant that even if I saved Devilla, my only reward would be a 6 x 9 cell, and that's if the judge was lenient.

The water continued to trickle down my back as soap covered my body. The bathroom fogged up while thoughts fogged my head. Then the bathroom door opened. I spoke through the curtain to thank the maid for bringing me a towel, but she didn't respond.

I thanked her again. Again no response.

Her silhouette showed through the curtain so I knew she was there, but why she wasn't responding was strange. I peeked my head out the shower curtain, only to make eyes with a sight that raised my blood pressure to the roof.

That silent intruder was not the maid, but Mr. Marcello who was standing by the sink.

And he was naked.

Butt Naked.

Butt booty naked.

Time stood still. I froze harder than a glazier. Told myself that my eyes were fooling me, that this man wasn't really naked in this bathroom, told myself that I was hallucinating, that this was nothing but a nightmare.

Or a wet dream.

Mr. Marcello was standing there with a smile on his face, a towel in his hand, and his penis stood semi erect, a long auburn-colored shaft with a light tan, full of girth.

He said, "Figured I'd be the one to bring you the towel."

I wanted to speak, but my mouth went numb.

He raised the towel in the air, and his penis jumped at me like a dog on leash. My flesh shivered.

He said, "So you want it or not?"

"Huh ... what ... what happened to the maid?"

"She's gone. I gave her the rest of the day off."

He tosses the towel on the back of the toilet, and that made his penis wave at me. Behind the shower curtain my clit waved back, stuck its face from my vulva to say hello. That meant I had to do one thing and do it fast: send him out the door. But my insides insisted I do something different; my insides begged for me to take advantage of his wayward penis, and as Mr. Marcello waited for me to throw him out the bathroom, his eyes circulated from my lips to my nipples that poked out the shower curtain.

I reached to close the curtain, but he blocked my hand in motion.

I stuttered. "What ... what are you doing?"

"Finishing our conversation from last night," he replied.

"That conversation ended with you saying you loved your wife."

"I know ... a love I lost a long time ago."

He pulls back the shower curtain to reveal my nakedness. My eyes widened, his eyes sharpened. I tried to cover myself, but D cups are impossible to hide with a wash cloth.

He tells me, "I'm through with pretending."

"What?"

"Last night you opened my eyes, Angel. You looked me in my eyes and told me the truth, that you don't see a man who loves his wife ... and you know what, Angel? You were right."

"So what are you saying?"

"I'm saying I no longer want my wife. I want this instead." He glared at my breasts. "I want all of this, every bit of your body."

I stood there in disbelief, thinking how I was ill-prepared for the situation at hand. Part of me was afraid to go through with this moment, mainly because it came sooner than I expected, not like I imagined. But the other part of me – the animalistic side of the brain – was warming my insides by the second.

He goes on to say, "I wrestled with my emotions all night long. Tried to convince myself that I could save my marriage, that Snow will always be the woman for me. But I'm tired of trying. Tired of pretending."

The shower ran briskly, water bouncing off my body and dampening his chest. Snow's lover didn't have the chest of a middle-aged man. It had perfect symmetry. Not too robust. Not too scrawny. A firm chest with a strip of hair running down the center, and with the water trickling on those hairs, the waterfall met with his well-endowed manhood.

Mr. Marcello continues to confess. "I was waiting for this moment."

My nipples became erect.

"Was waiting for my wife to walk out that door."

Clit got hard.

"That's the reason I was rushing her. Wanted to get her out this house as soon as possible so I could finish this conversation."

He steps into the tub uninvited, and that abrupt movement made me fidget and drop the soap.

Don't bend over, I told myself. Under no circumstances should you bend over.

He tells me, "I want you, Angel ... want you so bad that it hurts."

I glanced at his penis. "I can see that ... but what about your wife?"

"The hell with my wife."

He stares back at my body. Stares at my nipples that are staring at him, then he bites his lips and clinches his fist, his knuckles as hard as his erect shaft.

He says, "I want to do something."

"Yeah?"

He kneels down below my waist, dropping his head beneath my soaking wet vagina.

Caught off guard, my natural reflexes jerk back.

He tells me, "Relax, Beautiful. I'm just grabbing the soap."

He stands to his feet. "Want to wash you."

"But I'm already clean."

"Not quite."

Mr. Marcello turns me around to face the water, and he rubs the soap across my back. I don't resist his soft touch, his miracle hands that are warm and empowering. He rubs my shoulder, presses his fingertips into my collar bone to give a soapy massage, touching all the pressure points. Due to the circumstances, I tried not to let myself enjoy this moment, but I couldn't prevent my eyes from closing, couldn't prevent myself from envisioning him as my lover – perhaps in a different time zone or in a different place – him coming home from a long day's work, surprising me in the shower, doing my body justice while the kids play out back in the yard.

I let him run his hands from the nape of my neck to the dip in my back, the soap climbing that hump and sliding down my buttocks. I squirmed. Pulled my cheeks together as he left that spot. I took a deep breath, waited for his hands to climb back up that mountain of flesh, massaging me across my neck.

He whispers, "Your body is amazing."

"So I've been told."

"You work out?"

"Ghetto Palates."

"Come again?"

The ivory soap is placed on my ebony breasts. He washes them. Starts running his fingers around my alohas, fingers going in circular motions, figure-eights sketched across my breasts with traces of suds from the soap. Oh man does he know how to touch a woman. His fingers are delicate, receptive to a woman's arousal, very attentive, patient during the succession of stimulation. It was obvious that I wasn't the first woman he's done this with. A scientist conducts many experiments before prescribing the right dose, which means this level of affection didn't come over night. He's performed this treatment on other women, perhaps with his wife; there's no denying that. But his wife is not the woman in his arms right now. I am. My breasts are. And he's fondling these breasts with extreme delight, pinching my nipples, kissing my neck, bathing my babies while wetting the soap, breathing in my ear, pressing up against my body, his hands working wonders while his penis poked and prodded at my backside, begging me to open the gates of my buttocks, the gates that lead to the alley of sin.

He tells me, "On your knees."

I do as Simon says and drop on all fours. My rear sits high in the air, face to the floor, my back sloping deeper than a roller coaster at Six Flags. Mr. Marcello takes the shower head and points it at my backside; he stands at my ankles spraying water on my buttocks. I feel a sting. A stimulating sting. The water bounces off my flesh like its Wet-n-Wild, water soaking up the curtain, wetting up the floor. Then I felt a slap on my rear. I became startled, looked back. Behind me is an excited man with big green eyes, and he raises his hand to strike me again. I tightened up, waited for him to give me that exhilarating sting, for his palms to ricochet off each butt cheek. My hips gyrated, ass tingled, thighs shook from the constant slapping at my flesh. I tensed up, somewhat felt embarrassed, partly because this was different than other sexual experiences in my past, but I refused to stop the preface to his presentation.

He asks me, "Ever been licked by a Dominican?"

I quiver. "Not lately."

Mr. Marcello kneels behind me and parts my wet cheeks, looking through the core of my tunnel. He caresses that area gently, does that while tracing warm saliva around the epicenter of my flower, that opening leading to nirvana valley. He tastes my wetness. Relishes my sweetness. Then he lowers his tongue to that cautioned clitoris, licking the area that makes me cringe and leave planet earth.

I'm now in another world.

Dancing with the stars.

Ecstasy has confiscated my body and swallowed my soul. Senses are stirring. Vision is blurred. I'm starting to see things I've never seen before. Dogs are flying. Ducks are talking. At this point I'm more fucked up than a bottle of gin.

"You like that, mommi?"

"Yes?"

"You like this Dominican tongue? Huh, mommi?"

A man has never called me mommi before, but I dug it. Dug it deeply. Just hearing those words made me go insane, made me turn around and reply, "Yes, Papi ... Yes, Papi I like it."

He slaps me on the butt and bites that area, bites me like a man receiving his last supper. I keep my face to the floor. Vision inverted. The shower runs rapidly on my neck and flows down my back, flows down my cheeks, slides in between, water mixing with my juices to flavor that wetness, a wetness that drips unto Mr. Marcello's tongue. He consumes that bath water, savors the taste.

I repeat, "Yes, Papi. I like that."

He bites me again. "Hungry for you ... Very hungry."

I don't reply.

"Thought about your body all night long ... while I was in bed ... even while making love to my wife, I thought about you ... thought about your taste ... your scent ... the sweetness of these juices."

He feeds my ego that spoonful of arrogance.

I ask him, "Sweeter than your wife?"

"Much sweeter."

I smile in delight as he continues his journey, digging in my flesh like he's digging for gold. This tub is our playground. Our circus of lust. Water wets up my shower cap and rolls into my weave. This weave wasn't cheap. It was $67.36. But at this point I didn't care. I'll sacrifice the money for extreme pleasure. Perfect exchange.

Mr. Marcello says, "Come on, Ms. Angel. Let me take you to the bed."

"But I'm not—"

He swoops me in the air in mid-sentence, then he flips me upside down, 69 position, and now I'm staring at the floor, feet to the ceiling, my face now parallel to Mr. Marcello's penis.

My hungry lover carries me out the bathtub with the shower still running, his face in my kitty and my knees on his shoulders. We exit the bathroom with bodies all wet and hormones on fire. The man between his legs is steadily tapping my face with each stride he takes, and God knows I'm holding on for dear life.

Then I'm thrown on the bed. Thrown into sheets.

He spreads the legs of my tropical forest and nibbles on the forbidden fruit. Lips wrapped around that area, lips French kissing the outer lips of my Labia Majora. I breathe heavily. Breathe as he rubs his fingers across my kitty, then inserts a finger into my vagina.

I tell him, "I like that finger."

"You do?"

"Yes papi."

He inserts another finger to double the dose as I raised my neck to watch him in motion. We stare at each other endlessly. Stares magnetic. There's nothing like watching a man between your legs, the look on his face as he worships your pearl. It's a sense of empowerment. A sense of ownership. Like I own his body, or at least his tongue. Not every man puts their heart and soul into tasting a woman. Some do it unwillingly. Some do just enough to get by, or enough to get something in return. But Mr. Marcello was different. I can tell he enjoys pleasing a woman. I can tell by the look in his eyes, the passion on his face, can tell he understands the value of the clitoris – that if handled correctly, it's your greatest ally, but if handled incorrectly, it could betray you tenfold. Unlike others, this man licks a woman the way a woman should be licked.

With joy.

With honor.

With passionate pleasure.

And God knows I wasn't about to stop him. Not when I was seconds away from reaching the promise land, where I felt an orgasm coming on strong, but then, in the preface of that orgasm, Mr. Marcello never allowed me to reach that point. He stopped me in mid-relief and raised his head for air, but I stuffed his face back down my tunnel. "Don't stop now, baby. Don't you dare stop!"

I threw back my head from the effects of his tongue, his persevering lips applying much pressure.

Then I reached the end of the road.

Reached the dead-end to orgasm.

Intensity showed on my face and crawled through each orifice of my body, and as I strained to maintain, as I bit my bottom lip, as I lifted my neck to hold back the rush, I reached out to grab a fistful of sheets and screamed like a woman who was set on fire.

I was cumming out loud.

Cumming like a beast.

Cumming from the tongue of another woman's husband.

In that orgasmic moment of reverie, I wet up the room with my lustful liquids. Wet up the sheets. Wet up the pillows. Wet up the face of my Latin lover.

"Yes mommi! That's what I've been waiting for. Give me more! Give me more!"

Within those orgasmic liquids were all my emotions: Madness. Despair. Resentment. Hate. They shot out the hole of my turbulent tunnel, liberated themselves from a body of shackles.

Lips trembling, thighs vibrating, I struggled for a long breath of consciousness, my toes curling into their own cocoon.

I was becoming a free woman.

19

We lay in the bed naked, sheets damp, covered in our own transgressions.

My legs are still shaking from Mr. Marcello's performance, my clitoris steadily pulsating.

He asks me, "Are you okay?"

"You're kidding me right."

He smiles. "I'm sorry. Guess I got a little beside myself."

"A little?"

"Okay ... maybe a whole lot."

I sat up in the bed and crossed my legs, wrapped my arms around my knees and brought them to my chest. Mr. Marcello was lying at my feet. My eyes stare at the dresser that is congregating thoughts inside my head. Thoughts are racing against thoughts. All thoughts of Snow.

Mr. Marcello says, "You know what this means right?"

Afraid to ask what, I hunched over to drop my chin between my knees.

He goes on, "It means I have to tell 'er."

"Tell who? I hope not Snow. Are you crazy?"

"It's the only way."

"Yeah, the only way to death. In case you haven't realized it your wife is missing a few screws. To tell her this would only make things worse."

"I'm not referring to this. I'm talking 'bout the marriage ... I'm getting the divorce."

"You sure? I mean, you're not just saying that because we're—"

"Naked? No. Truth is, our marriage has been broken for quite some time."

"But what about the—"

"Prenuptial."

"Yeah. And stop finishing my sentences."

"At this point I'm through with protecting that money. Money is made to be spent, Angel. Not worshiped. So as far as I'm concerned, she can have whatever it is she thinks she's entitled to."

I ran my fingers through my tangled weave and let out a heavy sigh, knowing I had infected a union that was already tainted, the amalgamation of man and wife. Part of me – the malicious part – was saying that Snow deserved this infidelity. She deserved to be mistreated as much as I deserved a good orgasm, and that orgasm felt damn good coming from her husband.

That part of me was vindictive.

On the contrary, the other part of me felt dirty. I felt responsible for the death of their marriage, even if it was already hanging by a thread. I was officially a home wrecker. An intruder of love. And because of my selfishness, it was now too late to chase down the past. Can't run down the orgasm that ran from these walls.

But what I could do is disrupt the future.

The future that if I stuck with Snow's plan, Mr. Marcello won't live to see Tuesday, let alone see a divorce. His wife wanted to cash in his life and only I knew the pin number to that deposit. Part of me wanted to stop that bullet and save his life.

But saving his life meant risking Devilla's.

And that was a risk I could not take.

I told him, "Tell me something. How come you never had kids?"

"Kids?" he replied with an expression caught off guard. "Where did that come from?"

"It's just a question. I mean, fifteen years of marriage and no kids. Strange don't you think?"

I was testing him. Testing to see if he'd tell me the truth, that he neglected to father Snow's baby, all because that child was birthed from someone else, a move ultimately causing Snow to kill her own child for sake of a marriage. That was Snow's story. A story equipped with another side, the untold side. Now I wanted to hear the truth from the horse's mouth.

He answered, "Kids weren't part of the plan."

"Your plan or Snow's plan?"

He drops his head as if to gather a thought, then he looks at me with a melancholy face, the face of a man bearing a million regrets. "Wasn't part of God's plan," he said. "Truth is ... we tried ... tried to have a baby ... several times ... But never was I able to give her that gift ... almost happened once ... early in our marriage ... Snow was five months pregnant with my baby boy ... but she lost the baby. Lost it as easy as it came, all because of her constant smoking ... and I hated her for that ... hated her so much that we separated for a year to heal from the miscarriage ... truth is I was the one who needed that year ... I needed to get past it ... and when we got back together we tried it again ... but never was she able to get pregnant ... we saw dozens of doctors to rectify the problem ... some said it was due to a low sperm count ... others said it was stress-related ... whatever it was, it wasn't for us."

My curiosity asked, "Ever considered adoption?"

"Thought about it once, but the truth is, I'm too selfish to raise another man's child ... anything and everything that comes in my life, has to come through me, including children ... if it's not flesh of my flesh, blood of my blood, I'd always feel that the child belongs to someone else in the back of my mind ... I wanted my own child ... wanted to see my own eyes ... my own lips ... that's why I resiliently tried to have a child ... I wanted my own offspring ... but at some point you get tired of trying ... we all get tired of trying."

His pain was immeasurably vivid, as if his heart was painted on his sleeve.

"The worst part is not knowing what to tell people who ask me about children ... my friends ... my family ... the little family that's left in Dominica ... do you know how it feels to look your mother in the face and come up with a hundred reasons why you can't give her a grandchild ... it's the worst feeling on earth ... her dream was to have a grandson ... same as mines ... I often had dreams of watching my son take his first steps ... his first words ... wondering what his talents would be and how I could show 'im the ropes, maybe watch him take over my businesses someday ... I'd teach 'im the most important things in life ... things like love ... honor ... respect ... I'd teach 'im values, how to never disown where he comes from ... Dominica

Republic ... the most beautiful country in the world ... I'd teach him responsibility ... teach 'im ethics ... would show 'im how to love women and the true extent of their value ... I would've taught my son all of that and more ... would've been the perfect father ... the father that my father tried to be, but didn't know how."

He was putting it all on the table without holding back. Pain in his eyes. Regret on his face. Never before has a man expressed himself so ardently, takes a real man to unbutton his ego and fasten that genuine collar. And I respected him for that. Made him more of a man in my eyes.

I told him, "Maybe one day you'll get that son."

His face drew blank as if it was unattainable, as if hope had perished some time ago and the crumbs of that hope was a distraught man – a man who, regardless of money, was living a poor man's dream that would never be fulfilled.

I rested my palm on the smoothness of his chest as we drifted into the undercurrents of our thoughts.

Instead of letting those thoughts corrode the moment, he flipped the conversation by saying, "And what about you? What's your story?"

"My story?"

"Yeah, a beautiful chica like yourself ... no kids ... and single ... that's unheard of."

"And what makes you think I'm single?"

He gives a one-sided smirk. "Any real man can tell you are single."

I rose from his chest and folded my arms, gave him a bitchy unit.

He asks, "What's the matter, Senorita?"

"You tell me. You're the one that stuck your head in your ass. Here's your chance to pull it out. So go 'head. Tell me how you know I'm single."

He laughs. "You really want me to answer that question?"

I hold my sneer.

He goes on, "Okay ... for one, I can tell by the way you orgasm."

My eyes stand up straight. "What? What the heck is that supposed to mean?"

"Your toes curl in, you scream for Jesus, and you pulled out some strings of my hair, as if you haven't released in months. All signs of a single woman who doesn't get sex on the regular. Not to mention you couldn't even speak. But a woman use to being sexually fulfilled will tell you when they're reaching that point, and even after they've reached it, the only thing that changes is facial expressions."

I processed his mini lecture, and replied, "That's the most lopsided bullshit philosophy I ever heard of."

"Call it bullshit, but it's the truth."

"And what if I told you I faked it?"

"Faked what?"

"You know ... *it*."

Worriation spreads across his face like a plague. "Are you ... are you serious, Senorita?"

I wanted to say yes for the sake of argument, but I couldn't hold back the smirk, then the smile, then laughter that confessed to the truth.

That white lie made us laugh out loud together, our little liaison to intimacy. I wondered if he shared this chemistry with his wife. Do they laugh together? Probably not. That uppity-class bitch doesn't strike me as the playful type.

With that thought in mind, I told him something that I had to get off my chest. "Can I ask you something?"

"Anything?"

"What did you ever see in my cousin Snow? I mean, not saying she isn't pretty. Because she is pretty. But aside from that, she's a complete train wreck."

"You think so?"

"She's evil, conniving, condescending, and—"

"Loving."

"Huh?"

"Snow may be all of those things, but she loves me. Loves me more than any woman I ever had in my life. And I've had my share of women."

My forehead wrinkling, I tell him, "That's it. Just love."

"Love goes a long way."

"Obviously not far enough if you're getting a divorce."

He doesn't have a comeback.

I go on, "Besides, you could've found any woman to love you, especially an American woman." Then I thought of Cuqui. "I know a woman right now that'll give her left breast to be with a man like you."

He laughs, then says, "Sorry but I disagree. Women that see me only see what they can get out of me. They don't see me for who I am. But Snow does. She loves me for only me."

"And what makes you so certain of that?"

"Because she's done things to prove it. Things I could never mention, but I assure you that Snow has passed the test in many ways; she has stood by me during the darkest hours of my life and her testament goes beyond measures. My wife truly believes in those words, 'til death do us part."

"I bet she does," I mumbled.

"Excuse me?"

"Nothing."

I waited, added, "And as for the divorce?"

"Although we love each other our time has come and gone. Call it the nature of the beast but that's what has happened. It's like ... you see a woman one day, see what you want as your ideal wife, and before you know it that ideal wife has been reduced to just a wife, then reduced to a mate, then a companion, then a roommate, and then a person you only care for, and before you know it you're looking into the person's eyes trying to find love, but no matter how hard you stare, no matter how hard you wish, all you can see is your present situation."

"Sounds depressing."

"At first, until you see another woman that sets off the sparkle that you haven't seen in years, the same sparkle you first saw in your wife.

He looks into my eyes as if I was that sparkle, and I turned my face away like a little girl.

He says, "I'm sorry. Did I scare you?"

"Just caught me by surprise."

He toyed with my hair as I tousled with the hairs on his chest.

He said, "Well ... hypothetically ... could you see yourself being with a man like me?"

I smile. The smile of a woman that's caught off guard. "A man like you? That's hard to say. I mean, I couldn't."

"Which is it? Hard to say or you couldn't?"

I hesitate. "Are you for real?"

"At my age everything is for real."

Silence.

He goes on, "And if it means anything, know that if I was your lover, you'd be well taken care of."

"Taken care of?"

"If my father didn't teach me anything else, he taught me how to take care of a woman."

Ain't that the truth, I thought, my mind going back to him kissing my pearl.

I told him, "I'm not saying I wouldn't, it's just that ..."

"Go on. Go 'head and say it."

"We're ... we're from two different worlds."

"Maybe two different countries, but not two different worlds. You'll be surprised to know how much we have in common. For instance, what's your favorite color?"

"Okay, so now you're going elementary on me. Fine ... it's purple."

"You see. Mine is purple too."

"Really?"

He gives a sarcastic wink.

I laugh, tell him, "You're a goddamn liar."

"Okay, maybe not purple, it's really blue. But that's okay if we're opposite. As they say, opposites attract."

"Not in this case. It would never work out."

"Why not? Is it because of my age?"

"No."

"Because of Snow?"

I shook my head no. Then I turned away from him and stared into the eyes of the truth. Truth that I'm a woman who's wanted for murder and there's a timeline for my freedom. Perhaps we could've been lovers in a different world; a world where fear doesn't exists, where my mind is free of those demoralizing thoughts that constantly spiral inside. That world existed two years ago, when I was a law-school student on a road to greatness, a woman always looking straight ahead, never looking over her shoulder. In that world, where passion replaced paranoia, I would've made him my lover in a heartbeat, no questions asked.

But that world is now extinct.

Gone from my existence.

What's left of that world is a woman dealing with the austerity of the real world. I am a scorned woman. A woman who sold her life for the death of a man, and that is a scar that constantly hurts. Hurts to know I can never get back the life I had. Hurts to know I can never refund the life I've purchased.

I tell Mr. Marcello, "The bus stops here. Our bond can go no further."

20

Six hours later we had taken our conversation downstairs, now lounging in the coziness of the living room.

The sun was going down while evening was coming out the closet, and Mr. Marcello was in the kitchen cooking up a meal, told me he wanted to prepare me something special.

We had the house to ourselves.

And I ruled this nest.

With Snow being out of town and the maid having the day off, I was walking around half-naked, Vicky's lingerie with a long white housecoat, acting as if I was the woman of the house. The fire place was lit. Lights were dimmed low. I turned on the television and kicked back on the sofa, waiting for the man of the house to serve me diligently.

I picked up the remote and started flipping through channels. VH1. CBS. NBC. Then I stumbled upon a little girl's face that was showing on CNN. The featured girl was little Devilla, the daughter of the man I murdered back in Brooklyn. My brain relapsed as I saw Devilla's face. Wanted to turn the channel, but my eyes were glued to the television screen. Fear made me look over my shoulder for Mr. Marcello. He was still doing his thing in the kitchen.

I stared back at the television.

Stared at Devilla's face.

The newscaster was doing a special on missing children and Devilla's story was top on the list. He talked about her being kidnapped and last seen in Boston, then talked about her father, William Randolph, how he died in the hospital after being gunned down by a woman that was once his stepdaughter.

Died in the hospital?

That didn't add up. From what I remember that bastard was pronounced dead at the scene. There's no way he could've survived all the bullets I gave him that day, and I know because the officer checked his pulse right in front of my eyes.

I glanced back over my shoulder. Mr. Marcello was still in the kitchen preparing the food.

Eyes back on the television, CNN revealed that William Randolph was in a coma for a month, mentioned that someone had snuck into his room and finished him off on his deathbed with a .22. Cops said it happened at 2am, although cameras showed no entrance of an intruder that night. The FBI suspected me of being the hidden intruder and having an inside connection at the hospital, then they proceeded to show my face at the bottom of the screen.

Seeing that shocked me for two reasons.

One: I realized I wasn't the only demon from William's past that wanted him dead.

Two: That demon – whoever the demon was – was still out there, still lurking, which technically meant I wasn't William's killer. All I needed now was enough evidence to build myself a case.

Then I heard a voice. "Hey mommi, you ready to eat?"

Staggered, I nearly broke my neck to look over my shoulder. But he wasn't there. Mr. Marcello was talking from the kitchen. Make that leaving the kitchen and heading my way, tiptoeing while balancing a tray of food in his hands. I picked up the remote to change the channel.

But that channel never changed.

Then I shook the remote and tried it again, still no luck. Luck was laughing at my persistence on the opposite side of the living room, and after fiddling with the remote for a few seconds, I noticed it controlled the DVD and not the television. *Son of a bitch.* I glanced back at Mr. Marcello to mark his location. He was four steps from the living room. Four steps from seeing my mugshot plastered all over his 50 inch flat screen television. *Think, Angel. Think.* Panicked out, I leaped in front of the T.V. to power it off, never found that power switch, and with no other option, I yanked the cord out the wall, yanked it so hard that my arm flew back and hit Mr. Marcello right in the face.

He stumbled. Stumbled with shock in his eyes and a body unbalanced, and the tray of food he was carrying quickly tosses in the air and falls to the floor.

Plates broken.

Glass shattered.

Dinner is ruined.

Worst of all, Mr. Marcello is hunched over the couch with a hand to his nose that is bleeding indefinitely. He looks me in the eyes. The look of a man who has no forgiveness, eyes of a drug lord that just been hoaxed.

He tells me, "What the hell are you trying to do ... kill me?"

"I'm sorry. I'm so sorry. I didn't know you were—"

"Save it," he says with a tone that silences me.

I took a step back. So did my heart that hid behind my liver. Blood ran from his nose like water from a faucet, and his DNA begins to race down his face.

I tell him, "Wait right there."

I made a beeline to the kitchen in search of paper towels, also grabbed a dish cloth and ice from the freezer. When I got back to the living room Mr. Marcello was hunched over the couch with a hand to his nose, trying to stop the bleeding, waiting to be nurtured.

He said, "What were you trying to—"

"Not now," I told him, playing my role to the fullest.

I wiped blood from his face with thick paper towels, wiped him down like a man of my own. He let me take charge. Allowed me to lay his head back on a soft couch pillow, then waited as I wrapped ice inside the dishcloth to place it on his nose, hoping it would stop the constant bleeding.

As I continued to give him that southern hospitality, he said, "Why do I get the feeling that you're enjoying this?"

I smile. "Maybe I am. There's nothing like seeing a powerful man in pain."

He turns his head as if I've insulted him. "You call this pain. I've been shot three times and stabbed three more. This, Senorita, is nothing at all."

I rewind the tape. "You've been shot before?"

"Years ago ... got into some trouble back home."

"Well it must've been trouble with the devil."

He pondered a thought, then cleared his throat. "Although it might come as no surprise, I once worked for one of the most feared men in Dominica who employed crooked people."

"Crooked?"

"Friends in his presence, but when his back was turned these same friends wanted him six feet under, all so they could take over his empire ... As a matter of fact ..." He raised his head as if he was starting to feel the story, but I quickly reminded him of his bloody nose and positioned his head back on the pillow.

He went on to say, "I was the only one who remained loyal to my boss. But my loyalty almost got me killed."

"How come?"

"Because I wouldn't end his life."

"But that doesn't make since."

"It does if you're familiar with Caesar and Brutus."

"Backstabbing?"

"Yeah, but not from him. From someone else in our organization. Someone second rank under me."

I thought about Snow, about the conversation we had in the car while leaving the airport. The one about a war.

"You referring to Benito," I muttered.

Mr. Marcello's eyes widened. "That little bigot. All because of a lousy twenty grand that came up missing. Had he not—"

"Keep your head back. Don't want your nose to start bleeding."

"You wanna hear the story or not?"

I hushed.

"They conducted a drug exchange that entitled the buyer to 40 percent, ten percent more than our usual price, and they used me to do it, dressed it up as if the boss had given me permission."

"But why you?"

"Because I was the only the boss ever trusted. He looked at me like a son, took me under his wings, brought me into the business and showed me the ropes. And Benito resented that. He couldn't stand the fact that the boss put me second in charge, even though Benito had been there first. He couldn't stand the fact that I was the smarter one, the calmer one, and the one making tough decisions ... But still with all of this I loved him. Loved him like family, and even after I knew his intentions, I still wasn't willing to break Rule116."

"Rule 116?"

"The no snitch rule. Never rat out people in your own organization, no matter how corrupt their intentions are."

"Even if their plotting to kill the boss? What type of BS rule is that?"

"A rule that saves your life, Senorita. In the world of narcotics it's every man for his self, and you keep your mouth shut to save your own self ... Or so I once thought ... Once Benito found out that I wanted nothing to do with murdering the boss, him and the others double-crossed me just like that ... After tricking me into making the drug exchange, they placed twenty grand in the trunk of my car, twenty grand that matched the ten percent missing. Benito knew that this evidence would fuel the boss."

"But didn't the boss trust you? What about your word?"

"My word didn't stand a chance against half the organization. Nor did it matter when he tried to make an example out of me. He tied me up and tortured me for everyone's personal viewing. Then he branded me. Burned the first initial of his name into my back."

Mr. Marcello pulls up his shirt to reveal his scars. His light-skinned flesh is filled with knife slashes that form their own cemetery alongside his back, and in the midst of that cemetery is the wretched letter *A*, branded vividly, a marking so deep it made me cringe.

He tells me, "A stands for Alonzo, the name of my ex-boss. He placed the scar there as a lifetime remembrance of my disloyalty."

"And he let you live?"

"He didn't let me live. I survived. Just so happened that the police had been watching him for a long time, and they were getting ready to move in on him the same time he was torturing me. Wasn't long before the attention shifted from me and then to everyone else who engaged in a full-blown gun fight with the police. I got these wounds running from my own organization. And who was there to save me? The same police that I was taught to hate ... Isn't that ironic?" He shakes his head in discomfort, as if he's having a moment from the past. "Life is a trip ya know. All my life I was taught that cops were the enemies. But look at me now. I'm married to one. Guess it's true when they say to keep your friends close and your enemies closer."

With the ice still to his nose, he rises from the pillow and looks into my eyes. "If you don't remember anything else, remember this, Senorita. Fear is much stronger than love."

"Yeah. My mother used to say the same thing."

"And your mother was right. Fear will always be stronger than love. Why? Because with all the love I showed my boss, ten years of working for him, ten years of making him money, even killing people at his request, that love could never amount to the fear he had of my betrayal. Love got thrown out the window once fear walked through the door ... It's the same fear that causes animals to attack their owners. Or the same fear that makes a battered wife kill her husband."

Wake-up call. My brain switched gears and floored that pedal of panic as I juggled with the possibility of whether he knew about his soon-to-be death. Holding a straight face, it took everything inside of me to keep from coming clean, knowing this deadly game would be determined by the Ace I was carrying.

He goes on to stay, "Fear has no conscience or room for empathy, especially in the business of drug trafficking ... which is exactly why I'm getting out the business."

I came back to earth. "What did you just say?"

"I said I'm getting out ... Getting out the business for good."

"You serious?"

"Never been more serious in my life. After 25 years I'm giving it all up. Truth is I'm getting too old to have to constantly watch my back. I can't sleep at night. Blood pressure is up. Can no longer handle the constant paranoia. A man once told me that the people who last the longest in this business are the people who stay low-key. But over the years I've somehow neglected those words, and now that I'm on top, it seems like anyone and everyone is fearful of me. And I no longer want that life. For the rest of my life - the little life I have left - I want to live normal like everyone else."

That ball of guilt was still stuck in my throat, constantly begging me to spit out the truth.

Then I looked at Mr. Marcello.

Looked at a man who had no reason to die and a hundred reasons to live.

I said, "There's something I gotta tell you."

"Yeah?" he replied, his face going blank.

At the peak of me gathering the words, a cell-phone started to ring.

"Hold that thought," he said.

He answers the phone in an aggravated voice, that voice saying he was being disturbed. "Yes, My Love."

I swallowed hard. *My Love* was a pseudonym for Snow, meaning wifey was on the phone, my favorite enemy.

I sat up straight and braced myself while playing the third wheel, kept holding the ice-pack to Mr. Marcello's nose.

He tells her, "Oh I'm doing nothing ... just finished having dinner ... how did surgery go with my favorite mother-in-law ... Oh okay so she's doing good ... make sure you give 'er my best wishes ... wait wait, My Love. Hold for a second."

No longer wanting to hold the phone to his hear, Mr. Marcello places her on speaker and sits the phone on the table.

Speaker phone meant not caring about privacy, which meant he was more focused on me than the conversation with his wife. I smiled as I continued to hold the ice-pack to his nose.

She said, "I'll be home tomorrow evening."

"Why so soon?"

"No reason for me to stay. Mom's doing okay, and as you already know, that was my only reason for coming anyhow. Besides, don't you miss me?"

He hesitates, "Yeah ... I do a little bit."

"That's all? Just a little bit?"

I chuckled to myself. Desperate bitch.

He goes on, "Okay. I miss you a lot."

She asks, "You working tonight?"

"Have a meeting with my accountant. Don't think I'm going to make it though."

"How come?"

Because he's busy with me, I thought to myself. Now hang up the damn phone.

Mr. Marcello tells her, "Kind of tired. I might just do my usual and that's it."

I figured that *the usual* was going to the graveyard, that harshness reminding me of my reason for being here.

Snow asked him, "Did you reschedule the meeting with Benito?"

"Not yet. I doubt if I'd reschedule at all."

"I thought we talked about this, Honey. You told me that you were sending Sergio in your place."

"That was before I reconsidered."

"Reconsidered? Don't be foolish, Honey. The Columbians are our biggest suppliers and—"

"Was our biggest suppliers," he said, cutting her off. "As for now, there's gonna be some changes."

"Changes? How come you never told me about these so-called changes. After all, I am your wife."

His voice rises. "Didn't know I needed to consult with my wife about every decision I make."

"You don't. It's just ... well, what type of changes are you supposed to—"

"Drop it," he tells her. "We'll have this conversation tomorrow evening when you arrive."

The bark in his voice causes Snow to bite her tongue, nothing but air coming through the receiver.

After a moment of silence, she says, "Where's Maid?"

"Gave her the day off."

"For twenty dollars an hour she doesn't get days off."

"Yeah, well that's one of the changes I'm making."

"And my cousin? Where is she?"

He looks over to me, then tells his wife, "She's right where you left her."

"Let me speak to her."

The phone is taken off speaker and handed to me. I paused before answering, didn't want it to seem obvious that I was sitting right next to Mr. Marcello.

Snow told me, "And how's my favorite criminal?"

"Couldn't be better," I replied, smiling at her husband. "What is the deal?"

"The deal is your heart rate has been up and down for the last six hours. What's the problem?"

I looked down at the band aid, or the NM sensor, or whatever you call this high-tech device that was on my wrist, then I told her I was nervous about our plan. Would've said anything to keep her from suspecting the truth.

Snow said, "Without asking questions, I want you to listen carefully and nod your head to everything I say. The nodding is so you don't look suspicious to my husband."

"I'm listening."

"Our journey will end tomorrow morning at 9am. At 10am I want you to be waiting at the Starbucks across the street."

"Why there?"

"Told you no questions. Just nod your head."

"I'm nodding."

"Don't stand outside of Starbucks to bring attention to yourself. Order a cappuccino or something. I won't reach Vegas until 8pm tomorrow night, but one of my people will meet you at that location to deliver the girl..."

While Snow pitched the plan in one ear, Mr. Marcello was in my other ear, giving me light kisses. His kisses were unexpected, made me jerk away from the cell-phone and wave him off from distracting me.

He smiles, never backing off.

Snow says, "You listening? Nodding your head?"

"Yes."

"Look for a black SUV with tinted windows. It'll have a gold license plate."

"License plate number?"

"Nice try."

Lips travel from my ear to the side of my neck, the lips of a man who's trying to turn up the heat. I signaled for him to stop but he never let up, which meant I had to multitask between hearing Snow's voice and my innermost desires.

Snow says, "The SUV will be parked in the back of Starbucks beside the garbage dump. Inside that SUV will be your prize possession, little Devilla."

I thought of the fifty grand, told her, "Aren't you missing something?"

"What?"

"Think hard."

Silence rests on the line.

She says, "Oh ok ... you talkin' 'bout the money aren't ya." Then laughter in her voice. "I thought you didn't care about the money, Angel. Thought your only concern was the safety of Devilla."

I don't respond. Mr. Marcello's kisses are making me speechless.

She goes on, "Yeah, I knew that whole noble attitude was only an act. At the end of the day, you're just as dirty and greedy as me."

Lips travel from my neck to the center of my breasts, then down my stomach, down my belly-button, a tongue now journeying beneath that cherry tree of lust. I squirm. Tried my best not to moan in Snow's ear.

She yaps on, "Just like the girl, your money will also be in that SUV ... inside a black duffel bag ... all stacks of hundreds ..." My breathing got heavy. "If you knew what was good you'd take that money and leave the country ASAP, maybe start a life in Costa Rica somewhere. Or China. Or Japan ..." My kitty cat was starting to purr. "Hell, I don't care where you go, as long as I never see you again. Then you can go back to that poor excuse of what you call a life, I bet you're just counting down the seconds to where you can leave my house and finally be a free woman again."

I looked down at her husband's face that was buried between my legs, then told her, "Yeah ... Yeah you're right, couldn't agree with you more ... Are you done?"

"Yes. Now put my husband back on the phone."

Running From Redemption

"Uuum, I think he may have stepped outside for a—"

"Put 'im on the phone bitch!"

The vindictive part of me wanted to moan her husband's name, just so she could hear how much he was pleasing me. But instead I played by the rules. Stayed in control. I politely pulled my legs together and handed the phone to Mr. Marcello, watched him pick my pubic hairs from his mustache as he chatted with his legalized lover. The phone was no longer on speaker, but I could still hear Snow yapping through the receiver. She had taken the conversation backwards, telling Mr. Marcello how he never includes her on any big decisions, how he treats her like an employee rather than his wife, and how he couldn't afford to jeopardize some deal with the Columbians. They went back and forth like lawyers on trial, and eventually Mr. Marcello left the living room to take the conversation to the den, leaving me sitting all alone on the couch.

But I wanted to listen.

Needed to listen.

I rose from the couch and walked to the kitchen, the room that was closest to the den. As their bickering echoed, I pretended to make myself useful in the kitchen, started making hot water to start on some dishes. My ears were open, listening hard. Listened to Mr. Marcello's voice become a seesaw from pacing through the den, but that voice quickly went from dominating the conversation to now being submissive, as if his wife had finally gotten him to see her point of view.

I continued cleaning up everything in sight. Wiped down the counters, organized the cabinets, even cleaned out the refrigerator, Angel Inghram style. After thirty minutes of putting my stamp on the kitchen, I noticed that Mr. Marcello was now standing in the kitchen with his eyes locked on me. Pretending that I had not been listening, I kept playing the clean-up woman by sweeping the floor.

In that gigantic kitchen where I cleaned, he sauntered behind me to open the refrigerator. I continued to sweep. Looked in my peripheral. Vodka and Cranberry Juice is the result of the conversation that he had with his wife, that 80 proof drink being escorted to the kitchen table where his green eyes were staring at me.

"So I see that she cleans too," he said.

"One thing I can't stand is a dirty kitchen. And with the maid not being here, I figured I'd take it upon myself to finish the job ... You don't mind do you?"

"It's fine," he said, leaning over the kitchen counter. "You just keep on doing what you're doing."

For twenty long seconds those green eyes were still watching me as if I was his superwoman.

I said, "You ok? You act like you never saw a woman clean before."

"Not lately. I mean, other than the maid of course."

"Snow doesn't clean?"

He sucks his teeth. "Snow cleaning? I wish." Then he downs a shot of vodka. "Your cousin haven't cleaned in years. According to her there's never enough time ... Same goes for cooking."

"How unfortunate?"

"Household activities never crosses her mind. All that woman cares about is smoking those awful cigarettes and wearing expensive clothes from top-notch designers."

He took another sip of his potion, then requested I put the broom down and join him for a drink.

Any other time I would've taken that drink. But now wasn't the time. From the clock on the kitchen wall, it was time to get ready for the plan tonight. And in order to pull it off I would need all my senses.

I told him, "I'll pass on that drink."

"You sure. Because this is not regular Vodka. It's ... the good stuff."

"I know. The type of stuff that'll have me cuttin' up in here. White liquor tends to bring out the woman in me."

He smiles. "Is that so?"

"Besides, I got a date tonight. And I need to be sober."

That smile went sour, eyeballs enlarged. "You? A date? Tonight?"

"What is that supposed to mean?"

"Oh no, Senorita. Nothing like that. It's just ... you never mentioned it."

"Never felt there was a need. If you haven't noticed by now, I'm a very private person."

He looked away. Bit his bottom lip as if I had thrown a monkey wrench in his night, as if he didn't want me to go anywhere.

Then his eyes ventured back to mine. "So who is the lucky man?"

I almost said *him*. Almost.

Instead I said, "Nobody you know."

"What about my wife? Does she know 'im?"

I smirked. "Haven't anyone told you that being intrusive is a major turn off."

"I'm just protecting you, that's all. I mean, you've been in Vegas for less than a week and you're already hooking up with a stranger. Think about it."

"You're a stranger, and I hooked up with you. So what's your point?"

He reached a dead end.

I went on, "Besides, don't you have other things to do tonight besides worry about me?"

He sipped some more of his Vodka, did that as his cell phone began to ring again. He looked at the face of the phone, and in an aggravated voice he answered by saying, "What's the use of a vacation if you insist on checking on me?"

I knew who the caller was. It was Snow being Snow, calling to make sure her husband would be in the cemetery tonight.

I put down the broomstick and looked back at the kitchen clock.

Two hours.

Two hours before I did the unthinkable. Two hours before his final destination.

21

Ten o'clock came. Ten o'clock stayed. Ten o'clock locked my thoughts in a box, until 10:01 came with the combination.

Watching Snow's mansion from the house next door, I sat in the designated spot where she told me to be. Black Land Rover. Windows all tinted. I waited for the king to exit his castle, dressed in all black to fit the occasion.

The suburbs were quiet. Silent as air. Any sound of a car passing or a door closing was double the normal volume, paranoia had me turning my head every ten seconds to see if someone was scoping me out, my scalp being corn-rolled with fear.

I've been waiting in this truck for almost an hour, waiting long enough to see some company pull into Mr. Marcello's garage. I didn't get a good look at the company, but from this angle it appeared to be a bodyguard, probably setting up on a late-night post.

Minutes going by, I looked at the time. 10:05. 10:08. Then 10:13. At 10:18 I caught waves of suspicion, wondering why Mr. Marcello hadn't left the mansion. The bedroom light was still shining brightly. Shutters were open. Television flashed rainbows against the window, yet there was still no visual of my target.

But then I heard Macho barking out back.

And that told me his location.

Two minutes later the garage door opened with shiny headlights ushering out a tan Mercedes. I saw my target through the car of that Mercedes, but his head never turned, just kept looking forward while leaving his driveway, left his mansion without a worry in the world.

I immediately got focused. Sat up straight. Turned on my low beams and adjusted my mirrors before following him out of the suburbs, rode slowly with a pistol riding shotgun in the passenger seat.

The silent kill was on.

And so was my kill switch.

The cemetery was supposed to be twenty five minutes away. I gave my target some distance so I wouldn't look obvious, kept my Land Rover two car links behind his Mercedes as a Ford Taurus and a Grand Prix sandwiched their way in between us.

A slow left on 32nd Avenue, a right on Sax, and another right on Woodford, we drove pass all the fancy houses that Vegas had to offer, took ten minutes to leave planet rich and reach city limits, then another five minutes to veer onto the freeway.

Sitting high in this Land Rover allowed me to see far in front on this five lane highway. On the side we were driving there were very few cars exiting the city, yet traffic was bumper-to-bumper on the opposite side of the highway, a clear indication that everyone was rushing to a city where nobody left.

I ignored the scenery and stayed behind my target, trying to stay focused. Following death was nothing like following a cheating boyfriend. Unlike the thrill involved in that hunt, this here required more strategy and a lot more thinking. There's no anger involved. No constant cursing. No biting your lips at the preconception of how you'll react when you catch them butt naked. No anticipation. No ranting at yourself to lower your blood pressure. But even with all that, right now I'll prefer the cheating boyfriend any day.

I picked up my untraceable phone and decided to call up Cuqui. At this point I needed something to sidetrack me from thinking too much, also wanted her to know my location.

But Cuqui never answered, probably somewhere on her back doing ghetto palates.

Next I turned on the radio to search for good music, another approach to calm my nerves. On 86 FM they were playing a throwback, Guns and Roses, and on Blazin 106.3 Betty Wright was telling the world how she was through playing the Clean Up Woman.

Both songs worsened this drive.

I switched up to Reggae. Heard Bob Marley confessing of how he shot the sheriff. And that's when I turned the radio off completely. I had to do this alone.

No music.

No telephone.

No calling on Cuqui to keep me focused.

I trailed one car link behind Mr. Marcello in the HOV lane on the highway. Trailed behind a man going 60 slow miles in a 70 mile zone, a felony in the eyes of impatient drivers. Vegas night riders simultaneously flashed their bright lights for him to choose a different lane, but that didn't seem to faze him one bit. Just like his wife he drives as if the road is his monopoly board, like this route was designed for him and him only. Cars soon got fed up and decided to go around, making me switch lanes from driving directly behind my target to veering one lane over. Then two lanes over. But I quickly switched back once a semi truck tried to cut off my vision, and if that wasn't enough to get in the way then a Cadillac Escalade was, two Mexican men, both rolling down the windows to speak a language I'd never comprehend in this lifetime.

One flashed his tongue.

I understood that.

I flashed the middle finger.

He understood back.

I sped pass them to indicate how much I wasn't interested, then I slowed back down after passing Mr. Marcello, remained behind a jeep for the next five miles.

At 10:37 Mr. Marcello departed onto Exit 203. I broke my speed as we came to a red light, was hard as hell to keep my distance and remain discreet. We passed a few plazas on the left hand side. Outback Steakhouse. Big Lots. Glamorous Nails. Save-a-lot. And a Dollar Tree. On a road that had a dozen flashing traffic lights, it seemed like the road got longer and longer, maybe because I was driving five miles slower than he was. Almost lost him. Eventually did. I stayed on that road that got darker by the second. Traffic lights to streetlights. Streetlights to no lights. No lights to turning on my brights while thinking where the hell is a damn flash light, drove through thick fog, almost turned around until Woodlawn Cemetery decided to show its dark face, a graveyard hiding behind the great wall of China.

Once entering the gates of the silent cemetery I looked around for a tan Mercedes. Five miles per hour was the speed I was going, but

Running From Redemption   193

inside this darkness it felt like fifty. I love-tapped the gas pedal, eased up the hill, then headed onto a long unsteady road that wheeled me through death, death listening to crickets that sung from tall fragile oak trees.

That road through the graveyard was a road to remember. There were twists and turns with jerks and bumps. First rocky. Then smooth. Then rocky and smooth. Then dirt that chalked its own passageway of what it perceived as a road, I drove past graves that were older than the earth, no place for a girl to come mourning at night.

Then brake lights.

I saw them.

The mouse in the Mercedes was found by the cat, saw Mr. Marcello twenty yards ahead. He started backing up. I backed up too. I rolled back ten feet before coming to a complete stop. Waited for him to exit. Waited while I let down the windows and listened to oak trees singing in the night.

Mr. Marcello turned on his flashing lights and stepped out his car with the engine still humming, roses in his hand, roses for the dead. I watched him walk through the cemetery with a tailored suit that was dark as a closed coffin. Watched the night camouflage that suit as he found his father's grave, looked like a man that had found Jerusalem.

Turning off my engine, I stepped out the truck in my long black trench coat with a cap sitting low to cover my eyes. Gun at my waist. Keys in my coat pocket. Lips painted bloody red like the reaper with breasts, it was time to dispose of the garbage.

Only able to see him from behind, Mr. Marcello was about fifteen tombstones northeast of my truck. I acted as if I was here to pay my respects, did that by reaching down to snatch up the first group of flowers that laid on a grave, then I slowly moved towards my target, the .45 engaged, but the kicking of a branch triggered him to turn his head quickly.

I stopped in my tracks.

Looked down at a grave.

Pretended I was a loved one of Mary Cordell.

1934-1996.
Gone But Never Forgotten.
We Miss You Dearly.

Stolen flowers dropped from my hands and fell on that grave – and with my head down, I pretended to be praying. Seconds went by before I glanced back up at Mr. Marcello; he'd fallen for my act.

His back now turned, I watched him take one of his red roses and place it on top of his father's grave. He repeated that motion by dropping another rose. Then another. Dropped rose after rose until he dropped to his knees with pants covered in red, and he stretched out his arms while shouting to the skies, "Why father why??? Why father why???" Arms wrapped around the headstone with bodybuilder strength. "Answer me! Why'd you leave me???

His father never answered. But thunder did. Thunder answered with a light drizzle from the skies that quickly turned into a shower.

As rain began to soak into the pockets of my trench coat, I raised my .45 from twenty feet back, had enough power in this gun to put him in a grave so deep where earth worms wouldn't find him. I aimed at the back of Mr. Marcello's head. Almost pulled the trigger. But then he rose to his feet and continued to shout for his father, screamed at the heavens that brought down hell. I readjusted my aim, tried to get a better shot at my target that started moving around in a frenzy, his anger rising with the storm. I aimed carefully. Had a shot at the grizzly. Didn't take it. Wanted a better shot. Never got it. All I got was a fresh view of lightening while thunder resounded in the background. I stood there and waited for Mr. Marcello to become stationary, waited for a good twenty seconds that seemed like eternity. Eternity eventually came after my target kissed his father's headstone and stood up straight, then he stayed in that death stance for a couple more seconds, candyland for a trained assassin.

With wet fingers trembling on the trigger, I realized right then that I wasn't that assassin.

I was just plain ol' Angel Inghram, an ordinary woman that was dealt a bad hand, forced to take a life by trying to save another. It was right then that I realized how much I couldn't live up to my end of the bargain. Not in this graveyard. Not in this thunderstorm. Not with a man hovering over his deceased father, weeping for the dead to come back to life.

With the rainstorm getting louder, I counted my losses by placing the .45 back into the pocket of my trench coat.

Then a gunshot fired.

I fidgeted. That one shot hit the back of Mr. Marcello, a shot that never came from my gun.

Pop. Pop. Pop.
More gunshots.

Not believing my eyes, I watched Mr. Marcello fall to a slow-motioned death and land on top of his father's head stone, a corpse falling on top of another corpse.

Shockwaves of horror sprinted up my spine as I spun 360 to look for a shooter. I didn't see a soul. Only saw darkness. But I did hear footsteps running through the storm. Heard a car door slam. An engine cranked up.

Ears turned my head to that desolated sound that came from a big-wheeled truck. Not knowing or seeing who the intruder was, I raised my .45 at the ghost in the truck. Headlights flashed. Then bright lights flashed. The person blinded me before I could get off a good shot, but I shot anyway. Took out their front window. Thought I had wounded that ghost until the engine revved the sound of a howling wolf, and with that engine the tires began screeching in the mud, a car that immediately came speeding right towards my hundred pound frame.

My mind went blank. Eyes never blinked. I froze where I stood at death coming on wheels, became that deer now staring at headlights. If that deer had any human instincts it would break its stare to live another day. I dove to the ground, landed face-first into the arms of Mama Earth while the gun left my hands and fell into darkness, heard the truck slam into a loved one's headstone. I rose to my feet, rain pouring down, thunder roaring like a lion as I wiped my eyes all covered in mud. I looked for my gun. Couldn't find it. Glanced up and saw the truck making a U-turn in the land of the dead, a person on a mission to keep me in this graveyard without ever leaving alive.

The truck revved its engine. Started toying with me. Then it came flying at me like the headless horsemen, the23rd Psalm now playing in my head.

But in this valley of death it was no time to walk.

I needed to run. Was running in my head. Then shit hit the fan and I was running for real.

Running away from Goodyear tires that wanted their marks all over my pretty face, I jumped out the way for the second time and somersaulted towards a watery grave, only this time I landed on my gun that was trapped inside a muddied reef. I picked up my weapon and shot at the truck, took out the entire back window. Shot again. Told myself that whoever was inside the truck had better been prepared for a bitch like me, but that tough talk ceased once shots were fired back in my direction. Not normal shots. But machine-like bullets. Seemed like those bullets were coming faster than the rain that poured.

In the midst of Casper shooting back I jumped-roped with death by running to my truck, ran past tombstones, zipped through trees, shoes covered in muck from the dominating storm, my trench coat feeling like eighty pounds as I reached for the keys that swam in my coat, opened the door, cranked the truck, slammed on the gas to get the hell out of Hell.

And Hell was right behind me with lights shining bright.

In that pitch black cemetery, the big wheeled truck was coming after my miniature SUV, Tom chasing Jerry down that muddy path of horror. 45 mph was the speed I was going. I tried to go faster. But on this slippery dirt road - with the darkness and the rain pouring down – 45 mph was considered lightning bolt speed.

Out of nowhere the ghost rear-ended my bumper. Made me jerk forward, nearly bumped my head against the steering wheel and lost control. Another strike against my bumper. I hit the gas hard. Looked in my mirror. King Kong was literally trying to swallow my Land Rover, and if he didn't kill me, darkness surely would.

I did a few zigzags to try and throw off the hunter, swung right, then left, swung the wheel so much that I accidentally left that dirt road and started riding over graves, drove over the dead with Casper on my tail. I couldn't see a thing. Yet I felt everything. Felt rocks. Then bumps. Felt my tires go haywire from tearing down headstones. Vision pitch black. Windows fogged from the rain. Thunder was screwing the brains out of lightening while dropping babies from the skies, windshield wipers popping pills to keep up with the daunting storm.

Then pop-pop-pop-pop-pop.

Not only was the ghost still behind me, but it was now shooting at my truck. Shooting endlessly. I wanted to shoot back. But inside this darkness I couldn't afford to take hands off the steering wheel for one second. I tried to stay focused, kept swerving down Lucifer's Ave. Tires skidding through the mud as bullets came flying. I threw a hard right. Then another left. Almost ran into a tree from being so petrified, and the same tree I dodged was the same tree that Casper crashed into.

I glanced into the rear view. No longer saw headlights.

The front of that big-wheeled truck was now folded like a sandwich against the large tree, its wheels spinning incessantly while going nowhere, tree branches collapsing on top of the dented hood.

Seeing that I had slayed the hidden dragon, from that point on I never looked back. I stomped the gas pedal, almost popped-a-wheelie in the mud as I eventually found the dirt trail that led me out of Satan's den, my life spared from sudden death.

   Pulse-pounding, soaking wet, I fastened my seat belt and headed for the highway.

22

Five minutes later I was back on the highway, driving at the speed of sound.

I looked back in the rear view mirror, driver-side mirror, passenger-side mirror, was looking in three directions at once for a muddied up big-wheel truck. Never saw one. Kept telling myself that Casper was still on my bumper, although I know its fate was left spinning behind a tree in that graveyard.

The rain had packed its things and left this part of the world, although the highway was still wet, and so was my clothes.

With both hands hugging the steering wheel, my cell phone began to ring. It was Snow.

I answered the phone with a mouthful of rage. "Tell me right now what the fuck is going on? Why am I getting shot at?"

"You get my husband dead?"

"I thought we had a deal you backstabbing bitch?"

She calmly repeated, "You get my husband dead?"

"Oh he's dead alright. But not from my bullet—"

My voice began to fade in and out. Another caller was beeping in on her end. She paused to see who it was, never answered the beep, and what was a calm voice quickly went to her shouting, "Are you trying to run some kind of game on me, Angel???"

"Game? What do you mean game—"

"Thought you said my husband was dead!"

"He is!"

"Then why is he calling my cell right now?"

"Impossible! That's impossible!"

Her phone beeped again. Again she didn't click over.

"Don't screw wit' me, Angel! You were supposed to do a job for me. An assassination."

"For the third time, your husband is dead! Past dead! I saw 'im take four bullets with my own eyes."

"Did you check to be sure?"

"Are you insane? I was too busy trying to save myself. What part don't you understand that I was being shot at?"

"What?"

Her phone beeped again. This time she put me on hold to answer the beep. I carelessly switched lanes at a high rate of speed, cut off a Buick, slowed down to eighty, kept looking in my mirrors for a suspicious car that might've been trailing me. At this point, anyone could've been allies with the ghost I had dodged.

Snow clicked back over, told me, "I can't believe this. I send a little girl to do a grown woman's job, and this is what happens."

"What are you talkin' 'bout?"

"That wasn't my husband you followed to the graveyard, Angel. It was my husband's brother."

"Sergio?"

"Yes. My husband has a white Mercedes. Not tan. And he's still at home right now. Never even left the freakin' house."

"And does he know?"

"About what just happened?"

"About our plot?"

"My husband knows nothing. And that's how I want it to stay."

"But—"

"You said someone was shooting at you. Could you be more specific?"

I told her about what happened in the graveyard, about how Casper showed up in a blue suburban with a camouflaged appearance and a license plate number that I only saw a portion of, told her how that ghost tried to interfere with my job and put me in the same burial ground where Mr. Marcello's brother was left. Never told her that I refused to pull the trigger. That wasn't for her to know.

Her reaction was, "Did you say a blue Suburban?

"Could've been blue or black. Hard to tell."
"License plate number begins with SJK?"
"Uh huh."
"Now we're getting somewhere. Gimmie a sec'." She checked the rolodex on her end, whatever microcomputer that cops use to track one car from the next. Her search engine reported a total of four cars that shared that SJK prefix, one of them making her say, "There you are. Here's our shooter right there."
"Who?"
"The license plate came back with the last name of Wilmer. Wilmer is someone affiliated with the Columbians."
"Meaning?"
"Remember that call my husband got in the airport, about how one of the Columbian brothers was murdered last week?"
"Uh huh."
"Remember me telling you about the war that the Columbians and the Dominicans have been carrying on for years?"
"Yeah."
"Well it turns out that in their world, two wrongs do actually make a right."
"So they thought Mr. Marcello had something to do with the death of Benito's brother?"
"Exactly. And instead of coming for my husband, they decided to take out Sergio instead. A brother for a brother."
I took myself back to the graveyard. Back to the Suburban. Back to the ghost that was so eager to steal my breaths.
I told her, "But what does this drug war have to do with them trying to kill me?"
"Nothing that I can think of. Seems like you just so happened to be in the wrong place at the wrong time. And knowing the Columbians, they don't like to leave behind any witnesses."
"Are you telling me that the Columbians are now after me? Is that what you're saying?"
"Unfortunately yes."
I swallowed hard, snatched off my wig, checked my mirrors once more. No ghost in the rear view, at least not yet.
Snow went on, "Whoever was in that graveyard, did they get a good look at your face?"
"I don't know. I told you it was pitch black. But then again, they did catch me in their bright lights."
"Why weren't you wearing a mask?"

"A mask for what? How was I supposed to know that someone else would be at the cemetery?"

She blew out an aggravating breath into the phone, said, "Alright alright, what's done is done. The important thing now is to get you back in doors. How far are you away from the house?"

"Your house? You must be out of your mind. Your house is a death trap. I'd rather take my chances at a hotel."

"My house is the safest place for you to be right now, especially with my husband's bodyguards there. Anywhere else the Columbians will surely find you, then kill you, and I can't afford to have you dead right now, not with us having this unfinished business."

"Unfinished business? An innocent man, your step brother, has been killed for no reason and you're talking about unfinished business? This has gone way too far, Snow. The bus stops right here. Right now."

"The bus fucking stops when my husband is dead!" she yelled. "So what if an innocent man died? Deal with it, Angel! People die every day, and I don't care about Sergio or how much heartbreak it will bring my husband. All I care about is the agreement that you and I made, and that agreement is still incomplete. Now if I were you I'd drop the sensitive role, remember our deal, because if you forfeit the deal you forfeit Devilla's life."

I huffed, puffed, could've blown down a piggy's house with the rage I possessed, the phone in one hand, the other hand gripping the steering wheel as if it was Snow's neck. I knew that going to Snow's house wasn't the best choice, but with her playing the Devilla card, it was my only choice. Sometimes the safest place to be is in the arms of the enemy. The Columbians wanted my head. Cops wanted me dead. No matter where I went I was considered a marked woman, that resume getting longer and longer with every mile I drove.

The only thing that gave me any hope was little Devilla.

As long as she was alive, this war was worth living. With that optimism swirling through my membrane, I told Snow, "So what happens now? Is there a plan B for your husband? Because I was thinking we—"

"Let me do the thinking okay. Now are you still on the interstate?"

"Just got off, now coming up on 4th and Woodward."

"Perfect. I want you to make a right on Woodward. There's a small brick warehouse a couple streets up. Should be on the corner of 7th and McGriff. In the back of that warehouse is an alley. I want you to leave the truck there."

"And do what?"

"In the trunk is a box of matches and a can of gasoline."

"You're gonna burn the truck?"

"It's the only way. Can't take any chances with evidence that may lead back to me. Now did you bring an extra set of clothes like I told you?"

"Yeah."

"After changing clothes, I want you to burn the truck and leave everything inside, including the gun."

"Bullshit. The gun stays with me."

"Bad idea. Did you see the bullet that killed Sergio? What if it came from a .45? The same .45 you're carrying. That one mistake can come back to bite me in the ass."

"Like I said, the gun stays. I refuse to be on the news tomorrow from not being armed tonight."

She gave it some thought, then told me, "Fine, Angel. Keep the gun. But I want that truck to be nothing more than ashes by the time I get back to Vegas."

"Which will be?"

"Three days from now, giving me ample time to come up with another plan."

"Wait a second. How do you expect me to get back to your house after I burn the truck?"

"Be for real, Angel. With boobs like yours in a city like Vegas, I'm sure you'll come up with something."

Parked in the darkness of that dark alley, I wasted no time changing clothes, stripped off my wet clothes and slid into a tight pink dress with oxford style heels, one would've never thought I'd been in the fight of my life with the devil himself. I also had a spare wig in the bag. A short china-doll doo with pink highlights, it went over my soaking wet mane that stuck out the sides, tried my hardest to pack it under the wig to make it look presentable.

Snow wanted me to burn the Land Rover and everything inside.

I got out the truck. Looked down the dark alley with a strong vigilance, making sure the coast was clear.

After grabbing my .45 from the pocket of my wet trench coat, I shut the driver-side door and popped open the trunk. Matches were there. Gasoline was there.

But to my surprise, something else was there too.

On the floor in the backseat were the negatives of pictures from a throw-away camera, negatives that were all rolled up with no purpose. I instantly froze. Stared at the unknown. Heard that rational voice telling me to mind my business while the inquisitive voice was singing a different tune. I decided to reach for the unknown, and what I saw was a picture of Snow's face on every negative photo, saw her exchanging cocaine for money. Her and two other cops. Three of FBI's finest were caught on candid camera with their hands in the cookie jar, each unaware of paparazzi lingering in the shadows.

I thought back in time.

Back to the night that Snow infiltrated Shady Pines Apartments causing an uproar in the neighborhood. It was that night that Snow received a disguised package, a manila envelope exchanged for two hollow points that snatched the lives of two men.

I often wondered why she shot those men, and now it was right here in front of me, the clues spread inside this truck like a game of scrabble, waiting for me to piece the puzzle together.

Snow killed those men because they possessed incriminating evidence. These pictures. She knew if these photos were ever leaked, her fate would be nothing more than a prison cell, causing her whole life to go plummeting down the drain.

And that made me smile hard. Smiled at how a woman so careful, a woman that usually watches her every step, can carelessly allow something so vital to drop from her pocket and into my possession. Well she might be the detective, but no matter the cleanness of the cat, eventually they all leave behind a ball of fur, and with this fur in my possession I was finally considered a triple treat in her little world of blackmail. I could now play hardball.

I stuffed the evidence deep down in my purse and got back to the matches, then I backed ten steps away from the truck while pouring a trail of gasoline from the tires to the tip of my high heels.

I looked around again.

Coast was still clear.

One flick of a match ignited a small spark, and one drop of a match ignited a fire. I stood there to watch fire work its magic, watched it run towards the truck while lightening the alley, a view that sent me walking away.

Then an explosion.

I turned my back. Saw that SUV shoot up twenty feet in the sky, and it dropped back down like a meteor hitting earth. Knowing that a fleet of ambulances would be flying towards this alley in twenty minutes tops, I turned around, heightened my pace, and I left that alley the same way I entered.

23

Back at Snow's house, I was crawling out the backseat of a yellow cab. No money for the cabbie. But money wasn't an issue after the Turkish driver caught a glimpse of my tight pink dress that was riding up my thighs, a dress tight enough to be granted a free ride.

Or so I thought it was free.

After getting out the car, he asked for my phone number to replace the money, a proposition that came with a tour of Vegas if he could tour through my body. I gave him seven fake digits and sent him on his way. He drove into the night with a hustler's smile.

At the doors of Snow's mansion were two of Mr. Marcello's oversized bodyguards, thick and thicker controlling his property as if it were their own. The thicker one stopped me before I ever reached the gate. "Hold it right there. You here for somebody?"

"I live here."

"Since when?"

I reached in my purse and showed him a key. To him that meant nothing.

"Wait right here." he said.

His M&M physique strutted back up to the front porch where he told the other thick one to alert Mr. Marcello. After receiving confirmation from the king, the gates of the castle opened for my passing.

I timidly entered, went into the house.

Just as Snow mentioned, her husband had never left the house. Royalty was laid across the couch in his royal pajamas, a glass of wine in one hand, a remote control in the other, a man oblivious of what happened to his brother while the television displayed an old western movie.

Feeling like a teenager that was home past curfew, I headed for the stairway with a knot in my throat, my 4 inch heels click-clacking on the hard tile floor. Those annoying heels caught the attention of Mr. Marcello.

"So did you have a good time?" he shouted out.

I turned around. "Huh?"

"On your date? Did you have a good time?"

"Oh ... Oh yeah ... everything went great."

"Humph, doesn't seem like it, Senorita. You're home so soon."

"Well regardless of what you might've perceived of me, I still have my boundaries. And no sex on the first date is one of 'em."

He sat up straight on the couch, placed his glass of wine on the glass table and looked into my eyes. Even in the darkness of that living room those green eyes were radiant. More than just eyes. They were a reflection of what I witnessed in that graveyard, re-incarnation of the dead staring me down through the body of Mr. Marcello.

He told me, "Not trying to prowl, but where did he take you?"

"That sounds like prowling."

He smiles. "Okay then ... will there at least be a second date? For Christ's sake Senorita, give me somethin'."

I walked over to the couch with a slow silky stroll, picked up his glass and took in a sip.

I told him, "If you're asking me how he matches up with you, there's no comparison okay." That comment flooded his fifty-year old ego.

I asked him, "Anything else, because I'm feeling a bit restless?"

He smiled again and told me goodnight.

Following his interview I rushed upstairs to take myself a long hot anticipated shower. Scrubbing myself of any blood or dirt that might've hid in the pores of my skin, I replayed that graveyard scene over and over, and with each replaying episode I felt dirtier and dirtier, all the dirt possibly springing from guilt.

Twenty minutes into my shower I heard loud knocking below me, the sound of someone banging on the front doors of the mansion.

That shook me up.

A towel wrapped around me, I walked into the guestroom, half wet, my eyes going to the bedroom window where rainbow lights were shining through the blinds. I panicked at the sight of the detectives. Stopped moving upstairs. Heard voices downstairs, voices sending chills up my spine while causing the towel to fall to the floor.

Ten seconds later the voices were interrupted by a man screaming the loudest scream I ever heard in my life.

That traumatizing scream was the sound of a man who'd just been told his brother was dead.

24

5am.

While the earth suited up for today's race of time, my body was still running yesterday's hurdle. Once Mr. Marcello received the news about Sergio he hopped in the car and trailed behind his detectives to do what every loved one dread the thought of doing; he identified the body of his brother.

The front door of this haunted mansion was opening and closing the entire night. It kept me wide awake. Kept me hugging my .45 like a teddy bear in darkness.

I threw in the sleep towel and rose from the bed, noticed that my cell phone was carrying a text message from Cuqui.

Call me back. I finally received Snow's background check.

I called her back ASAP.
She picked up on the first ring.
I said, "What you got for me?"
"You're just calling me back at 5am! Where the hell you been?"
"Tell you later, it's complicated."
"Well did you at least follow through on the plan?"
"I couldn't."

"Why not? What happened?"

"Long story, Cuqui. Just tell me what you got for me."

She gave me the rundown on Snow's background check. Birthed as Snow Jenkins, for the last seven years she worked as a cop, and before that she worked as a correctional officer. A year done in Houston. Three years in Cleveland. Another four done in upstate New York. I inquired about the criminal part of her background report. According to Cuqui she was clean as a cat. Just one trespassing charge in the fall of 96. Misdemeanor crap, nothing serious.

Meanwhile I updated Cuqui on last night's episode. I gave her the watered down version. Never told her about the Columbians that wanted my head on a silver platter; that would've freaked her out big time.

When I told her to stay in doors for the sake of her protection, she answered with, "Oh now you wanna protect me? Should've thought about that before you dragged me up here. Now tell me what the hell is going on?"

"Just stay inside okay." I switched back to Snow's background report, asked her, "You find anything else?"

"Nope ... Wait. Actually, there is one more thing."

"I'm listening."

"Looks like your psycho detective has a phenomenal track record when it comes to narcotic investigations. In her short two years she took down some heavyweight drug cartels, managed to seize more than ten million dollars of cocaine."

"Well from knowing her husband, that doesn't shock me one bit."

"Maybe that won't, but this surely will. In that two year span she has also made over 200 arrests, which averages out to about two arrests per week. However, within the past two weeks she made no arrests whatsoever."

"Okay, so she didn't have to cuff anyone recently. Big deal. That doesn't mean anything—"

"Hold on. There's more ... Along with making no recent arrests, she also hasn't written any tickets. No cases have been assigned. No paperwork. No doughnuts. It seems she's been nonexistent in the cop world for the last two weeks."

"Wow. That's strange. But then again, two weeks is the length of time I've been in her possession."

"I know right."

"All of this showed up in the background report?"

"Actually no. I went down to the police station to request information about a domestic violence situation. But once I got down there - once I caught an employee staring at the jeans on this killer booty - general information turned into me prying for information on your favorite detective."

"One pair of jeans and you got all that. I don't understand."

"It's an ass thing, Angel. You'll never understand."

I pieced this information together with the rest of Snow's puzzle, questions swarmed around my brain like killer bees. No detective work for two full weeks. It made no sense, not unless she recently became unemployed.

Cuqui said, "I'll get back with you as soon as I find the answer to that riddle. In the meantime, I'm fixin' to go downstairs to the—"

"Cuqui."

"What?"

"Remember what I said. No leaving your hotel until this whole thing is finished. It's not safe."

"Yeah, yeah, yeah. Whatever you say."

She hung up.

I left the guestroom to go on a bare-footed trip to the kitchen for a glass of water, and with walking downstairs I ran into Mr. Marcello, saw him sitting on the same living room couch that I left him on last night. This time there was no remote in his hand, no television playing, and instead of watching old western flicks, he was staring into the flames of the fireplace. I couldn't see his eyes. Only saw his back.

I paused on the stairway to try and be quiet, told myself that at this juncture I could do without the glass of water, and rather than disturb him I slowly tried to turn around before he sensed my presence.

"Angel. Is that you?"

I stopped in my tracks, staring at the finish line of that stairway.

"Won't you come join me."

Wanted to ignore him, but that would've been rude, so I slowly turned around, cursed in my head, then motioned down the stairway to face him head on.

"Didn't want to disturb you," I told him. "I was just coming downstairs to get a drink."

No response.

He sat there like a lifeless man torn to pieces, eyes bloodshot red as he stared into the fireplace, his pupils mirroring the flames.

Never turning his stare, he said, "You know something Angel ... when we were kids ... about eight years old ... Sergio always wanted a fireplace ... it wasn't until we were 14, when papa first moved us to the states did we get a fireplace ... Seemed like yesterday you know ... Even when we became men, when I would come to my brother's house, he'd always be staring into his fireplace ... When I'd ask why he'd reply ... 'Sometimes you have to look into the past to appreciate the present' ... Unlike my brother I always felt different ... Never wanted to look into the past, always kept my eyes on the future." Those bloodshot eyes shifted to me, stayed there for a moment, then went back to the fireplace. In a crackly melancholy voice he said, "Well look at me now, Senorita. Look at ... me now ... appreciating ... the past."

Not knowing what to say, I stood in front of him like a book without words. Not even Webster could describe his disposition. His hair was sticking straight up in the air. Cheeks were past oily. Every wrinkle ever hidden was now visible. It's now that I see how old he really is, now that sorrow is beating down his door to steal the boyish glow.

After finding the right words, I told him the only appropriate thing to fit the situation. "I'm sorry about your brother, Mr. Marcello. I'm truly truly sorry."

He nodded at my condolence. Never commented. But somehow that nod was good enough for me. It let me know that in his eyes I wasn't his enemy.

But somebody was. The liquor and the gun on the living room table told me that somebody was.

His choice of a drink was a half empty bottle of expensive Vodka, no chaser, and lying next to the liquor bottle was a .44 magnum. Just the sight of it made me want to end whatever conversation he was trying to get started, made me tell him, "Well I'ma head back upstairs and—"

"Have a drink, Angel."

"I would but—"

"My brother just died. My wife's not here. The least you can do is join me for a drink."

Having alcohol at 5am. Before breakfast. Before roosters are singing their alma mater. Drinking right now was not a good idea. But then I looked at the gun on the living room table and that was enough to reconsider.

Grabbing myself a glass, I became Mr. Marcello's shoulder to lean on by doing something I haven't done in months, something I promised I'd stay away from because of what it does to my alter ego.

I sipped white liquor, joined him in the moment.

Mr. Marcello broke down and told me how he felt about last night, told me that the bullet that killed his brother was meant for him instead, that he should've did more to keep his brother alive.

When I told him he wasn't to blame for Sergio's death, he lashed out at me, "It was my job to protect him. My job and my job only. I promised my father before he died three years ago that I'd protect my little brother, promised my life ... See what you don't know is that my brother never wanted to be a part of the business. It was me that brought 'im in. He did this for me."

I kept my mouth shut. Didn't want to stick another foot in that mouth of mine.

He went on, "I knew something wasn't right, Angel. I felt it the moment he came over last night. Felt it so much that I refused to visit my papa's grave site, a ritual I haven't missed in three years. I tried to keep my brother from going there too. Told 'im not without bodyguards. But he insisted on going instead, told me that nothing would keep him from visiting his father. And you know what ... Like a fool I let 'im go ... I let 'im get killed just like that ... My little brother ... Only brother ... A bullet intended for me."

In the midst of his confession - in the midst of our drinking - a knock appeared on the living room door.

After Mr. Marcello gave permission to enter, through those doors came one of his bodyguards, the thicker one that held me at the gate last night.

"Hey boss, we just got word on where Benito will be today."

"I'm listening."

"His daughter is having a wedding rehearsal at 4pm, and it looks like he's gonna make an appearance. So tell us boss, what is it you want us to do?"

All liquored up, Mr. Marcello answered, "Nothing ... Nothing yet ... We wait."

Peanut M&M looked surprise at that answer. "Wait? Are you sure boss?"

"I'm sure."

"If I may ask, how come?"

"Do I look like the type of rat that go 'round shooting up weddings? Huh??? Do I???"

The condescending tone in Mr. Marcello's voice had silenced the intruder, no words detesting the order of Scarface.

Running From Redemption

"Now listen up and listen up good!" Mr. Marcello demanded. "We wait to avenge my brother's death. Another opportunity will present itself. But as for now, I want you and Reynolds to go home and catch up on some rest."

"Rest? No way boss. If we leave there'd be no one here to watch your back."

The boss picked up his revolver, raised it in the air, an insinuation that it was all the protection he needed.

"No one's gonna come inside this house. I'll be just fine."

"But what if—"

"Don't let me say it again. Now go home to your family, rest up, and I'll call you when I'm ready. Meanwhile, make sure my brother's wife and kids receive full protection."

"Done. And as for your wife in New York?"

"My wife is a detective. She can handle herself."

25

It took two full hours and three-fourths of a bottle of pure Vodka to fade away the thoughts of Mr. Marcello's brother, took three more swallows to change the conversation to something less depressing.

While the sun was steadily rising, I was a little past tipsy, one foot coherent and the other foot dangling in a incoherent universe. Hard to admit it but I missed this taste. Missed the powers it possessed. At a time when I should be most paranoid – a time when I'm wanted for murder, running from murder, and had witnessed a man who'd just been murdered – I never felt more relaxed in my life, all thanks to the Vodka.

Ten minutes later our conversation went from the living room couch to the kitchen, was now sitting at the table with the bottle of Vodka between us. The alcohol had Mr. Marcello talking in circles, first talking about Dominica, then about his father, then about how Snow never cooks, and when she does, it's usually a frozen dish that comes with heating instructions.

I asked him, "So whose idea was it to get a maid?"

"That was Snow's idea. Not mine."

"Really? That's surprising."

"How come?"

"I don't know. I guess you just look like the type of man who needs a maid around."

"Well look again because I'm not that type of man. Hell, I'm still getting accustomed to having a stranger walking around my house, doing my laundry, cooking my food. You know, all the things my wife should be doing." He shakes his head as if he's disgusted with the situation, sips more Vodka, then stares off in space for a brief moment. "You know, that's my only problem with American women."

I straighten up.

He goes on, "American women are lazy ... don't have a clue when it comes to taking care of home ... they're always—"

"Hold it right there," I said, thinking he must've had too much to drink. "Before you come out the mouth about American women, know that you're talking to one. All of us are not the same. The same way all Dominicans don't eat Jambalaya rice."

He laughs. "What? Where did that come from?"

"Just stating the obvious."

"Okay. So you wanna make it racial ... Okay then ... what about black people and their fried chicken. Or their kool-aid ... their watermelon ... collard greens and their sweet corn bread ... what about your endless love for pork chops."

"Kiss my ass. At least we have pigs to make pork chops."

"Hold on hold on hold on right there, mommi," he says, raising his tipsy finger. "Do your research 'cause we have pigs too."

"Yeah right. Ain't no pigs running round that little island where you're from, so don't even try to pretend. Y'all gotta take a boat ride to Cuba just to get a pig."

We laugh. Laugh with our alcohol content rising by the minute.

I tell him, "Besides, if you have so much of a problem with Americans, then why do you like black women so much? Why don't you go after the women in your own country?"

"Because the women in my country don't have enough ass."

"What?" I almost choked on my drink from laughing so hard. "So that's it? You only like me because of my booty."

"Just kidding, Senorita. The truth is I like you for many reasons."

"Okay ... I'm waiting patiently."

He sits down his drink, looks me in my eyes, and starts running his fingers around the rim glass of vodka. "I like a strong woman, a woman that doesn't fear. It seems like every woman I meet is intimidated by me in some type of way. Most women can't handle me, or don't have the stomach for what I do. But that's why I married

Snow. She could handle me for the long run, and I haven't seen that trait in another woman ... well, until I met you. I guess being a bloody chica runs in your family."

"Bloody chica?"

"It means ruthless ... A ruthless chica. I knew you were that from our first conversation."

I didn't know if being a bloody chica was a good thing, but at the present moment, that voice of his was as stimulating as the Vodka I was drinking, and although I might have been a little drunk, my mind was very coherent when it came to feeling Mr. Marcello. I was feeling this man. Feeling her man. And after another round of the good stuff, the Vodka told me to come closer to the man I was feeling.

I listened.

Got frisky by placing my hand on his thigh, then started running my fingers up Dicky Lane.

He raises a brow. "Finishing what we started yesterday?"

"Just being a bloody chica." I tightened my grip. "You got a problem with that?"

No answer.

"Didn't think so."

I dropped to my knees. The liquor brought me to my knees.

He looked at me like a helpless child as my aggressiveness caught him off guard, the reaction of a man that's not used to a dominant woman.

Then I pulled down his pants. Gnawed at his briefs. Saw his little man trying to get my attention. I love a man in briefs, no boxers allowed here. A man with boxers is a man unequipped, takes the resilience of briefs to hold back the power of a real hung horse.

Mr. Marcello was a horse.

And I wanted to ride that stallion.

But Before saddling up, I slid off those briefs so his hard-on could breath, a hard-on so erect that it smacked me in the face on impulse.

It's been a while since I came face to face with one of this size, an auburn-colored shaft that had a light fade, not only long but blessed with girth.

I asked him, "Ever received a head cocktail?"

"Huh?"

"Stay there and don't move."

I arose from my knees, grabbed the bottle of Vodka, and I poured some in a glass before kneeling back down.

He jerks back timidly. "What are you doing?"

"Don't move!" I demanded.

I dipped his penis into the cold glass of Vodka. That caused him to tremble. Caused him to look at me with a frightened face, my dominance making him become more erect.

"Don't move," I repeated. "Just relax."

More boyish looks covered his face as I dipped his penis back in the vodka. I licked it clean. Dipped it again. Repeated that cycle while savoring the taste, his penis becoming the perfect chaser to my 80 proof drink that drove him wild, made him squirm, I spoiled that shaft, Angel Inghram style.

After my experimentation was done, I sat aside the empty glass and decided to take him deep into my mouth, took that million-dollar dick to Never Never Land. I sucked him with passion. Passion and punishment. Sucked him as if I was bobbing for an apple that was buried under water. Sucked him like I never sucked a man before, until that schoolboy look encompassed his manly face, because it's now that I own him. And that ownership shows in his eyes as his pupils dilate, a man half-intoxicated and half-violated, his legs stiffening, fingers becoming hard fists, his shaft swelling harder and harder as he grabbed my head and begged for a release.

But I won't give him that release.

Not before intercourse.

Then he mutters, "What's ... what's gotten into you?"

"Should've never gave me white liquor."

I arose to my feet with his penis in my hand, never letting loose of that priceless possession. My insides are wet. Hellafied wet. So wet that I told him with hard breaths, "Want you ... inside of me ... right now."

He grabbed me by the waist and kissed me on the neck. Kissed me, licked me, touched me and sucked me, did everything but fuck me, kept teasing me by throwing rocks at the lions gate.

Then the lion came out of me. "Skip the foreplay. I wanna fuck!"

I pushed him on the kitchen table and climbed on top of him, forcing him to break the seal of this deprived woman.

He enters me.

Enters a woman that hasn't been entered in months, my body tensing up, my insides adjusting to the thickness of his deliverance as I rode him. Rode him right there on that kitchen table. Rode him with slow aggression and a strong desire, my eyes hardening like an empress on a throne as I looked down upon my Dominican Slave.

Inside that kitchen – a place where he eats with his wife – we made our own secret ingredients on that kitchen table. Every time he blesses a meal he'll think of me, and that thought alone made me more excited, more controlling, made me bite my bottom lip as I rode him with vigor.

Then that ride came to a halt.

With his hardness still inside of me, Mr. Marcello raised me from the kitchen table and carried me towards the living room, carried me while duck-walking with his pants at his ankles, duck-walking becoming duck-fucking, and I wrapped my legs around his waist to never stop riding, all while he carried me towards the window that had no curtains, then he propped me against the window seal, my ass against glass, and I held my sweaty lover with all I had, held him harder than Kate Winslet held Leonardo DiCaprico before going face down into the waters of the Atlantic.

"You like that mommi? Tell me you like it."

"I ... I like ... oh ... shit ... oh ... shit ..."

I came out loud against the window pane, came with my legs shaking and lips cursing, and as I dug my nails into his back, he carried me from the window pane to the living room sofa, then he entered my garden missionary style.

I embraced my lover. We embraced each other. Wet bodies merged together as we did the position of ancient lovers, my body becoming no match for his magnificence. I let him dominate me. Allowed him to force my knees up towards my shoulders, causing all my weight to shift on my spine, and as I strained in that ghetto palates position, it turned him on tenfold, caused the light in his eyes to become more aggressive.

He tells me, "Turn over. Want it from the back."

I did as Simon said and got on all fours.

"Lower!" he demands. "Face in the couch!"

The bark in his voice sent chills up my spine, turned me on so much that my insides became a Tsunami. He gripped my hips and began riding the waves of that Tsunami, did me deep doggy-style, did me while I tried to keep my knees steady, but the force of his strokes had me climbing the walls.

He tells me, "Don't move! Move and you get it harder!"

I moved on purpose. Moved so he could give me my punishment, then I told him, "Stop being a wimp and tame this pussy."

"That's what you want?"

"That's what I want!"

He grabbed my hair and gripped the back of my neck, then he slapped on my ass like a pimp does a whore.

I threw it back at him. Threw back my ass to match with his strokes, and eventually we were having World War III on the couch. Lots of slapping. Lots of swearing. Sweat pouring down my forehead and rolling in my eyes. I wiped the sweat from my face, bit my bottom lip, told him to give me every inch of that thing while looking back at my Dominican lover, veins popping out his neck, hell glowing in his eyes, saw his face becoming saturated with sweat as it dripped from his cheeks and landed on my back, us soaking the couch with our lustful liquids.

I moaned in the couch. Locked on the couch. I cursed and cursed and cursed and cursed. Cursed while he dipped that rod to the bottom of my canal, hitting my G spot, making me whine, then hitting the spot below my G spot, the spot that made my cougar stand up and roar.

And I was cumming again.

Us cumming together.

Intensity showed on my face and crawled through each orifice of my body, as this wasn't the type of orgasm that played violins. This orgasm was mean. Downright vicious. It rushed up my back like a tidal wave before rolling back down with raging force, and I screamed a silent scream, the type where your mouth opens up but nothing comes out, hoping the sex gods would hear my distant cry.

With our breathing heavy and our legs burning, we collapsed face-forward on the sweaty couch. Fell to our deaths. Surrendered our souls.

Then numbness again.

Numbness.

Numbness.

Five minutes later, me and Mr. Marcello were lying completely naked on the couch, me on my back, him on his stomach, trying to steadily catch our breaths.

After regaining strength, I opened my eyes and lifted my neck, only to notice a shadow coming from my peripheral vision.

My eyes swung left.

There was a woman standing in the doorway of the living room with wild dreadlocks and a fair-skin complexion. It was Vegas most feared detective, Officer Snow, frozen solid as if she stumbled into the wrong house, her eyes darkening, her crows feet spreading like wings.

"Shit!" I said, jumping upright on the couch.

"What is it?" Mr. Marcello asked.

I point towards the door, but Snow vanishes before Mr. Marcello can turn his stare.

He looks back at me. "Who was that?""

My teeth chatter.

"Who was it? Was that the maid?"

"It was ... It was ..."

His green eyes became dark as cognac. "Was that my wife?"

"Yes."

"You sure?"

"I'm sure goddammit!"

He jumps to his feet and goes after his wife. He runs fast. Runs wild. Runs out the door with his penis bouncing up and down.

26

"I can't believe you were fucking my cousin! In my house! In my goddamn house!"

"Let me explain."

"Explain what? Explain how your face was buried in her pussy? Well go 'head. Explain that."

Their voices could be heard across the street, but they were only in the dining room. Meanwhile, I was pacing in circles through the living room, pacing naked, looking for anything that could be used as a weapon, just in case this crazy bitch tried to get hostile. I searched under the couch. Searched around the T.V. Thought about the gun that Mr. Marcello was carrying by the fireplace, but I couldn't find that either. Then I thought about the .45 I had upstairs. Without second-guessing, I sprinted upstairs to go after my weapon, sprinted butt naked, titties bouncing with angst, nearly slipped on the cold tile floor before making it to home base.

After jumping into some panties and throwing on a robe, I flipped back the mattress to get my hands on the .45, the only friend I had at this moment.

The gun was miniscule enough to fit in the rear of my panties, and that's exactly where I stored it after inserting a clip.

Then I heard footsteps coming up the stairs. Footsteps chasing footsteps. Along with the constant stomping were voices of man and wife. Heard them arguing through the hallway, their voices now pounding through the walls of the guestroom.

"I'm sorry, My Love! I didn't—"

"Don't call me Your Love. Don't you ever call me that again!"

"It's not what it looks like?"

"Not what it looks like! For goodness sake, you're butt naked with a hard dick. Looks like infidelity to me."

"But—"

"But nothing. I don't wanna hear anything else you gotta say. You're a liar and a cheater, just like your damn father ... Fifteen years ... I gave you fifteen years and this is how you repay me, by fucking her on our couch, the couch where you just made love to me last week. Huh? Is this my reward? Answer me goddammit! Answer me..."

As Snow curses out her husband, her shadow moves recklessly around the doorway of the guestroom.

I remained ready.

Ready to bear arms.

Snow continued, "After all I've done for you. I've done things that no other wife would've done. Hid your drugs ... Protected your money ...I've imprisoned people that wanted to wipe you out clean ... People in your own organization ... Your own family ... And this is what I get for it? This bullshit?"

I waited patiently behind the door. Waited alongside an impatient .45 in the small of my back, hidden within my panties.

Snow continued her outrage. "You're nothing but a liar. Our whole marriage has been a lie... Just last night you told me you loved me."

"I do love you."

"What did you say?"

"I said I—" The shadow of a hand is raised in the air and it slaps the face of another shadow.

Snow says, "That's what I think about your love. Keep it!" She sticks her face through the door of the guestroom. "And as for you bitch,"—My fingers tickle the .45— "I want you out my house in the morning!" she yelled.

I didn't respond.

Mr. Marcello steps in, "Leave her out of this. She was only trying to—"

"Be there in a time of need? I know, that's usually how the story goes, so save it you son of a bitch!"

Snow gives her husband the middle finger and storms down the hallway like a mad woman. Mr. Marcello chases behind his wife, footsteps chasing footsteps down the stairs. I breathe hard. Breathed the breath of a dismantled dragon while hearing them argue their way out the house, heard the front door slam.

Then I heard something else.

The sound of a ringtone coming from the bed, saw the sheets light up from the shriek of a cell-phone. The face of that cell phone carried a text message from Cuqui: *Angel, get out the house quick. I've got the answer to Snow's riddle.*

The message had me flabbergasted. Throat got tight. Thoughts went a dozen directions as I took in the present circumstances.

Then I heard a gunshot.

The echo of a 9mm brought me to the bedroom window, and what I saw was Mr. Marcello being forced to his knees, hands in the air, pleading for pity while begging his wife not to shoot.

Another shot fires.

Then another.

The almighty Mr. Marcello hits the ground like a fish on concrete, his blood leaving its mark all over the front patio.

I screamed unintentionally.

Eyes looked up in my direction. Snow had finished off her husband and was now staring me down from outside the window, sneering like a leopard does a zebra in the wild.

She was coming for me, coming to end my life on a day that wasn't meant for dying.

I pulled myself together and shut the blinds. Threw off my robe and jumped into some sweats and a T-shirt.

It was time to run. Either run or be ran down, told myself that I only had seconds to get downstairs without crossing her path, had to maneuver my way to freedom.

At that instance the living room door burst open downstairs. I heard Snow entering the house, sounded like she was pulling something heavy. I glanced back out the window. A trail of blood followed the body of Mr. Marcello from the porch to the front doorstep, saw the lion dragging the corpse into the lion's den, heard the door slam and lock behind her. Next I heard her drag the body through the living room, through the dining room, into the kitchen, and within these thin walls, I heard more clicks of locks, followed by an alarm activation that said, *All exits are now locked and sealed.*

I swallowed hard. She now had me trapped in this chamber of death, my only exit being the windows or the attic.

Then her voice rang out. "You hear that Angel? That means you're not going anywhere. Now come downstairs so I can put a bullet through that pretty face of yours."

I refused to speak, was smart enough to know that the marking of my voice could cause her to shoot through the roof. No way was I coming to her. Let that bitch come to me.

She repeated her threat. "Come on out, Angel. Come to mama."

I grabbed the .45 and tiptoed towards the guestroom door, then I leaned my back against the wall and waited for her to make a move. Waited with my heart pounding at a rapid pace.

She carried on, "Fine then. You don't wanna come down. I have no problem coming up."

Feet slowly come up the stairs, feet taking a few steps and stopping midway, as if she was baiting me. "Where are you, Angel? Where is that pretty faced little girl? Are you afraid? Huh? I promise I'll be gentle … Just wanna play a little game … Now where are you … Where are you hiding you little bitch!"

Her constant taunting was igniting my temper, causing all the jitters to flow from my body and become replaced with rage. *The hell with this*, I thought. I'm through with the hiding. If this is what she really wants, then I'll give it to her.

With both hands on my death machine, I slowly stuck the gun out the guestroom door and stepped into the hallway, stepped cautiously, saw the head of her shadow around the corner of a curved staircase. The shadow became more vivid. What was a head became a full body that was creeping up the stairway with her frame ducked low, the silhouette of her dreadlocks moving like a predator.

"There you are," she said.

Her gun fires a bullet through the foyer, hitting the opposite wall of where I was standing. I locked my elbows and held my weapon against my chest, straightened up. She shoots again in the hallway and misses horribly, yet she blows off the head of her Marilyn Monroe painting.

She laughs, "I can do this all day, Angel! Lots of bullets inside this gun!"

"Well learn how to use 'em!" I hollered back.

This was her house. Her house meant her advantage, but when it came to the art of war she had no strategy. No patience. Just a wild woman overly-anxious to take me out.

Eventually a head peeked around the corner of the hallway, and that was my queue to take a shot at my enemy.

I aimed for her head. Barely missed. She ducked as I blew wood off the rail of the staircase, making her retreat back down the stairs.

I smiled as she backed away. Smiled as wood particles floated in the air.

"What's up now???" I yelled from upstairs. "Who's backing down now?"

"We'll see who walks out alive!" she replied.

I motioned through the hallway to start coming for the enemy. Fingers on the trigger. Senses on alert. I tiptoed down the stairs with my gun leading the way, eyes hunting for the deer downstairs.

What she didn't know is that she wasn't the only one who was trained to use a firearm. I've got medals to backup my tactical shooting. Medals from the shooting academy. Medals to prove that I'm not your average woman with a gun.

Midway down the stairs I saw Snow hiding under the stairway. I turned my shoulder to aim my weapon, but not before bullets came flying in my direction to try and claim my life. I floored down the stairs with gazelle speed, shot back at her blindly, heard bullets tearing through walls as I ran for cover, rounds from a 9mm chasing my tail. I ran into the living room and hid behind the love seat, got down low, then waited until I was able to regroup.

Thinking the coast was clear, I raised my head and glanced around the living room. No Snow in sight. All I saw was dismantled furniture and holes in the walls, the intermission to war.

Then I heard sounds. Heard steel and lead being merged together. Heard an authentic click.

I knew those sounds from anywhere. Those were the sounds of a reloading gun, the wolf being fed its Salisbury steak.

My eyes swung left to where the enemy stood, couldn't see her directly, but something told me she was kneeling behind the piano which sat in the corner of the living room.

She started to ramble, "What's with the wait, Angel? Let's get this over with so I can put a hole through your pretty brown face."

As she talked, I looked around the living room to determine what could be used during this heat of battle. Above the piano was a large chandelier, not big enough to kill, but heavy enough to cripple any human being. Snow's shadow was hunched beneath the chandelier with her mouth going a mile a minute. I shot at the ceiling to take her down, but she moved before the chandelier fell, and two hundred pounds of crystal dropped on top of the piano playing a fatal symphony. Glass shatters.

Snow ran behind the couch and shot in my direction, bullets ripped through the love seat of where I am hiding. I jumped back a few inches, then I shot back to return fire. We shot at each other, an all-out war, two women ducking and dodging while shooting to the death. No mercy involved. Either kill or be killed. May the baddest bitch win.

She shoots and shoots and shoots.

The love seat is now torn to shreds, and my first instinct is to run behind the Entertainment System where I'm now hiding behind wood.

Shots fired at the stereo and ripped up the VCR. The television explodes. "I'm gonna get you," she yelled. "I'm gonna get you little slut!"

While explosions propelled in my ear, I waited for accuracy as she drilled with quantity, waited for the one shot to end this madness.

The moment I had a good shot the gun went click. Then another click. No bullets remained in my .45, which was now considered suicide. Until I saw a miracle. Behind the entertainment system where I hid, I noticed another gun that was lying beside the torn up VCR. I picked up the gun, a .44 magnum, must've been the gun that I was looking for earlier, the one that Mr. Marcello was holding by the fireplace. I opened the cylinder and noticed six rounds, then closed it back up and looked for Snow.

Snow was still using the sofa as her shield, saw her continuously stick her head out behind the sofa like a bird in a nest. I fired at that woody wood pecker. Barely missed. Tried my best to blow the locks off that high-yellow bitch, then I put three more bullets through the sofa, forcing her to jump from behind the couch, then towards the back of a book shelf, but not before a bullet tears through her right thigh, now touched by the kiss of death.

She squirms like a wounded deer, yet she still attempts to flee.

I go after the wounded. Follow her as she hobbles to the dining room, limping, bleeding, her DNA leading a path for the hunter, the smell of blood heightening my senses like a vampire in thirst.

I walked into the dining room and caught her trying to switch weapons. She was reaching for a shotgun inside a glass door.

Her back is turned.

My gun is raised.

"Stop right there!" I yelled.

She freezes.

"Now drop the shotgun!"

She hesitates, tells me, "You sure you wanna shoot a cop? If you do you won't live to see—"

"Drop the weapon right now!"

She obeys.

"Now turn around!"

"Okay ... Okay ... Just gimme a—"

"Turn around goddammit!"

She faces me slowly, her eyes on my weapon. I force her to kick aside her shotgun, then I aimed my .44 magnum at her forehead and dared her to move; at this point she's nothing more than a eulogy waiting to be cited.

With rage in my eyes, I tell her, "You killed William Randolph didn't you?"

She smiles. "Actually, you killed William Randolph. Remember? New York City? Third floor apartment? Or did you forget?"

"Bullshit! William survived that day!"

"So you've been watching the news?"

"You finished 'im off in the hospital didn't you? Didn't you?"

"Yes! Yes! Yes! I put 'im out of his misery!"

"Why?"

"Why is not important. Just know that he owed me something."

"Owed you what?"

"Nothing that concerns you!"

"Yeah, well will see how much it concerns me when the cops get a hold of these."

I reached into my pocket to pull out the images of Snow and two cops doing a drug deal for money.

"Does this bring back any memories?" I asked, flashing the photos in her face.

She looks perplexed. "And what's that supposed to be?"

"Heaven for me and hell for you. Here, why don't you try taking a closer look?" Gun pointed at her forehead, I give her a better view of her dirty work, watched her while she clinched her teeth with regret, as if her fate rested in the palm of my hands. "What's the matter?" I asked. "You don't like seeing yourself on camera? Sucks doesn't it."

A suicidal glare crawls up her yellow face.

I continued to taunt. "I guess one woman's lost is another woman's gain ... lucky me ... So now that the tables have turned, it's either you play by my rules or play with the inmates in prison. And I know you don't wanna do that, because the inmates in prison would love to play with a high-class whore like yourself, especially after they find that you're a detective." I cut my eyes at her and smiled. "Do you know what they do to cops in prison? Oh I forgot, of course you do. There'd be four dikes on your ass before you could even make it to booking. Believe that! So unless you wanna shave that head and change your name to Butch, I suggest you do as I say."

"Fine. What do you want?"

"First, me and you are gonna make a trip to the bank so I can collect my other fifty grand."

"That was only if you killed my husband. That was the agreement."

"I know. That was the agreement when you were making the rules. But in case you failed to notice, I'm the one holding the gun, which mean the rules are what I say they are. And I say you're gonna get me that fifty grand."

She snarled.

"I'm not finished ... I'm also not leaving until I get little Devilla. Now where are you keeping her?"

"In a safe place," she said with a smirk.

I harden my tone. "Oh you think it's funny? You think threatening a little girl's life is funny? Well I got the perfect game that'll really make you laugh." There was one bullet remaining in my .44 revolver. I unloaded the bullet from the chamber, gave it a kiss, then placed it back into its natural domain.

Next I told her, "How 'bout a little game of Russian Roulette."

That smirk still hang-glides on her face as if she wanted to prove her bravery.

She says, "If you're trying to scare me, you betta come harder than that."

With the bullet in place, I spun that cylinder of death, then pointed it at the back of her head to show her I wasn't kidding. "There's only six chambers in this revolver. That means there's a 17% chance that this bullet can go through your head. Now if you don't want that to happen, you best tell me where you're hiding Devilla."

She tries to be tough, says, "You might as well lose the gat, 'cause I'm not telling you anything. If you wanted to shoot me you would've done it already."

"Very well then." I shot the gun and nearly scared the living daylights out of her, but nothing comes out but a click.

She jumps back in a frenzy. "What are you doing?"

I smiled. "You thought I was kidding? That number 17 has now went up to 34%. Now as I asked before, where is Devilla?"

She raises her hands and tells me to wait, but to me it's not good enough.

I shoot again. Another click.

"Stop it!" she begs.

"Your luck is running out! What was 34 is now at 51%, which means you betta pray to God that your cat pussy produces nine lives."

I took the .44 and forced the gun into her mouth. "Open up and open wide!"

Her eyes bulge with fright.

"Wider goddammit! Don't act like this is your first time." As I drilled the preliminary of death down her throat, she chokes on the gun like a deprived hooker, lips trembling, hands shaking, her body now dancing with fright. Demanding her full attention, my finger presses the trigger for the third time.

Another click. Her heart beats through her chest.

Then I give her the fiercest stare of her life. "What's it gonna be, Tough Cop? It's now at 68% Do you wanna die??? Do you wanna die??? Now where is Devilla???"

That frightened face mumbles for mercy, and in that moment of terror I take the gun out her mouth, allowed her to breathe, watched her chest go up and down as she chases the joy of fresh air. "Okay ... okay," she says. "Let me call 'er."

"Call who???"

"The person holding Devilla."

"Fuck calling her. I want you to take me to 'er! Take me to 'er now!

"Okay ... okay."

Something told me to raise the percentage and kill her right now, but saving Devilla is more important than my revenge.

Gun aimed at the back of Snow's head, I ordered her to slowly stand on her feet, forced her to start walking, and in that moment of taking a few steps, something falls in the corner of the room, something causing natural instinct to turn my stare for a split second.

That falling object is a book.

No threat at all.

Then I felt a hand grab on my arm, the hand of the enemy. Snow tight-gripped my elbow while reaching for the gun, then she dug her nails into the veins of my wrist.

The gun went off.

A bullet through the roof.

I tried my best to hold off the beast while holding the gun, but once our legs intertwined with knees locking in position, that awkward struggle caused us both to go plummeting to the floor, me falling face-forward and Snow falling on her back.

The .44 fell next to my hand, but the .44 wasn't the only gun lying on the floor. There was a double barrel shotgun lying right at Snow's feet, and without second-guessing, I grabbed my revolver as she reached for the shotgun.

Both guns were drawn.

Guns facing each other like dogs on a leash, waiting to be released by their rightful owners.

She smiles. "Looks like we have a situation. How 'bout you drop your weapon and I'll drop mine."

"How 'bout mama ain't raise no fool."

We started pacing in circles with our hands on the trigger, the guns staring us between the eyes.

She tells me, "I just have one question for you, little girl ... How can you shoot me without ammunition."

"What? What the hell are you—"

And then it came to me. Due to my game of Russian Roulette, the only bullet I had left was shot into the roof, leaving me completely defenseless, caught in a war without a solid weapon.

I swallowed hard.

Snow cocked her shotgun and gave me a malicious sneer. "Looks like Ms. Pretty is completely assed out," she said. "So now it's time to pay the price, I mean, unless you have something to give me of course."

"I have nothing."

"Oh don't play stupid with me. Those negatives ... I want those negatives. And unless you wanna die, you're gonna give them to me right now."

I hesitated before granting her request, thinking about the photos that were in my pocket, and how if I gave them to her, she'd have no other reason to keep me alive. I couldn't allow that to happen, not with so much at stake, not with me being so close to capturing Devilla.

"Hurry it up!" she said impatiently.

With the gun at my chest, I dropped my head before going into my pocket, and without second-guessing, the irrational part of me pushed her against the bookshelf, but not before her shotgun went off and nearly took off my head.

She struggled to regain her balance.

And I ran like hell.

I ran out the dining room. Zipped through the living room. Floored into the kitchen and hid behind the refrigerator.

Snow's voice rang out, "You've messed up now, little girl! You done really pissed me off!"

If she came into the kitchen I was sure as dead, especially with nothing to defend myself. I looked around enemy territory to get my hands on something useful, thought like a marine. There was a set of knives on top of the counter. Chef knife. Cleaver. Jagged-edge steak knife. I grabbed the cleaver, heard her footsteps nearing the kitchen while my pulse pounded with terror. There was nowhere to run. Nowhere to hide.

Think, Angel, think, I kept telling myself.

I noticed a round table sitting adjacent to the stove, right next to the pantry. The table was covered with a long table cloth, not big enough for a human, but at the moment it was the safest place to hide. I hid below the table and curled into a fetal position, heard the enemy enter the kitchen to look for my whereabouts.

A voice says, "Come on out, Angel ... Come on out so we can handle this like women."

At this point I can only see the tile floor; the table cloth has blocked half my vision, which gave me more of a disadvantage because I couldn't mark her location inside the kitchen. When one sense fails another sense gets stronger. My sense of sound told me she was on the other side of the counter, but that clue alone wouldn't keep me alive.

"I see you found yourself a weapon," her voice said out loud. "How cute. But didn't someone ever tell you to never bring a knife to a gunfight."

From nowhere her shotgun goes off and tears up a kitchen appliance. Sounded like a microwave, could've been a toaster.

Another shot fires.

I covered my ears. The sound of that gun was thunder in doors, made me cringe like a child who's afraid of the dark.

"You think you can outsmart me, Angel? Huh?" She puts two shell shots through the door of the pantry. The door flies open, and out from the door drops the body of a dead man, the body of Mr. Marcello.

I held my breath.

He was laying on the floor with his body facing me, head nearly splattered, eyes wide open like a corpse that fell out the casket. That nearly made me scream. I brought my hands to my mouth to keep from hollering, then closed my eyes tight and begged for a lifeline.

"Angel, come your black ass out right now!" Snow said in a skyrocketing voice. "You can only hide from me for so long ... Eventually I'll find you, and when I do it's gonna be hell to pay."

The sound of her double-barrel cocks like a cannon, and the echo of gunshots began to discharge. She shot up everything insight while I clinched my bare knuckles, appliances exploding, cabinets being blasted, glasses sung soprano and fell to their deaths, that along with milk and other liquids that covered the kitchen floor, drenched with specks of tomatoes and canned meat.

Laughter erupts out loud. "Having fun yet, Angel? Huh? You having any fun?"

The sound of her high heels click-clacked on the slippery floor, heard them clack around the counter until they showed the tips of her feet. Her feet made a right turn, faced me, then started to walk in my direction.

I grabbed my cleaver and squeezed it tightly as she kept tiptoeing in my direction, saw nothing but heels kicking up milk, my heart skipping more beats than a hip hop concert.

Then all of a sudden I heard knocking. Someone was knocking on the front door.

That made Snow stop dead in her tracks, her heels now pressed together.

The knocking grew louder, and it followed with a voice that said, "Angel! Angel! Are you inside? Open up the door! Open up the damn door!"

I recognized that voice from anywhere; it was the voice of my best friend Cuqui.

"You hear that?" Snow said. "Looks like you have yourself a visitor, Angel. Could that be your little ghetto friend?"

I was terrified and confused at the same time. Didn't know why Cuqui was here, why she would pop up without calling, and just like

Running From Redemption

that I found my answer. The phone is upstairs, which meant she probably tried to call a dozen times and got worried.

Right then and there the knocking went from banging on the front door to banging on the kitchen window. "What did you do with my friend, bitch???" Where is she at???

Snow ignores Cuqui and continues to talk. "You hear that, Angel? That's quite some friend you have ... I wonder if she would die for you too, 'cause that's what's next if you don't show your face right now. You got that? I'm gonna give you to the count of three to come out ... one!"

I had to do something quick; it was either end my life or Cuqui's, and if Cuqui got shot I would never be able to live with myself.

"Two!"

The sound of a shotgun cocks.

"Three!"

With no other card to play, I leaped out from under the table and ran towards my suicide, only to see Snow raising her gun towards the kitchen window, her back turned to me, and as she began to fire at the window, I saw Cuqui's face light up like a Christmas tree, saw her duck outside the window as I jumped on Snow's back to ward off her aim, and we both fell onto the wet kitchen floor with our weapons falling from our hands.

Before she could get up, I grabbed her by her locks and slammed her face into the floor, then started punching her in the back of her head, wanted to whip her ass ol' skool style.

Then I saw the shotgun lying above her head.

I climbed over her back and attempted to reach for the weapon, but before grabbing it I felt a hand on the back of my leg, a hand that made me kick her hard to try and shake her loose, but that jellyfish held me firmly, and she started pulling me back in her direction with my knees sliding in reverse.

"Get off my leg!" I kicked.

The power of my thrust forced her to let loose. I struggled to stand up straight on the slippery floor, did that while she gripped the back-end of my shirt and pushed me into the open door of the refrigerator, pushed me face-first into a bowl of spaghetti. I turned around to try and reclaim my balance, but I slipped again, and she charged at me like a bull with horns, her fists now swinging hard and wild.

In the door of the refrigerator, in that lopsided position, I fought back as best I could. She hit me in the stomach. I hit her in the face, then I lost my stance and attempted to block my face, tried to fend her off, but she pushed me back into the refrigerator and hammered me in the ribcage, forced me sideways and gave me all she had. Condiments fell. Mustard splattered. We tore up that refrigerator like wild cats.

Eventually I found enough strength to kick her in the stomach, causing her to fly back against the counter in the center of the kitchen.

I was now on offense.

And mad as hell.

So I reached into the refrigerator to get my hands on the first bottle I could find, because where I'm from there's no rules in fighting, and I gripped that bottle of Vodka with all my might, then broke it across her head like a drunk woman in a nightclub.

She takes a hard lick and falls back on the counter, disoriented.

I screamed out loud, "Payback bitch!" and I jumped on the counter and started wearing her ass out, grabbed her by the hair with one hand while the other hand dug into her face, bloodied her nose, I was literally trying to beat her to death.

"Get off of me!" she yelled. "Get off!"

After nearly beating her into a coma, she caught hold of my arm and sunk her teeth into my flesh, bit me harder than Mike Tyson bit Holyfield. I tensed up, kept swinging at her to let go, but the pit bull wouldn't release that bone from its mouth, made me scream, and as she locked onto my flesh with those jaws, she stretched out an arm to get her hands on a knife, brought it towards my face to make me jerk back, giving her the opportunity to flip me on the counter and climb on top.

I was now on the defense, holding back her arm while looking up at a blade that was inches away from cutting me in the face. I strained to hold back the knife from claiming my flesh, but it only got closer. Closer. Closer. Strength against resilience, she used both hands as I held my ground, then she pressed down on that blade with all her might, gritted with anger, showed me her teeth, the muscles in her cheeks spreading like wings.

She screamed out, "Die already you little bitch! Just die already!"

The blade went from looking me in the eye to now touching my cheek, death knocking at my door, that cutting edge trying its best to turn me into chopped liver. I strained and strained and strained, saw the devil in Snow's eyes, then with no more strength I released my grip and turned my face left, causing her to drill the knife into the marble countertop.

Before she could regroup, I swung my legs around and kicked her to the floor, saw her holding her stomach in pain while the knife remained on the counter. That natural instinct told me to pick up the knife and finish her off, but then I noticed she was lying right next to the shotgun. Before she could pick up the weapon, I leaped on top of the sink and climbed out the kitchen window, climbed like I was climbing Mt. Everest, then I fell onto a flowerbed outside of the kitchen window.

I got up and started running towards the front of the house, ran past the driveway, only to notice a car parked in the middle of the street, and standing beside that car was my best friend yelling, "Hurry up, Angel! Hurry so we can get the hell outta here!"

As I floored down the street, I heard a door bust open, and right then I knew the enemy was coming after me. I never looked back, saw Cuqui jump into the car as if she was fixing to leave me.

Then the passenger-side door popped open. "Get in!" she yelled.

I hopped into the car and told her to drive, said that as a bullet came flying through the back window, a bullet causing Cuqui to scream like a woman who was starring in a thriller.

"Drive!" I repeated.

Cuqui burned rubber, sped off as fast as our persevering heartbeats.

I looked in the rearview mirror. Saw Lady Lucifer standing in the center of the street. I saw her eyes. Saw her terror. Saw the shotgun resting at her side, her chest rising and falling.

27

Cuqui screamed, "Dammit, Angel! What type of wild, crazy, bizarre, insane, mess have you gotten me into?"

We were driving down Tobers lane, two blocks from Snow's house, driving recklessly towards an unknown destination. My face was sweating harder than an overweight woman in South Africa, hair playing hop scotch, and every two seconds I was glancing in the passenger-side rearview window for the first vehicle that resembled Snow's undercover car, paranoid by the colors of flashing lights.

Cuqui goes on, "Were you just gonna sit there and let her shoot me? Why didn't you give me a warning?"

"A warning? Didn't you see the gun?"

"I didn't see shit!"

Cuqui ups her speed to 70 in a 45 zone, her breathing getting heavy, her fingers starting to tap dance on the steering wheel.

I told her, "Slow down so you don't attract the police ... and where did you get this BMW?"

She snaps, "Never mind the BMW! You need to tell me what's happening? I thought the plan was to kill the husband, not you."

"It was."

"Then why the hell did we almost get our heads blown off?"

"Because..."

"Because what?"

Timid of telling her the truth, I decided to let the cat out of the bag. "Because I slept with her husband."

"You did what???"

Cuqui takes her eyes off the road and turns them to me. "What you do that for?"

"Watch the car in front."

She swerved. "Jesus Christ, Angel! What possessed you to do something so ... so stupid?"

"I don't know ... I mean it just ... it just happened."

"What do you mean it just happened? Out of all the men in Vegas, out of all the available dick in Vegas, why did you have to open up yo legs to that one? Hell, if I was her I'd try to kill yo ass too."

As our words played racquetball, Cuqui's cell-phone started ringing from the dashboard, the ring tone of T-Pain wanting to buy someone a drink. Cuqui picked up the phone, looked at the number, then she dropped it back into her lap without answering.

Seconds later T-Pain offered another drink, yet Cuqi refuses to accept it, ignoring the call again.

"Who is it?" I asked.

She shrugs her shoulders. "Dunno. The caller id shows private."

"Well aren't you gonna answer it?"

"Hell no. Let them have their privacy."

As we approach an intersection, the phone lights up once more, only this time it comes in the form of a text message that caused me to be alarmed. Cuqui multitasks between watching the road and reading the text, then she flips back her brownish-orange weave in an angry manner. "What the ... when the ... how the heck did this crazy bitch get my number?" she blurted out.

"Who is it?"

"Who do you think it is? It's Snow."

"That text came from Snow? Lemme see it."

"The hell with the text. I'm more concerned about how Ms. Psycho got my number. I swear fo' God I'm callin' Sprint tomorrow and gettin' my number changed ASAP..."

As Cuqui yapped away, I set my eyes on the text-message from Snow.

We both have something the other one wants. Meet me at Southside Park at 2pm. Come alone. And don't try to be smart. I promise you that if I even sense another cop, I'll send you a postcard of all Devilla's body parts ... you can count on it.

I glanced over at Cuqui who was biting her lips while holding the steering wheel, horrified of her potential fate.

She said, "Don't tell me you're actually thinking about meeting that woman, Angel."

I took a breath. "In fact I am. I think we should—"

"Hold up hold up hold up?" Cuqui says, her face swelling into a pumpkin. "What do you mean *we*? Last I checked, my birth certificate didn't come with a Siamese twin, which means *we* ain't 'bout to do a damn thing together. And if you had half a brain, you'd do what you should've done a long time ago."

"Yeah, and what's that?"

"Call the police for cryin' out loud!"

"I can't do that, Cuqui?"

"Dammit, Angel. Why fucking not?"

"Didn't you just see the text? She'd kill Devilla if I involved the cops."

"And what makes you think she won't kill Devilla anyway?"

"Because I got something she wants. Something she needs."

I reached into my pocket to show Cuqui the evidence, the uncensored pictures of Snow and the two cops exchanging money for drugs.

Cuqui asked, "Is this her?"

"In the flesh. Apparently to her these photos are a lot more valuable than killing Devilla, which gives me the upper hand."

Cuqui hesitated, said, "Oh okay ... So that must've been why she got suspended."

"Say what?"

"Remember when I told you that Snow hadn't made any arrests within the last two weeks?"

"Uh huh."

"Well I followed up on that, and it turns out that she's been put on suspension for a case that involved tampering with FBI evidence, her and six other cops."

"What???"

Cuqui tells me, "Look in the backseat and grab the white folder."

"What folder?"

"Behind the passenger seat on the floor. It'll tell you everything you need to know."

I reached into the backseat for the folder of truth, and inside were court documents of an investigation that involved five million dollars of cocaine missing from the FBI, cocaine that was evidence in the arresting of an overseas drug dealer. As of two weeks ago, Snow and six other detectives were suspected to be involved in the crime, but the case is still pending investigation. Until the FBI found probable cause to do their diligence, Snow was placed on suspension, and now everything is starting to make perfect sense.

Now I see why Snow wasn't handing out tickets to speeding drivers that passed us on the road. I see why the day she snuck me out of jail – the day we ran into her boss, the chief of police – he told her that he didn't want to see her on the clock until *this* whole thing blew over.

This meant the pending case.

This meant the stealing of evidence.

This meant whether she kept her job or was put behind bars the rest of her life.

I looked back at Cuqui driving fast but going nowhere. "How did you get this?"

She smiles. "Just because I ain't go to an Ivy League school, it doesn't mean I don't have a brain."

"Well how come your brain didn't tell you to send me this earlier?"

"I did, Angel. Didn't you get my second text message?"

"What text message? All you said was"—My mind backtracked —"Darnit!"

"What is it?"

"I left the phone upstairs in Snow's guestroom. The text must've come through then."

Cuqui sucks her teeth. "So that's how that crazy bitch got my number. And now because of you, Ms. Psycho is after me too..."

Another text-message came through Cuqui's phone, but this time it came in the form of a photo. I reached into Cuqui's lap to grab the phone.

Cuqui asked, "Is that her again?"

"Hold on."

"Is it?"

"Hold on!"

Before the picture had a chance to display, there were words above it that read: *Southside park. 2pm. Be there or be at her funeral.* I swallowed hard while waiting for the photo to upload, my mind spinning faster than the wheels on this car. Then the picture came to life, displaying a light-skinned girl with long tangled hair. Hands tied behind her back. Lips covered with duct tape. Eyes blindfolded.

It was little Devilla.

I couldn't determine her location from the poor contrast of the photo, but the closer I looked at the background the more I noticed something out of place, saw a brownish blur in the midst of sheer darkness.

I told Cuqui, "Quick. How do you enlarge this?"

"Huh?"

"The picture. I need to blow it up?"

After clicking on a button that tripled the picture in size, I brightened the contrast to get a better assessment of the object that was lingering in the background.

"What is this?" I thought out loud.

Cuqui reached for the phone. "Here, lemme take a look." Her eyes began to squint. "Wow ... it looks like ... some sort of a tail."

"A tail?" I snatched the phone back to do a re-examination. She was right. It was a mini tail of a Rottweiler, the tail of Snow's watch dog. Then another thought came to me. "Shit! If this is a tail, then that means ..."

"What?" Cuqui reacted. "What is it?"

"I can't believe it."

"Believe what?"

"All of this time! All of this time!"

"Bitch you bets get to talkin' 'cause you scarin' me."

I cleared my throat, told her, "Devilla is not being held at some secret location."

"She's not?"

"From this picture, it looks like Snow has her at the house, in the shed out back."

"Are you serious? In a shed?"

"In the back of Snow's mansion there's an old shed that Snow keeps closed up, told me that it's a place where she keeps all of her garden tools, that no one goes in there except her, not even her husband. What's ironic is that over the phone Devilla described her location as being a *dark place, a shovel, and a long knife*. What else could those descriptions be besides a shed or a garage?"

"Hell if I know," Cuqui replied. "All I know is that I should've never picked up that phone when you called me for help. Should've stayed my butt down in Miami."

"We've gotta go back."

"Say what?"

"We've gotta go back and get Devilla."

Cuqui slams on brakes. "Girl are you insane? I know you ain't talkin' 'bout going back to that haunted mansion, 'cause if you are, what type of weed are you smoking and where can I get a bag of it 'cause I ain't goin' no place where that crazy bitch Snow is at. I'm fixing to get on the first plane back to Miami 'cause it's too much shit going on at one time and I ain't even tryin' to understand it. Hell, little girl or no little girl, money or no money, I'm leaving 'cause this mess don't got nothing to do with me."

"But—"

"But nothing, Angel. You got me all out here in Timbuktu, following behind yo rabbit ass like we're a couple. Girl, I love ya but I ain't tryna take a bullet for ya. And I damn sure ain't taking one for some bad six-year-old girl that I barely even know. Shiiiiiiiiiiit ... There's only one child that I'll risk my life for, and her name is Shaquana."

Thinking her mind was already made up, I told her, "Fine then. Pull over."

"What?"

"I said pull over. You're absolute right. This has nothing do with you, so I'll go back by myself."

My reverse psychology was supposed to get her to feel sorry for me, but she reversed it back on me and said, "No problem. You ain't gotta tell me twice."

She pulls the BMW into the parking lot of Roscoe's Chicken and Waffles, never removing that uncompromising glare. Before getting out the car, I looked around for any cops that were on the prowl, then I took a deep breath and slowly opened the passenger-side door, giving Cuqui ample time to change her mind.

But she never does.

I exit the car. She rolls up the window.

Without saying a word, Cuqui skids off faster than a NASCAR driver, leaving dust blowing in my face from the burning tires. I stood in awe. Stood barefooted in the center of street like a homeless woman in search of shelter, watching my only friend drive off, thinking of another plan to execute. I reached into my jeans and pulled out my empty pockets. No cell phone. No money for public transportation. All I had to bargain with was my size D breasts, and even those weren't appealing enough to get me what I wanted right now. I started walking so I wouldn't bring attention to myself, kept wondering if I should throw in the towel and call the police, leaving the rest of Devilla's fate in the hands of the law.

But then I thought about Snow's text message.

Couldn't take that chance on Devilla's life.

There was only one way to end this. And that was by myself. So with no other choice, I picked up my pace and started heading back to Snow's house, only to hear a car approaching me from my blind side, a black BMW, and the driver of that car was an angry black woman wearing a multicolored weave, my best friend coming back to pick me up.

Cuqui slammed on brakes and pushed open the passenger-side door with a unit on her face that spelled out vexed.

I smiled in relief, told her, "I'm glad you—"

"Don't say shit to me. Just get yo' ass in the car."

28

Upon picking me up, Cuqui was sure to remind me that I was committing the dumbest act of my life and there's no way our plan would ever work.

Truth be told we had no plan. Nothing besides sneaking into Snow's backyard to try and save Devilla, and even if we did that without facing Snow, there was still Macho to worry about, a dog we both were frightened of.

Before dipping into danger, there were a few stops we had to make. First, I needed a gun and I needed one expeditiously, but due to the fact that I'm wanted for murder and Cuqui wasn't registered to carry a weapon, the odds of us getting one was slim to none.

We approached the corner of a Chevron gas station.

I told Cuqui, "Pull over."

"What for?"

"We gotta change into something sexy. Something promiscuous."

"But you have nothing to wear."

I point to her bag of clothes that's inside the backseat. She blows me off, then shakes her head to disagree. "I know you ain't thinking about wearing my clothes. You betta take yo self to one of them skinny heffa stores like Wet Seal 'cause ain't nothing for you in that bag."

"What's the problem? We use to wear each other clothes all the time."

"Girl that was back in the sixth grade. But in case you failed to look in a mirror lately, I'm a size 9 and you're a size 3. You know what that means? It means I'm built like a sista, but you ... well let's just leave it at that."

"First off I'm a size 6, thank you very much. And secondly, we can't afford to make a trip to any stores because time is against us. Now I'm sure you got something in that bag I can wear."

We went into the bathroom to freshen up, lotion up, and started getting dressed. While Cuqui jumped into her usual coochie-cutter jeans, I was busy skimming through her bag, searching for anything that would compliment my frame. I eventually got my hands on some thigh-grabbing shorts, a white sleeveless Sachi vest, matched them with a pair of 4 inch ankle-strap heels that made my calves look like drumsticks.

I stopped Cuqui in mid make-up, asking, "So what do you think?"

She started laughing. "I think those shorts are only made for women with hips and booty. You know, women like myself. So you bets take 'em off or get a safety pin to keep 'em up."

"Kiss my ass," I replied. "You just mad because I look better than you in your own clothes."

I completed my outfit with a dark brush-cut wig. Applied a little blush to my cheeks. Even put on a pair of Cuqui's extended eyelashes to give off that bambi-type look. I was now dressed for business.

We got back on the road and found a gun shop on 54th and Banniker Blvd called David's Guns, decided to park the BMW into the back, just in case it got serious.

Cuqui asks, "What make you so sure this plan w-ill work? What if—"

"Trust me, it will work," I assured her. "Just let me do all the talking. All you gotta do is stand there and look sexy."

"Who you tellin' girl? I do that better than anybody."

"Good. Now how much cash do you have on you?"

"About four hundred."

"That'll do. Let me have it."

Before walking into David's Gun Shop, I glossed the lips and undid the top button of my vest, told Cuqui, "Remember, let me do the negotiating."

We opened the doors to firearm heaven, inhaled the smell of gun powder from a place carrying every man-made weapon imaginable.

Behind each glass were weapons of mass destruction. Automatic guns. Sawed off shotguns. AK47's. Even saw a couple of grenades, as if the owner was ready for the worst. I wasn't interested in something big or powerful. I just needed something small and low-key, good enough to do some damage. As I looked for the perfect weapon, Cuqui kept cringing at the sight of every firearm, paranoid that the guns might accidentally fire off.

I told her, "Stop acting so scary and find something useful."

She snaps. "I ain't scared! Just being careful."

Her loud voice caught the attention of the middle-aged Caucasian man that was working behind the counter, a man watching us like women who stumbled into the wrong store.

"Can I help you?" he asked.

"Actually, you can," I replied. "Are you David?"

"Yes ma'am."

"Oh good. I just wanted to make sure I was talking to the right person ... Anyways, I'm looking for something that's not too over-the-top, something small enough for me to handle."

He asks, "Any particular reason why you ladies are purchasing a gun?"

"Do you ask everyone that question? Or is it just *us ladies*?"

"That question is standard ma'am. It allows me to better assist you when I know your purpose."

"Well since you wanna know, the gun is for my psycho ex-husband. I've got a restraining order against him, and the next time he pays me a visit I'm gonna blow his friggin' balls off ... Does that answer your question?"

He hesitates, then says, "Okay. Follow me. I keep my handguns over here."

Standing about six foot even, David resembled one of those military-type men. Square face. Boxed haircut. Wide broad Shoulders. He wore army jeans with pitch black boots, and a shirt that read, *War brings Peace*. He had a huge atoms apple that stood out for miles, and one of his arms was in a sling, as if it was recently injured in combat.

Like a typical salesmen, he takes me to the highest priced gun in the store to give me the lowdown. "Now if you really wanna do some damage, we have the Beretta Px4 pistol. Lightweight like you asked. It has rotating barrel locks and changeable back straps. And not only is it powerful, but it has a 3-dot sight system, you know, for use in the dark, and it can attach flashlights or lasers." He takes it off the rack and hands it to me. "Here why don't you take a look for yourself?"

I started rotating the barrels and playing with the parts, did that while he gave me the spill on another high-tech gun, the Kel-tec PF-9.

He tells me, "And just so you know, both of these guns are used by law enforcement."

"That's nice and all. But I'm looking for something a little simpler, something that isn't recoil operated, more so blowblack. Like a .25 or a .380."

"I see you know your guns."

"Guess you can say I have a little experience here and there."

He then looks at Cuqui. "And what about for you ma'am? You interested in anything?"

Trying to look sexy like I told her, Cuqui was caught off guard by his question, and she replied with, "Huh ... oh, you can just give me whatever she said."

The man presumes to the next gun, and when he turns his back, I bumped Cuqui on the shoulder and whispered, "Stop acting like a dumb blond and get yourself together."

"What do you mean? How am I supposed to know 'bout this stuff? Hell, I'm not G.I. Jane."

The man turns back around. We stopped bickering and flashed two smiles.

"And here we have the MP-25," he says. "It holds six rounds, plus another bullet in the chamber. Blowback like you asked. Comes in either chrome or black. And as you can see, it's very small, could possibly fit into your pocket."

I ask, "And what's the price."

"$61.25. Relatively inexpensive."

"I'll take it. As a matter of fact, give us two of those and a few boxes of ammo."

He motions to the register to total everything up, tells us, "That'll be $162.47."

"No problem."

"Registration?"

"Excuse me?"

"Your gun registration? I need that."

I looked at him as if I was surprised, told him, "Registration? I thought you didn't need a registration to purchase a firearm in Nevada."

"Maybe around the rest of the state. But in Clark County, you need to be registered."

"Wow. I didn't know that. Is that a new rule?"

"No ma'am. Rule been in effect since the beginning of time. I suggest you head twenty miles north. Nothing is required there."

"But I need this gun right now."

He shakes his head. "Sorry ma'am. No registration. No gun."

I dropped my face in disappointment, took a deep breath, and when I looked back up my face quickly turned into one of seduction.

I told him, "David right?"

"That's right."

"Well David," I whispered, leaning over the counter. "Seeing that we both are adults, maybe we could work something out, if you know what I mean."

I winked at him with my bambi clip-on eyelashes, causing his face to become filled with shyness, his cheeks turning red. Then he glances at Cuqui who licks her lips to play along with me, and now his face is shyer than a choir boy, as if he's never been seduced by two black women, double trouble.

He tells me, "Ma'am, I'm a happily married man, if that's what you're implying."

"Actually, I was implying something else."

I reached into my bra to pull out 4 c-notes, and as I slowly raised the money to his face, I allowed Benjamin Franklin to do the rest of the talking.

With double the asking price on the table, he swallows hard, tells me, "If anyone, and I mean anyone, ask you where you got these guns—"

"No worries," I said, silencing him with a finger to his lips. "I already know how this works."

Money on the counter. Guns in our hands. We left the store like two bad divas, our high heels clicking in unison.

Once getting in the car, Cuqui said, "Damn girl that was a close one. What was the plan if he had wanted the booty instead of the money?"

"Don't know. But I do know this, there are very few men that'll turn down sex, but you'll never meet a man that'll turn down money."

Ten minutes later we were driving up to the gated community of Snow's neighborhood. Wasn't hard to get pass the guard. He was more so focused on a sports magazine.

Once getting inside we rode cautiously through the area, the land of the rich. At noontime the place is quiet; the only sounds are those of lawnmowers and sprinklers watering the grass, and the only people out are those who are retired – people who lounge on a canopy, in their front yard, their eyes engrossed in a newspaper that reflects the ups and downs of the stock market, the rich getting richer while taking from the poor.

As Cuqui drove five miles per hour, I told her, "Stop acting like we're doing a drive-by and go faster."

"What for? I'm not in a rush to get there."

Nearing Snow's house, I caught a glimpse of her driveway from yards down the street, saw the usual Mustang. The Mercedes. Range Rover.

She was still at home.

Instead of riding up her block, I told Cuqui to take the back street, did that so we could approach Snow's house from the blindside.

We silently parked the car in front of a mansion that sat behind Snow's house. Regrouped while changing into sweats and sneakers.

Before exiting the car, I noticed an elderly woman that was watering some plants, her eyes watching our car like she was watching a hawk.

We waited for inspector gadget to go into the house, waited while a heavyset woman was walking a poodle, a poodle that made me think of Snow's watchdog.

Cuqui said, "Girl let's hurry befo' someone catches us."

"Wait."

"What the hell is it now?"

"Macho. Snow's dog. We need something to distract the dog."

Cuqui flashes her gun. "Nuff said."

"No stupid. If you shoot the dog then Snow will hear the shot. Instead we need something like ... didn't you have some chocolate candy bars in your suitcase."

"Yeah. So?"

"Good. We can use those."

She looks perplexed. "What the heck does candy bars gotta do with a dog?"

"Chocolate is toxic for dogs. If they eat it, it could be fatal."

"What?"

Running From Redemption

"Just shut up and grab the candy bars."

We walked towards the side of the unknown residence that led us to the back yard, strolled through sticker purls and ant piles before approaching a big brown fence that circled the back of Snow's residence. Connected to that fence was a gate that went up halfway, a gate that made it easy to climb into Snow's back yard.

I peeked through a hole in the fence. Saw Macho roaming the yard like a lion in an African jungle, also noticed the shed that was ten steps close to the fence.

I stood atop the gate to get a better view of the shed. Inside was a human being.

Saw tape.

Saw lots of hair.

Saw a little girl with her hands behind her back, her head twitching with fright.

"Oh my gosh," I blurted out.

Cuqui asked, "What is it? Do you see 'er?"

At that instance our voices set off the ears of Snow's watchdog, and with no chain around his neck, Macho came running in our direction. I jumped from the fence and backed away. Cuqui followed my lead.

I told her, "Quick. Gimme the chocolate."

"What you saw? Was it Devilla?"

"Yes."

"You sure?"

"I'm sure."

Without barking, Snow's watchdog is staring us down from the other side of the fence, daring us to invade the premises. A mouth big as my head, that savaging beast awaits our every move, and then he stands upright to open his mouth, allowing his teeth to cosign on what he'd do if we were to ever become bold enough to climb the gate.

I unwrapped the candy bar and threw it over the fence, then watched as Macho leaped in the air to catch the Hershey bar, watched his jaws tear through chocolate like meat thrown to wolves.

It took no more than five seconds for him to devour the treat, took less than that for him to stand again in that hunger position.

Cuqui muttered, "Are you 100% sure it was her?"

"Yes, bitch. Now gimme the rest of the chocolate."

I teased the dog by slowly unwrapping his gifts. He stands upright, eyes following my fingers, and as I tossed the remaining Hershey bars, he fetches the chocolate in full stride.

I tossed two more.

Another two eaten.

After the digestion of five Hershey bars, Macho the vicious dog was beginning to move sluggishly, his powerful legs now turning feeble, as if he was disoriented, like a man with an alcohol level above the legal intake.

Cuqui taps me on the shoulder. "Look girl look. It's working. I can't believe it's working."

"Lower your voice."

Eventually the dog stopped circling his territory to rest beside a flowerbed. His big round head had dropped like a poodle, eyes starting to droop, and two minutes later his eyes had closed.

I told Cuqui, "Okay, now all we have to do is get Devilla from that shed."

Cuqui stands alarmed. "Wait a second. What if the dog wakes up?"

"He won't."

"How do you know?"

"Because he's probably half-dead, if he's not dead already."

She shakes her head apprehensively.

I sucked my teeth. "Dammit, Cuqui. Do I have to prove everything to you?"

At that instance I picked up a stick and threw it across the fence at Macho, then I waited for the dog to react.

Macho never moves. Doesn't even open his eyes.

"See there," I told her. "Does that answer your question?"

Cuqui hesitates.

I tell her, "Never mind. I'll go. You just stay here and watch my back, and try not to look so suspicious. Is your gun loaded?"

"Uhhh...."

I took the gun from her hands, noticed that my stupid best friend still had the safety lock on. "Here," I said, fixing it. "That should do it."

As I turned my shoulder to climb the fence, I felt Cuqui suddenly reaching for the back of my leg. "Wait, Angel. Are you sure about this?"

"Girl stop acting so scary and watch my back. And watch where you're pointing that gun."

I jumped into the Devil's playground. Crept towards the large shed that stood beneath a sycamore tree, nearly stepping in dog crap that covered the yard like landmines. Once approaching the window of the shed, I heard the sound of lungs gasping for air, the frantic breathing of a human being.

I whispered through the window. "Devilla."

Her neck turns like an owl. Face changes colors. Cheeks fill with angst as if she heard the sound of the undertaker, her eyes blindfolded.

The shed had a wooden door. Wasn't locked. I pushed it open after giving a hard shove, then I walked into a spot that was cramped as a prison cell, and dark as hell. I inhaled the scent of a dog's bowels as Devilla sat blindfolded, her teeth chattering, and as I neared her, she kept shaking her head in fear, thinking I was Snow.

Devilla was tied to a chair with her legs dangling from her four-foot frame. Hands tied behind her back. Hands bound by a lock that clung from a thick chain, a chain bolted to a dirty white wall.

I reached to take off her blindfold, but instead of her being relieved to see me, she started kicking at me like a wild animal, as if she was traumatized from the blindfold.

"Get away from me!" she screamed. "Get away! Leave me a—"

"Shhhhhh," I said, covering her mouth. "It's me, Devilla. It's Ms. Angel." The kicking began to cease as she recognizes my face, and the terror in her eyes is suddenly replaced with tears, tears that wanted to hug me for dear life, but couldn't because of her hands being bound behind her back.

I embraced Devilla into my arms, then whispered, "You're gonna be fine okay. You're gonna be fine."

She's wearing the same Tinkerbell shirt from weeks ago. A Tinkerbell that was partially dirty. Half-laced shoes. Hair wilder than a newborn that just escaped the womb.

I looked her in those little brown eyes and asked her, "Did she hurt you?"

"No but ... she said that ... today I'll die if you don't give 'er what she—"

"Forget what she said okay. Now I need you to tell me something that's very important."

Knowing that Snow was getting help from someone, I asked Devilla to describe the person who kept her confined inside this death trap.

Trembling, Devilla answered, "It ... was a woman."

"Good. A black or white woman?"

"Black ... She was brown-skinned ... had on high heels ... and ..."

"And what?"

"That's all I can remember."

"You sure?"

She nodded yes.

Anxiety had her memory jaded, and instead of pressing her for a clearer description, I said, "You did good, Devilla. You did good. Now what I need at this moment is to get you unchained."

"On the dog."

"What?"

"The key is on the dog ... around his neck."

Shucks, I thought. "Are you sure?"

She nods yes.

Afraid to leave her, I said, "Okay ... okay ... Stay right here and I'll be right back."

"No, Ms. Angel! Don't leave me! Please don't—"

I covered her mouth. "Not so loud, Devilla. Now listen here, if I don't get that key you'll never get loose, so I need you to be strong while I do this okay?"

Eyes overflowing with fear, she drops her head.

I tell her, "How 'bout this. I want you to close your eyes and count to thirty. I promise you I'll be back before then."

Her head raises. "Pinky swear?"

"Pinky swear."

After giving her my word, I sauntered back into the yard to go after the key, saw the dog lying lifeless in the same spot. I motioned towards the dog as my heartbeat sped up, breaths got shorter, started sweating rigorously in my shirt from being so nervous. As I spotted the key around Macho's neck, I drew my gun in case he so happened to wake up, did that while the dog laid on his side, and then I lightly kicked the dog as a test of sureness, noticed it was as motionless as a rock.

Hands trembling, I reached around his furry neck to snatch the key. Did that successfully.

Afterwards, I glanced up to mark Cuqui's location. Wanted to ensure she was still watching my back from across the fence.

But there was no Cuqui.

No Cuqui in sight.

I panicked at the fact that Snow could've taken my best friend, and before I could think, I felt cold steel being pressed against the back of my neck.

"Drop it," a voice said. "Drop it right now."

Blowing out a deep breath, I dropped the key. Dropped that along with my bladder that wanted to run down my thighs.

Running From Redemption

"The gun too," she said. "Throw the gun in the grass."

I hesitated before sacrificing my only salvation.

"Do it now!" she demanded.

Gun tossed, I blew out a deep breath. "Anything else?"

"Now turn around."

"Huh?"

"Turn yo' ass around!"

I turned around. Faced the enemy. Took in all of her features.

But the person that's holding the gun isn't Snow.

It's Cuqui. My best friend. And to my surprise, she's pointing the gun directly at me.

29

"Cuqui, what are you doing?"

"It's sad that you haven't realized it, Angel. But you'll soon find out."

"Stop kidding around, Cuqui. Now put the gun down and let's hurry because Devilla is—"

"You're not going anywhere!"

"Say what?"

"I said you're not going anywhere," she repeats, holding the gun tightly.

I wanted to think she was joking, that this was some sort of prank. But the look on her face was serious. Dead serious.

I told her, "Cuqui, I don't know what's up with you but you've got three seconds to get that gun out my face or else I'm gonna—"

"What?" she said, gritting her teeth. "Or else you're gonna do what?"

Brick wall. Shock wave. The world has stopped turning.

My best friend takes her death machine and drags it from my chest to my forehead. "You're not gonna do a damn thing, Angel. And you know why? Because you're not the one who is holding the gun. I am."

"That's right!" a voice said from afar.

I turned my neck quickly. Almost got a whiplash from the presence of Snow, the devil intruding in this garden of Eden.

Her albino skin mirrored a pale python as she slithered through the grass with her snake-like walk. Duffel bag in one hand. Gun in the other. Her dreadlocks carried the color of blood, as if hell had come along for the ride.

Then she looked at Cuqui. "Nice work, partner."

"What can I say?" Cuqui replied. "I learned from the best."

They smiled at each other like reacquainted friends. The devil and the devil's advocate.

Cuqui asked Snow, "So you brought the money?"

Snow raises her black duffel bag in the air. "It's all here."

"Very well then. Let's get right to it."

Anger becoming a cyclone on my face, I screamed to Cuqui, "You stupid, stupid bitch! Do you have any idea what it is you're doing."

"Of course, Angel. I just became rich. How stupid does that sound?"

"Sounds smart to me," Snow said, jumping in. "I mean let's face it, Angel. She did something that you couldn't do. She kept her word and followed through on a deal. That's the reason I made her my business partner because I knew she'd do anything for money. Even if it took deceiving her best friend. So you see there, Angel. It's true when they say to keep your friends close and your enemies closer."

As I struggled to take in the moment, I thought about this nightmare that came to life. Cuqui had been the missing piece to Snow's puzzle, the help that Snow was getting all alone. She was the one who led me to Snow, the one tracking me from state to state, the only person who knew my whereabouts the entire time, and more than likely, she was the stranger that had picked up Devilla.

Not believing what I was seeing, I told Cuqui, "So you were the ghost in the graveyard that night? It was you who killed Sergio?"

She smiled. "I didn't want to Angel, but someone had to do it."

I stood in the outfield while the ball of betrayal came flying towards me, my hands glove-free from catching the hurt.

Judas betrayed Jesus.

Brutus betrayed Caesar.

Same story with a different face. And now my face is etched in that wall of treachery.

Coming in between our stares, Snow said, "I'm sorry, Angel. You look surprised. Did your best friend surprise you?"

I ignored Snow and kept my eyes fixed on Cuqui, didn't blink one bit as I stared down fifteen years of sisterhood that's completely gone up in smoke.

I said, "Just tell me why, Cuqui. Why would you do this?"

"Simple, Angel. She promised me two million dollars. Do you know how much money that is? Do you?"

"So you throw away our friendship for a few lousy dollars? Whatever happened to trust?"

"The hell with trust, Angel! This has nothing to do with trust! This is about getting' paid. It's about gettin' paid in any way I can. And if gettin' paid means betraying you, then so be it."

"And what about Devilla?"

"What about 'er?"

"You'll throw a little girl under the bus, all so you can get rich? Well I hope you burn in hell for that, Cuqui!"

"Maybe I will. But at least I'll burn with money." Cuqui turns to Snow. "And speaking of money, hand mines over."

"Money?" Snow replies. "What money?"

Cuqui grew rigid. "Don't play with me, Snow. You owe me two million dollars and I want it right now! We had a deal dammit!"

"You're absolutely right. I promised you two million dollars and that's exactly what you're gonna get."

Snow tosses the duffel bag at Cuqui's feet. Cuqui opens the bag to check her cash, and as she pulls out stacks of green, her eyes became filled with fireworks.

But fireworks fell short to a bullet.

A bullet shot from Snow's 9mm to enter Cuqui's chest, causing her to breathe rented breaths of time.

Cuqui falls on top of the duffel bag. Flops on top of her million-dollar death.

With her paymaster standing over her body, Snow tells her, "Sorry, Cuqui. But I don't make deals with criminals."

Running From Redemption

30

Twenty minutes later I was on my knees with my hands tied behind my back, wrists bound together, feet trapped in rope while waiting for the inevitable on Snow's back patio.

Devilla joined the party. Snow had lined us up together, and between Devilla's tears and my heavy breathing, one would've thought a beheading was set to take place.

I whispered to Devilla, "Just stay calm okay ... we're gonna be okay." Then I told Snow, "Why don't you just let her go? It's me that you want. Not her. She has nothing to do with this."

"You sure about that?"

Standing over us with a gun in her hand, Snow reaches into her pocket and pulls out a cigarette, then she sits in a chair to light up a blaze that follows with the crossing of her legs.

Silence rest between us as we longed for a lifeline.

Snow says, "Let me ask you something, Angel ... Did you really think you could just come into my house, take what you want, and then leave just like that? I told you before and I'll say it again. You can't outsmart me, Angel. I always know your next move before you ever make it."

On the patio where she kept us enclosed in rope, I scoped out my surroundings for something handy. Saw nothing but a lawnmower, a rake, and a weed eater. Nothing valuable enough to free us from this bondage.

I told her, "If you let us go right now there's a chance you won't go to jail."

She laughs. "Me go to jail? You're so funny, Angel. I thought we had this conversation once before."

"Not entirely. You see I know about your little situation, about how ten million dollars of seized drug money up and walked away from the FBI. I know about the investigation, how that little incident caused you to get suspended, and if your little problem goes to court, it may even cost you your life. It's the reason you needed those pictures wasn't it? The pictures of you and your crooked cop friends stealing all the evidence." I kept my eyes straight to give her the conversation she needed, did that while I secretly tried to squeeze my hands through the blistering tape. "I should've known something wasn't right about you and your job. I should've figured it out by your actions. How you never seemed to get a call on duty. And how you allowed every speeding car to pass you on the road. Too bad your partner Cuqui – or at least you thought she was your partner – gave me all the evidence I needed. Looks like she was getting ready to double-cross you the same way she double-crossed me."

Taking a hard puff of her cigarette, she rests the gun on her lap and started clapping her hands, clapping and smiling and clapping and smiling, and in a calm voice she told me, "Well done, Angel. I see you've done your research. But research with no proof is worth nothing."

"I won't need proof when the cops find out what really happened, that you not only killed your husband, but had his brother killed as well. And what about those two men in Shady Pines Apartments?"

"What about 'em?" she replied. "According to the evidence, you killed them too."

"What evidence? What are you talkin' 'bout?"

"I'm talkin' 'bout the .45 you used to shoot William Randolph. The same gun that I confiscated from you a couple of weeks ago, then turned around to not only shoot my husband, but I used it to wipe out those hoodlums in Shady Pines as well ... That's right, Angel ... Think back ... Think really hard."

My mind took me back to those encounters, and eventually it cosigned on the words she spoke. She was absolutely right. All of the evidence was pointing back to me.

She goes on, "So you see, Angel, unlike you, my tracks are always covered."

"But what about witnesses?"

"What witnesses?"

"There was an army of people who saw you kill those men at Shady Pines."

"Come on, Angel. You've lived in the hood before, and we both know that people in the hood don't talk. If freedom was based on their testimonies then there'd be no such thing as prison. No Scott Peterson. No Jeffery Dahmer. Everyone would be innocent ... So you know what that means right? It means I get away scotch free."

My emotions started getting the best of me, and after thinking about everyone she killed, including my best friend, I unintentionally screamed, "You murderer!"

She laughs aloud. "Murderer is such a strong word ... I prefer killer. You see murderers kill without motive. Without strategy. They just let their feelings get the best of them, you know, like when you shot William Randolph. But me on the other hand, I only kill for gain ... And I'll tell you something else, Angel. Something you don't even know." She sits up straight in her seat like a trained cobra, eyes protruding with venom. "The man you killed back in New York ... the man you know as William Randolph ... well that man was my fiancé."

"Your what?"

"My fucking fiancé!!!"

Baffled by her statement, I started fumbling over words. "But ... but how ... when did you ..."

"We met in prison. Upstate New York. Met 'im at a time when he'd just done five years behind bars, and had ten more years to go ... At that time he had no family. No friends. Everyone he'd ever known had completely turned their backs on 'im, everyone but a young naïve girl that worked as one of the security guards ... From the moment I saw him, I knew he wasn't your average criminal, I saw something genuine in him that I never saw in other men inmates ... I would bring him extra food, extra pillows, and eventually that attraction turned into brief conversations. I'd even sneak into his cell to give 'im the loving he hasn't had in years ... You see I was already married to a man named Solomon, Solomon Marcello, but once I met William, I saw what real love was supposed to feel like, and I noticed that Solomon wasn't half the man William was ... The only problem is that although I had found a new love, I was too afraid to leave Solomon, so I secretly got engaged to William in prison, thinking I could keep it a secret until he was released ... but then ..." Her tone softens from cement to clay. "Then I got pregnant ... Pregnant with William's baby, and eventually the secret came out ... Solomon was outraged ... He ordered me to terminate the pregnancy or he'd put me out, and when I chose not to and he did put me out. But I didn't care because I was pregnant from the man I wanted to marry, and with being three months pregnant, I decided to surprise William with the good news ... but what I didn't realize is that when I came to his cell, I was the one who was in for a surprise ... Before I could even tell 'im I was pregnant, he said he wanted to call off the engagement, gave me some cock-a-doodle story about how he wasn't ready for another marriage and how he wanted to get his life together, something along those lines ... I was devastated, was so hurt and upset that I quit my job and decided to never see 'im again, even tried to have 'im murdered before he got released ... the worst part is that it was too late for me to get an abortion, and now I was stuck with a child from a man that didn't love me back ... Me and Solomon separated for the next seven months, and then we got back together, re-united when I was seven months pregnant with another man's baby ... And Solomon hated me for that ... Hated me so much that he purposely added an infidelity clause to our prenuptial. Hated me so much that he wasn't in the delivery room when I had my baby, the one baby that he could never give me himself ... There's nothing worse than a mother being in the delivery room by herself, no man by her side, and no support whatsoever. But I did it. I had my baby all by myself. And on March 3rd"—her voice becomes rickety—"On March 3rd I birthed a seven pound baby named Devilla."

Dead silence.

A shock wave went through me as Snow looked at Devilla. "That's right, Honey. You are ... my daughter."

Devilla raises up her eyes at Snow, then she turned those eyes to me, hoping it wasn't the truth.

I tell Snow, "I don't believe a word you're saying. Devilla's real mother died while giving birth."

"Is that the lie William told you? He would've said anything to try and discredit me. But the truth is that Devilla is my child." She takes her eyes to Devilla. "I'm your mama, Devilla. When you were first born I ... I gave you up for adoption. It wasn't by choice, but it was something I had to do, and ever since then—"

"Don't do this to her!" I intervened. "Don't do this right now."

"This is between me and my daughter!" she snapped.

Devilla looks at Snow like she's the mother from hell, fear and confusion colliding in her childlike eyes.

Snow goes on, "I gave you up because I had no money. No sense of direction. And I didn't want to raise you by myself. So I gave you to the first family that could give you what I couldn't give you. A family ... I thought giving you away would make it easier, but it only got worse. Much worse. I took you to sleep with me every night, the guilt of knowing I had given my daughter to a pair of strangers, and with that guilt I decided that it was time to get you back. So for two years I started to look for you. I called Child Protective Services. Knocked on doors. Everywhere I went there was a little girl that reminded me of my little Devilla. At parks. At grocery stores. It's like you were all around me, but was never there. Then one day I saw William Randolph, your father. He was walking hand-in-hand with a girl your age, acting as if he was the perfect father. I don't know how he figured out that he had a daughter, but somehow he found you after prison and was determined to keep you a secret from me, feeding me some crap of how you were a child that he conceived from another woman. At first I bought it, but every mother knows their child, and once I saw your eyes – the eyes that I took to sleep with me for the last six years, the same eyes that gazed up at me in the delivery room – I knew right then that you were my daughter. But this time I'm not letting you escape me; this time it can just be us. Now I realize that I don't need your father, even if he left me for some low-down whore that was half my age."

She glances in my direction as if I was the whore she was referring to.

I told her, "You and William's mess has nothing to do with me."

"Actually, it has everything to do with you. From the time you stole 'im from me, it became your mess too."

"What are you talkin' 'bout? I stole no one."

She rises from her seat with a cigarette in one hand, the gun in the other, and she circles my body like a python does its prey, did that while I remained trapped on my knees standing half her height with wrists going numb from packaging tape.

She goes on, "You see, Angel, I had plans to reconnect with William again. But because you were fucking him he thought he was in love and somehow my plan got ruined. I mean, to leave me for some crap like you is beyond pathetic, and when I saw you two together, I thought it was even more pathetic."

"So that's what this is all about? Your jealousy of me and William?"

She hovers over my head like a massive dark cloud, the stare of an empress despising a peasant. "This stopped being about jealousy years ago, Angel. It's now about vengeance. Call it retribution. To get even with the two men that made my life a living hell, and to take everything they ever worshiped is my new redemption. For William it was Devilla. For my husband it was money. You just happened to be the victim that brought this whole thing in full throttle. And considering that you are a felon, it was to my benefit to use you like a pond in this little game of mine, but since you were too afraid to kill my husband, the game is now over, and you no longer serve me a purpose. So with that being said, where are those negatives?"

"Huh?"

"Don't play dumb. The negatives to the photos of me doing the transaction. The ones you supposedly have."

I hesitated, thinking of how those negatives were the last bit of evidence I had on her. In the midst of my silence, Snow drops her cigarette to the ground, steps on it, and with the 9mm in her hand, she walks over to Devilla and points the gun between her eyes.

Devilla screams.

"What are you doing???" I hollered. "For Christ's sake, she's your daughter!"

Snow positions the gun. "I'm not gonna say it again!"

"Alright. Alright. The negatives are inside my back pocket."

That angry woman goes in my jeans to take the evidence, and she snatches up the photos like money on the ground.

I told her, "You have what you want. Now let us go. Your business with me is finished."

"Not exactly," she replied. "You see I was serious when I told you that I cover all my tracks. And with you being on the loose you pose a serious threat."

She raises her 9mm to the back of my throat, did that as I swallowed a baseball. I glanced to my right at a crying Devilla. Then I looked back at Snow, back at her 9mm, thinking if there ever was a God I needed him now.

Before I could let out a single breath, a gunshot fired.

It fired at Snow. Fired hard and fast. It sent Snow falling backwards on the patio, falling to her death, falling with a bullet wound vacationing in her forehead, blood running through dreadlocks and filling the cracks of the concrete.

Devilla screamed as I looked around for the undisclosed shooter.

To my left was an elderly woman with thick salt-n-pepper hair, wore a cleaning uniform with a shotgun in her hand, a gun as big as her four foot frame.

The shooter was no other than the maid, Ms. Montreal, and she was still pointing the gun at Snow to ensure that the enemy was dead, a unit on her face like a slave seeking vengeance on her master.

I became speechless, totally shocked.

Panic intensified in her eyes as the maid rushed over to release me and Devilla from our bondage, then she reached into her purse to pull out a cell-phone, and after dialing 911, she screamed out, "Dey dead! Dey dead ... two bodies ... yes .... yes .... me dunno, dey dead wen me arrive ... yes ... herry herry get 'ere .... blood erwhere .... erwhere me turn ... 4400 Sou Wes Pelican Ro ... herry herry."

The phone clasped shut.

In that jaw-dropping moment, I told the maid, "What did you ... did you just do what I think you did?"

"Neva sey mi was a saint, Angel. Now yu bes leave fas' as yu cun. Cops come soon."

"I can't do that."

"Why?"

"I'm not leaving Devilla."

"She be fine. Me tek care 'er. Tek 'er bac to 'er fambly."

As much as I needed time to make the right decision, I didn't have time. Time had partnered with the law, and the law would be here any minute to do what they do best.

I turned my stare towards Devilla.

Before I could speak, she asked, "Are you leaving me, Ms. Angel?"

"Unfortunately yes," I answered, unable to look her in the eye. "But I'm only leaving for a little while. Just long enough to keep out of trouble. In the meantime this nice lady is gonna look after you. "

"No! No! No!" she cried, shaking her head. "I don't want to go with anyone else. I just want to go home!"

She said that as if it was non-negotiable, then she turned her nose up at Ms. Montreal, told her, "I'm not going with you lady. I don't know you—"

"Devilla, It'll be okay. Ms. Montreal will take you back to your aunts and uncles. Back home."

"But I'm afraid ... I'm afraid." She jumped up to hug me tight. Hugged me as if she was my biological child, and I embraced her like a mother, like my mother embraced me before she was stolen from this sinful world.

I brushed her hair from her face and dried her eyes. "You don't have to be afraid no more," I told her. "Now be strong ... Ms. Montreal is gonna keep you very safe. I promise." I glanced at Ms. Montreal to cosign on my promise. "You will keep her safe right?"

In her beautiful dialect, she replied, "Mi got five children un lots grandchildren. Mi tek good care of 'er. She be en good unds."

The maid ran her hands through Devilla's curly black hair.

She told her, "Firs' we get yu press comb. Den we get yu cundy. Yu like cundy?"

Devilla shrugs her shoulders. "Candy is bad for your teeth."

"Whad 'bout Fren' fries?"

"Okay," Devilla replied, ignoring her nutritional guidebook.

The maid smiled. "Gud. We get Fren' fries den."

I pulled the maid to the side, told her, "Whatever you do, make sure she doesn't end up in the system. If no one in her family will take her in, then I want you to take her in."

"As mi sey, yur gal be en good unds. Now yuh bes' herry en leev. Cops be 'ere soon."

I started to hear sirens. Heard that authentic cop-filled tune getting louder and louder, the police rushing to save the unknown.

"Here," the maid said, giving me a set of car keys. "Tek mi truk."

"You sure?"

She nodded yes. "Now leev. Leev now!'

I grabbed those keys and thanked her endlessly, did that as I turned my stare towards the body of Snow. The enemy's corpse was rotting on top of the one thing that held my ticket to freedom – the two million dollar duffel bag – and her DNA was soaking into the bag like a dirty sponge.

Without second-guessing, I pushed her body to the side and grabbed the bloody money, then I ran to the front of the house to climb into my ride, cranked up my get-a-way car and burned rubber on a full tank of gas. For an old truck that had a broken headlight, no tune-up, and the service engine light that was lit up, it sure did ride good.

Police cars started coming out of the woodworks. Sirens grew in volume - sirens causing traffic to stop on both sides of the street to yield to the law, and amongst those cops were two ambulances driving recklessly, panic making them oblivious to the old truck going in the opposite direction, the one waiting in line with the rest of the curious traffic.

American eyes watched the chaos like a funeral in passing. I attempted to look back too. But to my disadvantage, there wasn't a rear-view mirror in the truck, which meant I could only look in one direction. Straight ahead. And with Benjamin Franklin sitting in the passenger seat, that's exactly what I did.
 I drove fast.
 I drove hard.
 I drove unconsciously into the next phase of my life.

31

I stood in the checkpoint line of the Nevada Airport, Gate 4. Stood in my denim jeans, a purple T, and a baseball cap turned low on my face without every looking up.

My only luggage was the million dollar duffel bag. It was tightly gripped around my shoulder as I was getting ready to fly to the island of St. Croix (a virgin island), one of the most serene places in the world. I wasn't going for the beaches. Nor for the weather. But mostly for mama.

When I was a child my mother would take me out back to work in the garden, and my reward would always be sugar cane. Mama would educate me on my favorite treat. Told me that St. Croix had the best sugar cane on earth, then she'd go on to say how beautiful the island was – that the sands were white as snow and the waters were so clear that you could see a nickel at the bottom of the ocean.

While other kids were taking their annual trip to Disney World, my trip was the generic version of that reality, the dream world. Every night I'd drift into a world of being with my mother on the island of St. Croix. She'd be off to herself while I'd be playing with a little boy that spoke with an accent. Us building sand castles. Looking for jelly-fish. Playing Marco Polo as he chased me through the waters in my teenybopper bathing suit, and mama would be lying on a quilt sipping lemonade, yelling for me to stay in her sight before the current drifts me out to the deep end.

Then I'd wake up.

Back in the ghetto. Back in a place where the nearest beach was the water hose in the backyard and the nearest boy with an accent was Bernard down the street who couldn't pronounce his A,B,C's.

Nevertheless, with two million dollars I no longer had to envision. Now I could truly live the surreal life.

"Attention everyone! Please put your personal belongings in one tray and clothes in the other."

As the rules were explained to the passengers, I glanced at my black duffel bag that hung from my shoulders, realizing I was next in line. I tried to keep my items together by placing my shoes and duffel in the same tray, but the security guard quickly put me on blast. "Again! Personal bags in one tray and clothes in the other."

I watched as my items were sold into slavery. Told myself that no matter what, I wouldn't let that duffel bag out of my sight.

"Step forward please ma'am."

The security guard – a chubby middle-aged Latino that loved his job – told me to raise my arms and keep my feet apart, then he took his sensor and ran it over my body.

The sensor went off. His eyebrows flared up.

"Well well well," he said. "Are you carrying anything in your pockets?"

"Nothing but change."

"All change must be emptied into the tray. Now take two steps back and two steps forward again."

I emptied my pockets to walk back through, and again the sensor beeped at my mid-section.

"Your ring, ma'am. Rings and watches must come off."

Two steps back and two steps forward, I looked over to mark the location of my duffel bag, but I had no visual.

Again the sensor sounds.

"What is it now?" I asked.

"Do you have a metal clip in your hair?"

"Yeah, so what?"

"Step back through."

I blew out a hard deep breath before repeating this course of action that was more frustrating than chemistry. Now alarmed, the security swipes me up and down like a hoodlum in a club, his sensor treading my hips as if he's performing a cavity check.

The metal detector sounds once more.

"Your belt ma'am. The buckle on your belt is metal."

"For Christ's sake!" I screamed. "What else do a bitch gotta do for cryin' out loud? Get butt-naked?" Fed up, I tore off my belt then pulled down my pants, and now I'm left wearing nothing but a T-shirt and thong, my ass on display for the entire airport to see.

A mother covers the eyes of her son while the security guard's mouth drops to the floor.

"Jesus Christ!" someone yells.

Refusing to swipe me anymore, the security guard passes me along the checkpoint line.

I quickly suited up in all of my gear. Did that while I looked in the tray line for my black duffel bag.

But there was no duffel.

All the trays were empty, and security was placing the empty trays back in front for the next round of passengers.

Freaked out, I tapped one of the guards on the shoulder. "Hey Mr. I'm missing my bag."

"Your bag?"

"Yes. My black duffel bag. It just came through this line."

"As you can see ma'am, no bags are here. You might want to check at the information desk."

"The what? Oh hell no! My bag was just here and I know it's 'round here somewhere. So what I suggest you do is—"

"Ma'am!"

"What?"

"I need you to calm down."

"Then find my bag!"

"As I said, you must check with the information desk. If your bag is missing, I'm sure someone would've turned it in by now."

With two million dollars on the line, I replied, "Like hell they would've."

He blew me off and returned to his position, left me standing there vexed with 59 cents in my pocket, and that's when I started looking around to catch the chosen thief.

The airport traffic had gotten heavy. Noise grew in volume. Bodies brushed against bodies to rush to all parts of the world – hundreds of passengers with hundreds of bags walking in a hundred different directions, like staring in a maze, each person with a bag that was similar to my duffel. At this point the chosen thief could've already been on a plane, celebrating their luck while camping out in coach. The thought of that nearly gave me a hemorrhage.

I tried to stay focus and calm, took my stare to the wall to search the flight schedule. The next flight to board was heading for Sacramento. But that wasn't until the next ten minutes, which meant that whoever had my bag was still in this airport; all I had to do was sniff them out.

I looked into the cluttered crowd to detect any abstract behavior. In front of me was an Asian couple speed-walking with souvenir bags in their hands and hats that read, *Welcome to Vegas*. The hats fit the profile of tourists. But then again tourists don't usually walk that fast, which had my senses stirring, something was fishy.

The Asian woman turned her head to glance in my direction - her eyes beaming with guilt - then she turned back around and heightened her pace.

And that's when I saw it.

My black duffel bag was right on her arm, and the worst part of all is that her and her lover were speed-walking directly towards the escalator.

I ran down my money like an attic for a fix while pushing and shoving my way through the crowded airport. Before the target could step foot on the escalator, I grabbed her by her shirt, spun her around, and without intending to make a scene, I told her, "Gimme my money."

She didn't respond, just stood there and looked scared.

I snarled, "Gimme my money!"

"Uh ... Uh ... No Englis ... Me speak no Englis." She looked at her husband for support.

I told him, "Tell her to give up my money. And don't give me that no-speaketh-English crap either." Apparently he did speak English, or at least the generic kind, and he translated my words to his wife, did that while she raised her hands in a dumbfounded manner, then she translated back that she didn't have any money.

I told her husband, "Translate this! My money is in that black duffel bag and she's got two seconds to give it back before I whoop her narrow ass!"

He shook his head and defended his wife. "She has nothing ... we by bag ... souvenir store ... $24.99 ... $24.99." The hubby points toward the store but I'm still not buying it.

Right then and there, I snatched the duffel bag from the woman's tenacious grip, unzipped it, and I ran my hands through her paraphernalia as if it were my own.

What I found was absolutely nothing. No money. Nothing but tourist maps, chocolate snacks, and casino items.

Fresh out of luck, I gave her back what was rightfully hers, but not before she turned to her husband and held him tight, muttering in his ear, "Americans are crazy ... crazy crazy crazy."

I moved on to other potential targets, scoping people out like a carnivore for flesh. Eyes sharpened. Hawk-like vision. Every bag on every arm was a first cousin to my duffel, but none fit the profile exactly; either the strap was too long or the color was slightly off. And that drove me even more insane. Anticipation was heartless.

As the airport became blurry, I suddenly heard the voice of a security guard. "We have an unclaimed bag. Unclaimed bag!"

Without hesitation, I chased down the guard like a fleeing city bus, and that's when I started screaming out loud, "That's my bag! That's my bag!"

At this point I'd drawn the attention of the entire airport. But I didn't care. My only thought was retrieving that duffel no matter the cost.

The guard looked me in the eye. Coincidentally, it was the same guard that scanned me with the metal detector.

He asks, "Is this your bag ma'am?"

"Yes, yes, yes," I replied out of breath.

"Good. We're gonna have to check it."

"Say what? Wait a second. You already searched me once. Don't you remember? The woman that nearly got naked?"

Unsure of my face, he gave me an Alzheimer's stare, then went on to say, "Sorry ma'am, but a lot of people come through this airport."

"Are you kidding me?"

"I'm afraid not. Now before I search this bag, you mind verifying what's inside? Any liquids? Anything hazardous?"

"None of that. Just personal things."

"Such as?"

"Such as ... Tampons okay! A bag full of tampons, vaginal creams, and medications for my yeast infection."

Too much information caused a stunned reaction.

I didn't lie to him. I really did have a bag full of everything I mentioned. But I only had them to cover up the two million dollars that hid beneath.

Mr. Security Guard unzips my RX bag slowly, unzipped it as carefully as a body bag in a morgue.

His face wrinkles like a prune as if he hated his job, then he zipped the bag up with swelling disgust.

"You're all set, ma'am. Now have a safe trip."

32

After being on a plane for six hours, the island of St. Croix was well worth the wait, was well worth checking into The Palms Hotel at Pelican Cove.

I was lying on white sands with my knees up, staring into the sun as ocean waves hummed in my ear while filling my nostrils with salt-water scents.

This was the ultimate paradise. And walking the grounds of that paradise were men wearing nothing but Speedos. Chiseled bodies. Men with skin pigments that aren't black or white, just shades of brown where you have to guess their nationality. Every man walking by was staring at me as I lay on the sand. All shared the same routine. No conversation. No hi's or hello's. Just introverted smiles. I figured that eye contact was their way of trying to holla, but where I'm from, too much eye contact can be a major turn-off.

I guess I can't blame them for staring though. I was wearing the tightest, two-piece yellow bikini that money could buy, legs oiled for the sun, and my alohas could be seen through my top that was ready to free Willy. God knows I was feeling every single inch of myself.

I closed my eyes from the sun and envisioned Cuqui being here with me, the Cuqui I knew before the betrayal. We always talked about coming to this island with our bi-weekly checks and going half-

and-half on a master suite. I can picture her here; can hear her talking a mile a minute of how she'd do every penis that swings on this island, and how she'd impregnate herself so the child would come out with good curly hair. I can hear her persuading me to buy a Sex On The Beach, telling me that I might as well get drunk while I'm living because once I'm dead I've got the whole after-life to be sober. I can hear her laughing. Her bragging. Can hear her complaining that it's too hot to be getting a Suntan, that God had already made her black enough. That was the Cuqui I knew. The Cuqui I loved. And that makes this moment bitter-sweet. Makes me feel that there's no such thing as true happiness, even if two million dollars is lying in your lap.

After getting burned by the sun for nearly half an hour, my thirst had come to life, needed a drink badly. I wiped hot sands from my glistening skin before walking barefooted to the tiki bar with a towel around my waist.

Resembling a little brown hut with hay stacked atop the roof, that little tiki bar was the main attraction on this beach. Music gave life to this spot. Bob Marley was singing One Love, steadily convincing us all to get together and feel alright. I hummed along under my breath to co-sign on the chorus, did that while the DJ - a white chubby hairy-chested guy with a rock band haircut - winked in my direction while spinning the turn tables. Because of scarce seating I unfortunately had to stand. Every barstool was stolen by the rear of a man that was putting the moves on a young gullible woman. Older men. Established men. Men that needed the dollar bill to compensate for their lack of looks, and women sipping liver poison from fancy cups that came with roller-coaster straws.

But men weren't the only prowlers at the bar. Next to me was a man that was bunched in between two women who were twins, twins in bikinis. The women were six foot even with massive fake breasts, and they were working the man like hookers on the corner, anxious to show him the time they could give if he spent the right price. He muttered to them that his pockets were low, that he could only afford one of them, but then they muttered something back, something making him reconsider, and in the midst of his thoughts one flashed him a nipple. That sealed the deal. Was more than enough for him to leave hand-in-hand with the silicon twins and chase his fantasy up to a room.

Still needing that drink, I looked behind the bar for the bartender. Saw no one. Only saw Jack Daniels and the rest of his friends that were eyeing me down, begging me to climb across the bar and pop those bottles. I started getting antsy. Thirst came alive. Told myself that after all the stuff I'd been through this week, I don't have time for a bitch to clock in.

Subsequently I received a tap on the shoulder. My eyes went left. Went to a tall man with a pyramid of muscles, golden brown skin, clean-shaven head, shirtless, and from what I could see, pants less too.

Speedos. Booty-tight Speedos. That's all the clothing that covered his body, a walking exhibit outside the museum.

"Can I get you something to drink?" he asked.

"I can get my own drink."

"No seriously. I'm the bartender."

"Dressed like that? And I'm the tooth fairy."

"Oh I see, you a comedian huh. Well I'll tell you what—"

He reaches across the bar to pick up a menu, drops the menu into my lap, then he walked behind the bar to begin stirring up a vodka and cranberry before walking that over to an elderly man with an angry thirst. He collected ten dollars. Gave back four. Then walked back to that alcoholic basement, whipped up a Malibu on the rocks, motioned that million dollar body to a European woman that was joined by three friends, the four of them gawking at his body while saying what they'd do if they ever got him alone, one deeming him as her island aphrodisiac. Those same women were trying to reel him in by throwing out their bait. He never bit. Just smiled at them and walked back to me.

He said, "Figured out what you wanted?"

Fire brown skin. Perfect bone structure. An accent so sexy it could sweet-talk a swan, could talk a wild zebra right out of her stripes.

"I take that as you're still undecided," he said.

"I am a little. Anything you recommend?"

"Well, we have a really good Holy Moly."

"A Holy what?"

"Holy Moly. It's rum and chocolate, whipped cream, and a dab of Kahlua."

I looked at the menu, did that without trying to check out his package.

My choices consisted of a Sunrise Sunset. Greygoose on the Sunroof. Tila Tequila. Malibu thru-n-thru. Holy Moly. Sex on the Beach. Paradise Pointe. And Cocktail Crazy.

"A Malibu would be fine," I told him. "And go light on the chaser. Need extra liquor."

He smiles. "Long day?"

"Try life."

He saunters back to that alcohol basement to start working on my drink, began multitasking between fixing beverages and dishing out change. When he made his rounds back to me, I pulled five dollars out of my top, but he quickly said, "Save your money. The drink is on the house."

I checked him. "On the house or on you?"

He smiled a seductive smile. "Okay I'm guilty. On me."

"How sweet of you. But don't expect any booty in return."

"Any booty worth five dollars is booty I don't want."

We laughed.

He said, "Besides, everyone's entitled to a free drink their first time on the island."

"Oh I see. And what makes you think it's my first time?"

"Because I know every face that walks this island, and beauty like yours is impossible to go undetected."

I blushed. "Corny line, but I'll take it."

"So what is your name?"

"Let's not get into names. I'm still deciding whether I like you or not."

My comment stung hard.

He nodded his head. "Fair enough. Well they call me Ian."

"Nice to meet you, Ian. And where are the rest of your clothes?"

"What do you mean?"

"Do you always come to work like you're auctioning sex?"

He glances down at his half-nakedness, that bulge in his Speedos stretching the elastic. "Actually, this not my everyday job. I'm filling in for my uncle until he returns."

"Your uncle?"

"He is the owner. I'm just the dumb nephew that picked up the phone, and I'm doing him a favor for the next"—he looks over at the clock—"half hour. Only been here for twenty minutes and I'm already fixin' to throw in the towel."

"Hey bartender!" someone yelled. "Can we get a couple drinks over here?"

Ian cut his eyes at the impatient customers, then he walked off to quench their lingering thirsts.

Meanwhile, I got more acquainted with my Malibu drink that I strongly needed for twenty-four hours.

Alcohol. A relief liquid. It's the only medication that numbs all worries, can put your troubles into a temporary grave. But even with an unimaginable bank account and lying on a beautiful serene beach, alcohol wasn't enough to liberate my past.

Cuqui. Sergio. Snow. Mr. Marcello.

Those four haunted ghosts were swirling through the waves of my drink, reminding me that even though I was vacationing in a surreal world, the real world was just a boarding pass away.

I surrendered my thoughts to the tangy substance that's undefeated in the ring of tranquility, fed my thirst that Malibu drink while closing my eyes and savoring the taste. Then I sipped some more. And some more. Sipped that eighty proof anesthesia until it drove me into a sedated paradise, was so in tune with my drink that I never noticed Ian who was right in my face, staring me down with a palm to his chin.

"So what did he do?" Ian asked, leaning over the bar.

"Excuse me?"

"The guy you're thinking about. What did he do?"

"What make you think a man did something? Can't a woman just be on the beach to get some peace and serenity?"

He laughs an uncomfortable laugh, the type that said not to play on his intelligence.

Then he said, "If you look around this beach you'll notice a pattern. There are women here with other women. Women here with men. But a woman doesn't come to this beach by her lonesome, unless…"

"Go on. Unless what?"

"Unless Mr. Right turned out to be Mr. Wrong."

I sucked my teeth. "It's so typical of men to think that everything revolves around them."

"So tell me I'm wrong. Tell me that a sexy woman like yourself is here on this beach for another reason."

I glanced back at the world of my Malibu drink, that Styrofoam cup still carrying those ghosts.

Cuqui. Sergio. Snow. Mr. Marcello.

Those ghosts had swam to the rim of my cup like crabs in a bucket, all reaching out, eight hands persevering to strangle me subconsciously. With an aggravating thirst I downed the remaining contents in one large gulp, dumped those ghosts into a twelve-foot grave.

Eyes extended, Ian said, "If there's no men problems then what would you call that?"

"A deep-throat chick that loves to drink."

We laughed.

I said, "While you're all up in my kool-aid, tell me something about you. Are you married?"

"Divorced."

"Ran out on the wife?"

He scowls at my sarcasm. "Actually, she ran out on me. Out on me and our three little boys."

I swallowed that sarcasm. "Sorry to hear that."

"Oh it's no big deal. It's like my grandmother used to say, 'The upside to losing is receiving something greater."

"I dig that ... And as for you?"

"Huh?"

"What did you receive for losing your wife?"

"My life ... I got it back ... From my kids to my family, I got my life back."

No response. I just sat there as he said, "You know I gave up everything for that woman. My career. Money. Friends. Even went against my mother who told me not to marry her, a mother-son relationship that took years to patch up. I gave that woman everything that a husband can give a wife, and what does she do? What does she do? She ... she ..."

Words burn in his throat like salt on a wound, that sentence as hard as pulling a truck.

Eye contact is lost. Chemistry is broken. Then he looks away as if he's looking into a painful past. I wanted to comment, wanted to ask him why his wife up and left him like a Tyler Perry flick, but the fire in his eyes made me ditch the gasoline. I left that stone unturned.

Softening the moment, I said, "So you are a father of three ... that's very impressive."

"It is?"

"Of course. A single father that's handling his business. You should be honored."

"Wow, you make it sound like I deserve a humanitarian award. There are some single fathers still out there you know."

"Not in my neck of the woods. Where I'm from single fathers are like killer whales. Damn near extinct."

He laughed. That laugh lightened his mood as another woman walked up to order a Pina Colada, her third drink today, gave him a tip.

Ian asked me, "So what about you? Any kids?"

I thought about Devilla, remembered she wasn't mines, answered, "Not yet."

"Well if you need any just let me know in advance. I'll save you the nine months of pain and agony."

"Yeah right. You wouldn't dare give up your boys."

He raised a brow. "You sure 'bout that? With all the money they're costing me, I'll put them in a box and FedEx their butts to the highest bidder."

More chuckles that were interrupted by a few tourists that each wanted refills on their favorite island drinks.

The bar was starting to get crowded. The DJ had switched up the music from Bob Marley to Sean Paul's dance music, that uptempo beat bringing people to their feet with drinks in hands, caused people to grab a partner and get loose to their own ethnic rhythms. It was during that chaos that an elderly man walked up to Ian and slapped him on the shoulder, then gave Ian an immense bear hug that followed with a sun-filled smile.

"Er dere, nephew. Whaapm? Yuh treat dis bar right? Tek care mi customers?"

"Your customers are about to drive me insane. I don't see how you do it, Unc."

"Oh stop being pussyfoot. Lil' ezra work neva turt anti' one."

Like Ms. Montreal, Ian's uncle spoke in a patois dialect that skips and slurs, that beautiful broken English much richer than his nephews. Physically though, their features were identical. From the wide broad shoulders to the bowlegged stance to the dimple in the chin that sculpted their faces, it was no secret that Ian's uncle was dipped in the same bloodline, only difference is that the uncle's muscles had turned to flab. Looked like he was handsome in his early days, before time swallowed his youth and coughed up age. He wore dark brown Dockers with a Caribbean shirt, beat-up sandals as old as him. Head was bald on top, hair left on the sides. Shirt proudly unbuttoned with a pot belly, and on top of that belly was a chest of grey hair, growing into a garden of weeds.

Ian introduced the two of us, told his uncle, "Meet Ms. Anonymous."

"Ms. Anonymous?"

"Well I've yet to get the privilege of knowing her name so—"

"Angel," I intervened, reaching to shake his hand. "The name is Angel."

"Er gal. Whey yuh ah seh? Yuh firs' time on mi island?"

"Yes, Sir."

"Good. 'Cause ervy firs' timer deserve—"

"A free drink?"

"How juh knew?"

I smiled at Ian, told his uncle, "I guess your nephew already beat you to the punch."

He looked at Ian while rubbing his double chin. "Bounty bwoy neph. Always stealin' juice from yuh uncle. Well if yur gonna steal my lines 'least help me dis Saturday."

"This Saturday? That's completely out the question. I have a business to run and you know it."

"Oh dat right. Mi forget. Yuh gots run dat titty shack down de road."

Titty shack, I thought. Never said a word, just listened.

"So nephew, yuh gon' le mi pay dat lady island yurs visit."

Ian shook his head at his uncle, annoyance beginning to crawl up his face. "We've already been through this, Unc. You can't work at my place."

"Not even wun day?"

"Not even one minute. Don't need you scaring away the customers."

"Yur unc don't scerr way gals. Yuh mus' be crazy nephew. Mi might be ol' but mi sexy. Don't yuh know dat sixty is de new tenty."

"You mean thirty is the new twenty."

"Same tang."

"Actually, it's not the same thing."

"Mi sixty en still sexy. Ol' en sexy. Ain't a gal walkin' dat will tank mi not sexy."

"You sure 'bout that? 'Cause this isn't the seventies."

"Seventies, nineties, tenty-fucking-eleven, yur unc still be sexy. Yur yanky gal will even say so 'erself."

He looked towards me and flashed a wide grin, teeth a few winters from owning some dentures. "Now tell me sometin' sweet tang, is mi not de sexy ol' man yuh eva saw or wha?"

Ian quickly got in between us. "You don't have to answer that." Then he turned back to his uncle. "That's enough, Unc. Now if you don't mind, we're gonna get back to enjoying ourselves. Your cash is in the drawer. You're short on fives. And the Vodka is almost out."

After Ian passed his uncle the bartender baton, he joined me on a barstool to have another drink and I sipped a Tequila while he downed a Holy Moly. A new shift of cheating husbands had come to the Tiki Bar. They were greeted by the local hookers of this island – the silicon twins being the culprits of the bunch. Conversations were exchanged.

Big money quickly made its way into those conversations. The DJ had slowed down the tempo to Sade's sweet classic, *No Ordinary Love*, that symphony laying the charcoal for the soon-to-be heat that would later burn in hotel rooms. Ian started apologizing for his uncle's outbursts, but my mind was still on the past, on this boobie shack that his uncle mentioned earlier.

I told him, "So what does your real job consist of? You a Gigolo or something?"

"No no, I'm no Gigolo."

"Male Escort?"

"Oh be for real. Do I look like a Male Escort?"

I glanced back down at his Speedos. "You sure you want me to answer that question?"

He laughed. "I guess I set myself up for that one."

"He rub tit for living," his uncle said from afar. "Rub lot of tit."

Ian waved his uncle off, told me, "Don't pay that fool no mind. That's just the idiotic way of saying Massage Therapist."

"Oh I see, a Massage Therapist. So you feel women up all day."

"And men!" his uncle added.

Ian looked embarrassed. "He's just kidding around. I only massage women. The men are sent to my sister."

"Your sister?"

"I run a small business for Massage Therapy. It's family owned. Started by my grandmother twenty years ago and now it's left to me."

"Sounds like your job is the average man's dream."

"Or nightmare, depending on the client. Not every woman that comes into my shop is a Beyonce Knowles, if that's what you think."

"True. But that's still no reason to complain. Last I checked, ass was ass."

"Not ass full of dents, stretch marks, and twenty pounds of cellulite. That's no longer considered an ass. That's a woolly mammoth."

I cracked up. "You're wrong for that. Dead wrong."

"I'm serious. That's why I had to re-adjust my prices to match a woman's weight."

"What? You kidding right?"

"For a full-body massage, it's $75 for those under 150 pounds. 150 to 185 pounds is $90. 185 to 225 is $115. And anything over 225 is looking at $149 plus tax." He takes a sip of his drink as if he's said nothing wrong, and I reached over to stop him in mid-sip, followed by smacking him over the head.

I told him, "Could you be any more of a bastard?"

"Hey, I'm just making sure I get rightfully paid for my work."

"And how's that? By over-charging heavyset women. Whatever happened to equal opportunity?"

"Equal opportunity doesn't pay my mortgage. I mean, think of it like this. When you take a car to the repair shop, they don't only charge for the parts. They charge for labor too."

I shook my head in a baffling manner. "Is that your way of rationalizing your crooked massage parlor?"

"Business is business. And if you're gonna walk into my place of business with the body of a truck, then don't expect to get the price of a compact car."

"Yeah, well remind me not to ever go to your parlor."

We shared more laughs. Got better acquainted while refilling our cups with more island drinks. In that moment of truth, I found out that Ian was divorced and had sole custody of his three little boys. According to him the wife was a rolling stone, a stone that eventually rolled into the arms of another woman that was ten years their junior, then she fed him some lame story of how she wanted to explore other options, that after years of feasting on women it was time to let go of men. I found out that the entire dilemma caused him jail time for assault. Told me it was the first and only time he had ever put his hands on a woman, and ever since then he's been running from marriage like it's a plague. It's also why he came to the island. To have a new beginning. Create a new life.

Our conversation went on for another half-hour, a conversation conjoined with my second round of Tequila and another Holy Moly for my half-naked date. Although Ian was on some confession type stuff, I dared not to expose my reason for being here. Instead of telling him the truth, I led him to believe that his assumption was right, that men problems led me to this island alone. He smiled at the sound of that open door policy, but I quickly reminded him that I was off limits, no hanky panky going on tonight.

In the midst of that rejection his cellular vibrated.

Ian looked at the face of the phone, gritted his teeth, the type of aggravation that can only be caused by a woman. My ears zoomed in as he answered the phone, and I heard him say, "No ... no ... same place I was earlier ... on the beach with my uncle ... like I told you earlier, that's not my responsibility, I already did my part ... of course I'm sure goddammit ... okay ... okay."

Click.

That call ended in record breaking time, perplexity skating all over his face.

I told him, "Let me guess, the ex-wife?"

"Can you believe she got the nerve to call me ... me of all people ... fuckin' bombaclot ... She should try calling that butch looking thundercat she ran off with."

Anger. The tattle-tell of all emotions. It made Ian reach behind the bar to whip up a Cosmo and cure his frustration with an alcoholic dose.

I kept my mouth shut. His problem, his solution. It was obvious he wasn't quite over his wife. His eyes said he wasn't, voice said more. And I sat there and listened to him drag her in the ground, his face wrinkling, muscles tensing, but not even muscles can lift a heavy heart.

Ten minutes later, after the alcohol worked a miracle on Ian's temper, the Tiki Bar was starting to clear out. Every older man had struck a deal with their fantasy woman and each fantasy was either escorted to a hotel room or onto the hot sands of the beach. The silicon twins were the last women present. They were still on the grind, still searching for prey, determined to get rich before the day capped. Alongside them it was me and Ian, the DJ, and Ian's uncle who kept singing Bob Marley while wiping down countertops.

Laughter erupted in my peripheral vision. Laughter coming from four white men that stumbled to the bar, their potbellies out, tanned by the sun, and man boobs bouncing with every stride, looked like four whales that were drugged from the ocean. Wearing Mardi Gras beads around their necks, it was no doubt that these tourists were in search of some sin.

And sin quickly found them.

Sin that rose with the leopard's eye, the silicon twins going after fresh meat like lions on the backs of running zebras.

That illustration took me back to something I was curious about.

I told Ian, "So how much would you charge those women?"

"Come again?"

"As a Massage Therapist, you say you charge women according to their build. So if those women were to walk into your massage parlor, exactly how much would you charge them?"

He hesitates.

I went on, "On second thought, how much would you charge me?"

"You?"

"Yeah me."

He taps at his drink as if he's taking in my question.

"And don't BS me," I added. "Be honest."

"Well, Angel ... that all depends."

"On?"

His lips curl in like a little boy. "Tell you what, if you're here tomorrow, I'll be sure to give you one on the house. No charge."

I smiled. "You're so full of shit."

With two Tequilas in my system, my bladder was starting to overflow, plus all this seduction didn't make it any better. I left Ian sitting at the bar to make a trip to the bathroom around the corner. The bathroom was dirty. Make that filthy. Looked like a urine infestation had covered the toilet, and inside the toilet was another version of the Holy Moly.

I quickly flushed before untying my bathing suit bottoms, and without touching the seat I handled my business. Then knocking. Knocking on my bathroom stall. Saw a barefooted woman with really big feet.

I spoke out. "I'm using this stall. Go to the next one."

Those feet never left. Just stood there. Then suddenly the person kicked open the bathroom stall, a kick that made my eyes pop out like Roger Rabbit.

"What the—"

"Get on the ground!" the person demanded. "Get on the ground right now!"

I wanted to scream, but for some reason that scream turned around, fled down my throat, then it zipped through my uterus and out through my body to flush out the fluids I had left inside, fluids that thunderstormed into the filthy toilet.

"Get on the ground! Get your ass on the ground!"

Not a woman. But a heavyset man. It was one of the four whales that had walked to the Tiki Bar, the law in his eyes with a badge attached to his swimming trunks. *St. Croix Police.*

Embarrassed and frightened at the same time, I quickly tried to pull up my bathing suit, but I was bomb rushed before that could happen.

"Wait a second!" I screamed. "Wait a goddamn second!"

He grabbed both my arms in a forceful manner before slamming me against the urinated floor, my bikini bottom strapped at my ankles, my private parts now on display.

"Can't you see I'm naked motherfucker! This is police brutality!"

Pinned on that cold slippery floor, he ordered me to hurry up and pull up my bottoms, then he told me, "I'm with the St. Croix Police Department. And you're under arrest."

I tried to move.

"Stay on the ground, Ms Inghram! Stay on the ground!"

"Under arrest for what?" I yelled. "What are you arresting me for?"

"For the murder of William Randolph and the kidnapping of Devilla Randolph."

"But—"

"Stay on the ground! Don't you dare move!"

Handcuffs are slapped on one of my wrists. Handcuffs that made me go berserk for fear of the obvious, that if I didn't free myself now, I'll be staring behind freedom walls. I swept my foot around to kick him in the groin, kicked him good and hard. He ached and grabbed his balls, wailed like a man being burned to death. That genius kick allowed me some room to get up and run out the bathroom, but while running from the law, I ran into the web of another fat cop that was posted outside on the beach sands, couldn't dodge that spider for nothing in the world as the trailing spider was flagging me down. One strong-armed my free hand, the one that wasn't cuffed, and I bit into his forearm to try and break free from his tenacious grip. Bit into an arm of cement. An arm that gripped me like a dumbbell and spun me around, bringing me to my knees, making me retract.

"No resisting!" he shouted. "Try and resist and it only gets worse!"

"Wait a second! You've got ... the wrong person."

"Gimme that other hand!"

I refused to surrender. I kicked. Scratched. Bit. Pinched. Started fighting like a bull in a pin. Fought them motherfuckers with all I had.

"Taze her goddammit. Taze her!"

"I ain't tazing no woman."

"A crazy bitch is not a woman!"

I kicked some more. Bit and clawed. Flopped on the sand like a fish out of water. Kicked and scratched and swung and pinched, until 120 volts were sent through my ribcage, electricity that felt like a thousand lighting strikes.

I hit the ground hard. Squealed like a pig. Screamed louder than a woman in labor with twins, singing that song of agony.

"Now stay there! Try to get up and we won't hesitate to shoot!"

I raised my head up from white sand like a paraplegic, and what I saw above me was enough to take this nightmare into overdrive. *We* meant company. *We* consisted of three guns in three different hands, each pointed directly at me.

The owner of those weapons were the suntanned whales that came to the tiki bar, each affiliated with the St. Croix Police Department, each displaying mean units that dared me to escape.

One of the whales said, "You got her under control, Edgar?"

"She's not going anywhere. I got her pinned."

Cold metal is slapped hard against my other wrist. Metal stings me. Handcuffs tighten to control me.

In that moment of misery – with my chin buried in hot sands – one of the cops started saying my Miranda Rights, that declaration of imprisonment. "You have the right to remain silent. Anything you say or do can be held against you in the court of law..."

"Wait a second," I shouted out.

"You have the right to an attorney. If you can't afford an attorney, one will be—"

"Wait a goddamn second! You're making a mistake. You got the wrong—"

"—appointed for you. Do you understand your rights?"

"I'm tellin' you that you got the wrong—"

"Answer the question!" Do you understand your rights?"

With a graveyard of muscles on top of me, I raised my chin from the sands to look around for a getaway.

But every getaway was blocked, and all guns were still on me, the three whales biting their lips as if they wanted to finish me off right here; all they needed was a reason.

With nowhere to run, I cooperated by standing on my feet.

The Swimming Trunk Detectives walked me through the beach sands, then through the Tiki Bar, then walked me by people who were all standing by. Ian stood by. His uncle stood by. The silicon twins and the DJ stood by, witnessing my fate with box office seats.

Then Ian yelled to one of the cops, "What about my money? When do I get my money?"

In his hand was a sheet of paper that resembled a flyer. It looked like the same flyer I'd seen in the states.

Felon on the loose.
Armed and Dangerous.
$20,000 for any leads to her whereabouts.

Somehow that flyer had flown from the states to the shores of St. Croix Island, now resting in the hands of an informant with Speedos.

I thought back in time. Thought about the phone call that Ian received from his ex-wife, how he pretended to be angry, pretended to be vulnerable, pretended to be talking to a woman when he was really leading the FBI to my whereabouts, one little phone call costing my life.

One.

Fucking.

Phone.

Call.

Rage permeated in the pits of my stomach as the police escorted me pass the informant. I made an attempt to reach for his throat, but handcuffs made that reach impossible. I spat in his face. He couldn't dodge that. But from his reaction, twenty grand was worth the saliva that slid down his cheeks, and he repeated to the cops, "Where's my money? I need my money!"

The cops blatantly ignored his request. Maybe because they were too focused on their own prize, Angel Inghram, a prize they happily walked out the Tiki Bar and escorted through the parking lot, then opened the doors of the police car where I got in without putting up a fight. People followed the chaos like cheetahs going after gazelles, spectators coming and running from everywhere. Leading that crowd was Ian who flagged down the nearest cop he could find, the flyer in his hand and a concern in his voice. "My twenty grand! I need that twenty grand!"

"That has nothing to do with us," a cop said. "Now clear the way! Everyone clear the way!"

Parking lot full. All eyes on me. I became the *You Tube Video* on this little island, spectators coming from everywhere.

Police tried to handle the crowd. "Clear the way. Everyone clear the way."

"What's going on? Whose going to jail? Whose ... What did she do ... Murder ... When ... Why ... Kidnapping ..."

In the rowdy crowd, Ian was still yelling for his prize. "My money??? My money???"

"Like I told you, we don't control that part. Now move out the way! Official police business!"

Another police tapped on the window of the police car. Windows rolled down. "Hey Paul, is she cuffed securely in that back seat?"

"Secure as it gets."

"My twenty grand? You cops owe me twenty grand!"

"Sir, please clear the way! Everyone clear the way!"

"What did she do? She what ... Robbed a bank ... damn ... huh ... oh arson ... heard she committed arson."

"Everyone please clear the way! Clear the way!"

"My twenty grand? Where do I collect my twenty grand?"

"For the last time, move out the way!"

"But—"

"Hey asshole! You heard my partner. Clear the way or you will be arrested."

Staring out the backseat behind a thick window, I waited as the police car slowly backed out the parking lot to make its departure. Rainbow lights flicked on with the click of a button. Lights started flashing. Sirens started humming. But not even sirens could tune out the crowd.

"Please clear the way! Everyone clear the way."

"Twenty grand ... My twenty grand!"

33

I had made the front page of the New York Times.

The column read, *Judgment Day for Angel Inghram*, a paper shoved in my face from journalists and reporters who were all anxious to get their fifteen minutes of fame.

One reporter from Inquire Magazine asked, "Ms. Inghram, how do you feel the jury will rule today?"

"If they trust their instincts and don't be influenced by you people, then hopefully they'll make the right decision."

I'd never been so popular in my life. But popularity is a bitch when it's driven by controversy.

Me and my lawyer, a heavyset woman named Silvia Dawson – a woman who represented me before – were trying to fight through an enormous crowd before entering the courthouse of my awaited verdict, and after six months of ducking the press, after six months of going back and forth to court and receiving launch attacks from the harsh media, prison would be no harder than downing a cold glass of Chardonnay.

Today I felt confident. My lawyer did a fabulous job of proving that even though I shot William Randolph, it was an act of insanity, and my bullet wasn't the bullet that ended his life inside that hospital; Snow's bullet was.

But that wasn't the only thing I had to worry about. I also faced kidnapping charges. Charges that could bury me.

One news reporter yelled out, "*Ms. Inghram, although you rescued the little girl, do you feel there should be repercussions for committing the kidnapping?*"

"I was willing to endanger my own life to save the life of someone else. Now does that sound like kidnapping to you?"

"*But what about—*"

"*Ms. Inghram over here ... Over here ... Over here...*" My head turned to CNN. "*Do you feel any regret for what you did to your stepfather?*"

"Don't answer the question," my lawyer whispered.

Truth is my lawyer prohibited me from previously speaking to any reporters. Told me it was detrimental to the case. But how I saw it was that I had held my tongue long enough, and since the jury had finally reached a verdict, a little talking wouldn't hurt.

"*Ms. Inghram over here ... over here ... over here ...*"

People started closing in on me like an over-crowded elevator.

"*Ms. Inghram, are you afraid of going to prison?*"

"Oh course not. I can't wait to rub up against a hairy woman that hasn't showered in weeks."

My sarcasm solidified the stupidity of that question.

"*And what if you're acquitted? What's life going to be like for Angel Inghram after the trial?*"

"I've never given up on wanting to become an attorney. So when all this is over, hopefully my life will resume back to normal, and when I become a prosecutor, I can look forward to putting the real criminals behind bars."

"*But don't you think that goal is a little far-fetched, given the present circumstances?*"

I sneered. "Far-fetched? In case you failed to do your research, I was one of the top students at Brooklyn Law School before this tragedy occurred. As far as the present circumstances, I've learned what it means to think and act like a criminal, something that could never be taught in a classroom. So politics aside, if I don't meet the requirements of being an attorney, then quite frankly, who does?"

"Okay guys," my lawyer intervened. "We can only take one more question."

Her comments sprinkled peppers on the crowd, caused microphones to rush me like kindergarteners to a pinata.

"*What about Devilla?*" someone yelled.

I looked into the over-zealous crowd. A short stout woman from NBC was trying her best to make herself seen. "*What about Devilla?*" she repeated. "*If you could speak to the little girl, what would you tell her?*"

I paused for a brief moment, my words anticipated by every network on television.

I told the world, "I'll ask her for forgiveness ... yes ... just forgiveness."

Verizon's marching 500 was still trailing us towards the courthouse, but their tour ended at the front entrance. None were allowed inside.

The walk through the courthouse was one to remember. Felt like I was walking off a cliff while my soul lagged behind, no rush to get to the edge. Along that walk was a listing of the presidents of the United States. Their faces were lined up from oldest to current. Unfriendly faces. Faces that sneered at me with every step I took. By the time I reached Lincoln I was ready to sprint back in the other direction. Would've done so if it wasn't for my lawyer who kept reassuring me that everything would be okay.

She added, "And no matter the outcome, I'm still here for you."

I wanted to believe her, but after entering the courtroom and hearing the judge say, "*The State vs. Angel Inghram*," I knew right then that I was alone on this one. Completely alone.

The judge went on to say, "Has the jury reached a verdict?"

"Yes we have your honor."

"Very well then. Will the defendant please rise."

In a Democratic Nation, a nation where strangers are chosen to determine your fate before ever knowing their own, I stood up to face the jury. Stood in my long dress and waited for justice.

"When it comes to the charge of 1st degree murder in the case of William Randolph, we hereby find the defendant ... not guilty."

I dropped my head and squeezed my attorney's hand. Did that while the courtroom roared in celebration to show their support of the verdict.

"Order in the court ... I said order in the court ... This is not over. We still have another verdict..."

Silence swept through the courtroom as the juror began to read part two of my verdict.

Hearts stopped. Fingers were crossed. Eyes were frozen.

The juror proceeded. "When it comes to the charge of 2nd degree kidnapping in the case of Devilla Randolph, we hereby find the defendant, Angel Inghram ... guilty."

34

Inside every hell lies a piece of some heaven.
    My heaven was simply a Rubik's cube I kept turning and turning as I lay in my cell.
    A cell within prison.
    A prison from hell.
    I looked down at the pocket of my orange jump suit, saw the number A*06422* sewn on tight. Forget about my birth name. Forget about my alias. Forget any educated prefix that came with a degree. On this land of captivity – a land where wild sheep is controlled by shepherds – that DC number is all I'm known by, nothing else.
    Transferred back to Miami Florida, I was doing hard time in Dade County Corrections. Fifteen years was the time I received. Fifteen years for attempted murder and 2nd degree kidnapping that stripped me from a regular life, and just like Eve in the Garden of Eden, I feel naked. Exposed. Tainted from a fruit that's now illuminating the fruits of my labor, every day I walk through this prison.
    The guards heard about the getaway stunt that Snow and I pulled back in Vegas. This time I had a personal guard watching my cell in case the opportunity presented itself. I didn't know the guards name.

All I knew is that he was mean, old, and bald – a black sixty-year-old veteran that took no shit from anyone, not even from his own backside.

Like any prisoner there were things I could handle and things I could not. I could handle the food, could handle the guards, could even handle the sex deprived lesbians that wanted a sample every time I passed their cell block. But what I couldn't handle was the endless thoughts. Thoughts that for the first time ever I was facing regret, a word italicizing the tombstone of my disposition.

Mama used to say, *Behind every dark cloud lies a silver lining*. I used to think I knew what that comment meant, even once believed it, but prison has a way of questioning beliefs.

"On your feet," the guard said, tapping at my cell. "You've got a visitor."

I looked alarmed. "A visitor ... for me ... you sure?"

For an inmate, waking up to visitation is like waking up on Christmas. You never know what's wrapped under that tree, but the anticipation is a present within itself. Last time Santa delivered me Snow instead of those two front teeth that I requested. This time – while being escorted down that path – I kept my fingers crossed. But once I saw who it was – a short elderly woman with long thick hair, small waist, skin the color of honey, and saggy cheeks that could use a five grand face lift – I quickly went from a nonchalant inmate to an inmate who was trying to fix up her jumpsuit, hand brush her hair, and spit-slick her eyebrows to look less like an inmate as possible. Wasn't doing it for the woman, but for the little girl that stood beside her, little Devilla.

The guard said, "Thirty minutes, Inghram. Not a minute more."

Happiness illuminated my face as I stared at Devilla who'd grown a few inches. I put on a warm smile, the first smile I gave since entering prison.

But she wasn't smiling. And I had a feeling why.

"Hey there pumpkin," I told her. "You're getting tall."

She grimaced, said nothing, then put her head down.

"You been a good girl while I was gone?"

Still no reply, just a frightening stare.

"She bin fine," Ms. Montreal added, holding her hand. "She scerd of seein' yuh jail."

I shook my head as if I understood. I understood why Devilla was scared.

Wearing a high ruffled dress with Cinderella slippers, Ms. Montreal had transformed Devilla into a Catholic school girl. Her hair that was once wild and curly was pulled back in an orderly ponytail, making her deep cut dimples the heart of her face, and she had blue pearls around her neck.

I gave Ms. Montreal a much-needed hug, then told her, "I can't believe y'all are here. How did you get here?"

Out of nowhere, Devilla tugged at my jumpsuit and said, "We flew here, Ms. Angel. We rode on an airplane. A big big airplane."

"You did?"

"Yep. We were high in the sky, way above the clouds, flying at twenty million feet."

"You mean twenty thousand?"

"Twenty million!" she launched back, standing by what she believed. "And I got to sit by the window."

"You did?"

"Yup. And Ms. Montreal said we're flying back too. I can't wait to tell all my friends in school. They ain't never gonna believe me. I'm gonna take pictures to prove it."

"Sounds like fun."

After the ice was broken, I asked her about the new school that she was attending. She replied with Mayberry Elementary, then went on to brag about how she was voted class President of the 2nd grade class. I asked about her friends in school, about the teachers, about little boys, about her grades, about her favorite subject, and about how she wanted to grow up and be an actress. I asked her everything that could be asked in thirty minutes, tried to play catch up and adviser in so little time.

Everything was okay until she asked me, "So when are you coming home, Ms. Angel?"

Reality hit me like a bullet. "Soon. I'll be home soon."

"Will you be there in time for my play?"

"Your play?"

Ms. Montreal intervened. "She character en Shrek play dat dey have en school."

"That's right," Devilla said. "And this time I'm playing Princess Fiona."

"Wow. Princess Fiona. That's wonderful."

Last year she played a lioness. I remembered it like yesterday because I took her there at the last minute, because William had to work that night. I played the parental role by squeezing her into her lioness costume, put on her make-up, helped her rehearse her lines, and when it was time for someone to represent her for an award, when the

Running From Redemption 295

principal told the mother to stand in the audience, I did that too, without hesitation.

But this time everything was different.

This time I could only wish I was there.

In the best way I could, I explained to her that I wouldn't make it to the play, and like a typical child, no reason on earth was good enough for her to excuse my absence, not even being in prison. I told her that I'll be there in spirit, but those words made her face turn upside down, as she slowly replied, "That's what my daddy used to say."

I swallowed, said nothing.

In that moment of silence it felt like I'd been hit by a rock, but that was nothing compared to the stone that flew next.

"Why did you ... why did you shoot my daddy, Ms. Angel?"

My throat tightened, lungs ran to hell and back like a breathing inferno.

With a hard swallow, I said, "I didn't mean to ... it's just ... I got very upset about something in the past ... about someone who was very dear to me."

"Did daddy hurt that person?"

"Yes. But that still doesn't excuse me for what I did. Two wrongs don't make a right, Devilla. Always remember that, okay?"

She nodded yes, her face starting to redden, tears standing in line to fall off the solemn cliff.

Ms. Montreal patted Devilla's back as I wiped her little cheeks. I told her I was sorry for hurting the first man she ever loved, for stealing her joy that I couldn't replace. I knew at this point my apology was invaluable, but I said it anyhow, because had I kept that apology hidden inside, it would've haunted me forever.

Trying to get past the moment, I muttered, "Do you still like Tinkerbell?"

She nodded yes.

"Well guess what? Although I can't make it to your school play, I have something else in mind."

"You do?"

"I hear that Tinkerbell has some new shoes on the market?"

Her face came to life. "How do you know?"

"I saw them on television. And guess what?"

"What?"

"I'm gonna buy you the new Tinkerbell shoes."

Those little brown eyes exuded all happiness.

She asks me, "Are you for real, Ms. Angel?"
"That's what I said."
"Oh my gosh. And can they be purple?"
"Purple it is."
"Yes yes yes!"
That made her day, as if being on a plane wasn't enough to celebrate already.

After Devilla went into intricate details of what she wanted on her Tinkerbell shoes, I gave her a long-lost hug and kissed her on the cheek. But while this moment was sweet for her, it was bitter-sweet for me, because I knew it was only a matter of time before her sweetness turned sour, only a matter of time before she got old enough to hate me for the death of her father, the unpardonable sin, time ticking for that human to transpose into vampire.

Five years.

Maybe ten.

At some point that stone will certainly be turned.

The guard reminded me that I had fifteen minutes left on the clock. That was my queue to wrap it up with Devilla. I told her I loved her. Told her that one day I should come after her, then I looked her in the eyes and asked for forgiveness, that one day she'll understand why I did what I did.

She nodded as if she understood, as if I was forgiven, as if Tinkerbell shoes could compensate for a life.

One minute later that dimpled freckled-faced girl was on the other side of the visitation room playing ice hockey. With fifteen minutes remaining for visitation, I wanted to spend my last minutes with Ms. Montreal.

"So what made you come way out here to see me?" I asked. "I had no idea you were coming."

"Me needer," she replied. "Was not mi idea, Angel."

"It wasn't?"

"Devilla ... she wanted to see yu since day yuh left. She ask me wen yuh cum bac."

I dropped my head. "And what did you tell her?"

"Dah truf, Angel. Mi tel 'er yuh come someday wit' wings on yur bac, fly like Tinkerbell."

We both laughed out loud at her little joke, laughter that lifted my spirits.

I asked, "So where are y'all staying now?"

"Chicago."

"Chicago. Why there?"

She told me that Chicago is where Devilla's Aunt was living, the relative willing to take Devilla in. Not only did she take in Devilla, but she helped Ms. Montreal to find an apartment in the neighborhood, a way of showing gratitude for bringing Devilla to the family. Devilla joined the house with a little boy cousin, a boy younger than her, and because Devilla's Aunt was constantly working the graveyard shift, the kids spent a lot of nights at Ms. Montreal's apartment. According to Ms. Montreal the apartment was in a drug infested neighborhood a notch above section 8, but aside from the drugs outside her apartment, inside there were strict rules to abide by. She limited Devilla to one hour of television a day, another hour of mandatory reading, and bedtime was set for 8:30 every night, took care of Devilla like her own flesh and blood.

When I asked Ms. Montreal about her real family, she told me, "Da res' mi fambly live New York. Keens."

"Queens, NY?"

"Yes. Me use live der tenty years bac, before second husban'."

"You were married?"

"Muny times," she answered, shaking her head. "An mi regret erv one dem bastards."

I giggled, then changed subjects. "What about your job? Did you find another one?"

She smiled. "Foun' new job ... Mi clean new munshen, but few hours. Ten hours week."

"And the boss?"

"Youn' ... Nice ... Sexy."

More laughs.

She went on to tell me about Devilla's life, how she was so involved in theater and musicals at school. Two months earlier she played Snow White in a Christmas musical, and watching from the audience was a director from The School of Julliard, the most prestigious school in the country when it comes to producing actresses and singers. Ms. Montreal tried to inform me that the director was so impressed with Devilla's singing that he wanted her to attend The School of Julliard in New York City, plus the school would take care of her tuition.

However, like every good deal, there was always a catch. Although Julliard was willing to cover Devilla's schooling, they weren't willing to fund an apartment for Ms. Montreal, nor for Devilla's Aunt. It was another classic case of money getting in the way. For money gets in the way of everything, including a child's education.

I said, "Well what about your life in Chicago? I mean, with only working ten hours a week, how you pay bills, buy clothes, feed yourself every day?"

Food stamps. Government housing. Uncle Sam was her answer to this money riddle, which made me feel even worse because a person her age should not have to struggle so hard. Being of age with little education, she represented the people of this country who were stuck in the middle, the ones that can't land good jobs because of their age, and couldn't receive their pension because they weren't old enough.

Knowing I could change this, I told her, "What if I told you that you're never gonna need Government Assistance again."

"Whad yuh mean?"

"It means I have a lot of money that could do you some good."

She touched my forehead with her palm, then answered, "Yu whack out yur mind, Angel? How yu len mi money wen yu in jail?"

"Because I'm not lending you anything. This money is yours to keep. All two million dollars."

"Whad yuh say?"

"I'm giving you two million dollars."

Her pupils became solar systems, a face more delighted than a winner on an episode of *The Price Is Right*.

She said, "Two ... two million."

"The day you helped me escape in your truck, do you remember the bag that I had with me?"

"Uh huh."

"Well that was a bag full of money ... Snow's money."

The prison guard signaled from afar. *Two minutes left, Inghram.*

Ms. Montreal asked me, "But why didn't cops—"

"Get the money?" I peeked over my shoulder to mark the guard's location. Then I whispered, "Cops didn't know about the money. They only wanted me for murder and kidnapping. Good thing I hid it before they arrested me."

"Hid where?"

"St. Croix of the Virgin Islands. It's buried in the sands of a beach condo. Approximately the fifth condo down from the tiki bar. That's where you'll find it."

Not believing what she was hearing, the smile on her face began to double in size, but after some seconds that smile decreased.

"What's the matter?" I asked. "You should be excited."

"Me cunt tek yur money."

"What?"

"Money for yu, Angel. Yuh earn it."

"No, Ms. Montreal. You earned it. And you're gonna take it. That money can't do me any good in prison."

"But yu gettout soon? Whad yuh do wen yuh gettout? Mi know yu smart gal but no comp'ny hiah crem'nal. Yu need money to get yuh on yur feet. Maybe yu cun start business."

I thought about what she was saying. It made a lot of sense. In fifteen years I'd be a middle-aged woman. That age might be tapping at Botox in the beauty world, but in the corporate world, it is still considered wet behind ears, could still have a future. With two million dollars I could work many wonders. Could start my own firm. Invest in some stock. Could sit back and watch my money grow roots of wealth, maybe even fund my own best-selling book about the life of Angel Inghram, the woman that got her chances stripped because of circumstances.

But then I thought about Devilla.

And that made me rethink.

I'd rather fund her future than refund my past, because unlike me, Devilla's life is just beginning, and unlike me, her chances will not be ruined because of circumstances.

I now see what mama meant when she said those words: *Behind every dark cloud lies a silver lining.*

You see I was mama's lining.

And now Devilla is mine.

Staying with my decision, I told Ms. Montreal, "The money is all yours. Just make sure you enroll Devilla into that school of Julliard."

She smiled. I smiled back.

Then our smiles got bullied by that bastard called Time, taking me back to write a bestseller.

FOR ADDITIONAL COPIES OF

RUNNING FROM REDEMPTION

Visit your local bookstore along with the following websites:

www.cyrilgillion.com
www.amazon.com
www.barnesandnoble.com